FURY

THE VIGILANTES, BOOK SEVEN

STONI ALEXANDER

SILVERSTONE PUBLISHING

Published in the U.S. by SilverStone Publishing, 2024
ISBN 978-1-946534-30-9 (Print Paperback)
ISBN 978-1-946534-31-6 (Kindle eBook)

Respect the author's work. Don't steal it.

NOVELS BY STONI ALEXANDER

THE TOUCH SERIES

The Mitus Touch

The Wilde Touch

The Loving Touch

The Hott Touch

In Walked Sin

Dakota Luck

THE VIGILANTES SERIES

Damaged

Vengeance

Savage

Wrecked

Broken

Rebel

Fury

BEAUTIFUL MEN COLLECTION

Beautiful Stepbrother

Beautiful Disaster

Available on Amazon or Read FREE with Kindle Unlimited

ABOUT FURY

THERE'S A RAZOR-THIN LINE BETWEEN LOVE AND HATE

Carrera

I live to chase evil. Signed up for the job. And I do it damn well. The bad guys think I'm one of them. Every. Single. Time.

When tragedy strikes the Santini family *again*, I'm done. Flat-out done. No more playing by the rules. I become an assassin, hunting down and eliminating monsters, all while being one of the good guys.

Welcome to my Jekyll and Hyde life.

Even with the mayhem, I got this. What I *don't* have is the stunning blonde who's back in my life. She was my first. The one who stole my heart, then ruined me for any other woman.

Years ago, when I learned the truth about her, I dumped her. And I never looked back.

Biggest. Mistake. Of. My. Life.

Now I gotta prove I'm the one she's meant to spend her life with. Hard to do when she hates me with a passion.

There's a razor-thin line between love and hate. All I gotta do is tip the scales in my favor...

Slash

I live life on *my* terms, but it wasn't always that way.

Years ago, life was good. Then it turned into a raging dumpster fire, and I plummeted to hell. Climbing out took everything I had... and the kindness of a stranger. That stranger turned out to be someone I would walk through fire to keep safe.

I'm a fighter and a survivor. I depend on no one, distrust most, and I'm beyond loyal to my ALPHA family.

You got an issue with me... I don't give a damn. So when Carrera Santini returns from who-the-hell cares, I don't give him a second thought.

I do, however, give him a second glance.
But that's all I'm gonna give him...

Until the universe throws me a curve ball.

To my devoted readers who've asked again and again
for a story about Slash...

This one's for you.

1

MARA

One year ago, June

Carrera

Carrera Santini exited the beltway toward his sister's house and called his younger cousin Theodore.

"Yo," Teddy whispered. "I can't talk."

Carrera cracked a smile. "Why'd you answer?"

"I thought you might be here," Teddy whispered.

"Are you at Mara's?"

"Why would I be at her house?"

Carrera stopped at a red light. "To help move her furniture."

"Why would I do that?"

"Because you *like* helping family."

"I do?" Teddy asked.

Carrera's patience had ended. The light turned green and Carrera powered through the intersection. "Bro, where are you?"

"Outta town," Teddy whispered.

"On a hit?"

"Dude just walked in."

The line went dead.

Who answers the damn phone on a hit?

My idiot cousin.

Carrera pulled into Mara's Falls Church neighborhood, a busy suburb of Northern Virginia that boasted a quick twenty-minute commute to downtown DC. His sister had asked for help moving some furniture. In exchange, she was cooking him dinner. That could go either way. Her lasagna was to die for. Same with her wok stir-fry. If she had steaks, he'd grill 'em. Once, Mara had charred the meat into leather. Then, there was the time she served him a porterhouse that was still mooing when she set it on his plate.

Mara wasn't just his sis, she was his business partner. Together, they owned and ran Carrera Cruises, a DC-based company that offered daily excursions along the Potomac River and on the Chesapeake Bay near Annapolis, Maryland. Working with Mara was a great fit. She was reliable, punctual, and organized.

Their vessels included party boats, several forty-foot yachts, and one specially-designed sixty-foot ship that hailed as the star of their fleet. The spacious stern had been built to accommodate special events like weddings. It could comfortably seat up to thirty guests with room for the bridal party and was booked months in advance.

He parked in front of Mara's small townhouse. After grabbing his work gloves off the passenger seat, he exited his four-door truck, made his way to the front door.

Just after seven on a beautiful Friday evening in June, and the sun had started its graceful descent below the horizon. He rapped on her front door.

No answer. He called her.

Also, no answer.

Where the hell are you?

She'd asked him to help her weeks ago, so there was no way she'd blow him off now. He punched in the garage code and waited while the door rose. As he eyed her car, his frustration morphed into concern. He strode over to the door, tried the handle. To his surprise, it was locked.

She never locks this.

Urgency had him fishing out his keys and shoving the spare into the lock. Darkness filled the lower level. Out of habit, he reached for his weapon, tucked in the back of his pants, but he'd left it at home.

Who needs a gun when they're moving furniture?

He hoofed it up the stairs and into her kitchen. Also dark. His guts churned. He grabbed a long kitchen knife.

"Mara!"

The silence was deafening.

He cleared the first floor. No sister, nothing out of place. He checked the front door. The bolt was flipped closed, no sign of a break-in. Though concerned, his blood pressure didn't jump, neither did his pulse.

Maybe she's sleeping.

She *had* been putting in long hours at work.

He flew up the stairs, flipped on the hall light. His sigh of relief filled the quiet space. Though her bedroom was dark, hall light spilled into her room. There she was, in bed, buried under a comforter. Time to get her lazy ass up.

"Wake up, sis."

She didn't stir.

"Mara, let's go."

He pulled back the comforter and recoiled. Her naked torso was covered in dried blood, a single gunshot wound to her abdomen.

His heart cried out, anger surging to the forefront.

God, no.

Her face ashen, her eyes lifeless. She was gone, but he had to try. After not finding a pulse, he removed her pillow and craned her head back to open her windpipe. Thirty compressions before he breathed life into her.

Nothing.

Another thirty. Two more breaths.

Thirty compressions, two breaths.

Still nothing.

Dread flooded him.

He pounded on her chest. "Mara, come on! Breathe. We got this. C'mon, sis, don't leave me."

Nothing.

Her lifeless body was taking the assault like a champ. Like a Santini.

He stopped pounding, but he couldn't see, couldn't hear.

His eyes clouded with tears and he released a gut-wrenching scream. Then, he kissed her cold forehead, his heart shattering into a million pieces.

"Who did this to you?"

He waited for God to whisper the answer into his ear, but he was met with an eerie silence. He pulled the blanket up to her neck, sat on the edge of the bed, and gently closed her eyelids.

She looked like she was asleep. He wanted to remember her this way. And she would want that too.

His slaughtered heart mourned while the anger morphed into fury—a rage so powerful he wouldn't push it back down, even if he could.

Fury drove him. That made him excellent at his job. Kept him chasing after the walking evil, day in and day out.

But... this feeling was new.

Fury cloaked his soul in a darkness so severe, there would

be no escape. He wanted to exact his revenge on the evil who had done this to her, and to his family.

His broken, broken family.

"Mara, I will find the monster who took you from us." Then, he reached under the blanket and clasped her pinky in his own. A stupid childhood ritual going back decades.

"Pinky promise."

One gentle squeeze before he let her go, his heart wrecked, the need for revenge taking over his soul. He covered her face with the comforter. In that moment, all the color in his life melded to black.

Nine months after Mara's murder, March.

Carrera

With his worn, leather duffle in hand, Carrera strode inside the J. Edgar Hoover building in DC and made his way to security. Once cleared to enter, he rode the elevator upstairs.

The last nine months had been a whirlwind. He'd taken an undercover assignment in Delaware, then another in Tucson, then another in Seattle, then another in... he couldn't fucking remember.

Anything to keep moving. Slowing down allowed the pain of losing his sister to slither back in. He needed to stay sharp on those undercover gigs, so he worked 'til exhaustion, slept for a few hours, then did it again. The routine had turned him into a machine. A machine hell-bent on revenge.

He exited the elevator, made his way toward his department. Truth was, he was burned out, he missed his family, and his cruise line company wasn't thriving like it had been.

Time to return to ground zero and face reality.

He entered the Violent Crimes Unit, tossed a nod toward

one of the Special Agents before making his way toward his boss's office. Stopping in front of her closed door, he knocked.

"Come in," she said.

He entered, his gaze sliding from hers to the man seated across from her desk.

"You want me to come back?" Carrera asked.

"No," she said. "Now's good."

The man rose. "Thanks for your time."

After he left, Carrera stepped in.

"Good to see you, Carrera," his boss said. "Have a seat."

Carrera's phone rang. It was the homicide detective from Mara's case. His fingers twitched to answer, but he'd wait until he was done talking to his superior.

He silenced the call, sat in the chair across from her. "How are you doing, ma'am?"

"That's my question for you," she replied. "When did you get back?"

"My flight just landed."

She glanced at his single piece of luggage. "How was Philly?"

"We made the arrest."

"Nice work." She broke eye contact, clicked around on her computer. "I've got a few undercover assignment options for you."

"I need to stay in town."

She nodded. "Understood. Any updates on your sister's case?"

The fury circled like vultures over the dead. "Nothing."

"I'll transfer over some local cases in the next day or two. It'll be a good change for you." She hesitated an extra beat while her gaze floated over his face.

He'd seen that look before. Whatever she was about to tell him wasn't good.

"I have an update on a case you worked two years ago," she

began. "Richard Allen Glazer was arrested for heading up a New York sex trafficking ring."

"I remember. Glazer's DNA was all over that house where the women were being held."

"His trial ended. He was found not guilty and released a few days ago."

The familiar jolt of anger slammed his chest. Instead of releasing a string of expletives and telling her what he *really* thought about the criminal justice system—he stayed silent. What the fuck good would talking do?

"I heard he's suing for wrongful arrest," she added.

"What a cluster," he ground out.

"We're keeping an eye on him," she continued. "We're concerned he might go after the arresting officers." Then, she quickly added, "But you're not in danger since your testimony was videoed with your voice and appearance altered."

Carrera wasn't scared. He was pissed. And an angry Carrera was much more dangerous. "Thanks for the heads up."

She rose. "I'll be in touch about your caseload."

He grabbed his leather bag, stood. "Thanks for your time."

As Carrera made his way toward the elevator bank, he thought about Glazer. It had taken months, but Carrera had infiltrated that crime ring, gotten the evidence the Bureau desperately needed. Days later, they'd moved in for an arrest. Carrera actually believed it was a slam dunk. How could it not be?

Once outside, he inhaled the chilly March air as he called the detective. Just because he'd been out of town for the past nine months didn't mean he'd been out of touch.

At present, there were no clues and no evidence. There had been no fingerprints at the house besides his and Mara's. Her bedroom had been wiped down, same with all the doorknobs. Neighbors hadn't heard or seen anything. Not one damn thing.

"Jurgenson," the detective answered.

"It's Carrera Santini. Anything new?"

"Let me pull the file."

A growl shot from Carrera's throat. His beloved Mara had been reduced to a goddamn case file.

"I'm back," Jurgenson said. "Did I tell you Mara's kitchen slider was unlocked?"

"No."

"That's pretty common, you know, for people to leave that door unlocked."

"Not my sister."

"I finally got the results from the second M.E. She ruled the intercourse as nonconsensual. I'm sorry."

An explosion of fury ripped through Carrera. Pain shot through his chest, but it was nothing—*nothing*—compared to what Mara had been forced to endure. Sexually assaulted in her own bed, then shot and left to die.

A growl shot out of him. He wouldn't just kill the mother-fucker. He would rip his heart out and stomp on it.

"Months ago, the unsub's DNA was sent to three database companies for any familial hits. Unfortunately, nothing came back."

Carrera wanted to scream at the detective, but the man was doing his job. Mara's case was one of many, and Carrera didn't get special treatment because he worked for the Bureau.

"I'm sorry, Mr. Santini," the detective said. "If anything changes, I'll let you know."

Now Carrera knew the vicious truth. His sister had been sexually assaulted and murdered. Then, the son of a bitch had breezed out the kitchen door, down the steps, and into the night.

Like the devil himself.

Shrouded in a veil of hate, Carrera Santini was done bringing the wicked to justice.

So. Fucking. Done.

Rather than call a rideshare, he started walking. Anything to burn off his anger. As his feet ate up the pavement, he made a decision.

He unearthed his phone and speed dialed the familiar number.

"Carrera, hold on," said his older cousin, Luciano Santini. A few seconds later, Luciano returned. "Are you back?"

"Yeah."

"How'd it go?"

"This one'll probably get off on a technicality or some fucking loophole."

"I heard about Richard Allen Glazer," Luciano said.

"How?"

"I make it my business to know when a monster walks free," Luciano replied.

"Mara was raped." Carrera let the words hang in a heavy silence.

"Jesus, no," Luciano whispered. "We'll find him. You have my word."

"I'm done playing by the rules," Carrera said, the fury slicing through him.

His cousin grew silent for several seconds. "That's your emotions talking. Go home, sleep it off."

"No," Carrera ground out. "This is your *one* opportunity to get your claws in me."

"I've waited a long time to hear you say that," Luciano said. "Are you leaving the Bureau?"

"Hell, no." Carrera replied.

"Are you sure you want to work with me?"

"One-hundred-percent."

"Welcome to the *real* family," Luciano Santini said with a smile.

2

THE ASSASSINS

Three months later. June, present day.

Carrera

Sunday evening, Carrera studied the faces of evil on the wall-mounted screens. The leader—Richard Allen Glazer—and the five loyal men who worked for him.

Carrera, along with his cousins, Luciano and Teddy Santini, had been squirreled away in Luciano's Great Falls mansion for the past hour. This hit was days in the planning, and Carrera could not fucking wait.

"Once released from prison, Glazer moved to Maryland," Luciano said. "and he picked up right where he left off. Trafficking women."

"Ballsy," Teddy added.

"He thinks he's untouchable," Luciano said.

"Up till now, he has been." Carrera clicked on the laptop in front of him and read through the men's long list of atrocities.

Kidnapping, sex trafficking, prostitution, sexual assault, and murder, though no arrests had been made for that last crime.

"He sued every law enforcement agency that had anything to do with his arrest," Luciano explained. "Claimed his civil rights were violated."

"We got this," Carrera said closing his laptop.

"Are we in agreement?" Luciano asked.

Carrera slid his gaze from the screen to his older cousin. "Hell, yeah."

As Teddy tied his long, blond hair into a man bun, he flicked his gaze from Carrera to Luciano, but he didn't speak.

"What's going on with you?" Carrera asked.

"I got a bad feeling about this," Teddy replied.

"You want to sit this one out?" Luciano asked.

"No," Teddy said. "I'm in."

"How long until law enforcement arrives?" Carrera asked.

Luciano's upper lip curled into a snarl, and Carrera bit back a smile. His cousin hated law enforcement, with the exception of a few select individuals.

"ALPHA gets there at three," Luciano explained.

Carrera pushed out of his chair. "It's one in the morning. Let's do this."

"Teddy, turn your phone *off*," Luciano said.

On a huff, Teddy turned off his device. "Happy?" he asked.

"I wouldn't know happy if I fucking bumped into it." Then a sinister smile lifted the corners of Luciano's mouth. "But I know pain and misery."

"Then, let's go inflict some," Carrera rasped.

"My driver's taking us," Luciano said.

"Not for a hit," Carrera pushed back. "I got this."

All three slid Glocks into their ankle holsters before checking their primary weapons. After grabbing their go-bags, they entered Luciano's six-car garage.

Like his cousins, Carrera was dressed in black, his body armor beneath his tight black shirt.

"Teddy, vest?" Luciano asked.

"Duh," Teddy bit out. "Just because I never *used* to shut off my phone doesn't mean I'm not in body armor. I'm not stupid."

The annoyance in Teddy's voice had Carrera placing a hand on his shoulder.

"We want you safe, bro," Carrera said before getting behind the wheel of Luciano's SUV.

Luciano rode shotgun. As Teddy climbed in the back, he mumbled something in Italian under his breath.

Carrera headed down the tree-lined private road to the front gates. They swung open, and Carrera drove through the upscale neighborhood with the headlights off. Once on the main road, he flipped on the lights. Though he could not wait to take this monster out, he took his time getting to their destination.

"G-ma drives faster than you," Teddy said from the back seat.

Luciano chuckled. "You *could* go a little faster."

"I'm driving five miles over the speed limit," Carrera said.

"You know, people get pulled over for going too slow," Teddy said.

"Speaking of G-ma, she's got a birthday this week," Carrera said.

"Eighty-five," Luciano added.

"Damn, that's up there," Teddy added. "I thought she was younger, like sixty or somethin'. I mean, still old, but not *ancient*."

The men fell silent as Carrera jumped on the beltway, then onto I-95 north. An hour later, he drove into the older suburban Maryland neighborhood and past Glazer's house.

A light was on in the front room and another upstairs.

"We gotta kill the lights," Luciano said.

"I'll take the basement and kill the breaker while I'm there," Teddy said.

"I'll cover you," Luciano said.

"I don't need—"

"At the Delaware house, Glazer kept the women holed up in the basement," Carrera said. "You can't kill the electricity and watch your six at the same time."

"Whatever," Teddy said.

Per their plan, Carrera drove into the empty parking lot of a small neighborhood park. While the area had surveillance cameras, Luciano confirmed those had been disabled hours earlier.

Carrera parked in the shadows, cut the engine. After Teddy opened the hatch, each man pulled on a ski mask, strapped on his helmet equipped with night goggles and a two-way comm, attached the silencer to his Glock, then covered his hands in black gloves.

The sounds of chirping crickets and rustling leaves in the early summer breeze had Carrera inhaling a calming breath.

Tonight was not their first hit. Wouldn't be their last.

They made their way out of the quiet park and down the street. As they approached Glazer's, they veered into the back-yard. Once there, the men lowered their goggles. Now, Carrera's world took on a greenish hue. He tried the slider. Locked.

"There's a door," Teddy whispered, gesturing to one ten feet away.

Luciano tried the knob. Within seconds, he had a pick inserted into the lock. "Got it."

The security alarm pierced the silence, the blasts of noise heightening Carrera's already-alert senses. Undeterred, the men rushed inside. With their weapons drawn, they made their way down a pitch-black hallway, then into a large room filled with sofas and mattresses strewn across the floor.

Three men had been sleeping on them. Now, they were sitting up, their eyes wide with surprise. One reached for his weapon.

Carrera fired his Glock.

POP! POP! POP!

The bullets pierced their skulls between their eyes.

Teddy vanished around the corner in search of the electrical breaker, Luciano doing a three-sixty to keep his brother safe.

The alarm stopped.

"Who's there?" A man yelled down the basement stairs.

The basement lights came on blinding Carrera. He flipped up his goggles and moved against a wall, his Glock at the ready.

Someone whispered before a stampede of footsteps pounded the stairs.

BANG! BANG! BANG!

The scumbags were shooting their way into the room.

C'mon, Teddy. Find the breaker.

As the first guy rounded the corner, the room went black. Carrera flipped down the goggles, eyed the men. Neither were Glazer, but he recognized them both.

POP! POP!

He hit the first between the eyes, shot the second on his forehead. Both men went down, but the second one raised his arm to fire his weapon. Carrera fired—*POP! POP!*—hitting him twice in the chest.

"Fuck, it's a bloodbath," he bit out.

His cousins appeared at his side.

"Glazer's upstairs," Luciano said.

On the main level, they found the front door wide open. A car flew out of the driveway and sped away.

"Fuck," Teddy bit out.

In seconds, they cleared the first floor, bolted toward the stairs.

A woman's scream pierced the night.

"You come up here, she's dead." A thug stood at the top, his elbow locked around a woman's neck while he pointed a large hunting knife at her chest.

A man with a flashlight appeared next to him, temporarily blinding Carrera and his cousins.

They flipped up their goggles.

"Three, two—" Carrera whispered.

POP! POP! POP! POP! POP! POP! POP!

Luciano pumped flashlight guy with bullets. Teddy hit the man with the hunting knife in the hand. The second he jerked his hand away, Carrera unleashed a torrent of bullets into him.

POP! POP! POP! POP!

He shoved the woman down the stairs as he dropped.

Luciano grabbed her while Carrera and Teddy thundered upstairs. Into the first room they flew.

Empty.

"Clear," Teddy murmured.

Second room, a naked man stood over a mattress where two naked women huddled close.

"Consensual?" Carrera asked.

One of the women shook her head.

"Close your eyes," Teddy said to the women.

The second they did—*POP! POP! POP!*—Teddy dropped the guy.

"Take them downstairs," Carrera said.

"I need to clear the last bedroom with you," Teddy said.

"Go. I got this."

Carrera bolted out of the room, heading toward the closed door at the end of the hall. With his gun drawn, he opened the door, but kept his back flush against the wall.

Silence.

He waited.

"Hello?" called a woman. "Are you police?"

Carrera knew he could be walking into a trap, but he would take that risk. With his gun at the ready, he stepped into the room, and his brain stuttered to a stop.

Three mattresses lay on the floor while eight women sat on them, their feet chained to the floor.

"What the fuck?"

"Bathroom," one of the women whispered.

Carrera cleared the closet, then strode into the bathroom. Glazer crouched near the toilet.

What a fitting way to die, like the piece of shit he was.

"Glazer," Carrera bit out.

The man looked up, fear shining in his beady eyes.

"Any last words?" Carrera asked.

"I was cleared of any wrongdoing," Glazer bit out. "I'm innocent."

"Sure you are." Carrera raised his weapon.

"Spare me," Glazer bleated.

"Tell the devil I'm gonna chase him until the day I die."

POP!

A single bullet pierced his forehead. Dead eyes stared up at nothing.

Killing was wrong. Carrera knew that. He also knew that justice doesn't always win. Sometimes the bad guys steal the prize. He was righting the wrongs that society couldn't.

Rules are rules are rules.

And then, there were the Santini Assassins.

"ALPHA's here," Luciano said through the comm. "Gotta fly, brother."

Carrera strode out of the bedroom. "Don't let these monsters win," he said to the chained women. "Make it a good life."

"Help us," pleaded one of the women.

"The rescue team is here." And with that, Carrera left the bedroom, and took off down the stairs.

In the living room, Luciano spoke quietly with a man people either loved or feared. Sinclair Develin, known in the DMV—DC, Maryland, and Virginia—as The Fixer.

Both men shifted their attention to Carrera, but no one in ALPHA knew he was working with his cousin. His face concealed behind a ski mask, he hoped Sin couldn't ID him.

"Let's go," Carrera murmured to Teddy.

Luciano shook Sin's hand before Carrera raced down the stairs, Teddy close on his heels. Once outside, Luciano caught up to them.

At the SUV, they removed their helmets. Carrera wiped the perspiration from his brow before getting behind the wheel. He eyed the two black SUVs and the white van as they drove by the house.

The drive back to Luciano's was quiet. Once there, the men shook hands. That was how Luciano did business. A simple handshake at the beginning and end of each business transaction.

That's all these hits were to Luciano—business.

While Carrera had a conscience, he was convinced his cousin did not.

Luciano retreated inside, then Carrera and Teddy hugged it out before Teddy took off. Carrera drove toward home, his thoughts floating from the chained women in the house to his sister, Mara. He wanted to think about happier times, but the image of her lifeless body crashed into his mind.

Instead of turning right into his Alexandria neighborhood, he took a left. Several short blocks later, he stopped in front of an end-unit townhome. While he could *not* stand its sole occupant, he promised his G-ma he'd keep an eye on her. Kinda hard to do from the outside, but he wasn't going in, and hell would freeze over before he got an invitation.

Five minutes later, he was in his trendy neighborhood. Two turns, and he drove down his street. He tapped the garage door opener, pulled in, killed the engine, and got out.

With his go-bag in hand, he said, "Computer, close the garage door."

The door rattled and squeaked on its hinges until it stopped.

The retina scanner cleared him and he made his way into his home office, retreated into his walk-in closet, and instructed his security system to open the panel door.

The back wall slid open, and he stepped into his inner sanctum. There, he set his go-bag on the bench, pulled out the Glock, and exited.

"Computer, close the panel door."

The door slid closed.

It was just after four-thirty in the morning. He should sleep, but he was wound pretty tightly. Upstairs, in his bedroom, he set his weapon on the dresser before changing into a bathing suit. His beloved grandmother would have several choice words for him if she knew he swam alone, but she didn't know. So, he dove in.

The water cooled his heated skin, and he swam the first several laps with ease. Forty minutes later, he'd tired himself out. He dried off while catching his breath and headed inside.

After showering off, he tugged on shorts and left the bathroom.

That's when he heard glass shatter.

He grabbed his weapon, bolted downstairs. The house was dark and quiet. Too quiet. He slunk into the kitchen and a stabbing pain seared his foot. Shattered glass from the kitchen window lay everywhere.

Movement caught his eye as a baseball bat loomed into view. He jumped out of the way, grabbed the wooden bat, and flung it over his shoulder.

Then, he raised his Glock. "Down on the floor, or I'll shoot!"

"You cock-sucking motherfucker! You killed my brother!" The intruder charged at him.

Carrera opened fire. *POP! POP! POP!*

The man dropped.

What the fuck was that?

He pulled the shard of glass from the bottom of his foot before confirming the man was dead. Then, he charged upstairs to grab his phone. He dialed. The phone rang and rang.

"What?" Teddy grumbled. "I'm sleeping."

"Clean up on aisle five," Carrera said.

"Shit, are you for real?" Teddy asked.

Carrera stayed silent.

"On my way." The line went dead.

Carrera eyed the trail of blood from his foot before he pulled on boots and strode into his garage for a tarp. Back in the kitchen, he dragged the man onto the plastic covering, pulled up IDware—Stryker Truman's facial-recognition app—and held his phone to the dead man's face. Then, he wrapped him in the tarp. Seconds later, the software came back with a result.

The man who tried to kill him was Glazer's brother, and most likely the man who fled from Glazer's house.

He tailed me home.

Luciano had a rule. No phone calls, emails, or texts about jobs. But Carrera needed to let his cousin know, so he called him.

Luciano answered right away. "Santini."

"Clean up on aisle five."

"Are you alone?"

"Teddy's coming over."

"Understood." Luciano hung up.

Carrera cleared the shards of glass from the floor, the kitchen counter, and from the sink.

Ten minutes later, Teddy showed up with a scowl and an attitude. "What the fuck happened?"

"I was attacked in my home."

"Who is it?"

"Glazer's brother." He showed him the pic on his phone. "I need to board up my window. Can you move the body without me?"

"No prob," Teddy replied.

Carrera rolled his motorcycle into the corner of his three-car garage so Teddy could back his truck in. Once the garage door closed, Carrera boarded up his window while Teddy tied rope around the tarp, then dragged Glazer's wrapped body into the garage.

Together, they lifted it into the SUV.

Fifteen minutes later, they arrived at the crematorium in Franconia. Though owned by ALPHA, they had access to it.

A man named CK lived in the house next door. Teddy stopped at the gated entrance and pressed the buzzer.

"Yeah," answered the gruff voice.

"Delivery."

"Name?"

Turning toward Carrera, Teddy raised his eyebrows.

"Pied Piper," Carrera said.

The gate opened. Teddy drove through, and Carrera instructed him to drive around back. The metal fire door had been propped open. They carried the body inside.

CK shook Carrera's hand. "How you been?"

Carrera pressed cash into his hand. "Good. You?"

"Can't complain." CK eyed the blue tarp. "Unwrap the deceased."

Carrera untied the rope, opened the plastic. He and Teddy carried the man into the back, laid him on the cold slab that would be rolled into the fire.

Wasn't the first time Carrera had done this. Wouldn't be the last.

Carrera closed Glazer's eyes. "Your bad decisions led you to this."

CK chuckled, displaying his stained front teeth. "Everyone ends up here or six feet under, even if you're a goddamn saint."

"Maybe so," Carrera said, "but heaven doesn't accept sinners."

"We're all sinners, my friend," CK said. "We're all sinners." Then CK flicked his gaze from Carrera to Teddy, then back to Carrera. "You can go."

Carrera shook his head. "You know I stay. Burn him."

"Don't trust me still?" CK asked.

"I don't trust anyone," Carrera replied.

3

HAPPY BIRTHDAY!

Slash

Slash— real name Amanda Maynard—held Elsa Santini's hand as they left the exam room en route to the waiting area. While Elsa was relatively sure-footed, her wellness check-up tired her out.

Elsa Santini was the matriarch of the Santini family. Small in stature, she was a strong-willed widow who wore her gray hair short, her makeup light, and her couture clothing wrinkle free. She was kind to everyone, but she was no pushover.

Pausing at the counter, Slash handed the medical admin Elsa's folder before lifting her phone from her pocket.

"Do you want to book your six-month follow-up now or call us when you're ready to schedule?" asked the woman.

Tucking her long silver hair behind her ear, Slash regarded Elsa. "What works for you Elsa?"

Elsa smiled. "My schedule is much more flexible than yours."

Slash jumped ahead six months, selected a date and time.

Once the appointment had been booked, she clasped Elsa's hand and they left the office.

"You don't have to hold my hand, honey," Elsa said.

Slash stopped in front of a pothole in the parking lot. "Look down."

Elsa did.

"That's why I hold your hand. I've got you before you hit the ground, or I steer you around it."

Elsa smiled. "You take good care of me."

"Goes both ways."

At Elsa's Mercedes, Slash asked, "Are you riding shotgun?"

Elsa laughed. "Always," she said as she walked over to the passenger side.

Slash got behind the wheel, headed out of the parking lot. "How are you for groceries?"

"I went to the market yesterday."

"Did someone help you bring the bags inside?"

"Carrera did."

Slash's upper lift curled. Rather than make a snide comment, she changed the subject. "You had another great physical, Elsa." She stopped at a red light. "What's your secret?"

"I refuse to die."

Slash laughed. "Nice."

"What did you decide about my birthday dinner?" Elsa asked.

Before turning down Elsa's tree-lined, Old Town, Alexandria street, Slash glanced over. She loved this woman with her whole heart. Adored her with every ounce of her being. But there was no way in hell she was attending a Santini family event.

"I thought we'd celebrate together tonight. Just the two of us, like we usually do."

Slash pulled into Elsa's driveway, tapped the garage door

clicker, and waited for the door to rise before pulling in and parking.

"I want you there," Elsa pushed back. "And I'm the birthday girl. When you turn eighty-five, you get everything you want."

Though Slash wanted to be there for Elsa, she wouldn't go anywhere near that celebration. Slash had a hard line she would *not* cross, not even for Elsa.

She stayed silent as they went inside. It was only four-thirty, but after washing her hands, Slash started prepping for dinner.

Elsa picked up the mail in her foyer, sat at the kitchen table sorting through everything. Forty-five minutes later, they were seated at Elsa's kitchen table. After Elsa said grace, Slash lifted her wine glass. Elsa did the same.

"Happy birthday, Elsa. I wish you a happy, happy year. I love you."

A smile wrinkled Elsa's beautiful face. After clinking glasses, they sipped the red wine.

"This is good," Slash said.

"Yes, but I liked the other one better."

"This *is* the other one." Slash showed Elsa the bottle. "This is a Santini Chianti, your favorite."

Elsa smiled. "Oops, my bad."

Slash laughed. "Stop showing your age. It freaks me out."

"I didn't think anything freaked you out."

"Thinking about you not being here does." Slash sliced into the chicken breast, forked a piece into her mouth.

"Dinner is delicious," Elsa said. "I like the potatoes."

"Eat the protein, Elsa."

"Tell me about work."

Though Slash never discussed her job with anyone, she broke that rule for Elsa. "I did a rescue mission last night for a group of women who were being sex trafficked."

"That sounds scary." Elsa put a small piece of steamed broccoli into her mouth. "Why no butter on the broccoli?"

"Because you have a pound of butter on your potato." Slash shook her head. "Less butter, more vegetables."

"Were you scared when you made the rescue?" Elsa asked.

"No, but it helped that there were several of us, and we were armed."

"Are you afraid someone will recognize you?"

Slash pulled out her phone, showed her a photo of the team, all dressed in SWAT gear, including helmets with night goggles.

After studying the photo, Elsa said, "You're the third from the left."

Slash eyed the picture. "How'd you do that?"

She sipped the wine. "I would recognize my favorite grand-daughter anywhere, no matter how disguised she is."

Love filled Slash's heart, especially since she wasn't even Elsa's biological relative. She was a broken, broken stray that Elsa had plucked from the depths of hell.

Pushing out of her chair, she walked around the kitchen table and kissed Elsa on her cheek. "I have a present for you. Be right back."

She retrieved it from her handbag, set the card on the table. After tugging it from the envelope, Elsa read it out loud.

Dear Elsa,
You make my life better...

Elsa opened the card.

Simply because you are here.
All my love, Amanda May

Elsa smiled. "Thank you, honey. I love it." Then, she opened the folded piece of paper and read Slash's homemade coupon.

Two tickets to the Washington Symphony
John F. Kennedy Center
for the Performing Arts

"This is wonderful. So thoughtful, especially since you don't listen to classical music."

"It's a Saturday matinee, so after, we'll go out to dinner."

Elsa reached across the table and patted her hand. "I can't wait." She glanced at the handmade note. "When is it?"

"Next month. I'll add it to your calendar."

After they finished eating, Slash cleared the table and did the dishes. Then, she went in search of Elsa, who was watching the news in the living room.

When it ended, Slash said, "A few months ago, you asked me to do something."

"Did you do it?" Elsa asked with a gleam in her eyes.

"Do you remember what?"

"Can I get a hint?"

Slash chuckled. "You asked me to color my hair back to my real color, the blonde I had when we first met."

"Ah, yes, I remember that. I used to call you Sunny because it was bright, like the sun."

"Well, I did it, for you."

Elsa stared at Slash's long silver hair. "Get me my other glasses because it looks like you're still coloring it that silver I don't like."

Slash pulled off the wig, pulled the hair tie and clips from her head, and shook her long, blonde hair free. As she pushed her long bangs to one side, Elsa started clapping.

"Now *this* is my favorite birthday present!" Elsa exclaimed. "You look like my Sunny girl. I love it."

"I haven't had it like this in so long, I don't even recognize myself."

"You went through a lot of colors," Elsa said. "Blonde, then you made it brown, then black. Then you started with the exotic colors. You had purple for the longest time, then you had blue and pink. Green, but that didn't last. Then silver. You look beautiful."

She smiled. How could she not? She loved making Elsa happy, and this was an easy way to do it. "Great memory." With a smile, she said, "I'm going to cut two pieces of that chocolate cake I brought over."

"Can you make me a decaf, dear?"

"You got it." Slash returned to the kitchen, popped the pod into the coffee maker, then pulled the store-bought cake from the box.

As she slid a few candles into the soft frosting, the doorbell rang.

"G-ma, it's Carrera," he called from the front door.

Ah, crap.

Slash's day was ruined. Biting back a groan, she went to retrieve the just-filled mug from the coffee machine.

"How ya doin'?" Carrera's sexy voice rumbled through her. "I'm Carrera Santini."

Slash turned to face the one man she hated with a passion.

That familiar hit of adrenaline powered through her, followed by a slow wave of nausea. Nothing like that two-punch effect from Carrera Santini.

If he were the only person left on planet earth, she'd find a different continent to live on. That's how much she loathed him.

Carrera's eyebrows jutted into his forehead while he pierced her with his bedroom eyes. Large, brown orbs that could hypnotize with a simple glance. Only she wasn't like every other woman who'd ever met him. She couldn't stand the sight of him, let alone being in the same room.

"Whoa, it's you," Carrera blurted. "You... you changed your hair."

"Your brilliance astounds me," she hissed.

Elsa joined them at the counter. Probably to ensure Slash didn't grab a kitchen knife and slice him into bite-sized pieces.

Carrera swept his grandmother into his arms and hugged her. There was a time when Slash loved those ripped, muscular arms around her, loved how his handsome face split into the most breathtaking smile whenever he looked into her eyes.

But those days were gone. Long gone.

"Are you hungry?" Elsa asked him.

"No, he's not," Slash bit out.

Carrera sauntered over to check out the leftovers. His manly, leathery scene filled her lungs but she refused to move. He was invading *her* space. She would stand her damn ground.

"I was here first," she murmured.

"Amanda May, play nice," Elsa said.

"I'm not playing," Slash bit out. "We're in the middle of a birthday celebration."

As if he'd been invited, Carrera pulled a plate from the cupboard, piled it with chicken, potatoes, and broccoli, then got too damn comfortable at the table.

With another movie-star grin cemented on Slash, he said, "Happy birthday, G-ma."

"You've gone cock-eyed, Carrera," Elsa said, and Slash laughed. "I'm over here, but I see you noticed how pretty Amanda May looks with her new hair color. She did it for me, for my birthday."

"He *is* cock-eyed," Slash grumbled.

Elsa sat back down at the table and slid the card over to Carrera, along with Slash's simple homemade coupon for the symphony.

If Slash had a thing for Carrera, she would have snatched that coupon so he wouldn't laugh at her rudimentary handiwork, but she didn't give a fuck what he thought about her... or about anything at all.

She steeled her spine, set the mug of coffee in front of Elsa, along with the cake. After lighting the candles, she sat, but she refused to even glance in his direction.

Every cell in her body wanted to flee the scene, but she wouldn't leave just because this asswipe showed up. As far as she was concerned, Carrera Santino wasn't even in the room.

Only he was.

She could feel his one-of-a-kind thunderous energy rolling off him, she could smell his baseline scent, and she could see his guns out of the corner of her eye. Large, cut biceps and triceps of granite-hard muscles. Her thoughts jumped to him planking over her, while she ran her fingers over his soft skin.

A growl ripped from the back of her throat.

They looked at her.

"Make a wish, Elsa," Slash said.

"We gotta sing first," Carrera interjected.

Elsa smiled, then hummed the first note.

"Happy birthday to you..." Carrera began, his perfect pitch catching Slash's ear.

She joined in, her gaze cemented on Elsa. Looking at Carrera would only piss her off. When they finished, Elsa applauded, then she fixed her attention on the candles.

"Make the wish count, G-ma," Carrera murmured.

Elsa's gaze floated to him, then to Slash before she closed her eyes. A few seconds later, they fluttered open. She heaved in a breath and blew out the candles.

Slash smiled. "Good job." She retrieved dessert plates, small forks, and a sharp knife before returning to the table. With the knife in hand, she shifted her gaze to Carrera, and tightened her grip.

"Go easy with that," he said as if issuing a stern warning.

She removed the candles, sliced through the cake. After cutting two pieces, she sat back down.

"Where's my dessert?" he asked.

"Yeah, right. Like I'm gonna serve you." She forked in a piece. Creamy chocolate and sweet sugar flooded her taste buds. If she had a weakness, it was chocolate cake with chocolate frosting. Simple, yet delicious.

Elsa took a small bite before sipping the coffee.

"When are you going to the symphony?" Carrera asked.

Slash glanced his way, only this time, sadness filled her soul. Sadness and loss. So much loss. Her afternoon with Elsa had been great. Now, she had to sit there and play nice with this douche. While she could pretend like it was okay that Carrera was there, it was not.

"Why don't you tell your grandson about your wellness visit today?" Slash suggested.

As Elsa prattled on about her good health, Slash left the table. She would have preferred to stay and enjoy the celebration, but her stomach had soured. It was time to bolt before she and Carrera removed their gloves and started flinging shit.

It was inevitable.

Rather than ruin what had been a wonderful afternoon with Elsa, she would take off. Feeling that familiar pang of loss at leaving, she shouldered her vintage hobo handbag, and walked back over to the table.

Elsa's expression fell. "Please don't go."

"We had a great afternoon together, and a special birthday celebration," Slash said.

"Will you come to the party the boys are throwing for me?" Elsa asked.

Shooting daggers at Carrera, Slash shook her head. "No." Then, she kissed Elsa on her cheek. "I love you. Happy birthday."

Elsa rose and hugged her. Slash melted in her loving embrace, gently hugging her back. "I'll text you tomorrow, then swing by over the weekend."

She walked over to Carrera, bent down and whispered, "Go fuck yourself, Santini."

"Language," Elsa exclaimed.

"*You* go fuck *yourself*," Carrera bit out.

"That's enough!" The sternness in Elsa's voice snagged Slash's attention.

"I'm outta here." Slash stormed to her ALPHA SUV, parked at the curb.

She hated leaving before their celebration had ended, hated that *he* was back in town. As she buckled, tears pricked her eyes.

No crying.

When she glanced up at the house, Elsa stood in the doorway, waving. Slash rolled down the passenger window. "Love you."

"Love you, honey. Drive safely. Thanks for making my birthday so special."

A single tear rolled down Slash's cheek as she drove away. Slash couldn't remember the last time she'd cried.

I would be lost without her.

∾

Carrera

CARRERA HAD a mouth full of food when G-ma marched back into the kitchen. "What is wrong with you?"

He shrugged, finished chewing, then swallowed. "I don't want to talk about her."

"Why don't you just admit how you feel?"

"I have," Carrera replied as he cleared his dish from the table. "I can't stand her and you know it. I'm polite for your sake."

She followed him to the sink and swatted his arm. "Amanda May is very, very good to me."

He stayed silent. No point in discussing her. Yes, he *had* feelings for her. Once. A long time ago. Yes, his feelings were strong, but c'mon, she was his first. They had teen love, then he learned the truth about her, broke it off, moved away for college, and kept his distance ever since.

But damn... she looked fantastic. I mean, beyond gorgeous.

She'd probably find her way into a late-night fantasy, but for the moment, he'd pull his mind from the gutter and try to get his grandmother to stop talking about her.

"You asked me to look after her, so I swing by her house every night," Carrera said. "Isn't that enough?"

G-ma grunted. "Even I could do that. How do you know she's home?"

"Sometimes her lights are on."

Shaking her head, she said, "Do better, Carrera." After a beat, she added, "Do you want a piece of cake?"

He grinned. "And a cuppa coffee."

She made him a single-serving cup while he cleaned up the dishes. Then, they sat at the table and he wolfed down a huge piece of cake.

"I'm going to be in a TV commercial," G-ma said.

"How'd you manage that?" he asked before sipping the hot drink.

"Russell's event."

He checked his phone calendar. "That's tomorrow night."

"Will you be there?" Elsa asked.

"Wouldn't miss it."

"Good. I need a ride home."

"How are you getting to his restaurant?" He sipped the coffee.

"Russell's picking me up." She smiled. "I'm getting my hair

done tomorrow and I have a new outfit. It's exciting. He said the media will be there."

"Why?"

"He said he has a big announcement."

"Maybe he's opening a second restaurant," Carrera said.

After a beat, she patted his hand. "Do better. For me."

He nodded as the image of a very sexy, very blonde Slash flashed in his mind. Though he couldn't stand her, he couldn't deny that she looked good. She looked damn good.

On his way home, he stopped in front of Slash's townhouse. The outside light was on, as was a light on the first floor, and both upstairs. He pulled over. Blinds hung closed on the first floor, but light spilled from the upstairs rooms.

He cut the engine. If he rang her doorbell, would she invite him in? What would he even say? They hadn't spoken, really spoken, in years. Would he apologize? If he did, would she even accept it? As he sat there running through the scenarios, she appeared in an upstairs window. Like an angel, backlit in bright light, she peered outside, then slowly closed the blinds. Seconds later, she appeared in the next room and closed those as well.

If she saw him, she didn't let on. From what he did know about her—professionally—nothing got past her.

He got out of his truck, made his way across the quiet residential street. As he was walking up her yard, the front door opened. She stepped outside, hitched her hands on her hips, and glared at him.

She'd pulled her cascading blonde hair into a ponytail, her long bangs draped over one eye. She flicked her head, sending the hair flying off her face.

"I'm sure you're here because Elsa asked you," she bit out. "Be warned, I will *never* play nice with you."

He continued toward her as if pulled by a powerful force. Inches away, he glared down at her.

"I'm not scared of you and I will *never* be intimidated by you," she said.

"You'd know if I was trying to do either," he growled.

She narrowed her eyes.

He gritted his teeth.

"I meant it when I told you to go fuck yourself," she growled.

Then, she glanced at his mouth, her gaze hovering on his lips before she peered into his eyes.

Fuck me.

He lowered his head to kiss her, but she palmed his chest with both hands to keep him at bay.

"If you even *think* about kissing me again, I will knee you in the nuts so hard, you'll see every fucking star in the universe before you pass out on my front lawn." Then, she removed her hands. "Now, get the hell off my property and don't come back."

With a fiery gaze that screamed "fuck off," she stared into his eyes while angry energy swirled around them.

He stood there glaring back.

She walked into her house, shut the door behind her.

"What the hell was I thinking?" he grumbled as he made his way back to his truck.

But he knew exactly what he was thinking.

He might hate her, but he couldn't ignore the attraction, now more powerful than ever.

4

SLASH SAYS YES

Slash

Slash parked her Suzuki Bandit 650 motorcycle at ALPHA, removed her helmet, and dismounted. She collected her things from the bike's saddlebag and made her way toward the employee entrance, located in the rear of the building.

At seven-ten in the morning, only a handful of cars peppered the parking lot.

Normally, she rolled in around eight-thirty or nine, but since she'd gotten no more than three hours sleep, she decided to get a jump on the day.

She could thank her *lack* of sleep on that dickwad of a man, Carrera Santini. If there was anyone who could ruin her day or suck the life out of a fun event, it was him. But last night, as she tossed and turned, she couldn't shake his gorgeous face or rock-hard body from her thoughts. That man had it goin' on.

That man is an asshole.

Pushing him from her thoughts, she stood in front of the

retina scanner. The light turned green, she yanked open the door, and walked inside.

ALPHA was located in Tysons, Virginia, a bustling suburb located twenty minutes outside DC. While the top-secret, off-the-books organization was a part of the Department of Justice, very few within the federal government knew of its existence.

The warehouse-like structure sat tucked at the end of a quiet street. The windowless building bore the sign ALPHA MEAT PACKING over the front door.

The only thing an ALPHA Operative packed was heat.

After years with the Bureau, she'd been selected to be an Operative, something she took great pride in. Then, more recently, she'd earned a coveted spot on ALPHA's BLACK OPS rescue team.

Between those gigs and her regular ALPHA caseload, she was stretched pretty thin. But she didn't have a man in her life, she had no kids, didn't even have a pet, so she put all her energy into going after the worst criminals in the country. She'd made a career of chasing scum. And she was damn good at it.

Sometimes, she'd make an arrest. Other times, she'd get called in for a specialty mission. Those were her favorite, and they included hunting down and eliminating a serial killer or serial rapist. Might be a pedophile who needed to be taken out. Some had been arrested, then released on a technicality. Some had escaped the slammer. Whatever their poison, she lived to chase evil.

As of late, she'd segued from having a regular caseload to becoming more of a specialist. Her area of interest was violent crimes committed against women. She believed these criminals had a special place in hell, and she was more than happy to help them get there.

She turned the corner, entered her office, and set her bags down. Once she connected her laptop to the large monitor, she logged in and got to work.

Space at ALPHA HQ had been tight for months. At present, Slash was sharing her office with Brit Skye Dillinger and Addison Skye Hawk, sisters who had become two of her closest friends.

Her top priority was finding a convicted serial rapist who'd intentionally injured himself in prison. From there, he'd been taken to a nearby hospital. Two days later, while guards were escorting him to the transfer van, he'd escaped with the help of an unknown accomplice. Her concern was that he was going to start assaulting and attacking women while he fled from authorities. Her mission? Find him before the police did, and shut him down for good. That hunt had proven harder than she'd anticipated.

At some point, Brit walked in.

"Hey, mama," Slash said.

Brit set down her things. "I feel like I haven't seen you in forever. How was your mission?"

"Good," Slash replied. "We rescued the women. But check this out... the traffickers had all been killed."

"Hmm," Brit said before pulling her laptop from her computer bag. "By us?"

"No. Sin went in first and he spoke with someone in a ski mask."

Brit scowled. "Who?"

Slash tucked her hair behind her ears. "No idea."

"Did you ask around?"

"No." Slash stood.

"Break room?" Brit asked.

"Yeah, babe."

"I'll go."

As they made their way down the hallway, Brit said, "Joaquin and I are thinking of having a dinner party this Saturday. Will you come?"

They entered the break room.

"Sure." Slash pulled a bottle of water from the fridge. "Rebel's close with Carrera. Will he be there?"

Brit filled a mug with coffee. "What's up with you? You never care about stuff like that." Brit sipped the hot drink. "Ah, soooo good."

Slash opened the bottle, chugged a few mouthfuls. As the chilled water filtered through her, she knew she needed a hit of caffeine to shake the cobwebs from her head.

Slash poured herself a coffee. "Carrera and me in the same room is not a good scene."

"You work all the time," Brit said. "Come over early. We'll go for a run. You love seeing the twins, and they adore you."

Slash smiled. Brit and Rebel's babies were the absolute cutest. "Sold, but be warned... if Carrera's there, it'll get ugly."

"Just freeze him out," Brit said. "Men hate that."

Slash laughed.

Providence Luck breezed into the break room. She and Cooper Grant ran ALPHA.

"Good morning," Providence said. "I just sent out an email for a meeting at ten. Are you both here?"

"I am," Brit replied.

"Depends on the meeting," Slash replied.

Providence and Brit laughed.

"Small conference room." Providence filled a mug with coffee. "Don't be late."

"She looked right at me when she said that," Slash said biting back a smile.

"We know you," Brit said.

"You only *think* you know me," Slash said. "I'm here and it's barely eight in the morning."

"She's got a point," Providence said.

"What's the meeting about?" Slash asked.

"An undercover gig," Providence replied before leaving the room.

"I'll take the bait," Slash said as she and Brit followed Providence out. "What else can you tell us?"

"Ten o'clock." Providence vanished around the corner.

Slash and Brit returned to their office to find Addison working away. The women spent a few minutes catching up, then got busy.

At five minutes 'til ten, they headed for the conference room. Danielle Fox and Emerson Truman joined them. When they entered the room, a few other Operatives were already seated around the conference table.

"This should be interesting," Slash said. "Women-only meeting."

"Maybe it's an HR issue," Addison said.

Slash's shoulder's fell. *What a time suck.*

Providence entered the room, glanced around, and shut the door. "Good, everyone's here. Thanks for being on time,"—she shot Slash a smile and the team cracked up.

Providence eased down at the head of the table. "There's a members-only gentleman's club in Arlington called The Blue Suit Club that popped up on our radar."

"That's a high-end strip club," Emerson said.

Providence nodded. "Months ago, the Bureau got a tip that the club was running a prostitution ring, so they sent in a special agent to check it out."

"Musta been fifty guys who fought over that gig," Slash said.

The women started laughing.

"An agent went there for two months, but he was never approached," Providence explained. "When he inquired about special services, he was told the club offered nothing more than lap dances, but he'd seen a few guys get escorted into a room marked Management Only."

"Doesn't sound like much to go on," said one of the Ops.

"What does this have to do with us?" asked another.

"The Bureau isn't asking a woman to take the case because

it's unethical," Providence said. "They won't ask a female agent to strip."

"Here we go," Slash mumbled under hear breath.

"The undercover gig was passed through the necessary channels to us." Providence let her gaze drift from one woman to the next. "It's not like any assignment we've ever had, so rather than eliminate it, I'm letting you decide if it's something you'd be interested in."

"What's involved?" Danielle asked.

"You'd apply to be a dancer."

"Yeah, that's not happening," Emerson said.

"I had a feeling this wouldn't fly," Providence said.

Emerson stood, as did Danielle, Brit, and Addison. They were out, along with all but two Ops. In the doorway, Brit turned back to Slash. "If anyone has the balls to do this, it's you."

Slash raked her fingers through her hair, moving her long bangs aside. "Talk to us, boss."

"It's simple, really," Providence replied. "The Bureau will create a legend for you. Most likely, you danced out of town. You'll apply to be a dancer. If you get the gig, you'll start working there. The second anyone propositions you, they'd move in for an arrest."

"How's that gonna work?" asked the other female Op. "We can't wear a wire unless we put it in our thong."

"I'm not gonna screw some john so the agency can make an arrest," Slash said.

"I hear you," Providence said. "I don't think the Bureau anticipated anyone would even ask these questions. From what I've been told, they're probably going to send another Special Agent in there."

The other Op stood. "I'm out."

"I understand," Providence said.

The employee left, shutting the door behind her.

"Is this coming from Z?" Slash asked.

"It is," Providence replied.

"I'll check out the club and let you know." Slash pushed out of the chair.

"Let's get your legend set up first," Providence said.

"I'll use the name Lavender Young," Slash said.

"Thanks for even considering this."

"Whatever it takes to get the scum off the street." Slash left the office unfazed over the possibility she'd be ogled by some horny losers.

Shaking my titties to shut down a prostitution ring is no big deal. There was a time when I did that for real.

～

Carrera

CARRERA SPENT the morning familiarizing himself with his new caseload.

It felt great being back in DC. Truth was, he'd gotten burned out from being on the road. Living in motels, eating out all the time had grown old. He missed his family, missed his friends. Taking a break from undercover was exactly what he needed. What he *didn't* need was the lack of sleep he got from the fiery blonde who'd kept him up half the night. He'd fall asleep, dream about Slash, then wake back up.

He hated—fucking hated—that she'd gone back to being a blonde. He liked it better when she had blue or purple or pink hair. He'd always found her stunningly beautiful, but the hair color didn't work for him. That little change made it easier for him *not* to think about her.

Easier, but not impossible.

Carrera's cell phone rang, and he answered. "Hey, Dad, are you cruising the Potomac?"

"There's been a mix-up," his dad said. "This afternoon, I'm captaining a family reunion, but I just hung up with Evangeline Develin from Develin and Associates. She got an email confirming the company's cruise tonight. Only it's *not* tonight, it's tomorrow. No one answered at the office, so she called me. I don't even know how she got my number. Anyway, I called the office, but had no luck."

"What do you mean, no luck?"

"No one answered."

"Did you call Jazz's cell phone?"

"She didn't take my call," his dad replied.

Dammit.

Carrera grabbed his sunglasses, strode out of his cubicle. "I'll handle it."

Several agents nodded or said hello as he made his way out of the department. Bypassing the elevators, Carrera headed for the stairs.

"Are you in town?" his dad asked.

"Yeah, just got back." As he trotted down the steps, he asked, "Has this happened before?"

"Oh sure, but Jazz got it straightened out."

Jazz—short for Jasmine—was Carrera's baby sister. She'd worked for him since graduating college. Currently, she was his executive director.

"Are you on your ship?" Carrera asked as he made his way to the parking garage beneath the building.

"Yup," his dad answered.

"I'll call you back." Carrera hung up.

He jumped in his truck and drove out. In the bright June sunlight, he slipped on his shades, rolled down the windows, and headed toward his executive offices in Georgetown.

Traffic clogged the streets, so he called his sister. Her phone rang, no answer. When he got voicemail, he hung up. Then, he called Gracie from marketing, and also got no answer.

Where the hell are they?

Fifteen minutes later, he parked in the lot and strode into the office building at The Washington Harbour. He took the stairs, two at a time, to the third floor, strode down the hallway to his business office. As he suspected, the door was locked.

After keying his way inside, he called out, "Jazz," before walking through the quiet space. The lights were on, but he couldn't find a single employee. No receptionist, no marketers, no accounting team, no customer service reps. At the end of the hall, the executive director's office door stood wide open. His sister wasn't sitting at her desk.

The business office was open daily from ten 'til seven. Clearly, he'd missed the news that his business was closed today.

He sat at his sister's desk, plugged in the password, and got to work. First, he cleared up the confusion as to which group was cruising when. Then, he called the contacts to clarify.

During his phone call with Evangeline Develin, another line started ringing.

"Sorry again, Evangeline," Carrera said.

"No problem," Evangeline said. "Thanks for calling me yourself. Will I see you Saturday at Joaquin and Brit's dinner party?"

"Wouldn't miss it."

A second line started ringing.

"We'll talk Saturday," he said. "Enjoy your cruise." He answered the second call. "Carrera Cruises. Can you hold for me?"

"Sure," said the caller.

He answered the first call, apologized for the long wait, and helped the customer.

Thirty minutes later, the phones finally stopped ringing. He leaned back in the chair and swiveled to stare out at the

Potomac river. A massive headache pounded like a bass drum in his temples.

The front door chimed. Pushing out of the chair, he made his way toward reception.

Jazz was back, as were his employees. All of them—the men and the women—were wearing cheap flip flops, their shoes in hand. From what he could tell, everyone had just gotten a pedicure. They all stood there like bumbling idiots.

Jazz broke into a lopsided grin while she hid her stilettos behind her back. "Heyyyy, brother! Whatcha doin' heeeere?"

Dammit, she's been drinking.

"Conference room," Carrera said. "*Now*."

"Oops," Jazz blurted.

Once there, he stood at the head, placed his palms on the tabletop, and eyed his employees. "What's going on? It's four in the afternoon and you've been gone for a while."

Jazz huffed. "I took my employees out for lunch, then we had a mani-pedi day."

Carrera stared at her. "C'mon, Jazz."

"We took a few hours off, so what is the big deal?" his sister pushed back.

"If you do that again, you're terminated," Carrera said. "All of you."

"I'm sorry," said one of his employees.

"Same," said another.

"You can dock my pay," said a third.

"If you need time off—" Carrera said.

"It's not about that," Jazz interrupted. "We're here five days a week, week in and week out. I thought it would be nice—"

"It's called a job, Jasmine," Carrera said. "No one here works weekends. I've got a different team for that." He eyed his employees. "If anyone needs time off, do you take personal days or vacation?"

Nods from everyone, but his sister. She sat there giving him a glassy-eyed glare.

"I might not be on site, but I'm available if any of you have an issue or need to talk to me." Carrera confirmed that everyone had his number before he dismissed them.

Putting Jazz in charge had *not* been a smart move.

Alone with his sis, he shut the conference room door. "Jasmine, you're the boss."

"Yup, and I'm a damn good one."

"Dad called because there was a mix-up with cruises. I get that people make mistakes, but you can't shut the office, not answer your phone, and not give me a heads-up."

"Whatever. Look, it won't happen again."

"This isn't the first time."

She glared at him. "Save the lecture."

Two months ago, Jazz had gone out of town for the weekend —which he knew about—but she didn't show back up for work until Friday. No one could locate her. Like today, she hadn't answered her phone.

After what had happened with his late sister, Mara, his family was freaking out. Carrera had been out of town on an undercover assignment and couldn't get back.

Though his dad *hadn't* wanted to step up and run the company that week, he had.

"This is the sixth time something like this has happened," Carrera said.

"Ohmygod, you're keeping track? Seriously, Carrera! And what is the big deal? It's not like the company goes under or anything." She glanced at her finger. "Oh, damn, my polish got messed up. Crap, now I'm gonna have to get that redone."

"Jasmine, I gotta let you go."

With a grin, she shot out of the chair. "Thanks! I'll get my nails redone, but I'll be back tomorrow."

"No, I'm firing you."

Her smile dropped. "For real?"

"Yeah. This isn't working out. Give me your office key."

She pulled a keyring out and flung it at him. He snatched it just before it sailed into his eye.

"That woulda hurt," she sneered. She stormed out, then marched right back in. "You're a jerk. This was a stupid job anyway."

Seconds later, the front door slammed shut so hard, he expected the glass to shatter. To his surprise, it didn't.

At twenty-five, Jazz wasn't ready to lead his company. He loved his sister, but she wasn't the best person for the job. After too many chances, he had to let her go. Even so, he hated doing it. She was family, and to a Santini, that was *everything*.

Carrera needed to find a replacement. For the next few days, he hoped his existing team would step up. Time to find out.

He left the conference room, stood in the middle of the office. Within seconds, all eyes were on him.

"Jazz doesn't work here anymore," he said.

"Oh, boy," someone muttered.

"If anyone else is unhappy working here, we can talk in her old office." He didn't want to put anyone on the spot, so he offered an encouraging smile before walking down the hall to her corner office.

He could hear plenty of whispers, but he wanted to give them time to take in what had just happened. A few minutes later, one of his marketing reps appeared in the doorway.

"I'm sorry about today," Gracie began. "It won't happen again. If you need help, I can fill in until you find a replacement."

"Call me for any reason," he said, "and let me know if Jazz shows up telling you she has her job back."

"I will," Gracie replied.

Carrera spent the next few hours working with Gracie.

They cleared out emails and followed up with any outstanding customer-related issues. She appeared responsible, but the gnawing in his gut wouldn't go away. He wasn't going to quit his job at the Bureau, but he couldn't abandon his business either. He'd trial her while he figured out next steps.

Then, he checked in with the rest of the team. They'd sobered up and were taking care of business. At seven that evening, his employees left, and he locked up behind them.

On the way to Russell's restaurant in Arlington, he remembered back to when he and Mara had first decided to open the business.

Just ten months apart, they'd been best buds as kids. Both went to the University of Pennsylvania. He studied criminal justice, she, business. After graduating, he accepted a position at the Bureau. She worked for a marketing firm until they came up with the idea for the tour boat cruise line. They pooled their savings, borrowed money from G-ma—which they repaid with interest—and grew it from an idea on a napkin to the area's most popular boat excursions.

I miss you, Mara.

He knew it was wrong to compare his sisters. Jazz and Mara were completely different. Mara was all about being responsible. Jazz was a free spirit. Mara squirreled her money away while Jazz spent hers, then went in search of more.

He loved both his sisters, and he ached for his loss, for his family's loss.

His thoughts were pulled back to the moment when he drove into the parking lot of Russell's. Local news vans made it impossible to find a spot. Carrera drove around back and parked.

As he made his way around the building, he spotted Russell escorting G-ma toward the entrance while the camera crews captured their moment.

He dropped some pounds.

In addition to slimming down, Russell had cut his hair military-short. His dark suit, white shirt, and power-red tie were a change from the Khaki pants and golf shirts he used to wear.

Carrera had only seen Russell a few times in the six months since his friend had moved back. Between his tight schedule, and Russell's new restaurant, they'd been keeping in touch through texts.

Before entering the eatery, Russell addressed the news crews. "Helping others is what gets me out of bed every single day."

"Is that your Grandmom?" asked one of the reporters.

"Elsa is a close friend's grandmother," he replied, "but I've known her most of my life, so yeah, I think of her as my G-ma."

"Russell Fitzpatrick is a hard-working, trustworthy, young man," G-ma said before painting on a smile.

Carrera bit back a laugh. Russell had asked her to say that.

Russell kissed her cheek. "Aww, thanks G-ma." He smiled at the television crews. "Come on in and we'll get you set up with some incredible appetizers."

With another ear-to-ear grin, Russell vanished inside with his grandmother.

Carrera held the door while everyone traipsed past. The restaurant was busy, but not filled to capacity. After Russell seated G-ma at a table, he started saying hello to the seated customers. Carrera made his way over, sat next to his grandmother at a four-top.

"Hey, G-ma. You look pretty."

She smiled. "Thank you, dear. Russell wanted me to say that line. How'd I do?"

"You rocked it out," he said, and she laughed.

A server delivered a tray of appetizers. Sliders, fried calamari, grilled peppers, and macaroni salad. Even though Carrera had been hungry for hours, the food didn't look very appetizing.

G-ma leaned up and he put his ear next to her mouth. "The macaroni salad is bad. Don't eat it."

He raised his brows.

She nodded. "Rancid. I can smell it."

He grimaced. "Have you eaten?"

"Homemade lasagna."

His stomach growled. "I can wait." Rather than dig into the sliders, which looked meh, he glanced around the room.

"How long has Russell had the restaurant?" G-ma asked.

"Five or six months," Carrera replied. "He bought it when he moved back."

"Where'd he go?"

"He went to live with his mom in Boston last year."

"How's the restaurant doing?"

Carrera shrugged. "First time here."

"Excuse me," Russell said into a mic. "Can I get everyone's attention?" The room quieted. "Hello and welcome to Russell's. I'm Russell Fitzpatrick. Thanks to everyone for being here. I hope you're enjoying the appetizers." He paused, his gaze canvassing the room. "As many of you know, in addition to running my successful restaurant, I've been very active in our community." He started reciting all the community activities he'd been involved with or had spearheaded. "It's my great honor to announce that I'm running for United States Congress!"

I wasn't expecting that.

He and G-ma exchanged glances.

Several in the room started cheering.

Though surprised to hear, Carrera applauded. He thought Russell had zero interest in politics, but maybe that had changed since he'd gotten involved in the community. Carrera couldn't fault his friend for wanting to make a difference.

"I'm going to work hard for my constituents, put your needs first, and fight hard to make sure that the good people of

Virginia get the tax breaks they need," Russell continued. "If you want to be a part of my campaign, talk to me or to my campaign manager."

A man standing next to Russell raised his hand. "I'm the campaign manager."

"A round of drinks on the house," Russell said. "And I hope I can earn your vote through hard work and an honest campaign. God bless." He turned off the mic and start shaking hands with everyone standing nearby.

"That was exciting," G-ma said.

A server came by. When she made eye contact with Carrera, she smiled. "Hi, would you like a glass of champagne to celebrate with the future congressman? Or maybe a shot?"

"I'm ready for that lasagna," Carrera said to his grandmother.

"Oh, did you order lasagna?" the server asked. "Wait, we don't have that on the menu."

"I need to make a stop before we head home, so we should probably go," G-ma said.

"We're gonna pass on the drinks," Carrera said.

The server's expression dropped. "How 'bout a coupon for a free appetizer?"

"We're good, but thanks," Carrera said.

Russell walked over, a wide grin covering his face. "Is this great or what?"

"Congratulations," Carrera said as he extended his hand.

As the two men shook hands, Russell said, "Well, I haven't won yet." Russell addressed G-ma. "Thanks for joining me today, Elsa. It means a lot."

"I hope you win," G-ma said.

"Carrera, I was hoping you'd join my campaign, maybe take that pretty mug of yours and go door-to-door talking to the good people of Virginia."

"I wish I could help, but I'm stretched thin."

Russell shot him a smile. "I'll get you to change your mind." After a hearty laugh, he squeezed G-ma's shoulder. "Thanks for being here."

Russell moved on to the next table as the server handed Carrera a business card. "It's for free appetizers." Her cheeks pinked. "I put my number on the back, if you ever want to have coffee or something."

A patron called out, "Excuse me," so she hurried off.

"Ready to head out?" Carrera asked his grandmother.

"I need to stop by Luciano's on my way home."

As he stood, Carrera dropped the coupon card on the table.

"You're going to break that girl's heart," G-ma said. "She seemed like a sweet person."

"That's why she *shouldn't* be hanging with me."

He guided her outside, then stopped on the sidewalk. "I had to park out back. Do you want to wait here?"

"I'm fine. Amanda May holds my hand, so I don't fall."

Carrera clasped her hand.

"Did you stop by last night and see her?" G-ma asked.

"I did."

"You're a good boy."

"She threatened to knee me in the groin."

G-ma laughed. "What did you do to deserve that?"

"I thought about kissing her."

"Can't blame you, honey. She was a catch all those years ago and she's double the catch now."

Carrera released a growl.

Frustration festered as he brought G-ma to his truck, then helped her climb in. After closing the truck door, he got in beside her.

"Does Russell have family?" G-ma asked.

"He's got a sister who lives in Washington state. His mom died while he was in Boston and his dad passed several years ago."

"That was an exciting announcement. Why don't you help him with his campaign?"

"I'm too busy. I had to let Jazz go, so I've got to put in extra hours at the cruise line."

"What did she do?"

"Not work," he replied.

"I'm surprised she didn't stop by to see me."

"She will when she runs out of money."

G-ma chuckled. "Probably tomorrow."

A short ride later, he pulled up to Luciano's gated entrance. "Carrera and Elsa Santini."

The guard made a call, then opened the gate. "Mr. Santini is expecting you."

As Carrera drove forward, G-ma said, "It's like we're entering the gates of heaven."

"Or hell," Carrera added.

She swatted his arm. "All my boys are good."

Carrera wondered what his grandmother would say if she knew what her "good boys" did in their free time.

Once inside, Luciano kissed their grandmother on both cheeks, then brought them into his kitchen. He opened a fifty-five-year-old luxury brandy, poured a little into three snifters and handed them out. "Alla famiglia."

They tapped glasses and sipped. The delicious liquor awaked Carrera's taste buds. He savored the drink before swallowing it down, feeling the warmth all the way to his stomach.

"Delicious," G-ma said. "Let's talk business."

Together, they made their way to his home office. There, she settled into one of two guest chairs across from his massive desk. Rather than sit, Carrera stood behind the second chair.

"What can I do for my G-ma?" Luciano asked.

"I need to confirm you made the changes to my estate," she said.

"Of course."

"Show me."

Luciano walked over to the bookcase, tapped a button hidden under a shelf. The door swung sideways, he stepped into a room. A moment later, he returned with a bound leather notebook. Back at his desk, he sat in the guest chair next to her, opened the notebook, pulled out several sheets of paper, and handed them to her.

She grew quiet as she read through all of them. When finished, she kissed his cheek. "I had another dream I went to be with the Lord."

Carrera's stomach dropped. He and Luciano exchanged glances.

"Have you been going to mass every day again?" Luciano asked.

"Just a few times a week," she replied. "What does that have to do with anything?"

"This has happened before," Luciano said. "You're gonna live a long, long time, Elsa Santini."

"I hope so. Someone has to keep an eye on you boys." A sadness fell over her. "Luciano, I made lasagna. Come back with Carrera and me for supper."

"Save me a piece," Luciano replied. "I'll swing by tomorrow for breakfast."

Her jutting eyebrows wrinkled her forehead. "Breakfast?"

"My stomach doesn't know the diff," he replied before turning toward Carrera. "We need to talk. Can you find time in the next few days?"

"Who the hell knows."

"He had to fire Jazz," G-ma shared.

Luciano walked them out. "I'll be in touch."

The drive home was quiet. Back at G-ma's house, she heated the lasagna, they ate at the kitchen table.

"This has gotta be your best," he said.

"I'm glad you like it." Her gaze lingered on his face. "I have a question and I need an honest answer. I always come to you for the truth, Carrera."

He nodded, his mouth filled with delicious seasoned meat, homemade red sauce, a blend of cheeses, and thick lasagna noodles. He swallowed it down.

"Is Luciano an assassin?"

His brain stuttered to a stop. Unsure how to proceed, he studied her face. If he lied, she'd know. But he would never break the vow he made.

Rather than muddle through some bullshit answer, he said nothing.

She nodded, once. "Are you?"

More silence.

"That's what I thought." With her eyes still locked on his, she added. "Are you searching for Mara's killer?"

"Always," he replied.

"When you find him—and I know you will—put a bullet in him for me."

"You got it, G-ma," he said. "With pleasure."

5

THE BLUE SUIT CLUB

Slash

At ten-fifteen that evening, Slash entered The Blue Suit Club wearing a black, leather halter top and hot pants. She'd pulled her hair over to one side and around her shoulder, holding it in place with a clip. She wore no jewelry, had no ID. In her back pocket sat a burner she'd picked up on the way.

She shadowed her eyes with smoky makeup, lightened her lips with gloss, and added a small amount of blush. Beyond using the name Lavender Young, she was keeping her story very basic. The less said, the better.

Excitement pounded through her. It had been years since she'd gone undercover, something she'd loved doing. Sometimes life was easier when she pretended to be someone else. Someone who had no problems, no issues. Someone who wasn't lonely, someone who could outrun her demons. Just some girl named Lavender, or maybe she'd call an audible on the line and change her name to Candy. Her name never mattered. What mattered was doing her job, doing it well, and moving on to the next one.

In this case, her only goal was finding the prostitution ring. If it existed, she'd help shut it down.

The Blue Suit Club was the premiere gentleman's club in the area. She strolled around, checking out the vibe and taking in the scene. The music was rockin', the lights were low, but all four stages were well lit. Three of the four dancers wore thongs, one was a total nudie.

It was one thing to put her boobs out there, but no way would she dance naked. As she meandered around, she eyed the clientele. The split of men to women looked to be seventy-thirty.

There were several dancers giving lap dances while the men ogled them. But it wasn't just men getting the up-close-and-personal attention. A dancer was giving a lap dance to a woman at a table of women.

Male servers were shirtless, their pants held up by blue suspenders attached to blue dress pants. Female servers wore a blue bikini top, except for two who wore blue pasties. All wore shorty shorts.

She hadn't spotted any surveillance cameras in the bar, but two ceiling-mounted cameras were posted near each of the four stages. Maybe management wanted to make sure no one groped the dancers. As she wandered down the hall toward the restrooms, she saw no cameras. What she did see was the Management Only door. She tried to open it.

Locked.

No surprise there.

A digital card reader had been screwed into the doorframe.

Rather than return to the main room, she ducked into the restroom.

Shiny marble floors and countertops reflected the chande-lier hanging in the middle of the room. The private stall smelled of lilac. If she ended up going undercover, she couldn't complain about the digs.

Back through the club she went, stopping at the long bar in the front.

It was large enough to keep all four bartenders hopping busy. Both men were bare chested, dressed in blue suspenders and blue pants. The women wore blue bikini tops and blue hot pants. A woman, wearing a blue shirt and blue pants, lifted the counter and stepped behind the bar.

Slash's brain skidded to an abrupt halt. She'd recognize that strawberry-blonde bob anywhere. It was Karen Woodside, former ALPHA Operative. Not only had she gotten herself fired, she'd been arrested for obstruction of justice. Because Karen had been a law enforcement agent, her sentence had been reduced to time served. But the real punishment was that Karen could never work in law enforcement again.

That would effin' kill me.

Slash watched from a safe distance as Karen spoke to a male bartender before heading toward the back of the club. Pulling her long bangs over her eyes, Slash followed Karen until she entered the hallway that led to the restrooms. Instead of stopping in front of the Management Only door, she swiped a keycard outside the office marked GM. Karen entered and shut the door.

Damn crazy world.

As Slash made her way toward the front of the club, she kept her head down.

Slash was the one Operative who'd been willing to work there, but there was no way in hell Karen would hire her. Not only did Karen blame Slash for getting fired and arrested, Karen would know she was there as an ALPHA Op.

Frustration pummeled her. She hated having to walk from the gig before it even got legs.

Slash sidled over to the bar and got the attention of a

female bartender. After waiting on someone, she dropped a napkin on the bar in front of Slash.

"What can I get you?"

"Who does the hiring around here?" Slash asked.

"The GM for the dancers, and Bradley for the bartenders and servers." She pointed to a man at the other end of the bar. "That's Bradley."

"What's the GM's name?" Slash asked.

"Karen, or KW."

As Slash slunk out of the club, she started brainstorming ways she could get Karen to hire her, a challenge Slash could not pass up. A smile lifted her lips as she climbed into her SUV and drove way.

She was determined to find out if Karen Woodside was running a prostitution ring.

THE NEXT MORNING, Slash got to ALPHA early again. As she exited her vehicle, Providence parked nearby. Slash waited, and the women walked toward the entrance together.

"I checked out the club last night," Slash said.

"That was fast," Providence said.

They each stood in front of the retina scanner, the light flashed green twice, and they went inside.

"I ran into an obstacle, but I've got a workaround," Slash said.

Providence ran the overall business and managed the other teams, and Cooper managed the Operatives.

"Let's talk now," Providence said. "I'll run it by Cooper during our morning sync-up."

In Providence's office, Slash set her bags on one of the guest chairs, stood behind the other.

"Karen Woodside is running The Blue Suit Club," Slash said.

Providence tucked her short hair behind an ear. "Wow, that's a surprise."

"I need to get fake fired," Slash continued. "We need a few Ops who're in on it, and we need everyone in the company to know I got canned, so I gotta create a scene."

Providence regarded her for several seconds. "I'm listening."

"Karen hates ALPHA, and she blames me for getting fired and arrested. She also knows I love working here. If I get fired, I'll be angry as hell, so she and I can bond over our common enemy. If she calls to verify—and she will—anyone here can confirm I'm gone."

Providence broke eye contact for a second. "That's well thought out. Unfortunately, there's a problem with that."

Slash nodded. "She's got motor mouth, so she could talk about ALPHA at the club. I can try to contain the convo to her office, but she could bring it up in front of anyone."

"Let me run this by Cooper."

Slash shouldered her bags. "If that won't work, you'll have to send another Special Agent."

Providence shook her head. "I don't want to do that."

Slash opened the office door, turned back. "I can do this."

As Slash made her way down the hallway, Providence called out, "Meet me in Cooper's office in ten."

A smile lifted Slash's lips. "You got it."

Carrera

AT NINE IN THE MORNING, Carrera made his way down the dock, eyeing each of his tour boats, nestled in their slips. Most days all eight were in use, sometimes twice daily. Some days, a company would book an early-morning breakfast tour.

While he loved what he and Mara had built, the past year

had been rough. Losing his sister had been heart wrenching. Losing his business partner had forced him to put his business up for sale. Three days before closing on the sale, his dad had offered a helping hand.

His dad appeared on the stern of a vessel, snapping Carrera back to the moment.

"There's the captain," Carrera called out.

His dad waved. "Hello, son."

Paul Santini hadn't yet dressed in his captain's uniform, so he looked relaxed in a golf shirt and pants. These days, his dad wore his smile with ease, but it had been a long and hard-fought road for the elder Santini.

Standing a few inches shorter than Carrera, Paul kept his graying hair short, his face clean shaven, and his physique as trim as he could for a man who enjoyed a daily dose of sweets.

After a hardy hug, his dad stepped back on board, Carrera close on his heels.

"You just missed my sponsor," his dad said. "He joined me for breakfast."

"That's great, Dad."

"Are you hungry?"

"I could eat," Carrera replied.

Into the ship they went. The crew was already on board, the chef and his staff getting organized in the galley.

"Good morning, Mr. Santini," said the chef. "Eggs and toast?"

"That would be great, Chef," Carrera replied.

Ten minutes later, Carrera and his dad were sitting outside, the morning sun warming Carrera's skin.

"Doing your monthly ship visit?" his dad asked.

"No, I'm here because I need your help."

His dad sighed. "Jazz told me what happened. She's got a temper like your mom, and boy was she flaming mad."

"So, about that." Carrera sipped the coffee. "I know you love cruising in the summer months—"

"I had a feeling that's why you texted me," his dad said.

"I've got my senior marketing rep—Gracie—running things, but you did a great job after Mara died. Dad, I can't work full time and run the cruise line. I trust you—"

His dad smiled. "Thank you for saying that. I'll do it, but I'll still captain my ship on the weekends."

Carrera extended his hand and his dad shook it. "Dad, you're a lifesaver."

To his surprise, tears clouded his dad's eyes. "That means a lot. There was a time when I couldn't tie my own shoe."

Carrera glanced down at his dad's feet. "And now, look at you. Shoes tied *and* you came through for me... again."

As he wiped his eyes, his dad chuckled. "Is there someone at the office I can train to take over, so I can return here?"

"Gracie stepped up," Carrera explained. "She's a hard worker, so if you see potential, let her run with it."

"Being outside every day is good for my soul. This job saved me."

"It helped, but you saved yourself."

"Actually, I stand corrected. God saved me. And I got sober. You gave me a chance, and I think it would be difficult for me to be in an office long term. I'd be counting down the days until I can retire."

Carrera finished the last bite of toast. "I appreciate your doing this. Can you start Monday?"

"Yeah," his dad replied. "I'll call Gracie and let her know. She was very helpful last go-round."

Carrera downed the rest of the coffee, said goodbye to the crew, and hugged his dad. On the pier, he said, "Call me for anything."

"Always do," his dad replied. "I take it you're in town for a while."

Carrera nodded. "It's good to be home."

"It's good to have you home, son."

Slash

AT JUST PAST four that afternoon, Slash walked into Cooper's office. Brit, Addison, and Emerson were already there. The stage had been set, the plan in place. Now, it was up to them to carry it out.

She shut the door and extended her hand to Cooper. "I'm the last person to get mushy, but I'm going to miss you guys. If you give away my job—"

"That would never happen," Cooper said as they shook hands. "You're irreplaceable. You and I go back—"

"Way back," she said and swiped a tear.

Brit hugged her. "I won't let anyone take your desk."

"We'll see you Saturday at Brit and Rebel's dinner party," Addison added.

"Not if I'm working," Slash said.

"Tell Karen Woodside you've got a pre-existing commitment," Brit said. "You're already giving one-hundred-percent by even doing this. You deserve *one* night with friends."

"I agree," Cooper said. "Who will I do a Jell-O shooter with?"

Slash laughed. "We haven't done those in years. Alright, I'm in for Saturday." After steeling her spine, she said, "Let's do this."

Cooper held out his Glock. "I'm going to ask for your weapon, so give mine back to me."

She tucked it into the back of her pants.

Cooper opened the door. "How dare you talk to me that way!"

"You deserve it!" Slash said. "I worked that case for months and you're taking it away from me?"

"It's taking you too damn long," Cooper yelled. "You've got too many cases and you're spread too thin. Plus, we've had some complaints about the way you're talking to witnesses."

"You need to do a reality check." Slash carried the argument into the hallway. "We're done with this convo, and I'm not giving you that case."

"You don't have a choice," Cooper said, following her. "I took it, and if you continue disrespecting me, you won't have a caseload."

"Fuck you, Cooper Grant!"

Providence came rushing around the corner. "I can hear you on the other side of the building! What's going on here?"

"Mind your damn business," Slash hollered. "You don't manage the Ops, but maybe you should because he sucks at it."

"That's it! I've had it," Cooper exclaimed. "You're terminated for insubordination."

"You're firing me? Are you out of your mind? You don't need a reality check, mister, you need an effin' sanity check!"

Cooper got in her face. "Give me your weapon."

Glaring, she handed his Glock back to him.

As she stormed past the employees who stood there with their mouths agape, Slash shouted, "I'm fired, so you dumb asses better watch what you say or do. If you step out of line by a damn inch, he'll fire you too!"

She strode down the hall, grabbed her handbag from her office, and hoofed it outside.

Cooper followed her into the parking lot. "I already deleted you from the organization. Good luck finding work in law enforcement."

Those words, though untrue, cut to her core. Heaving in a breath, she jumped in her SUV, started the engine, and hauled ass out. Once she cleared the parking lot, she pulled over.

Her heart was pounding out of her chest. While the outburst had been planned down to the reason for her being fired, it was still hard to hear. Outside of G-ma, Slash didn't have family. Her family were the people she worked with. She loved them all, treasured the relationships she'd built with each of them.

From her days of working cases at the Bureau with Rebel, to her early days at ALPHA with Dakota and Sin, she'd made friends for life. She'd been the first female Operative, so she especially treasured her female friends.

I can do this.

Shaking off the bad vibes and reminding herself that she hadn't really been shit-canned, she put the SUV in gear and she drove away. As soon as she got home, she pulled her computer bag from the floor behind her seat where she'd hidden it hours ago.

She sat at her kitchen table, logged into ALPHA's secure network and shot off an email to Providence and Cooper. "I'll keep up with progress reports."

Then, she sent a separate one to Brit, Addison, and Emerson. "Did I pull it off?"

Within seconds after sending it, her email binged with a reply.

"That was great!" Brit said. "The entire office is talking about it. People are stunned. STUNNED! Miss you already. Come by early on Saturday and we'll hang."

Her email binged with a reply from Cooper. "Thanks for the laugh. Stellar performance."

In anticipation of her upcoming gig, she created an online file, then pulled up a daily report. She added today's date, fully anticipating she'd be returning to the club that evening, and she would have news to share.

Then, she went for a beast of a run. Forty-minutes later, she returned home, soaked in perspiration. She wanted to go for a mind-clearing motorcycle ride, but Friday rush hour was the worst time for that. She made a mental note to get up early Saturday morning and ride when the streets were less trafficked.

It was eight-twenty when she entered The Blue Suit Club, this time fully prepared to meet with Karen. Forcing herself not to roll her eyes at the thought of that woman, she beelined toward the bar. The place was already busy, dancers shaking their booties on all four stages while servers bustled around delivering drinks and eats.

Filled with determination, Slash slid onto a stool, caught the head bartender's attention.

"How's it going?" he asked.

"I'm lookin' to dance," Slash said.

"I manage the bar," he said. "Are you interested in serving drinks?"

She shrugged. "Lookin' to pay the bills. What pays better?"

He shot her a smile. "Depends on how hard you hustle. My team does pretty damn well—"

Slash leaned forward. "Don't bullshit me." She glanced at his name tag. "Bradley."

"Dancing. Not gonna lie, having you back here would be good for business."

"Why's that?"

"You're gorgeous."

"Yeah, okay, so can I talk to your GM?"

He pulled out his phone. "She's in her office. I'll text her." After he finished, he shot her another smile. "Good luck. You'll clean up here." He pulled a bottle of white wine. "On the house."

"Water," she said.

He poured her a sparkling water and added a lime wedge. She flashed him a smile, watched his cheeks flush before he moved on to serve someone else.

She swiveled to watch the dancers and the wicked memories came racing back. A chill rippled down her back, but she wasn't deterred. She had come so far since her life had splintered into a million slivers. She'd only been sixteen when she'd started dancing. A fake ID, along with her unwillingness to take no for an answer, had her working the stage at a shithole strip club.

What Slash hated were the lap dances. She hated gyrating on a pervert, hated the way they eye-fucked her, hated their hard-ons even more. But, back then, she needed a way to survive. It had sucked, but being in that foster home had been much, much worse.

Until she got offered a lot of money to screw one of the patrons.

That's when she hit rock bottom.

"Here comes the GM." The bartender's words crashed into Slash's ears.

Slash followed his gaze as Karen Woodside zoomed into focus.

"What the hell do you want?" Karen asked.

"Ah, fuck me," Slash bit out. "I came here for a job, but that's not gonna happen." Hoping Karen would take the bait, Slash pushed off the stool and took a step into the crowd.

"Whoa, whoa, wait a sec," Karen said. "You need a job?"

Slash turned. "At least your ears still work."

Karen's lips twitched.

C'mon, bitch, ask me why I need a job.

"Is this a joke?" Karen asked.

Slash got up in Karen's face. "I'm here. I need a job. Either you give me five fucking minutes of your time, or I'm out." With a hand on her hip, she glared at Karen.

"You want to dance?"

"I've danced. I've also served booze. I can do either. You hiring or not?"

"Sure, what the hell. Come on back," Karen said. "This, I gotta hear. You packin' heat?"

"No," Slash replied.

But she did have her switchblade. One flick of her wrist and the blade expanded to a seven-inch knife. She'd had it for so long, it was an extension of herself. Normally tucked in a sheath around her ankle, she'd stashed it in her hobo bag.

She tossed the bartender a nod before following Karen, her reddish-blonde bob swinging back and forth. The clubbers were seated at round tables, their attention locked on the mostly nude dancers on stage while several others gyrated on laps, hoping for big tips. Servers whizzed by delivering food and drinks. The place was humming with energy, while lust hung heavy in the air.

Down the hall Karen trudged. She stopped at the door marked GM, swiped her keycard. The light flashed green and they entered the office. Once inside, Karen sat behind her desk, crossed her arms, and said nothing.

Rather than sit, Slash placed her hands on the back of the guest chair. The barebones office was in stark contrast to the upscale club. Facing into the room sat a black desk with a computer and a swivel chair, two guest chairs, that looked old as fuck, and a gray sofa with stains on one of the cushions.

"I got fired from ALPHA," Slash said.

Karen's shrill laugh made her skin crawl. "Spill it."

"Cooper accused me of taking too long to solve cases, told me I was hard on witnesses. He yanked cases. I cussed him out. We got into a screaming match and I'm fired for insubordination."

More chuckling from Karen. "At least you weren't arrested."

"Yet," Slash said. "Guy's a total tool."

"I hate ALPHA," Karen said.

"We finally agree on something. I hate ALPHA too."

"Why are you here? There are strip clubs all over the DMV."

"Blue Suit is a cut above. I need to make decent money, and I'm ready to cut loose."

"Hmm, well, I gotta say, your hair looks a lot better."

Slash didn't give a fuck what Karen thought of her hair, but she needed to play nice. "Maybe your clientele will like it too, especially when I shake it in their faces during all the lap dances I'm gonna give."

"Why don't you come back tomorrow night and I'll trial you."

"My baby bro is getting married, so that's not gonna fly," she lied. "How 'bout I get up on stage tonight?"

"Are you a topless-only or a nudie girl?"

"Topless."

"Show me your tits."

Yeah, right.

"On stage," Slash pushed back.

Karen studied Slash. "I'll take you back for an audition. If one of the girls will give up a time slot, you might have to split your tips with them."

"Whatever it takes."

"Wow, you're desperate."

"You have no idea," Slash replied.

Slash followed Karen to the other side of the club, and down a hallway toward a door marked Dancers. To Slash's surprise, the door wasn't even locked.

She didn't like that these women were vulnerable to the clientele. Any perv could just walk back here.

The large room had over twenty stations. Each came equipped with a well-lit mirror, a small counter, and a chair. Rather than use a dressing room, the women were getting dressed or undressed at their station.

Karen stopped at a station halfway down. "Use this one."

There was a photo of a woman taped to the mirror.

"Whose is this?" Slash asked.

"Terri, but she ghosted on me. Her and five others." Karen rolled her eyes. "Too much damn turnover. If things work out for you, you can't ghost on me too." Karen arched an eyebrow as she gave Slash the once-over. "It's no secret I don't like you, so don't get your hopes up."

I'll get this gig.

"How can I make money besides dancing? You got VIP rooms?"

"Yeah, and they're managed by me." Karen glanced around the spacious dressing room. "Girls," she called out. "I got an audition. Who's willing to give up a spot?"

Most didn't even glance over.

When Karen's request was met with silence, Slash called out, "You can have my tips."

Heads whipped in her direction. Several women hurried over as Karen headed out.

"Hey, I'm Slash."

"Deb," introduced one. "I'm up in ten on the main stage. "You can keep half your tips."

"You sure?" Slash asked.

Deb's spray tan was done well, her long dark hair fell down her back, and she had several piercings and tats.

"Melody?" called a woman nearby.

Slash flipped her gaze towards her as the woman moved into view.

No way. Could it be?

"Melody, is that you?" the woman repeated.

I haven't heard that name in years.

"Jilly?" Slash asked.

"Yes, it's me!" Jilly hugged her. "Damn, girl, you look good."

"You too," Slash said. "I go by Slash now."

"Love the name," Jilly said.

"Did you dance together somewhere?" Deb asked.

"We knew each other a while ago," Jilly replied.

It had been fifteen years since Slash had seen her one-time foster sister. Jilly Linder hadn't changed much. Her ebony skin shimmered in a light dusting of gold glitter, and false eyelashes made her warm brown eyes pop.

Jilly was a little taller than Slash, a fuller-figured woman with long, black hair. What Slash remembered most about her friend was that she had the heart of an angel.

"I tried to find you," Slash said. "But I couldn't."

"I keep a low profile," Jilly said. "You got time to catch up tonight?"

"I'd love that," Slash replied.

Jilly gave Slash's outfit a stern look-over. "You're not auditioning in that, are you?"

Slash had worn the same outfit as the night before. Black leather halter top and hot pants.

Slash glanced down at herself. "Guess not."

"We'll find you something," Jilly said.

Five minutes later, Slash was ready. Between Jilly and Deb, they'd found her a tiny string bikini that covered the essentials. The scant outfit provided an eyeful without her having to remove the top. It was the five-inch stilettos that worried her.

"What's the deal on topless?" Slash asked.

"Most of us do," Jilly said.

"Bigger tips when you show the nips," Deb said, and she and Jilly laughed.

"You can lose the top on stage," Jilly said.

"Thanks for your help." Before Slash left the dressing room, she flipped her head over, ran her fingers through her hair, then flipped it back. She glanced in the mirror, eyeing her now-mussed hair.

Then, she headed toward the stage entrance.

Despite what she was about to do, her pulse hadn't quickened. She had every confidence she could pull this off.

All four stages were connected with small walkways that led from one stage to the next. The farther out a dancer walked, the larger the audience, which is why Karen was placing her on the main stage.

One shot to get this gig.

It had been a lifetime since she'd danced, and she vowed she'd never do it again. Tonight, however, she was doing it in the name of justice, so she held her head high, and she stepped into the spotlight.

The stage lights blinded her, but she kept her gaze on the lit walkway, and strutted on stage.

The first dancer was wrapped around a pole. Rather than pass her by, she danced over, ran her fingers over the woman's shoulder, offered a demure smile into the crowd, then continued on to the second stage.

Might have been her attitude, which screamed, "I don't give a fuck." Could have been her confidence. Maybe it was her wild, blonde hair or her toned physique. From the second she walked onto that main stage, she took command of that room.

Bring it on.

In her other life, she'd learned to look the men in their eyes. After several shimmies and sensual gyrations, she strutted over to the silver pole, wrapped her fingers around the cold, metal. and swung herself around.

Hello, old friend.

She was much stronger than she'd been all those years ago, so in seconds she was hanging from the pole and bending like a gymnast. The music changed, this song had a slower beat, so she adjusted her dance. Then, as she moved away from the pole, she pulled the bikini top away, exposing one of her nipples.

And the audience started hooting and hollering like they'd struck gold.

Truth was, she loved having this kind of control over them. Loved that she could hypnotize them with her movements, with her body. Being free with hers gave her *all* the power. She wasn't hung up on anything like she'd been before she lost it all. Back then, she'd been a regular teen who loved hanging with her soccer team, loved spending time with her mom and dad. She liked boys, but she was pretty shy and kinda awkward around them.

Fast forward through so much pain and suffering to now. She didn't need this job. She didn't need the money from it either. She had a home, she had friends. She had Elsa. She had her health and she had a career she loved.

She also loved how the audience lusted after her. How they wanted to fuck her, wanted a piece of her. She loved that she didn't care about any of them. She didn't need them to survive. This time around... she had *all* the power.

As she swept her gaze around the room, a shock of adrenaline charged through her.

What the hell is he doing here?

She had a stalker.

Leaning against the wall stood a beast of a man with a killer face and dope body. Someone she loathed with every fiber of her being.

Carrera Santini.

The only man she ever truly loved. The one man who shredded her heart and reminded her of her fragility.

If she could go over and slap his face she would do it. But she was there to get the gig, so she would shut him out. She'd work the stage, make love to the pole, and use the damn audience for her professional gain. This had nothing to do with *him*. Nothing at all.

Back then, she'd closed her heart. Now, she didn't have one. That's what gave her the ultimate edge.

Several men walked to the stage, bills in their hands. Slash blinked back to the moment, sashayed over and waited while they tucked bills into her thong.

One of the guys let his fingers linger on her skin an extra beat before he stepped away. She hoped that made Carrera green with envy, though she doubted he gave a fuck about her. If she had to guess, she'd say that Elsa asked him to keep an eye on her.

Watch all you want, asshole. You had your chance and you let me get away.

Moving her hips to the sensual beat, she untied the string straps around her neck, and let the thin layer of fabric fall away. Now, her breasts were on full display. She ran her fingers over her nipples, squeezed her breasts together with her arms, and put the full focus on her girls.

All while eye fucking as many of the patrons as she could.

And that's when a long tip line formed.

Her sesh ended when the next dancer appeared.

She tied her bikini straps around her neck and, with an extra sway in her hips, made her way toward the back. Once behind the curtain, she removed her shoes, dropped the facade, and walked with purpose back to her station. Jilly and Deb started clapping.

"How'd I do ladies?" She tugged out the bills from her thong.

"Fantastic," Jilly said. "Where'd you learn to dance like that?"

"I used to dance." Slash counted the money, offered half to Deb and the other to Jilly.

"No," Jilly protested, "you keep it."

Slash held out the money. "Take it."

"Wow, thanks," Jilly said.

As Slash changed into her street clothes, Karen moseyed into view.

"Here comes the boss," Deb murmured.

"Didn't she do great?" Jilly said as Karen joined them.

"Whatever," Karen replied.

"C'mon, boss." Deb held up the wad of cash. "She cleaned up. This is great for biz."

Jilly held up the other half. "She killed it."

"Yeah, so I don't think you're a good fit," Karen said.

Slash needed to keep chill. If Karen wouldn't hire her, the Bureau would have to send in another Special Agent. "No prob. Thanks for the—"

Karen's phone started ringing and Deb startled. "Damn, that's loud."

After glancing at the screen, Karen's face split with a smile. "It's my boyfriend." She answered, put the phone to her ear. "Hey, you." As she listened, her smile fell away. "Well, I don't think—" Her eyes narrowed. "I disagree." Then, she sighed. "Of course, you're right. I can't wait to see you too. Byeeeeeee." Karen hung up and sighed. "He's the best."

"C'mon, KW, you gotta give Slash the job," Jilly said.

"You're lucky my sweetie puts me in the best mood," Karen said. "The gig is yours, but you can't ghost on me. In the past few months, I've lost six girls."

Out of the corner of her eye, Slash saw Jilly shaking her head.

"Dancers work on tips only," Karen continued. "You can access the schedule through the dancers-only portal on the club website. You start next week."

"That'll work," Slash said.

Without so much as a smile, Karen marched out.

"We don't like her," Jilly whispered.

"She's a total B," Deb added. "We make good money, so we put up with her."

Biting back a smile, Slash added, "I knew someone like her at my last job. There's one in every group."

"If you two wanna catch up, I'll take your next shift, but you'll have to close," Deb said to Jilly.

"No problem," Jilly said. "We'll sit at a table up by the bar."

Slash stepped into her biker boots.

As she and Jilly left the dressing area, Slash spotted a surveillance camera in the corner, and a chill swept through her.

What's with the camera in the dressing room?

While walking through the club, Slash refused to scan for Carrera. Perv-man, lurking in the shadows was not her problem.

A customer approached and held out a twenty.

"I really enjoyed your performance," he said.

Slash took the money. "Thanks."

A few more steps before another guy asked if she was dancing again.

"Not tonight," she replied.

"How 'bout a lap dance?" he asked.

"No," Slash replied.

Twice more she was stopped and given tips.

After Jilly found a two-person table in the corner by the bar, she flagged over a server. "Coffee."

"Sparkling water," Slash said to the server.

After she left, Slash set the tip money in front of Jilly. "For you."

"No, you keep it."

"I told you and Deb you could have my tips tonight." Slash flashed a smile. "Take it, 'cause you won't get free money from me again."

On a laugh, Jilly scooped up the money. "Thanks."

"Catch me up on your life," Slash said.

"I'm single, no kids," Jilly said. "I'm taking college courses online. It's taking forever but, fingers crossed, I'm supposed to finish up this year. I'd like to work in marketing, maybe sales. I've been dancing for a while now and I'm totally burned out. That's me over the last fifteen years. Tell me about you."

"I bounced around for a while, did some dancing, lived in my car," Slash said. "Then, I met someone who changed my life. I went to college—"

"What did you study?"

Slash graduated with a double major in criminal justice and psychology, but she couldn't tell Jilly the truth. It had been years since she'd needed a cover for people outside ALPHA. Elsa knew she'd been a Special Agent with the Bureau, so when she made the jump to ALPHA, she never mentioned it.

"Liberal arts," Slash lied. "I was in sales. When my last job didn't work out, I was hoping to make good money here."

"You'll clean up," Jilly said. "This place is busy every day of the week. I pick up day shifts when I can, but my classes keep me super busy."

The server returned with their drinks.

After she left, Slash asked, "Why'd you shake your head when Karen mentioned how the dancers ghosted on her?"

A man approached the table. "Hi, how you ladies doing?"

"Whatcha need?" Slash asked.

"If your shift isn't over, I'd love a lap dance," he said.

Her guts churned. She hated giving lap dances then. Wasn't gonna like it now either. "My shift ended."

"Tell me when you're back and I'll be here."

"The schedule hasn't been worked out," Jilly said. "Slash is new."

"What about you darlin'?" he asked. "You're a hottie. How 'bout we get some alone time?"

"No, that's not my thing," Jilly replied.

"You got great tits," he said. "I'd love to fuck you—"

In seconds, Slash had the douche in a choke hold. She

forced him outside, pulled her knife. One snap and the blade jutted out. "You need to get the hell outta—"

Jilly ran outside. "Melody... *Slash*, stop! Let him go!"

Slash released him, closed her blade.

"Whoa, you might be gorgeous, but you're bat-shit crazy." The guy raised his arms in mock surrender, walked backwards into the parking lot before jogging away.

Jilly stared at Slash. "You gotta take it down a few, 'kay?"

"Sorry. I flashed back to when we lived together and I did nothing to defend you," Slash explained.

"We were just kids back then," Jilly said.

Slash slipped her blade into her bag.

"Most of the customers are cool," Jilly said. "Horny as hell, but they try to keep their hands to themselves. Not gonna lie, we've got some who like the turkey *and* all the trimmings, if you know what I mean."

Slash stepped close. "Are you talking about prostit—"

"Do *not* say that word." Jilly glanced around.

"Is that what you're talking about?"

"I was offered the opportunity to make more money, but I said no," Jilly confided.

Nausea clouded Slash's thoughts. If she was going to get to the truth, she'd have to go deep undercover. Screwing a stranger would never happen, so she'd let Providence know she was out.

"We should get back inside before Karen finds out you put a customer in a choke hold, then pulled a knife. You're definitely a badass." Jilly paused. "If you don't want to get fired, you gotta chill."

When they returned to their table, the head bartender hurried over. "Everything okay?"

"This is Slash," Jilly said. "She's one of our new dancers. Our head bartender, Bradley."

"Yeah, so I saw what happened," Bradley said. "You can't attack customers like that."

"Won't happen again," Slash said.

"How 'bout a refill on your drinks?" Bradley asked.

Both declined, and Bradley returned to the bar.

"We get hit on all the time," Jilly said. "You get used to it."

"When Karen told me I couldn't ghost on her, you shook your head," Slash said. "Has the club always had high turnover?"

"No, the last owners—a husband and wife—they were great. The dancers and servers stayed on for years. We were treated like family."

"What changed?"

"They left, and Karen started working here."

"When?"

Jilly paused. "Five months ago."

"Are dancers leaving because she's a bitch?"

"The women *haven't* ghosted," Jilly murmured. "They've gone missing."

6

THE BABYSITTERS

Carrera

Carrera wanted to put his fist through a goddamn wall. He couldn't believe what he'd just seen. Slash had just brought down the fucking house with her sexy dance moves. And when she started shaking her tits, he thought he'd lose his ever-lovin'-mind.

When he'd agreed to keep an eye on her, he never imagined it would lead to The Blue Suit Club.

It was bad enough he was there. Strip clubs weren't his thing. He was more of a hands-on man. Watching felt skeezy. From the looks of the packed room, he was in the minority.

Between his undercover work, his hits with Luciano, and his cruise line business, he had zero time for dating. Didn't mean he didn't want to, but when the hell was that gonna happen?

Being back home gave him a better shot, but as he watched Slash on stage, he admitted the truth. He wanted *her*. That had never changed from the moment he'd set eyes on her.

But her truth had changed him. So he'd let her go and he moved on.

Only he hadn't moved on, not really. His feelings of love had turned to anger, then a sense of loss and betrayal had settled into his bones.

After Slash's set ended, he went outside and waited in his truck. Fifteen minutes later, she dragged some guy outside at knife point, and he laughed out loud.

Badass.

While he was confident she was there for work, he knew ALPHA didn't do undercover gigs.

She could be on loan to the Bureau.

As he ran through the people who would know, Slash retreated back inside. Not long after, she reemerged, got in her truck, and drove away.

Following from a safe distance, he trailed her home. After pulling into her garage, she sauntered out, stood in the middle of her driveway, and flipped him off.

Though he'd stopped several houses up the street, it was impossible to pull one over on her. All he could do was chuff out a laugh before he continued on home.

G-ma, I love you, but I gotta cut her loose. Amanda May can take care of herself.

THE FOLLOWING AFTERNOON, he parked his truck in Rebel and Brit's long driveway, pulled his duffle from the back seat, and headed toward the front door. He rang the doorbell. A long minute later, the door swung open.

Adrenaline spiked through him as he took in the scene.

Slash—looking phenomenal in a tank top, shorts, and barefoot—stood there with a crying Willow in her arms and a crying Clark sitting on the floor a few feet away.

Her expression fell. "I'm kinda busy. Go away." She started

to close the door, but he grabbed the doorframe and stepped inside.

Willow stopped crying and reached out for him.

"Even worse, she likes you," Slash grumbled.

"I can take her." Carrera held out his arms and the baby leaned toward him.

"Hold her while I change Clark." He loved the bite in her tone. Didn't matter what she said. Being around him frustrated the hell out of her.

Join the damn club.

When he took the baby, his hand brushed against her breast.

"Seriously, you had to do that?" she bit out. "That peep show you got last night wasn't enough?"

He smiled at Willow. "Why don't you tell Auntie—what do they call you?"

"Nothing, yet." Slash picked up Clark and the baby grinned at her.

When she smiled at the little one, energy powered through him. He loved her smile. Always had. Her smile spread across her face, lighting up her eyes. She was already an extraordinarily beautiful woman... but man... that smile sent him to the stratosphere.

Every. Single. Time.

"Clark, tell Auntie Amanda May that I didn't mean to touch her breast," Carrera said. "While it's a fantastic breast that too many pervs got to ogle last night, it was an accident. If it were smaller, that wouldn't have happened."

"Tell Uncle A-hole all I heard was blah-blah-blah," she said before heading toward the stairs. "I have to change him. A bomb went off in his diaper."

"Where's Rebel and Brit?" he asked as he followed her up the long staircase, his eyes cemented on her fine, fine backside.

"Stop," she growled.

"What?"

"You're checking out my butt."

He bit back a smile.

Into the twins' bedroom they went. There, she laid Clark on the changing table and smiled down at him. He grinned up at her and she kissed his cheek. "Who's the most handsome boy in all the land?"

"I am," Carrera replied.

"Clark, that's not true," she said as she removed his shorts, then his diaper. Urine shot into the air and she covered him back up. "Nice job, Clark. The poop isn't enough. You've gotta show off your peeing talents too?"

She smiled at him and he giggled. When she removed the diaper, Clark didn't start peeing again.

"That is the stinkiest poop," she said. "I'm so *not* cutout for this."

Carrera loved watching her. This was the first time he'd seen her maternal side... and it was crazy hot to watch. She talked to Clark, smiled non-stop, and was wicked fast.

After putting on the clean diaper, she pulled on his shorts, lifted him into the air and spun around in a slow circle. "Clark, you're an airplane. Wheeeeeee."

Belly laughs erupted from the little one.

He loved this carefree side of her.

Willow watched her brother with a cool indifference. "She's pretty mellow," Carrera said.

Slash held Clark in her arms while she cemented her piercing blue eyes on Willow. "Willow, what sound does a pig make?" Slash started making grunting sounds and Willow burst into gales of giggles.

"What the hell was that?" Carrera asked.

"A pig." She smiled at Willow. "What about a horsey?" She neighed several times and Willow belly laughed again.

He chuffed out a laugh while his gaze jumped to Clark who had no reaction to the animal reenactment.

"Children are fascinating," Slash said. "Why don't you change her since we're up here?"

"Me?"

"Yup."

"So damn bossy."

He laid Willow gently on the changing table, pulled up her dress, removed her diaper, and placed a new one under her. Then, he taped it together, and pulled her into his arms. "Another first. How'd I do?"

Slash's eyes grew large. "You've never changed a diaper before?"

"Nope, that was numero uno. You get all my important firsts."

Sadness flashed in her eyes but her gaze never left his.

Willow started babbling. He kissed the baby's cheek, then started making frog sounds. Her laughter touched a part of him that had been dead for so long.

When he looked back at Slash, her gaze was fixed on his. He stared into her eyes while the air turned turbulent. Like the other night, the overwhelming desire to kiss her took hold.

"Why are you here?" she asked before turning on her heel and heading into the hall.

Down the stairs they went and into the family room. Once they put the children down, Slash started stacking squishy blocks.

"Rebel and I were going to the gym, then for a run," he said. "What about you?"

"Brit and I were going shopping, but her mom called. She and Z were playing pickleball together."

"Are they dating?"

"No, they're close friends. They take care of the twins on

Fridays." Slash stood. "Watch them, I'm going to fill two sippy cups." Once in the kitchen, she said, "Either one or both had a pickleball accident. Rebel and Brit went to the hospital."

She returned with two plastic cups. Clark reached up and she handed it to him, but Willow shook her head.

"You try," Slash said to him.

"What's in it?"

"Vodka," Slash replied.

He laughed. "Way to go."

"It's water, *idiot*."

She handed him the cup, he offered it to Willow. She took it, dropped it next to her.

After a pause, Slash said, "Stop stalking me."

"What were you doing at the strip club last night?" he asked.

"Giving the clientele their late-night fantasy. What do you think I was doing?"

"I didn't think ALPHA did undercover work."

She said nothing, so he started playing with the babies.

The tension between them was driving him crazy. Being this close to her turned him into a rabid ball of need. She'd always been his dream girl, but it was easier to forget her when he wasn't around. But he was back... and they were sitting inches away, playing with children that could have been their own.

Her scent wafted over and he breathed deep, savoring everything about her. She smelled of spring, of the outdoors. She smelled like someone he used to know... and used to know well.

But that was a long time ago.

"I'm going for a run in the neighborhood," he said.

She'd been playing on the floor with the babies, but her gaze found his. Intense blue eyes drilled into his. "Rebel and Brit could be a while. Why don't you take off? If they end up having their dinner party—and you're gonna be here—I'll leave."

"You stay," he said. "I'll go."

He said goodbye to the babies, made his way into the foyer, and opened the door. The sun was shining, the sky as stunningly blue as Slash's eyes. He shut the door, strode back into the family room. "Do you have workout clothes with you?"

"In my SUV."

"We're putting the babies in the stroller and we're going for a run," he said. "I'll get your bag."

He went outside, pulled her duffle, returned to the house.

She stood in the family room, her hands on her hips, daggers shooting from her eyes. "I'm not doing *anything* with you. I can't effin' stand you."

The sexual tension had turned him into a beast. Unable to stop himself, he stormed over, snaked his arms around her, and kissed her, fully expecting to get kneed in the groin.

A risk he was willing to take.

Instead, she groaned into him, sandwiched her body against his, and kissed him back. She pushed her tongue into his mouth and thrust it against his while she started grinding on him. He firmed, and was racing toward a steel boner when she fisted his hair and tugged. Then, she ran her hand down his groin and cupped his erection, beneath his shorts.

He held her close, ran his hands across her beautiful back, desperate to strip her naked and drive himself inside her.

She broke away, panting. Her electric gaze boring into his. "Happy?"

"I'm moving in that direction."

"Good, 'cause you got something those losers didn't. Now, you're one step ahead of 'em."

"Whoa, what is your problem?"

She got in his face and stared up at him. "*My* problem? You, for starters. You're my problem. I don't know what kind of game you're playing, but it's not cool, Carrera. Not cool. You dumped me after you *blamed* me, and then you acted like a total dick. We haven't talked in years, but when we do, we're spitting fire. Ever since you got back, you've been following me around. Also, not cool. Then, the other night, you were about to kiss me—"

"You stared at my mouth."

Her eyebrows crowded her forehead. "I stared at your mouth? So what? If I'd stared at your dick, would that mean it's go-time?"

He smiled, shrugged. "I don't know. Would it?"

She glanced at the clock on the wall. "I've got to feed the babies. Brit said they like a snack around now. Since you're here, and you're clearly interested in doing *something*, you can help me."

First, Slash cleaned Willow's hands, then she cleaned Clark's. He loved how gentle she was with them. One minute, she was grinding on him, then she's chewing him out. Now, she was smiling and telling them a story about some puppy named Kevin.

After she put Willow in her highchair, she said to him, "Do what I do."

He put Clark in his highchair.

"How old are they?" Carrera asked.

"Nine months."

He heard the garage door rise as Slash opened the fridge. She pulled out three containers, set them on the counter, and placed their contents on two plastic toddler dishes. With two spoons in hand, she pulled up a chair and started feeding Clark.

"Here's a spoon," she said. "Feed Willow."

A moment later, Rebel and Brit walked in.

"Hey, look who's here!" Rebel said.

After the men hugged it out, Carrera hugged Brit. "The babies are adorable."

The little ones saw their parents and started grinning. Clark raised his arms toward them, and Brit kissed both children.

"Thank you so much, Slash," Brit said. "I'm sorry we left you."

"You had a helper," Rebel said.

"Not exactly," Slash bit out. "Are your parents okay?"

"My mom sprained her ankle," Rebel said, "but she's fine otherwise. Z took a tumble as well, but he's okay."

"Badly bruised ego," Brit added.

"Our kids look like you," Rebel said. "Willow's got Slash's blue eyes, and Clark has Carrera's brown ones."

"Ugh." Slash rose. "I'm gonna take off."

"No, I'll go," Carrera said.

"What is going on with you two?" Rebel asked.

"We can't stand each other," Slash said. "And I break out in hives if I come within ten feet of him."

Rebel and Brit laughed.

"I didn't know you knew Carrera," Brit said.

"Bad blood from a long, long time ago," Slash replied.

"In a galaxy far, far away," Carrera added.

More laughter from Rebel and Brit.

"You and I—we're not friends, so don't stick your tongue down my throat again." A low rumbly growl escaped her before she set down the baby's spoon.

After kissing each baby on their food-stained cheeks, she said to Brit and Rebel, "Have fun tonight. I'll see you guys next week."

"Stay," Carrera said to Slash. "I'll take off."

"The party is still on," Brit said. "Our part-time nanny is coming over to watch them. You guys have to stay, but you don't have to talk to each other. Slash, we're going for a run. Babe, please finish feeding the twins. After they digest, put them down for their mini-naps. You and Carrera can go for a run or to the gym when we get back."

"The queen has spoken," Rebel said.

Carrera laughed. "Works for me. Slash, you good with that?"

Slash ignored him, her attention on Brit. "As long as I don't have to talk to him or even look at him, I'll stay." She stood and glanced over at him. "I'll change in the guest room."

She's still crazy about me.

Excitement pounded through him.

After the women left, Rebel said, "You could cut the sexual tension with a knife. What's goin' on with you two?"

Slash

As she and Brit jogged through the beautiful McLean neighborhood, Slash inhaled the warm summer air, turned her face toward the sun. Fifteen minutes passed before the tension in her shoulders and the knots in her guts started to subside.

"Something's going on," Brit said. "You want to talk about it?"

Slash wasn't much of a talker, especially when it came to her past. She lived for the moment, looked to the future, and kept all the yesterdays in the rearview mirror.

"You're a good friend," Slash said.

"Same," Brit said. "We've come a long way since the day we met."

Slash laughed. "You mean when I saw you at ALPHA and pulled my Glock on you."

Brit smiled. "Yeah, but in that split second—"

"You saw your life flash before you?"

"No, I knew I liked you."

"Why's that?"

"There's a saying in the Navy—Ship. Shipmate. Self. I loved that you were protecting and defending ALPHA and everyone who worked there."

"Thanks, but looking back, it was a little extreme."

"We're coming up to a fork," Brit said. "Right or left?"

"Same distance?"

"Left is longer. I'm good with longer."

"Same. It's too beautiful to be inside today."

"I'm here for you, even if you don't want to talk about whatever is going on between you and Carrera."

"It's not gonna change anything."

"Talking helps me get clarity, then I can let it go."

Slash grew silent as she thought about talking to Brit.

"I've never talked to anyone in our circle about what happened," Slash said. "We're already a close group, especially since we're in BLACK OPS—"

"I wouldn't tell anyone. Not Addison, not even Joaquin."

More silence as Slash wrestled with her demons.

Tell her. See if it helps.

"Carrera and I were together our senior year of high school," Slash began. "First loves, you know, the V-card for both of us."

"Wow, that's so special."

They rounded the corner, continued jogging.

"Why did you break up?"

"He dumped me when he learned who I really was."

Brit looked over. "What does that mean?"

~

Carrera

AFTER REBEL LAID out a large blanket in the backyard, the babies started crawling around. Clark moved off the blanket and was staring at the grass, so Rebel lifted him up, and zoomed him around like an airplane.

"So I'd fallen in love with her," Carrera said as he stood Willow in front of the activity walker. After helping her grip the bar, she took a few steps, then plopped down in the grass.

"Did she love you?" Rebel asked.

"Yeah, she did. I thought she was the one."

"Why'd you break up?"

"It's complicated," Carrera replied as he set Willow on the blanket and placed a stacking ring in front of her. After removing all the rings, he handed one to her.

She placed it on the tower and it slid down.

"Good job, Willow."

Rebel set Clark in front of the activity walker and he took a few steps forward. "Way to go, Clark."

"I found out that Slash—who went by Amanda Maynard— wasn't really Amanda," Carrera continued.

"Who was she?"

"She was the reason my mom was dead, and my dad had started drinking. He lost his job, and couldn't take care of us kids."

"Whoa," Rebel said.

"Yeah, it was bad," Carrera said. "Rock-bottom bad."

Slash

SLASH AND BRIT returned to the house. Into the kitchen they went, still breathing hard, each guzzling a large glass of water.

"That was such a good run," Slash said.

"You know, you're in the middle of your story," Brit said.

"Yeah, let's get out of these sweaty clothes—"

"I have a feeling this story calls for a glass of wine."

"More like an entire bottle." Slash glanced around. "Don't we need to start cooking for your dinner party?"

"It's being catered by Joaquin's hotel."

"Nice," Slash said as she looked out the family room window. "The guys are outside with the kids."

Brit joined her. "Let's shower. Joaquin will either put the babies down or we'll do it once we're ready. Do you want to come into my bedroom when you're finished or should we meet downstairs? I don't want you to be uncomfortable around Carrera."

Slash smiled. "I'm okay. Talking is helping, which I never would have believed."

They went upstairs. On the way down the hallway, Brit said, "Fresh towels in the bathroom closet. There's shampoo and conditioner, plus hair dryer. If you need anything—"

"Thanks for being there for me." After Slash walked into the guest room, she shut the door, and stripped down. In the en suite bathroom, she turned on the faucet, dropped a towel on the bench, and stepped into the doorless, walk-in shower.

As the warm water rinsed away the sweat, her thoughts jumped to Carrera. Their circle of friends was tight, so she wouldn't be surprised if he started showing up everywhere.

And thanks to Elsa, he's stalking me now too.

She sudsed up, tried not to think about him, but his stunningly handsome face would *not* go away. She'd been looking forward to this dinner party all week, so she'd ignore him like he wasn't even in the room.

Yeah, like that's gonna work.

Despite hating him, she was crazy attracted to him, even all these years later.

On auto-pilot, she washed her hair, then worked the conditioner through.

As long as I stay clear of him, I'm good.

As she rinsed the conditioner from her hair, the bedroom door shut. Seconds later, Carrera walked into the bathroom wearing only black boxer briefs, the cotton material clinging to him like a second skin.

Every cell in her body came alive. Hit after hit of adrenaline raced through her while she soaked up all that hotness. She had a front-row seat to absolute male perfection.

Her gaze floated from his thick brown hair to his piercing bedroom eyes. A chiseled face with cheekbones to die for had her biting her lower lip. She soaked up his sculpted broad chest, his bulging guns, his eight-pack abs, his hardening bulge, and those ripped, massive thighs.

More than her next breath, she wanted to jump his bones and screw him for days. Get lost in those piercing bedroom eyes and his strong embrace.

She needed to stop staring, but she couldn't look away. No matter how hard she willed herself, she could not.

His hard-as-fuck body, the sexy tattoos snaking their way down his arms and across his chest, and that face. God, that face.

Seconds passed while they eye-fucked each other so damn hard. Then, the room went all wobbly. She placed her palm on the wall to steady herself, and she breathed.

Without a doubt, he was a stunningly beautiful beast of a man.

"You're back," he said as he stood like a statue in the middle of the spacious room.

A shadow darkened his eyes, turning them black with lust, while he raked his gaze over every inch of her. Very, very slowly.

"You've taken stalking to a whole new level," she said after she'd found her voice.

"You are so fucking beautiful," he bit out.

So are you.

"What are you doing in here?" she asked.

"I'm changing, and I need to pee."

"Pee away," she replied.

He walked into the water closet. She didn't care that he'd seen her naked. What she *did* care about was her reaction to him. It was over-the-top. For a woman who kept things chill, he'd stolen her breath… and her mind.

That was a first.

Forcing herself to focus, she turned off the shower, and rung out her hair. When she finished, she found him standing in the middle of the room, gawking.

"Hand me the towel," she said.

"What?"

She walked over to the bench in the dry part of the stall and picked it up. "This one." Then, she started drying herself off. With that done, she wrapped her hair, and stepped out

What she did next, she did for him.

She sashayed up to him, pressed her naked body against his, and grabbed his muscular ass with both hands. Then, she pressed her lips to his and kissed him hard. His raspy growl turned her wet with need.

Her tongue slayed his. He bit her lip. She sunk her fingers into his hair.

Lust and desire jumped to a feverish pitch. She ground against him while his strong arms held her close.

Her moan ripped from the depths of her soul, and she realized she was losing control. He was sucking her into a black hole from which there was no escape. Pushing off him, she stood there, catching her breath. Desire ran rampant through her. She wanted him, but her need ran much deeper than sex.

Jesus, get it together.

He inhaled a slow, deep breath, his perfect pecs expanding as he filled his lungs.

Steeling her spine, she hitched her hands on her hips.

"If you hadn't made the biggest mistake of your life, I'd be on my knees giving you a blowjob." Then, to drive her point home, she stroked his long, thick erection through his cotton boxers. "If you were mine, I'd swallow you down."

"Fuck," he murmured.

She stepped away, creating the distance she desperately needed to get her shit together. After removing the towel from her head, she turned her full attention on him.

"You blame me," she said. "Now... you only have yourself to blame. You and I both know the truth. I was just as innocent as you when our lives spun out of control."

She hitched an eyebrow and sauntered out, his heated gaze burning a hole through her as she entered the bedroom. There, she slipped on a black thong. As she was hooking her bra, he stalked into the bedroom.

The fury rolling off him could have scared her, but she knew the truth. He was angry at himself. Angry because, all these years later, he knew she was right.

They dressed in a seething silence. She slipped into a black, sleeveless, one-piece romper. He tugged on running shorts and a T-shirt. He was ready in seconds, but he waited for her. When she finished, he opened the door.

As she walked past him, he murmured, "It's better this way."

You got that right.

Silence followed her until he caught up with her. "I'm a monster," he murmured. "I could never make you happy."

"You don't know me, Carrera. Not anymore. I'm not a teen. I'm a thirty-one-year-old woman who had to figure shit out alone. My life would have turned out very differently if it hadn't been for your grandmother. She is the absolute best thing that has ever happened to me."

"I know," he murmured.

"You," she said, "are still a jackass."

A tornado of hostility followed them down the stairs and into the kitchen.

"Hey," Brit called from the family room.

Brit and Rebel were on the sofa. He, on the middle cushion, while Brit sat beside him, her legs draped over his thighs.

"We can get outta here—" Carrera said.

"You guys were up there a long time," Rebel said.

"Sorry about the confusion," Brit said. "We meant to send Carrera downstairs to the in-law suite."

"No worries," Carrera said. "We're all adults."

"Nope," Slash murmured. "Not you."

Rebel cupped Brit's chin. "We're going for a run. Back in an hour, wife." He dropped a tender kiss on her lips. "Love you."

"Love you, baby," she said before kissing him and pushing off the sofa.

"I'm getting the party started with a glass of wine," Brit said.

After the guys left, Slash eased onto a stool at the kitchen island. Brit set down the baby monitor before pulling a bottle of white from their wine cooler and a bottle of red from the mini-bar off the kitchen. When she set them both on the island, Slash pointed to the white.

"My choice too." Brit handed Slash the corkscrew before pulling two glasses from the cabinet.

"How long do the twins sleep?" Slash opened the wine, filled two glasses.

"An hour, maybe a little longer." Brit grabbed the baby monitor. "Let's sit on the screened porch."

Outside, Slash raised her glass. "Love you, Brit. Thanks for being there."

"Love you back," Brit replied. "You haven't even finished telling me what happened."

"It's okay."

Brit smiled. "Just tell me and we'll move on to what *really* happened upstairs in the guest room."

Naked bodies. That's what happened.

Brit curled up on the sofa, but Slash stood by the screen, peering into their expansive yard.

Pausing, Slash sipped the chilled wine, savoring the bouquet of flavors. "Where was I?"

"He dumped you when he learned you weren't Amanda Maynard," Brit said. "What's your real name?"

"My legal name is Amanda Maynard. For the first sixteen years I was Melody Donaldson."

Brit offered a sweet smile. "You can call yourself whatever, but you'll always be Slash to me."

Slash smiled in return. "I was a star soccer player for my high school. I also played on a travel team. I was hoping for a full ride on a soccer scholarship and had even considered playing professionally. Soccer was my life."

"Okay."

"Carrera's mom was my travel team coach. Several parents were in a carpool rotation for the games. One time, my mom couldn't take us, so my dad did."

She hadn't thought about this part of her life in a long time. Shuddering in a breath, she took another sip of wine.

"My dad met Carrera's mom, and they started having an affair."

"Did you know?"

"No idea." Slash's heart started pounding harder and she sat next to Brit.

"Take your time." Brit held her hand. "I can see this is hard for you."

"My parents got into a huge fight one night. My dad said he was leaving my mom for Carrera's mom."

"Oh, no," Brit whispered.

Slash started trembling, something unfamiliar to her. She was always tough as nails, good on locking down her feelings, but as soon as she spilled her damn guts, a myriad of emotions came rushing back in.

"The next day, I got home late from school," Slash said. "I found my parents and Carrera's mom, shot dead. My mom killed them, then turned the gun on herself."

Brit set down her wine, put her arms around Slash. Slash melted into her as tears pricked her eyes. She hated showing weakness, fought it every chance she got. After a beat, she broke away, set down her own wine glass, and rose.

"I need some water," she said, wiping away a tear.

Inside, she drank some down and returned to the porch.

"The next few months were a blur," Slash said. "It was tough. I was alone, although some of the soccer families took me in. I couldn't pay the mortgage and I lost the house. I lived in my car for a while."

Brit's eyes grew large. "That's rough."

Slash held up her hand. Normally rock solid, she was trembling pretty good. "Carrera's dad fell apart. He didn't know his wife had been having an affair, then she gets murdered by my mom."

"How do you know what happened to him?"

"Because his mom, Carrera's grandmother, was the one who saved me. She says that God saved me and she was just doing His work. When Carrera's dad hit rock bottom, their family fell apart. Carrera blames me for *everything*."

Brit's mouth fell open.

Silence.

After a long moment, Brit said, "I don't even know what to say."

"Yeah, so, you got the short version, but now you know why we hate each other."

"Britain," announced the security system, "a white van has parked in front of the house."

"Thank you for opening up to me," Brit said. "I respect and

admire you even more than I already did. You're a fighter and a survivor. I hope you know I will never share that with anyone."

"Unknown people are approaching the front of the house," said the security system.

The doorbell rang.

Slash smiled. "Thanks for listening., I do feel better, and I don't care who knows. I wasn't to blame, and I stopped hating myself a long time ago."

As the women made their way inside, Brit said, "Maybe it's time for Carrera to stop hating you too."

7

THE DINNER PARTY

Carrera

While they continued their run, Carrera finished telling Rebel what had gone down with him and Slash all those years ago.

"If this wasn't your life, it would make for a great movie," Rebel said.

"Sucks that it's real," Carrera said.

"Did you know she worked at the Bureau?" Rebel asked.

"Yeah, but we were in different divisions, so it was easy to stay out of each other's way. It worked better when I was out of town on undercover gigs. It's harder now that I'm back. She and my grandmother are super close. Slash takes her to her appointments, checks on her a few times a week."

"She's like your sister."

Carrera laughed. "I walked in on her in the shower. There's *nothing* sisterly about that woman."

"You gotta work it out, or stay clear of her when we're all together."

"That's just it," Carrera said as he picked up the pace. "I

don't want to avoid her. I regret letting her go. It's always been her."

"I'll help any way I can," Rebel said.

"Thanks, brother," Carrera replied. "This is on me. I fucked up, and I gotta find a way to win her back."

A FEW HOURS LATER, the dinner party was in full swing. Carrera kept clear of Slash without making it obvious. If they made eye contact, which happened a lot, he'd offer a smile—which wasn't reciprocated—or he'd hold her gaze until she broke first.

Her beautiful naked form was forever tattooed on his brain. He couldn't shake it, no matter how hard he tried. But the fiery look in her eyes, the confidence in her voice, and the way she pressed close and kissed him made him crazy with need. She'd grown from a pretty girl into a gorgeous woman.

A woman he was determined to make his.

While he was talking to Sin and Dakota on the porch, Slash walked outside.

A hit of adrenaline sent blood whooshing through him.

Dakota smiled. "There she is. My former ALPHA partner." He pulled her in for a warm hug. "I heard you're kicking some serious ass these days."

She slid her gaze from Dakota to Sin, to him. "Should I assume Carrera was talking about my performance at The Blue Suit Club?"

The twins regarded him.

"You didn't tell us you were there," Sin said to Carrera.

"Strip clubs aren't my jam," Carrera replied.

"Then, why—" Dakota began.

"He was stalking me," Slash said, and Sin and Dakota started laughing.

"For real?" Sin asked.

"Guilty," Carrera said.

"Did you make any progress with the case?" Dakota asked Slash.

"Someone did proposition one of the dancers, but she turned him down. When I mentioned prostitution, she told me some men like the turkey and all the trimmings."

"Did you see anything suspicious?" Sin asked.

"Nothing, but I was only there to audition."

"How'd that go?" Dakota asked.

"She killed it," Carrera said.

"I never mix biz with pleasure, but I was hoping to talk to Providence," Slash said. "Any idea where she is?"

"Downstairs with our nanny and the babies," Dakota replied.

Slash tossed him a nod before heading back inside. At the door way, she turned back. Carrera was waiting, his gaze locked on hers. She arched an eyebrow before vanishing inside.

"That was an invitation, if I've ever seen one," Sin said.

"She hates me," Carrera said, "and it goes back years."

"What did you do?" Dakota asked.

"All the wrong things," Carrera replied.

Slash

SLASH FOUND Providence in Brit and Rebel's finished basement. She and a middle-aged woman were feeding the twins. Both babies were in high chairs.

All four turned as Slash moseyed over. "Hey."

"Hi," Providence said. "Come join us."

Providence offered Willow another spoonful, but she shook her head. "All done? Okay, well you did a great job."

Slash smiled at the woman. "I'm Slash."

"Miranda. Lovely to meet you."

"Same," Slash replied.

"Miranda is our nanny," Providence said. "She's been with us since it was just Dakota and Sammy. Now, she takes care of Willow and Clark too." Providence smiled at the twins. "We love Mrs. Morris, don't we?"

Both children started babbling.

"I love you too, don't I?" Miranda asked the twins as she fed Clark. "I love you to the moon and back."

"I was hoping to talk shop with you," Slash said to Providence. "Maybe later?"

"Now works." Providence regarded Miranda. "I'll just be ten minutes."

"You're supposed to be upstairs at your party," Miranda said. "Take all the time you need."

"Let's go out back," Slash said.

Out of earshot in the yard, Providence said, "I read your progress report. Good job getting hired at the club. Must be a challenge working for Karen Woodside."

"She's a mess," Slash said as they strolled around. "I've run into a challenge. If I'm propositioned, I won't have sex. Even *I* don't love my job *that* much."

Providence laughed. "Not taking one for the team?"

Slash chuckled. "I was going to bail and have the Bureau send in another case agent, but there's something else going on there."

"I'm not surprised. Drugs? Money laundering?"

"Women are going missing."

Providence stopped in the middle of the yard, her full attention on Slash.

"Karen mentioned that six women have ghosted in the past few months, but one of the dancers thinks they've gone missing."

"Maybe there's high turnover because no one likes working

for her. We know she's difficult to get along with. What's the pay structure?"

"Tips only." Slash wasn't giving up so easily. "While this is just another gig, it's personal to me. I hit a bumpy patch during my teens and worked at a strip club for a while. Those girls could have been me."

Providence nodded.

"I checked police reports on two of the women, Terri and Kim Billiawitz. Sisters, whose parents filed missing persons reports. A detective stopped by the club and talked to Karen. She said they ghosted. He followed up with the parents. That was it."

"I can't assign you missing persons cases," Providence said. "It's not something ALPHA does. Since there's no rescue, it's not BLACK OPS either. You'll have to work the prostitution case from the front of the club and let us know what you learn."

"Hey guys!" Brit called from the porch. "We're serving dinner."

"I'm sorry, Slash," Providence said. "You ready to head inside?"

"You go. I'll be right in."

Slash stood in the middle of the freshly-cut lawn. She didn't like being told she couldn't do something, but this wasn't the first time a request had been denied.

When Elsa had plucked her from the depths of hell, she vowed she'd pay it forward.

As she made her way through the yard toward the porch stairs, she ran through her options.

Between her regular caseload, her BLACK OPS missions, and this new gig, neither Providence nor Cooper Grant knew where she was most of the time. It would be easy to start poking around.

I'll work the cases on the down-low.

She needed to get propositioned so she could check out the VIP rooms. How else could the Bureau move in for an arrest?

Slash returned to the party, but her thoughts were too focused on the missing dancers and the bullshit orders about working the case from the front of the club. Why bother to send her in if she couldn't actually *do* anything? Shaking her titties and gyrating around a steel pole wasn't gonna shut down a damn prostitution syndicate.

Starting around ten-thirty, some of the couples headed out. Everyone else moved onto the screened porch to dance.

Her close friend and fellow ALPHA Op, Antonio Herrera, made his way over to her. "Hey, chica, you've barely smiled all night. What's up with you? This is a parteeeee. Why won't my amiga cut loose and have a little fun?"

She smiled at her longtime friend. "I miss working cases with you. How's South Carolina?"

"We're loving it," he replied.

"Where's Estrella?"

"She's in the limbo line." He waved at his wife and she blew him a kiss.

The music changed to a slow song and Herrera held out his hand. "Dance with me, old friend."

She placed her arms over Herrera's shoulders and they started moving in place. Though Herrera put his arms on her waist, they were so far apart, Slash almost laughed out loud.

"What's going on with you?" Herrera asked.

"Boring work crap. Nothing I can't manage."

Standing eye level with her, he chuckled. "There's the woman I know and love."

As she glanced around the room, several other couples started dancing nearby. Normally not an envious person, Slash watched as Addison and Hawk, Brit and Rebel, and Emerson and Stryker held each other close and moved as one to the love song.

Carrera appeared next to them, his large frame hijacking her attention. Her heart skipped a beat, then took off in her chest.

"Good to see you," Carrera said.

Herrera extended his hand. "Brother, it's been a while."

"Any chance I could cut in?"

Herrera regarded Slash. "Do you know Carrera Santini?"

"Unfortunately," Slash deadpanned.

Herrera broke away. "Good to see you, amiga."

"Same," she said to Herrera before he took off toward his wife.

"Dance?" Carrera asked.

Slash's heart was still beating too damn fast. "Ugh."

With a smile that made her head buzz, Carrera slid his arms around her, pulled her flush against him, and peered down. "I won't bite."

"I will, and I have razor sharp teeth."

"I can take it."

"You deserve it," she murmured.

His breathtaking smile sent zing after zing of attraction charging through her, but it was the light shining in his eyes that had always melted her the most.

Things had been easier when he'd been gone. Now that he was back, it was a struggle to even breathe. Her fingers tingled to touch him—run her hands down his striated triceps or granite chest—or stare into those dark, alluring eyes.

Be strong. Do. Not. Cave.

Moving tentatively, like she was about to touch a hot stove, she placed her fingers on his shoulders, and her heart found a home.

"There you go," he murmured. "Easy does it."

When her gaze settled on his, every damn thing in her life fell into place. Being with Carrera had once been her happy place. Didn't matter what they were doing, as long as they were together.

She loved when they'd made Elsa breakfast on Saturdays. Attending Mass on Sundays with them made her feel safe and loved. Another favorite was when she and Carrera played soccer together in Elsa's backyard. He was good, but she was better. More than any of those, she loved when he'd sneak into her room in the middle of the night and love her.

She blinked back to the moment, the memories of yesterday replaced with the reality of today. He caressed her back, his gaze never leaving hers. It was exactly like it used to be. Like she was the only girl in the world.

But she wasn't a girl. She was a woman. A woman who'd learned that life doesn't go according to plan, that it's critical to have a back-up plan, and that nothing lasts forever. Not the good, not the bad. Everything has a beginning and an end.

"Thank God for Elsa," she whispered.

He cocked his head. "What about her?"

"Did I say that out loud?"

He nodded. His eyes roamed over her face, over her long hair and long bangs that always seemed to find their way over one eye. With a tenderness that made her heart sing, he moved her hair away from her face.

"I wish I could fix us," he murmured.

His eyes were filled with a mix of honesty and sadness, the muscles in his cheeks were flexing. He did that when he was angry.

The song ended and another slow one started up. While she wanted to press close and let his delicious scent wash over her, she was a realist. Like everything else, this dance had an end.

"I'm taking off," she said.

"I'll walk you out."

"I'm gonna say goodbye to Brit and Rebel."

But she hadn't broken away from him. Hadn't released her now vice grip on his shoulders. This was the kind of effect he'd always had on her. He had this magical way of breaking down all her barriers until she'd bared her soul to him.

He leaned down, dropped a light kiss on her lips. "Thanks for the dance."

"Go fuck yourself, Santini," she whispered.

A grin spread across his beautiful face.

Damn him. Damn him to hell.

"I think *you* should do it," he said as she stepped away.

"You wish," she said.

She thanked Brit and Rebel, grabbed her duffle, and left. While Elsa's home wasn't on her way, she drove over to check on her.

The front light was on, as was the living room. Rather than use her key and scare her, she shot off a text.

> Elsa, are you awake?

Dots appeared.

> Yes TV

> I stopped by on my way home. Can I come in?

> Of course

Slash keyed her way in. Once inside, she found Elsa relaxing in her recliner in the family room. Dressed in her bathrobe and covered in a blanket, Elsa's sleepy smile warmed Slash's heart.

She leaned down, kissed her on her cheek. "How are you doing?"

"I'm fine. You can watch my show with me."

Rather than sit on the sofa, Slash eased onto the floor. She removed one of Elsa's slippers and gently rubbed her foot. Elsa was watching her favorite crime show, so Slash stayed quiet.

"That feels great, honey," Elsa said.

Several minutes later, Slash slipped on her slipper, removed the other, and repeated the gentle foot rub. When the show ended, Slash fitted Elsa's slipper back onto her foot.

"Are you sleeping down here tonight?" Slash asked.

"Oh, no. Upstairs in bed."

Though Elsa was sure-footed, Slash had once asked if Elsa would consider moving to a single-level home or even into an assisted-living building. Elsa loved her home, she didn't need assistance, end of discussion.

Slash went upstairs with her and waited in her bedroom while she brushed her teeth. Once Elsa got into bed, Slash sat on the edge of the bed.

"Can I stop at the store for you tomorrow?"

"I'm going after church with my friends, but thank you, honey. You can join us."

Slash nodded. "Any appointments next week?"

"No, but come by for dinner any night."

"Can I ask you something?"

"Always."

"If I forgive him, will that matter?"

After a few seconds, Elsa said, "It will matter to you. You'll lighten the burden you've been carrying around. Then, you can start to heal. Maybe even stop all the swearing you two do at each other."

They shared a smile.

"I still love him," Slash said.

Elsa patted her hand. "I know."

"I hate him too," Slash said.

"That's just how you protect your heart. He has to earn your trust, earn back your love." Her eyes fluttered closed. "Forgive him."

One more kiss. "I love you, Elsa.

"I love you, angel."

"I'll bolt you in." Slash turned off the bedroom light, but left the hall light on. She wished Elsa wouldn't live alone, but at eighty-five, Elsa did what Elsa wanted.

Elsa Santini took orders from no one.

Back in the kitchen, Slash confirmed the stove burners were off, left the light on over the stove. She locked the front door, exited, and pulled it closed. After throwing the deadbolt, she made her way to her SUV parked in the driveway.

As soon as she was on the road, she made a call. "I have a problem. Can I swing by?"

"I'll let security know."

The line went dead.

Fifteen minutes later, Slash pulled up to the iron gates with the giant S, rolled down the window and spoke to the night guard seated in the booth. "Slash for Luciano."

"Mr. Santini's expecting you."

The gates opened, and she drove up the long driveway to the lit fountain out front. She rang the doorbell and waited. It was a moment before Luciano Santini opened his door. He wore a silk bathrobe and silk pajamas.

She stepped inside, kissed both of his cheeks. "Where are the bunnies?"

"Bunnies?"

"The Playboy ones, Mr. Hefner."

His deep laugh filled the two-story foyer. "I'm alone."

She didn't believe him, but she wasn't there to inquire about his sex life. She was there because she had a problem. Most of the Santini family didn't like Slash. Like Carrera, they blamed her for what had happened.

Only Elsa and Luciano held no grudge.

He dropped an arm over her shoulder. "How 'bout a cognac?"

"Only if it's Santini liquor," she replied with a smirk.

Luciano owned Santini International. His conglomerate of businesses included a designer clothing line for men, a luxury liquor brand, and a vineyard in Italy that produced the best Chianti in the world.

He brought her into his lounge. The large room made cozy with dark green walls, dark furniture, and a table lamp set on low. Rather than sit on the sofa or relax into an upholstered chair, she eased onto a leather stool at his bar. The house was quiet, except the symphonic melodies playing from speakers built into the walls.

"It's Saturday, why aren't you out?" she asked as he opened the brandy.

"How do you know I wasn't, or that I'm not hosting a party now?"

She listened, but couldn't hear anything beyond the music. He poured the liquor.

She raised the snifter. "Santini," she said.

That made him smile. He tapped her goblet, and they drank.

He moved to the sofa, she swiveled toward him. "I got myself hired at The Blue Suit Club, but I have to work the case from the front."

"No sex for you."

"That's my life these days."

"Your choice," he said. "I know several men who would love to date you."

"Thanks, but no thanks." She sipped, set down the glass. "There are six women who've gone missing from there. Law enforcement isn't putting much focus on them, maybe because they're strippers—"

"Maybe they're overworked," Luciano said.

"Are you actually defending the men and women in blue?" she asked.

"You know I dislike law enforcement," he said. "Too slow, too many rules, too much bureaucratic bullshit, too many bosses, too much paperwork."

"If only Luciano Santini ruled the world."

"I'm working on it." One more sip before he turned his piercing gaze on her. "How can I help?"

She told him about her friend, Jilly, and Jilly's missing friend, Terri. "Terri has a sister, who also went missing. According to Jilly, Terri never missed her shifts. In the four years she worked there, she called out three times."

"So, you want to rescue these women?"

She regarded him. "I want to find them."

"You can't save everyone," he said matter-of-factly.

She tapped her fingernails on the shiny bar. "Where would I be if Elsa hadn't come along?"

"You're a fighter. You would have done okay."

She sipped her cognac. "Let's give Elsa a little credit. I want to pay it forward."

"I can't help you."

She stood. "I'll go it alone, then. I'm not afraid." Instead of leaving, she sat beside him. "How are you?"

"Ruthless, arrogant, wealthy, power-hungry."

"Most people say, *I'm good*. Or you could say, *great, thanks*."

A devilish smile filled his face. "A leopard doesn't change its spots."

His phone buzzed. He pulled it from his silk pocket, replied to the text, and set the phone on the sofa cushion.

Luciano was very handsome. Tall, muscular, and tan, he looked like he'd been vacationing on his yacht in the Riviera. He kept his almost-black hair shorter on the sides and longer everywhere else. Always looking impeccable in his designer clothing, he drove the most expensive cars, lived in a stunning Great Falls mansion once owned by Colton Mitus, and he paid a gazillion dollars for round-the-clock security.

Without so much as a single hair out of place, he always looked photo-shoot ready. Like he could glide onto a movie set and assume the leading-man role, simply by how he carried himself, the deep timbre of his voice, the way he commanded control. There was an essence of danger that surrounded him no matter where he was, what he did, or who he was with.

She adored him, but she wasn't attracted to him. Plus, she imagined every woman within a two-hundred-mile radius of DC was vying to get her talons into him.

He caressed her cheek with the back of his hand. "Did my cousin upset you today?"

She held his gaze. *Not going there.*

"My gut tells me the missing women are connected to the alleged prostitution ring," she continued. "I'm concerned they've been trafficked."

"Not backing down?"

"Hell, no."

"I might have a solution," he said.

She smiled. "I knew you'd come through for me."

"There's one man who might help you out."

"He better be good because it's gotta look real."

"He's the best at what he does."

"There are cameras in the club, and I saw one in the dressing room," she said.

His upper lip curled into a snarl. "Find the eyes behind the camera, you'll find the prize."

"Exactly. So, is it someone who works for you?"

"It's me," said a familiar voice behind her.

She spun around, and her traitorous heart leapt into her throat.

Carrera stood there, all man, all muscle, no more than twenty feet away.

8

THE AGREEMENT

Carrera

"You again," Slash bit out. "I'd rather work with the devil himself."

As he studied her face, her expression belied her words. Though she'd never admit it, she was happy to see him.

"Perfect," Carrera replied. "I've always wanted a helper."

As her gaze jumped back to Luciano, a growl ripped from her throat.

A throat Carrera wanted to place his mouth on and kiss.

"Figure it out." Luciano kissed both her cheeks before he rose. On his way out, he shook Carrera's hand.

Carrera poured himself a brandy, eased onto the sofa beside her. "I'll help you."

She sipped her drink, slicked her lower lip with her tongue before leaning back and crossing her legs.

He followed her movement, appreciating every little thing about her. Her arched eyebrow, the way her eyes stayed locked on his. He wanted to rake his fingers through her golden hair, pull her close, and kiss her for days. Then, take her home with him and bury himself inside her heat until they both surrendered to the mind-numbing ecstasy.

Hunting a predator would come naturally to them both. Being together would be like the fucking fourth of July. White-hot fire, scorching heat, and explosions for days.

His junk moved and he grunted. Common sense told him to move away from her. But he couldn't. Beyond her beauty, her determination, and her independent nature, she needed help. This was his chance to step up and be that man. The universe was handing him a Get-Out-Of-Jail-Free card.

Do it.

"Whatever you need, I'll help you," he said.

She laughed. The sudden and unexpected joy on her face sent a powerful punch of adrenaline racing through him. Her throaty laugh was sexy, yet the happiness in her eyes was what he used to live for.

Making Amanda May happy.

That's what G-ma had called her, so that's what he used to call her too.

They learned *from* each other and *with* each other. It was a wild, wild time in their teenage lives. It had been magical and one of a kind.

"Here's what I know," Carrera said. "You want access to the VIP rooms and you need to make it look real. Is there anything else going on like money laundering or drugs?"

"All I know is that six dancers have gone missing. Two from the same family. The GM insists they all ghosted, but I don't believe that."

"Okay," he said. "What else?"

"The police did a basic check, but no real follow up. I can't let this go. If it hadn't been for Elsa, that could have been me."

What the hell is she talking about?

She nibbled her lower lip. That was one of her tells. That was her telling him she'd said too much.

He wanted her to start feeling comfortable around him, so he didn't push for information. Instead he said, "Tell me what you need."

"I need a man to proposition me for sex."

That made him smile. "I think every man at that club would love to do that."

"And I need to tell my B of a boss—the one who got shit-canned from ALPHA and blames me—" She paused. "Why am I the one who's blamed when *other* people fuck up?"

That sliced his heart.

I'm guilty of that.

She flicked her head as if shaking off that painful memory. Her hair went flying around her like a mane.

So. Fucking. Beautiful.

"I need to get into the back, or wherever the hell the dancers are taking these johns."

"I'll do it," he said.

She crossed her arms which squeezed her breasts together. He did *not* look.

She growled. "I'm *not* having sex with you."

He looked around the room. "No one else here, babe. You want to arrest your bitch boss, you're gonna have to screw me."

"Maybe you're a john who just wants someone to talk to."

"No."

"What about a foot fetish?"

He shook his head. "If you want to make this gig look real, we have to work together. Are you in?"

The intensity in her gaze had him hypnotized. He had to kiss her, so he leaned over. Only this time, he waited so see if she'd pull away.

She did not.

Her warm breath heated his cheeks, her bright blue eyes like exotic island seas.

Their mouths came together in a tender kiss. One, two, on

the third, he placed his hand on her cheek, deepened the embrace. Her breath hitched, she thrust her tongue against his, and she released a long, sexy groan.

Heat filled his chest. His trapped cock firmed, the need taking hold. She slowed the kiss, broke away, but she stayed close.

Dangerously close.

"Nice audition," she murmured. "We can pull this off."

Dammit.

That kiss meant nothing to her.

But this opportunity meant *everything* to him. He'd won her love once. He would do it again. Undeterred, he sat back.

She pulled her phone from her back pocket. "I'll text you my schedule at the club. What's your number?"

He gave it to her.

Leave, now.

If he didn't, he'd have her naked and purring in seconds. He'd take her to the brink, over and over, until he sent her over, the orgasm a promise of all the ones to come. He owed her that. Pleasure in exchange for all the pain he'd caused her.

He pushed off the sofa.

She rose, eyed him with a cool disdain. "You're *not* one of the good guys, so don't expect me to play nice."

"Bring it on."

She extended her hand. He shook it. The deal had been made. There was no backing out now.

"I don't just scratch," she said. "I bite."

That made him smile. How could it not? This was going to be the best undercover job of his life.

Maybe even legendary.

Luciano entered the room, his gaze jumping from one to the other. "What's the plan?"

"We're working together," Carrera replied.

"And it's going to be ugly and vicious," Slash added.

Luciano smiled. "Sounds fun." After a beat, he said, "Carrera, I need to borrow you."

"I'm out," Slash said.

After flipping Carrera off, she stopped to kiss Luciano on both cheeks before exiting the room.

Luciano held up his hand until the front door shut. Then, he tapped his phone. "Let's make sure she gets to her car."

One more tap on his phone and a screen rose from the credenza across the room. Up popped a live feed of Slash walking to her truck. Rather than getting in, she stood at the lit fountain, staring into the bubbling water.

"Things will get complicated between you two," Luciano said.

"I got this."

"I hope so, because she's very special to G-ma."

Both men watched as Slash jumped into her SUV and drove away.

"Who's our target?" Carrera asked.

Luciano set his laptop on the bar. A few quick strokes and he displayed a man's face on the screen. The man wore a suit, no tie, his dark hair mussed, his eyes beady.

"This is Garren Butler," Luciano explained. "He was in the area when Mara was killed, but I don't think he murdered her."

Mara's lifeless body popped into his thoughts. Pain and fury flooded him, and he curled his hands into fists.

"Why not?" Carrera asked.

"He's known as The Red Rose Killer. He leaves a single rose with his victims."

Carrera's blood ran cold.

"Law enforcement brought him in for questioning, his lawyer got involved, and he was released. The trail went cold, until now." Luciano pulled up a video.

Carrera watched as Garren Butler entered a woman's home in the middle of the night. Luciano fast-forwarded as he sexually assaulted her, shot her in cold blood. Then, he left a red rose on the other pillow.

"Jesus," Carrera bit out. "I'm in."

"My jet is waiting at Dulles."

"Where are we going?"

"Charlotte."

Carrera had come prepared. He'd swung by his house, changed into a black shirt and pants, pulled on body armor. Beneath his black jacket sat a shoulder holster with his Glock. A second weapon filled his ankle holster.

He knew about the hit when he drove to Luciano's. The beautiful blonde had been a surprise.

An hour later, they were boarding Luciano's private jet. His cousin spoke with the pilot and copilot while Carrera got comfortable in the back.

Luciano's easygoing smile faded as he sat next to him. "They think we're going to visit a sick aunt."

"Nice."

They taxied to the runway, the bird gained speed before lifting effortlessly into the night sky.

"He's staying at a rental property," Luciano said. "He should be alone, but we assume he's not."

"Meaning?"

"He makes friends easily," Luciano said. "Could be other men there. Could be a victim." A sinister smile lifted his cousin's lips. "A surprise awaits us."

When on an undercover assignment with the Bureau, a lot of planning goes into making an arrest. While he understood the value of that, he meshed with Luciano's methods better. Go in, make the hit, leave.

No discussion of what could go wrong, what back up plan was in place. Definitely riskier, but much more fluid.

An hour and a half later, the plane landed and they made their way to a black sedan, parked at the curb, outside the private aviation terminal. A lanky woman stood nearby on the sidewalk.

"Good to see you." Luciano shook her hand.

She offered a tight smile, but said nothing.

After they sat in the back, she got behind the wheel. He gave her the address, but she didn't enter it into her phone or into the vehicle's GPS system. She said nothing as she drove them to their destination.

After pulling into a neighborhood, she cut the lights, drove to the end of the street, and parked at the curb. In the dark car, the men opened their go-bags. On went their helmets, night goggles up. Gloves on their hands.

They left without a goodbye, slinking into the darkness like the assassins they were. At three in the morning, the neighborhood was quiet. The beautiful June night allowed for open windows. He and Luciano made no sound, spoke no words.

Their goal? Leave no breadcrumb trail.

They passed the house where Butler was staying, walked around to the back. The house was bathed in darkness.

They moved their night goggles into place. Luciano tried the back door. It was locked, but within seconds he picked it open. Once it gave way, Luciano turned the handle. Even if the home had a security system, they'd move forward as planned.

Fortunately, it did not, and the silence stayed with them as they entered the home.

Rather than split up, they would stay together. They cleared the pitch-black basement. No one on the first floor. Up the stairs they went, Carrera first. One of the steps creaked, the wood screaming out from his weight.

They stilled.

Then, they heard something being dragged off a table and hurried movement on the hardwood floor. Carrera charged toward the sound, coming from the bedroom on the right. He stormed into the room—

Butler stood there in his underwear, a Glock in his outstretched hands.

BANG!

The bullet pierced Carrera's vest, the force thrusting him backward. Luciano stopped him with his body, moved around him, and raised his weapon.

BANG! BANG!

Butler fired off two more rounds, hitting Luciano dead-center in the vest.

Carrera fired.

POP! POP! POP!

Butler dropped.

"Rot in hell," Luciano rasped.

Carrera rushed into the bathroom. A woman lay dead in the bathtub, soaking in her own blood. The stench from her rotting body made his stomach lurch.

Jesus.

He strode out, went in search of Luciano.

BANG! BANG!

POP! POP! POP! POP!

Carrera bolted into the bedroom, eyed the scene. Luciano stood over the bodies of a man and a woman, the gun still clutched in the dead woman's hand.

They opened the closet, found two more bodies. They cleared the house again, this time checking the closets for corpses. In total, eight women had been lured there and slaughtered.

"What a fucking bloodbath," Luciano bit out.

He pulled his burner, made a call. "Three killers, eight vics." He hung up.

They exited through the back. As they made their way back to the black sedan, Carrera noticed lights on in two homes that had previously been dark.

"They heard the gunshots," Luciano whispered.

They slid into the sedan. The second Carrera pulled the door closed, the driver took off. After they left the neighborhood, she turned on the headlights.

"I got grazed by a bullet," Luciano murmured.

"Where?"

"Shoulder."

In the dark car, they removed their helmets, stored them in their go-bags. Off came their gloves. They said nothing more on the ride back to the airport. Once the plane was airborne, Carrera asked to see Luciano's wound.

"I'm fine," his cousin pushed back.

Carrera went to the back of the plane, pulled the emergency kit off the wall. Back in his seat, he opened it. "Let's just cover it, so you don't bleed all over the white leather seat."

That strategy worked.

Off came Luciano's black shirt. Carrera cleaned the wound, put ointment on it, and covered it with a gauze patch.

"You gonna see someone about that?"

"I just did."

"It could get infected," Carrera said.

"You've been hanging around G-ma too much. I'll douse it in whiskey."

"I'd rather see a doc and *drink* the booze. Are you talking about the whiskey you sell for a thousand, or the cognac you sell for ten?"

That made Luciano smile. He came from nothing. Dirt poor. Now, he had more money than God. But Carrera knew the truth about his older cousin. Even all the money in the world didn't make him happy.

"Who was the couple?" Carrera asked after he put the med kit back.

"Butler's sister and brother-in-law. I didn't think they'd be there."

"Why not?"

"They've been hiding in Mexico."

"What's their stories?"

"They helped Butler lure his vics."

After a long silence, Luciano said, "I have another assignment for you."

"Whatever you need."

"You're gonna like this one."

"If it gets me one step closer to finding Mara's killer, I'll love it."

"This one will put you at the front of the line," Luciano said with a smile.

The plane landed at Dulles, they made it through the small terminal reserved for private jets without incident.

It was just past seven in the morning.

"I arranged a meeting," Luciano said as they approached the large, black SUV waiting at the curb.

Luciano's personal driver opened the back door. On a nod, Luciano ducked inside.

After Carrera sat beside him, he asked, "Do you instruct them not to talk?"

"They learn to use their words sparingly, and they never say my name in public."

"Why the hell not?"

"I have enemies everywhere," Luciano explained. "Why draw attention to myself?"

He had a point.

Once en route, Luciano suggested lunch on his yacht.

"I gotta work," Carrera said. "How 'bout dinner?"

"Lunch."

"I can't."

"Trust me, Carrera, you can."

"Is this like that crap you used to pull on me when we were kids?"

Luciano laughed, something he rarely did.

"No, this is lunch," Luciano said. "That was me pranking you. Go to work. We'll meet on my yacht at noon. All we need is an hour."

"We?"

Luciano fell silent. Conversation over.

While Carrera would never admit it... he was curious. Curious enough to take the bait.

AT TEN PAST TWELVE, Carrera stepped onto Omega, his cousin's sixty-foot, Princess Skybridge yacht. Luciano and Sin were relaxing on the stern, each sipping a glass of red wine.

"So, this is what DC's power players do in the middle of the week," Carrera said before easing onto a chair.

Luciano offered him wine, but he refused.

Carrera didn't want to act like a jerk, but he had a shit ton of work to do, he needed to check in with his dad at Carrera Cruises, and he wanted to research The Blue Suit Club. If he was going to partner with Slash, he needed to be of value.

That, and fuck her like she'd never been fucked.

"Help me get her into the water," Luciano said.

Carrera and Sin untied the ropes from the pier while Luciano climbed to the second level and motored out of the slip.

It was a crystal-clear day. Blue skies, low humidity. As they moved up the Potomac River, Carrera spotted one of his cruise ships.

"My employees had a great time on one of your cruises last week," Sin said. "First class all the way."

"Thank you," Carrera said.

"I heard you're working with Slash," Sin said.

"How'd you find that out?"

Sin smiled. "I've had you on my radar for a while."

Carrera waited for Sin to say more, but he flicked his gaze out over the water and said nothing.

After ten minutes underway, Luciano dropped anchor away from the steady stream of boaters.

"My chef put together lunch," Luciano said. "We'll eat on the bridge."

They retreated inside, filled their plates, then took the stairs to the upper level. The breeze flowed through Carrera's hair. The heat of the day had him removing his jacket, loosening his tie, and rolling up his sleeves.

The men dug in.

"We have an opportunity," Sin said.

Carrera eyed both men. "I gotta tell you, I can't add another job, assignment, hit, or anything else. Seriously, I appreciate it, but it's a hard no."

Luciano looked amused. "You haven't even heard what it is."

"Philip Skye —Z—is retiring," Sin said.

"Addison and Brit's dad?" Carrera asked.

Sin nodded, once.

"He *already* retired and he owns Two Sisters Art Gallery," Carrera said.

"He does own the gallery, but he's *not* retired," Sin said. "He's a Deputy Director at the Bureau. Years ago, he and another man started ALPHA."

Carrera set down his fork, leaned back.

"Back then, he had no idea the group would grow to the organization it is today," Sin said. "With the addition of BLACK OPS and the rescue team, ALPHA wields a lot of power."

"Non-existent on paper, but powerful nonetheless," Luciano added.

"Several brass at Justice, the State Department, and the White House can't wait until he leaves next month," Sin continued.

"Why's that?" Carrera asked.

"He set up a group within Justice that *doesn't* follow the law," Sin said. "He trains assassins and he controls a lot of what goes on in federal law enforcement."

Carrera regarded Luciano. "What does this have to do with you? You're not law enforcement. You're not in ALPHA."

Sin and Luciano exchanged glances.

"There are jobs LEOs can't touch," Sin explained.

"Like the one last night," Luciano added.

"Over the past year and a half, Luciano and I have teamed up," Sin said.

That was unexpected.

Carrera regarded both men. "What does this have to do with me?"

"We want you to take Z's place," Sin said.

Silence while Carrera chewed on those words.

Then, he laughed. "That's a good one. You two got me."

"Not a joke," Luciano said. "You're the one."

Carrera shook his head. "You just said the higher ups can't wait for Z to leave. No one's going to agree to this, especially not the Director or anyone at the White House."

"If I say it'll happen, it *will* happen," Sin said.

"And what, exactly, would I do?"

"Whatever the hell you want," Luciano said.

Luciano and Sin laughed.

Carrera did not.

"You decide which cases get funneled to ALPHA, which go to Luciano," Sin said. "You'd be the liaison between the FBI and ALPHA, so you'd be quietly recruiting ALPHA Ops as positions open up, and you'd be training lone-wolf assassins."

"There's no way the Director will agree to this."

"Let me worry about him," Sin said. "Your formal title will be Deputy Director Special Projects."

"And to whom do I report?"

"That's where things get gray," Sin replied. "On paper you

report to the Director, but in reality, you, Luciano, and I will be working together."

Carrera laughed, his hearty chuckle floating away in the gentle summer breeze. "When he stopped laughing, he regarded both men. "You're kidding, right?"

"This isn't a joke, Carrera," Luciano said. "Z wields a lot of power. Power neither Sin nor I are willing to let go of. You're loyal, you're smart, you're hard working—"

"And you're ruthless," Sin said.

"The perfect storm," Luciano added. "Do you want to think about it?"

Carrera stared out at the boats, then at the sun's glare reflecting off the river. This position was beyond anything he'd ever imagined for himself. But was it where he wanted to take his career?

I'd be a fool to turn this down.

After a long moment, he shifted his focus, first to Luciano, then to Sin.

"I'm in," Carrera replied. "I'm all in."

9

YOU. ARE. MINE

Slash

S lash entered The Blue Suit Club at eight-thirty ready to work. Beneath her oversized shirt and yoga pants, she'd worn a skimpy black bikini. She'd packed her stilettos in her bag, along with a different bikini. Though she couldn't bring weapons into the club, her switchblade was stashed at the bottom of the zippered side section. As she passed the clubbers seated at the bar and at high-top tables, she scanned the room for Carrera.

He wasn't there.

Frustration started to take hold, but she shoved it down. If he didn't show, she'd work the damn case on her own.

I got this.

Once in the dressing room, Slash passed Jilly's station, but it was dark. At her station, she slipped off her outerwear, fastened on her shoes, tied a sarong around her waist, and shoved her duffle in the nearby locker.

She'd be dancing on the fourth stage.

Tucked in the far corner, this stage didn't draw as big of a crowd as the main stage, but Slash strutted up there like she was the boss lady.

As she danced around the stage, made love to the pole, and pretended like she lived for these performances, she maintained an awareness of the hallway that led to the VIP rooms.

As she continued dancing, most guys tossed a bill on stage, but the bolder men and women ventured to the front and waited for her to step close. Once she did, they tucked the bill into her thong. While her skin crawled every time a customer's fingers grazed her skin, she wasn't deterred. It would take a lot more than that to scare her away.

Karen loomed into view as she led Deb—the dancer who gave up her spot for Slash's audition—and a man, down the hallway.

As soon as Slash's set was over, she collected the cash and her sarong, and returned to the dressing room. She stashed the bills in her locker and wrapped the sarong around her waist. Back on the floor, she sauntered over to the Management Only door. She waited, but she heard nothing.

I gotta get back there.

Back in the main room, she swept her gaze in search of her target. Carrera was seated at a table, his heated gaze drilling into her.

Hit after hit of adrenaline pounded through her and her heart skipped a beat.

Damn him.

The effect he had on her was immediate, intense, and utterly infuriating.

Dressed in a dark sport coat and dark dress pants, his bright white shirt made his tanned skin pop. Her fingers tingled to caress his bearded cheeks, press her lips to his, and kiss him.

And she hated that she wanted to do those things to him.

From the looks of things, Carrera had amassed quite the

harem. Three female clubbers flanked him at the eight-person table while four dancers were all vying for his attention.

Was it his looks? The way he dressed? The confidence he wore like a second skin?

Slash didn't know, didn't care. She needed him to gain access to a VIP room. Then, if the universe was spinning in her favor, she'd be one step closer to finding out if sex was on the menu.

He flashed her his killer smile and she bit back a groan.

As Karen hurried over to him with a dancer, Slash got flagged down by a member at the table next to Carrera's.

"How's it goin'?" he asked.

"Goin' alright," Slash replied. "Enjoyin' your evening?"

Slash didn't give a fuck how his night was going or how his day had been, but she needed to play along. If someone complained about her, Karen would fire her ass.

She forced herself to smile, but that's exactly what it felt like.

Forced.

He held up two fifties. "I'd love a lap dance."

She glanced over at Carrera to find him and Karen staring at her. And an idea took hold that she could *not* resist.

She wanted to make Carrera crazy with desire and wild with envy. She wanted to tease him with her body, torture him with what could have been. She wanted to make him pay for the hurt and the heartache he'd caused her all those years ago.

"My pleasure." Slash took the customer's cash, slid it into her thong, then started dancing seductively to the beat of the music.

The patron moved his chair, giving her full access to his lap. While gyrating her hips, she slowly untied the sarong and draped it around his neck. When she turned her ass toward him, she locked eyes with Carrera.

The lust in his eyes left her breathless. As she slithered and wiggled over this guy, Carrera tapped his fingers on the table.

Impatient? Annoyed? Either works.

Whatever it took to get under his skin, make him angry, or make him regret the damage he'd done to her would be well worth her efforts.

With an arched brow, she turned back toward the guy and lowered herself onto him. His audible moan made her want to grimace, but she stayed focused on his face.

"Can I touch you?" he asked.

"No," she replied as she continued teasing him with her body.

"My god, you're even prettier up close," he said. "I would cut off my right arm for a shot with you."

She wasn't impressed.

When the song ended, she stepped away.

"That was great," he said. "I was hoping my hundred would get me a little contact."

"That's not happening." She retrieved her sarong and tied it around her waist.

To her surprise, Karen had pulled a chair over and was chatting it up pretty good with Carrera.

As she sashayed by him, he didn't even glance in her direction. For a woman who kept her emotions on lockdown, Slash wanted to scream.

No one on the entire planet infuriated her more than Carrera Santini.

Carrera

CARRERA'S AGITATION was front and center... but he only had

himself to blame. Slash had danced on that guy to piss him off. He was sure of it.

Why else would she be eye-fucking me?

He hated watching. It took all his willpower *not* to pull her away. But Slash wasn't his and that kind of behavior would kill their partnership. He had a plan, so he sat there, gritting his teeth through her sexy performance.

Tonight, however, he was Claude Amos, a wealthy out-of-town businessman. Dressed in duds from Luciano's designer line, he'd worn a $7600 sport coat, a $1500 pair of black stretch pants, a $700 white dress shirt, and a pair of $2900 dress shoes.

When he first arrived, thirty minutes ago, he asked to speak with the manager. Karen Woodside had been talking his ear off when Slash strutted onto one of the stages.

And his brain shorted.

Sensual, stunning, and commanding, she strutted around like a woman who was in complete control. Second to no one, her sexuality drove him wild with need.

After he introduced himself to the GM, she paraded a steady stream of dancers his way, hoping to entice him into forking over $5000 for a membership.

Then, he had to endure Slash's fucking lap dance... on someone else.

"Mr. Amos, you've got the most beautiful brown eyes," Karen said.

Glancing around the room in search of his target, he said, "You're making me blush."

Slash had been called over to the bar by a few guys. He wasn't fazed. The sooner he could get her into a VIP room, the faster he would have her writhing beneath him and begging for more.

"What do you think about the women you met, Mr. Amos?" Karen asked. "Are you ready to become a VIP member?"

"I'll tell you what," he said, "Arrange a lap dance with the blonde at the bar, and I'll consider it."

Karen jerked her head in that direction, her gaze jumping from person to person. When she stilled on Slash, her shoulders dropped. "Are you talking about the dancer with long, blonde hair and the sash covering her ass?"

Carrera peered over. As if she felt him staring at her, Slash turned in his direction. While she didn't flip him off, he had no doubt she wanted to.

Biting back a smile, he said, "Yeah, that's the one. What's her name?"

"Slash. She's former law enforcement."

Wow, she's got a big mouth.

"A lap dance isn't illegal," he said, keeping his voice chill. "If she does a good job, I'll consider forking over the membership fee. He pulled out two, crisp, $100 bills.

"I'll bring her right over." Karen beelined toward the bar.

Karen spoke with Slash, then pointed in his direction. While the men didn't want her to leave, she said something to Karen, then made her way over.

Her steely gaze stayed cemented on his. With each step she took, heat blasted his chest while blood whooshed through his veins. He raked his gaze over every sexy inch of her. She looked phenomenal in her string bikini, and he could not wait to peel it off her.

She stopped directly in front of him. "Mr. Anus?"

He laughed. "It's *Amos.* Claude Amos."

She leaned over, pressed her soft lips against his ear, and whispered, "You will *always* be an anus to me."

In that moment, he knew he'd met his match.

"I'd love a lap dance."

"Money first," she said.

As he tucked the bills into her G-string, he grazed her skin with his fingers. "You're hot."

"I'm soooo horny for you."

She loved messing with him, and it showed. Her eyes gleamed with a playfulness he hadn't seen in years.

After straddling his lap, she pressed her breasts against his chest. A blast of heat suffused him. Again, she pressed her sultry mouth to his ear. "I want your long, thick shaft deep, deep inside me. I want to fuck you so good, you won't remember your own name. You'll come so hard, you'll see stars while you take me for your own pleasure."

Jesus.

He firmed.

As she started moving on him, she kept her eyes locked on his. Seconds later, she'd looped the sarong around his neck, twice, and pulled.

His breath hitched. There had been a time when she liked tying him up.

Then, to his surprise, she untied the top of her bikini, letting the strings fall over her breasts. The thin fabric fell away, leaving her tits fully exposed.

He shouldn't look. He couldn't *not* look.

As he dropped his gaze, she whispered, "No one sucked them like you. The girls miss their daddy so, so much."

She started moving on him. When his gaze found hers, a shadow darkened her bright eyes, made smoky by the makeup. She undulated on him, shook her tits in his face. He sat there like a goddamn statue while his raging boner sat trapped between his legs.

The ultimate punishment.

Maybe this was just the beginning of the torture she'd put him through. Payback for how he'd treated her all those years ago. And he'd take it like a man because her torture was better than anything he'd get from any other woman.

She pushed up, her toned thighs hijacking his attention. Then she turned around and wiggled her ass at him. His fingers ached to touch her soft skin, stroke his hand over the thin fabric covering her sweet, sweet pussy.

As the song came to a crescendo, she turned back around and shimmied, sending her full breasts bouncing. Before he'd caught his breath over that little move, she sat back down and mimicked gliding on him.

His balls were blue, his shaft starting to hurt from the tight confines of his pants and the way he was sitting. She shook her head, sending her hair flying in every direction, her sun-kissed mane framing her beautiful face.

The song ended.

She tied her bikini straps, removed the sarong from his neck, and stood. "Mr. Anus, that was fun. Let's do it again some-time." With a smile that sent another burst of heat pounding through him, she kissed his cheek, then the other, before saun-tering toward the back of the club, and disappearing out of sight.

This wasn't just another undercover job. Working with Slash had become his reason for being.

He pushed out of the chair, freeing his boner, but he buttoned his sport coat, hoping to hide the bulge. Time to find the manager.

At six-two, he could see over most everyone. When he didn't spot her, he flagged down a server.

"Yes, sir," said the woman.

She wore pasties over her nipples, shortie shorts, and thigh-high boots. Strange how he would normally check out her, but not now. Now, he was on a mission to lock Slash down.

"Find me the GM," he said.

While waiting at a high table in the bar area, a dancer approached him. "You look lonely," she said. "How 'bout some company?"

"I'm waiting for the manager."

"Is there a problem?"

"I'm good, thanks."

Her gaze lingered on his. "I gotta say... you're killer hand-some, and I'm not just saying that for a tip." She gave him a once-over. "Those are some serious threads. I used to work at a men's clothing store. That sport coat had to cost you a few thousand."

Karen hurried over. "I hope you've got good news, Mr. Amos."

After the dancer left, he said, "I've got a proposition for you."

"Let's chat in my office," Karen said.

He followed her through the spacious club, glancing at the stages. As he walked down the corridor toward Karen's office, Slash exited from the dancer's dressing room and crashed into him.

He wrapped his arms around her, pulled her close. "My apologies," he said. "Are you okay?"

"She's fine," Karen blurted.

"Hello, Mr. An—"

"Amos," he said. "Claude Amos."

Her lips twitched.

She loves giving me a hard time.

"Slash hears my proposition." To ensure she didn't bolt, he clasped her hand.

The second they connected, that last puzzle piece clicked into place. She'd been his missing link, the one thing he desperately needed, but didn't know it. Probably because he'd been too busy hating on her.

Karen eyed their clasped hands. "Don't you two look cozy."

"Hardly," Slash said, tugging her hand away.

"It's *my* club, so Mr. Amos and I will talk privately," Karen said. "If I like what I hear—"

"You'll love it." Carrera smiled at her, and Karen's cheeks pinked with color. "And Slash stays."

Slash, on the other hand, looked non-plussed. He wanted to make *her* cheeks flush, *not* Karen's. Karen narrowed her gaze at Slash before continuing to her office.

Karen held open the door for him. "Have a seat, Mr. Amos."

Carrera gestured for Slash to sit in one of the guest chairs across from her desk. When she walked past him, he breathed in her fragrant scent, and a whoosh of memories flooded his mind.

Karen sat at her desk, cleared her throat, and fixed her gaze on him.

"I'm interested in becoming a VIP member," Carrera said.

"Wonderful," Karen exclaimed.

"But I'm not paying the five thousand."

Karen harrumphed. "I'm sorry, but—"

"I'm offering you twenty for free use of Slash."

"Ohmygod," Slash murmured.

Karen blurted, "Twenty? Twenty *what*?"

Slash

Oh. My. God. What is happening?

"Thousand," Slash bit out. "He's offering you twenty grand for me."

"Holy crap," Karen whispered.

Carrera raked his hand through his hair. "Half for you, half for Slash."

"She gets five, the club keeps fifteen," Karen explained.

It was rare that something shocked Slash.

She wanted to congratulate Carrera for going too damn far. From what she knew about his career as an undercover agent, he liked to push the envelope. But this? This was insane. Over-the-top crazy.

"Fifty-fifty or I walk," Carrera pushed back.

The confidence rolling off him was a total turn-on. Aphrodisiac overload. He commanded the space with his energy, the power in his eyes had her hanging on his every word. As if he had nothing but time, he stroked his beard with his index finger and his thumb, running his long digits over his whiskered face.

He shifted his focus to her and the air got sucked from her lungs. This was not the teenager she knew from yesteryear. This was a man brimming with a heady mix of determination and composure. The magnetic energy that passed between them had her biting back a moan.

Stop staring at him.

She could not.

Karen cleared her throat, breaking the spell. They both turned toward her.

"You've got a deal, Mr. Amos."

"Here's the kicker," Carrera said. "I want her exclusively. No more stripping unless I'm here. No lap dances for anyone but me. And as much time in a VIP room as I want."

He's out of control.

Karen's eyebrows jutted into her head. "For how long?"

Leaning back, Carrera crossed his legs, turned toward Slash. He raked a ravenous gaze over her face, her hair. He eyed her breasts, her shapely legs to her stilettos. Then, he traced his journey back until he was staring into her eyes.

Damn, that was good.

Slash's insides burned. Hours and hours of screwing him was something she'd imagined... more than once. Just because she despised him didn't mean she hadn't fantasized about him. Sex and love didn't always coincide at the intersection of happily ever after.

"Three months," Carrera said.

Slash shook her head. "That's not happening."

Carrera's surprised expression made her want to laugh. Undercover gig or not, she needed to weigh in.

Karen grunted. "What is it, Slash?"

"I'll do it for a month and a half," Slash said. "Six weeks."

"That'll work," Carrera said. "Who owns the club?"

"I run it, so it's pretty much mine."

She didn't answer his question.

Karen turned her attention to her computer. "Mr. Amos, I'm setting up your account. When can I expect the cash?"

"The next time I'm here."

Knock-knock-knock.

"Come in," Karen said.

Her head bartender, Bradley, walked in. "I have a guest who's had too much to drink. I called him a ride, but he won't leave."

"Two minutes," Karen said.

Carrera walked over to the door. "Slash, I'll wait outside."

Carrera and the bartender left, shutting the door behind them.

Slash's fingers twitched. It would be so easy to take Karen out... and so damn satisfying. But killing Karen wasn't part of her plan.

In an unexpected twist of fate, sex with Carrera had become the main course. And to sweeten the deal, he'd asked for free use.

On a huff, Karen asked, "What is it?"

"If I'm only making ten grand, what am I supposed to do?" Slash bit out.

"Not my problem."

"It's about to be when I refuse this gig."

"What a bitch!" Karen barked, the heat rising from her neck to her cheeks.

Slash arched an eyebrow and waited.

"Talk to Bradley about bartending." Karen pushed out of the chair.

Before Karen made it to the door, Slash got in her face. "*You* talk to Bradley or I'm out."

Slash needed to pick up bar shifts to ensure Karen didn't see through the ruse.

As she made her way toward the dressing room, a group of guys stopped her for a table dance.

"My shift's over," Slash said.

"C'mon, baby," said one of them. "I'll be fun."

Slash stepped close. "What would be fun is *me* using my switchblade on *you*."

Fear filled his eyes. "Whoa, you're crazy."

"You have no idea," she said and continued through the club.

When she returned to the dressing room, Jilly had just come back from dancing.

Slash stepped close. "I had a thing happen," she murmured.

"Did you get propositioned?"

"Karen set up an arrangement between me and a VIP member, so I'm gonna pick up some bartender shifts."

Jilly furrowed her eyebrows. "That's weird."

"No shit." Slash opened her locker, grabbed her duffle. "Do you have time to get together?"

"Sundays work best."

"I'll text you." After exchanging numbers, Slash pulled on her street clothes, made her way through the club.

Once outside, she found Carrera leaning against the building, head down on his phone. With his sport coat draped over his arm and his shirt sleeves rolled up, she had an easy line-of-sight to his tattoo sleeve.

Damn, he's hot. Total eye candy.

And now she was about to enjoy some no-strings fun. An unexpected perk of the job.

As she made her way toward him, she had the strongest urge to jump in his arms, attach herself like a monkey, and kiss him for days. With each step, her body burned for him.

Despite the major crap he'd pulled in Karen's office, she couldn't wait to unleash herself on him. No longer a seventeen-year-old girl, she was all woman.

And from the looks of him, he was all man.

She stopped inches away. The hunger in his eyes couldn't be denied.

"You're mine," he said.

"You wish."

"You. Are. Mine." He tugged on a chuck of her hair. "Every time we're in a VIP room, I own you."

Her insides came alive.

"This arrangement isn't for me." The smooth timbre of his voice rumbled through her. "It's for you."

Yeah, right.

"Sly, like a fox," she said.

"Your job is to uncover the truth," he murmured, his warm breath heating her forehead. "Mine is to bring you pleasure, over and over, night after night." He tipped her chin, gazed into her eyes with an intensity that left her breathless.

Her insides were quivering, the desire to fuck him hijacking her thoughts.

"I'm gonna take such good care of you, you'll never want to leave me," he whispered.

That smacked her back to reality, and she reeled back.

Fooled me once... never again.

The group of guys from the bar walked outside.

"Hey, it's the sexy dancer with the great tits," said one of them.

"Honey, why don't you come home with us?" asked another.

Ignoring them, she said to Carrera, "As much as I *don't* like this partnership, let's talk tomorrow—"

"Dinner, my place," Carrera said.

The guys moved close. She reached into her duffle, pulled out her switchblade, and snapped it open. "If you think I'm joking, try me."

One of them backed up. "I'm out."

The second laughed. "You're outnumbered."

In less than two seconds, she had him in a chokehold, the knife poised at his throat. "If you so much as breathe in my direction, I will make your scariest nightmare come true. Now, get the hell out of here."

The third guy grabbed her arm, yanked her away. "You're fucking with the wrong guy, bitch."

Carrera moved so fast, it was a blur. He had the guy pinned against the wall of the building. "Go home, asshole, and leave the lady alone."

"She's no lady, she's a whore."

Carrera clocked him in the face.

The guy rubbed his cheekbone. "Motherfucker, I'm gonna have you arrested for assault."

"His name is Anus," Slash said. "*Mr.* Anus to you."

Out of the corner of her eye, she saw Carrera biting back a smile.

She shoved the guy she had in a choke hold into the one Carrera had just punched, then she walked backward into the parking lot, her switchblade still in hand. "Mr. Anus, you're with me."

At her SUV, he said, "I'm following you home."

"I can't shake you, can I?" she asked before climbing in.

He leaned in, kissed her goodbye. "We're gonna have some fun in that club, you and me."

"It's you and I," she said, and pulled the door shut.

She couldn't miss his smile as she backed out of the spot and drove away.

10

THE PROMOTION

Carrera

The following morning, Carrera exited his truck at the circle near Luciano's fountain, strode up the steps to the front door. He had a definite pep in his step, but he didn't deserve to feel this good.

Years ago, he'd hurt Slash. Now was his opportunity to make things right between them. Show her he hadn't just changed, but that he was the absolute right man for her.

He tapped the doorbell.

Seconds later, his cousin opened the door, and Carrera stepped inside.

"Thanks for doing this," Carrera said.

"No one can know," Luciano said.

Carrera glared at him. "Don't insult me."

In the center of Luciano's grand foyer stood a large round table with claw feet. A family heirloom from Italy that had been handed down from generation to generation, going back centuries. It looked like an old table to Carrera, but to Santini, it was one of many treasured pieces that filled his home.

On the table sat a black duffle. After Luciano tugged on gloves, he unzipped the bag, pulled out bundles of tens and twenties. "Ten grand. Use gloves."

"How the hell am I gonna do that at a strip club?"

Luciano retreated down the hall. Moments later, he returned with a tiny spray bottle. "This is hydrolyzed silicone sealant. Spray it on the pads of your fingers. It dries instantly and masks your prints."

Carrera took the bottle. "Where'd you get this?"

"I had it made," Luciano replied. "Wash it off after. For the transport home, wear these." Luciano handed him a pair of skintight black gloves, which Carrera tugged on.

"What's your plan?" Luciano asked.

"Which one? I got several."

"Start with the money," Luciano said as a woman sauntered into the foyer, her stilettos clicking on the marble floor.

Her black hair was pulled into a tight bun. She wore black lipstick and a black jumpsuit. Her skin was so translucent Carrera saw a vein running the length of her temple. In her hand, she held a black cell phone. Her long fingernails, painted black, caught Carrera's attention.

She offered a single nod in Carrera's direction, then stopped close to Luciano. He kissed her, once on each cheek. She left without a word.

"The walking dead," Carrera said, and Luciano smiled.

Carrera zipped the duffle, picked it up. "I'm dropping this in my safe room, then meeting Sin at Justice. He's introducing me to Z, then I've got to get some work done. You know, my *real* job."

"How's Slash?"

"Doing what she does best," Carrera replied. "Hating me."

"I'd hate you too." Luciano opened the front door, stepped outside.

"How can you be in sunlight?" Carrera asked.

Luciano laughed. "I'm in shade."

"Good to know, Nosferatu."

"Take good care of her," Luciano said.

"Of Slash? She can take care of herself."

"Don't break her heart again. Elsa would never forgive you, and neither would I."

"I know what I'm doing." He tossed his cousin a nod. "Thanks for the help."

"I have to get back to my coffin." With a wink, Luciano walked inside and shut the door.

Carrera drove home in silence, his thoughts focused on the million things he had to get done, like yesterday.

In his house, he made his way to the basement, pausing at the retina scanner outside his safe room. After the light turned green, he entered. He set the spray bottle next to the duffle and removed the gloves.

Thirty minutes later, he was parking in the underground garage at the J. Edgar Hoover Building in DC. After passing through employee security, he scanned the lobby.

Sin stood in the corner talking with a sharply dressed Black man. Both men wore dark, tailored suits. Sin wore a blue tie, the stranger a red one.

As he made his way over, Sin turned in his direction.

"Good to see you," Carrera said shaking Sin's hand.

"Carrera Santini, Luther Warschak," Sin said.

"Mr. Warschak." Carrera shook his hand.

"Please call me Luther. Good to meet you, Carrera. I've heard good things about you."

"Luther and Z started ALPHA," Sin said.

"We set up a clause in the job description that we would choose our replacements," Luther explained. "I retired a few years ago, but Philip—Z—wasn't ready. I trust Sinclair's decision, and I've read up on your career. You should expect pushback."

"From whom?" Carrera asked.

"From Philip, from the Director," Luther said. "Hell, it might be from your Special Agent in Charge. The claws come out when it's time for a promotion. You're level jumping so many rungs, you'll probably get called to The White House."

"Is Z expecting us?" Carrera asked.

"No," Sin said. "Surprising him is better." Sin glanced at Luther. "Ready?"

"I'll meet you upstairs in the executive conference room," Luther said.

Luther headed toward the elevator bank, but Sin suggested they take the stairs. At the scanner, Sin said, "I reprogrammed your card remotely. See if it works."

Carrera held his government ID against the wall-mounted scanner. The light turned green, Carrera turned the door handle and stepped into the stairwell.

One flight down, Sin directed him down a corridor and around the corner, stopping in front of a closed door.

Knock-knock.

"Come in," Z said.

Sin opened the door.

Philip Skye—known to many only as Z—was on his computer. With a remote in hand, he clicked a button and the four monitors on his wall went dark.

After Sin stepped inside, Carrera stood in the doorway and glanced around at the shithole office, if he could even call it that. Nothing but an old metal desk, an executive chair from decades ago, a harsh desk lamp, and a computer. The musty smell, paired with the depressing digs, had Carrera wondering what the hell he was getting himself into.

Z slid his gaze to him. "Is this your choice?"

"It is," Sin said.

"Where's Luther?" Z asked.

"Upstairs," Sin replied.

As Z pushed out of the chair, he expelled a sound that sounded like a growl-sigh.

Clearly, I'm not his first choice.

As they made their way back to the lobby, Sin asked, "How are the babies?"

Z beamed like he'd won the lottery. "Adorable, hysterical, stubborn, and life changing. As much as I've enjoyed my career, I'm looking forward to this next chapter even more."

"You deserve it," Sin said.

On the executive level, Sin pulled Carrera to a stop as soon as they walked through the glass doors.

Luther had been talking with the FBI Director, but when he saw Z, he came right over. The two men shook hands, then Luther pulled Z in for a hug. Two men who had gone rogue, creating a secret organization that went against everything law enforcement stood for. They spoke quietly for a few minutes until Luther waved them over.

All four men walked into a small conference room and shut the door.

Z sat at one end, Sin at the other. He and Luther sat across from each other.

This felt more like a standoff than a meeting.

"Sin, I understand you're partnering with Carrera, but doing so from outside the organization," Z began.

"Yes," Sin said.

Z glanced at Luther. "While Luther has green-lighted this decision, I have not, nor am I okay with Mr. Santini. He's too green to have this kind of power."

A tense silence fell over the room.

After several long seconds, Luther said, "Philip, Carrera is loyal to the Bureau. He's a risk taker and he's fearless. More so, he's doggedly determined. He's an excellent team player, and he's got a degree from our alma mater."

"You went to the Penn?" Z asked.

Carrera nodded slowly. "I did."

"He graduated summa cum laude," Sin said. "I sent over his resume."

"I didn't read it," Z said.

Luther chuckled. "That's the Philip I know and love."

"And it's just the two of you?" Z asked.

Oh, boy.

If either of them knew Luciano was involved, the deal would be DOA. His cousin's white-collar crimes were legendary. And from the bag of counterfeit money sitting in Carrera's safe, they still were.

"If there were anyone else, wouldn't that person be here?" Sin asked.

Carrera couldn't look at him, so he kept his gaze firmly cemented on Z.

Note to self, answer a question with a question.

This meeting was better than any of his psych classes.

"Carrera will take an office up here," Sin continued.

"His title?" Z asked.

"Deputy Director Special Projects," Sin said.

"I just invited the Director and his wife to join my wife and me on our yacht for a Sunday cruise," Luther said.

"What for?" Z asked.

"To grease the wheels when he rejects our replacements," Luther replied. "I think Sinclair is going to be a harder sell than Carrera. At least Carrera is a career agent. Sin has never worked in law enforcement."

The conversation continued for several more minutes. Carrera spoke only when directly asked a question. Otherwise, he stayed silent, his vibrating phone in his pants pocket a reminder that he had a shit ton of things to do.

After a pregnant pause, Z said, "Alright, you've got my blessing." He shifted his attention from Sin to Carrera. "Welcome to the dark side."

Relief mixed with excitement washed over him.

In a matter of minutes, his career had drastically shifted from a cog in a well-oiled wheel to a position of tremendous power.

"Our organization is in good hands," Luther said. "We can walk away knowing that the next generation will carry on with our intended mission."

"Carrera, stop by whenever you're in the building," Z said. "I'll show you everything I'm privy to, then we'll start transitioning the decisions to you."

"Will do," Carrera replied.

"We'll tell the Director our decision, then I'm taking you to Rudy's for lunch," Luther said to Z.

After handshakes all around, the men exited the conference room.

Luther spoke with the Director's assistant, then they waited. Ten minutes later, the Director exited his office.

"Director, this is Carrera Santini," Luther said.

"Good to meet you, sir," Carrera said shaking his hand.

"Let's talk in my office," the Director said.

Everyone got comfortable around the conference room table, with the Director sitting at the head.

To Carrera's surprise, Sin sat at the other end, leaving the chair next to Carrera empty. That ballsy move got Sin a disgruntled look from the Director.

"As you know, I'm retiring," Z said. "These are our replacements."

The Director slid his gaze from Carrera to Sin. "Carrera, you're a Special Agent, yes?"

"Yes, sir, for the past nine years, which includes undercover work."

"Sinclair, I have a hard time condoning you in this position because you don't have any law enforcement or legal background, but I would be a fool to refuse The Fixer. I'm confident a time will come when I'll need your team to save my ass."

Sin nodded, once.

"Congratulations, gentlemen," said the Director. "Carrera, are you taking Philip's office in the basement?"

"Undecided, sir," Carrera replied.

"He can take my old office," Luther said.

"Someone's working in there," the Director said.

"I'll move in next week," Carrera said.

Silence.

All eyes on him.

"That's going to ruffle some feathers," said the Director.

Not my problem.

"Let my assistant know on your way out." The Director stood signaling the end of the meeting. "Carrera, your cousin is Luciano Santini. He cannot know what you and Sin are doing."

"Why would I tell my cousin about a top-secret organization that doesn't even exist?" Carrera replied.

The Director smiled. "Good answer. I like this man."

~

Slash

SLASH ENTERED THE APARTMENT BUILDING, walked up the stairs, and exited on the second floor. She'd worn her brown wig, non-prescription glasses, and a dark blue pantsuit. She had her FBI badge—one of many ALPHA-provided three-letter agency IDs —along with her Glock, concealed in its shoulder holster, and her switchblade tucked in the sheath strapped to her ankle.

She stopped in front of an apartment, knocked. Not long after, a woman opened the door.

Slash flashed her FBI badge. "Mrs. Billiawitz, I'm Agent O'Reilly."

"Agent O'Reilly, come in." The woman welcomed Slash into her home.

"I wanted to ask you about your daughters, Terri and Kim."

Mrs. Billiawitz led the way into the kitchen, sat at the table. Slash pulled out a chair, eased down. She set her small pad and pen on the table.

"I'm following up on the missing person reports you filed on your daughters. I know a detective spoke to you, but I'm giving the case another look."

"They just vanished," the mom said. "First, Terri, then a month later, Kim." Tears filled her eyes. "I feel so helpless, not knowing where to look, or what could have happened to them."

"Did your daughters live with you?"

"No, it's just me and my husband here. The girls share an apartment in Arlington."

"Is it possible they left town?"

Mrs. Billiawitz looked surprised. "No. Neither of them would ever just leave. That's not like them."

"What about boyfriends?"

"Terri had one, but he ended it last year."

"Did they keep in touch?"

"He moved away and she doesn't talk about him. It was hard on her at first, but she wouldn't have moved with him. Her friends are here. Her dad and me are here. She and Kim are close."

"Did they talk to you about their job?"

"I knew they worked at The Blue Suit club. Terri didn't say much. Kim is my chatterbox. She told me about the tips and some of the men she'd meet. She was going to cosmetology school and she was trying to make as much money as she could to pay for school."

"I read the police report," Slash said. "You'd mentioned that Kim got offered a lot of money from a customer. Can you tell me about that?"

"She was all excited because a club member had tipped her $500. She told me she ran into him at the grocery store. They got to talking and he asked her to dinner." The mom wiped her eyes with a tissue. "That was the last time I talked to her."

"Did she tell you his name?"

"She never told me anyone's name from the club."

"Did she have dinner with him?"

"I'm not sure. She might have."

"Did Kim describe him?"

"She didn't mention what he looked like but she did say he was sweet. She might have called him shy, but I'm not sure. She told me in the VIP room, he just talked to her. Men usually want to touch her or watch her dance, but this one didn't."

"What did they talk about?"

"She said he asked her a bunch of questions about herself. He was very interested in getting to know her."

"Had she seen him there before, you know, like a regular?" Slash asked.

"She didn't say." Mrs. Billiawitz offered her a glass of water.

Slash declined. "Did the same thing happen to Terri?"

The mom shook her head. "I don't know."

"Did either of your daughters journal?"

"Terri used to when she was younger. When we moved their things back here, there might have been a few journals."

"Could I see them?" Slash asked.

"They're in the guest room," the mom said. "Why don't you come back with me?"

Boxes filled the room. Folded clothes and clothes on hangars covered the bed.

"Are these Terri and Kim's things?" Slash asked.

"Yes, we couldn't afford to keep their apartment, so the landlord let us out of the lease without penalty and told us the girls are welcome back. They always paid on time and were such good tenants."

The mom started sobbing and Slash put a comforting hand on her shoulder, gave her a little hug.

"I'm sorry," Slash said. "I know this is tough. Anything we learn might help in the investigation."

Mrs. Billiawitz opened several boxes until she found a few journals. "These are Kim's. I hate betraying her trust by reading them."

"I'm only interested in seeing what she wrote right before she went missing," Slash explained.

Slash flipped through the first one. Wrong year. The second journal was from years ago, so she set that aside. The next two were also from a few years back. When Mrs. Billiawitz found a journal from this year, she skipped forward to the end and handed it to Slash

"Here's something," Slash said as she skimmed the entry. "I met a sweet guy named Greg. We were in the VIP room. First guy who didn't ask for a hand job. He just wanted to talk. He said he was with the CIA, so he couldn't talk about his job. After an hour, he gave me a huge tip! $500! YAY!"

Slash scribbled a few notes, before jumping to the next entry. No mention of Greg, so she turned the page. She continued reading out loud.

"Ran into Greg in the parking lot at the grocery store. Small world! He was even more shy than I remember and stumbled through asking me out. Adorbs. He wants to take me to dinner. I'm excited."

Slash flipped a few pages. "That's Kim's last entry."

She asked if she could take pictures of those pages, but Mrs. Billiawitz wasn't comfortable with that.

"I understand," Slash said before she jotted down more notes.

"We're so grateful you called," Mrs. Billiawitz said. "I hope you can find my daughters."

Slash was a realist. In truth, she held out little hope that

Terri and Kim were still alive. If they were, they'd been trafficked. Probably another city. Maybe even out of the country. Her heart ached for this family. A happy outcome was unlikely.

"I know this is a very stressful time for you and your husband. I'm going to do everything I can to find your daughters." Slash offered an encouraging smile. After thanking her for her time, Slash left.

After jumping in her SUV, she checked her phone. A text from Carrera sent a wave of excitement rushing through her.

Easy. It's just a text about work. Work that involves sex.

Her phone rang with a call from Providence.

"Hey, boss," Slash answered as she drove out of the parking lot.

"How's the case?" Providence asked.

"Karen is a pain in the ass, but I learned the owner let's her run the club."

"Is the owner on site?" Providence asked.

"I don't know. She's pretty tight-lipped. I saw her escort a dancer and a member into a locked room. I'm thinking it's the VIP rooms."

"Hmm, any chance you can get back there without risking your own safety?"

A very sexy Carrera popped into her thoughts. "I'm working on that."

"Let me know if you need anything." Providence ended the call.

As Slash slogged through rush hour traffic, she thought about Terri and Kim Billiawitz. She now had the name of a man—Greg—though that was probably an alias. And she had a man with a possible M.O.

He invites them into a VIP room, doesn't want sex, tells them he's a spy. Instead of running his mouth, he gets them to talk, gains their trust... then bumps into them outside of the club and asks them out.

She hated that people were so gullible. That they believed

others were good. She used to be like that, until her life went sideways and she found out that evil lurks *everywhere*.

In her townhouse, Slash stripped out of her pantsuit and pulled on shorts, a running bra, and a tank top. On went her running shoes and her armband phone holder. Before inserting her phone, she remembered that she'd *forgotten* to read Carrera's text.

That made her smile.

There was a time when she lived for texts from the best boyfriend in the world, who ended up being the biggest shit on the planet.

Now, he was her partner, working a case neither had been assigned. Enemies going rogue together.

That's a recipe for getting our asses sacked.

She tapped on his text and read it.

> Looking forward to tonight. Dinner at 7?

It was almost five-thirty.

> Just got home. Going for a run. 8 is better.

Her phone rang, and her heart did that annoying little flippy thing when she saw it was him.

"Talk dirty to me," she answered.

"I can do a lot more than talk." His deep voice rumbled through her like thunder.

"I'm not sure you can even do that," she replied.

"I'll go running with you."

"Yeah, so that's not happening—"

"Be over in five." The line went dead.

What the hell?

She called Elsa. After several rings, Elsa answered.

"How's my angel?" Elsa asked.

"In a heated conversation with the devil," Slash replied. "Were you napping?"

"I'm doing a word game on the computer while my chocolate cake bakes in the oven. Why are you talking to the devil?"

"I'm having dinner with your grandson tonight," Slash said.

"You and Luciano are good friends," Elsa said.

"Not Luciano."

Silence.

"*Carrera*. I'm having dinner with him."

"That's a surprise."

"It's for work."

"I hope you can get through the meal without swearing at each other," Elsa said.

"I thought you should know in case I get murdered."

Elsa laughed. "He's not going to kill you."

"Do you need help with anything tomorrow?"

"I'm good, dear. Come by for chocolate cake. Oh, there goes my timer. Love you, Amanda May." Elsa hung up.

Slash slid her phone into the armband, grabbed her switchblade, and left through her garage. While waiting for it to close, she started stretching.

Carrera pulled up, parked at the curb. When he exited his truck, she gave him the once over. A ratty T-shirt and running shorts covered his perfect physique.

With more swagger than one man should have, he stalked over to her, her heart pounding faster with each step. Then, he shot her a smile that lit her insides on fire.

"Hey," he said.

She hit the timer on her sports watch. "Let's see if you can keep up."

"I'll do my best," he replied.

They started out at a brisk pace. While she normally ran alone, she didn't mind having a running partner. Her issue with this one? They were too close, he was too damn sexy, and he smelled phenomenal.

It was an overload to her senses and a big distraction. She ran to clear her head, to sort through work issues, to think about whatever. Now, as they fell into a steady rhythm, he was interfering with her ability to think at all.

Just one big, muscular magnet pulling her closer and closer. Their arms brushed. A zing skittered through her.

"Which way at the corner?" he asked.

"Left," she replied.

More silence as their breathing fell in line.

At the corner, when he turned left, she turned right.

In a few easy strides, he caught up with her. "Nice try," he said.

"I can't shake you, can I?"

"After I make you purr like a kitten, you won't want to."

Her whisper-soft moan floated in the air between them. She tried covering by clearing her throat, but she could feel his eyes drilling into her.

It had been easy to hate him when he wasn't around. Easy when she never once heard from him. Harder since she'd run into him at Elsa's.

The heart wants who it wants.

Now, as they ran side by side, she wondered how long she could continue to mask her real feelings. And how long it would take before he shredded her heart all over again.

She was pushing hard to keep up with him. He had a good seven inches on her, plus he was long-legged and all muscle.

As if he could read her mind, he asked, "How you doin' over there?"

"I'm good."

"I can slow."

"For me or for you?" she asked.

"I usually run slower for longer," he said.

"That'll work," she replied.

They pulled back a little, but they were still doing a pretty good clip. As they rounded the corner, he said, "This is my street."

"Yup."

"You run past my house?"

"When I take this route."

"Did you know I live here?"

"Knew, didn't care."

"Do you care now?"

"Nope."

More silence.

"I'm sorry," he murmured.

"*Now* what did you do?" Slash asked.

"I'm sorry for ending us, but I'm more sorry for *how* I ended things."

Did I imagine that?

She'd waited so long to hear those words, she wasn't sure they were real.

"What did you say?" she asked.

"I'm apologizing for being the biggest ass. My name *should* be Mr. Anus. I'm sorry for how I treated you. I was angry, I was immature, I was fucking stupid."

She looked over at him. Even perspiring, he was still a stunning sight. When his gaze found hers, his beautiful brown eyes tugged and tugged and tugged. She wanted to press her sweaty body against his and slide all over him. For hours and hours.

Stop.

"We're going to be working together," he said. "If we get physical, I don't want things to get awkward."

There it is. We're gonna be working together.

"Why would it?"

"Sex," he replied.

"We're doing our jobs, that's all."

Tears pricked her eyes, but it was easy to mask the pain. If they rolled down her cheeks, it would look like sweat. He'd never know the difference.

She would work this case, then return to ALPHA and to the BLACK OPS rescue team. There, she was valued and appreciated. There, she had friends who were family. There, no one would ever rip out her heart and shred it to bits.

Because the one person who had done that was right beside her, completely oblivious to how vulnerable she was to him. She'd never stopped loving him. She could date limitless men, but no one would ever hold claim to her heart.

Even all these years later, if she wasn't careful to guard it, he'd wreck her all over again.

God, help me.

11

GET IT ON

Carrera

Carrera knew what he was getting himself into. He needed to earn back Slash's trust, then slowly remind her that loving him had been her favorite thing to do. And his.

He should *never* have stopped loving her. But he was getting way ahead of himself. The word love shouldn't even be on his mind. They had a mountain to climb before they could see the valley below.

They finished the run in silence. As she returned to her street, she touched his arm. "I'm gonna slow down, then walk it off."

He followed her lead until they got to her house.

"Do you want some water?" she asked.

"Sure."

He'd never been invited into her home. Ever. This was a win.

They entered her townhouse through the garage. Up the stairs she went. He tried *not* looking at her ass, but he couldn't help it. Only this time, her shapely legs caught his eye. Defined muscles under soft skin. He'd always loved her legs, especially wrapped around him.

In the kitchen, she set her switchblade on the counter, removed her phone and armband, before filling two tall glasses with water.

"Where was the blade?" he asked.

"In my hand."

"Why don't you strap it—"

"No good if I'm attacked."

"Have you ever been—"

"Not on a run, but I'm ready if someone jumps me or tries to pull me into a car."

"Badass," he said.

"Just trying to stay alive in a fucked-up world."

She had a point.

"I spoke to the mother of the two sisters who went missing from Blue Suit," she said after draining her glass.

"How'd that go?"

"She let me look through one of the sisters' journals."

She told Carrera about Kim's final entries about a guy named Greg.

"Great work. Seriously, that's impressive." He stepped close, peered down at her. "Why don't I wait while you shower, then I'll drive you over?"

He loved that she didn't back away. She stared into his eyes for several seconds while the air grew charged with desire. He wanted to pull her into his arms, kiss her, love her for hours.

A *real* apology.

"I'll drive myself."

He set his glass in the sink. "Come over whenever you're ready."

She walked him to the front door.

Once outside, he turned back. "Do you trust me?"

"You? Hell, no," she replied.

"If you didn't know me, and we were working together, would you trust me then?"

She shook her head.

"If we're gonna pull this off, we've gotta trust each other. We've gotta act like what we're doing is real."

"I'll fake it so good, you won't even know." She shut the door, snapped the bolt into place.

He chuffed out a laugh as he trotted down the stairs.

You won't be faking a thing, I can promise you that.

Five minutes later, he pulled into his garage. Five minutes after that, he was standing in the shower, his raging hard-on interfering with his ability to think. Being around her had turned him into a savage, but he was going to keep the focus on her and only her.

Ignoring his boner, he washed off, then turned the water to cold and tried to freeze his libido. Even the chill didn't tamp out his desire, so he turned off the water and dried off. After running his hands through his wet hair, he pulled on worn jeans, shrugged into a collared blue shirt and buttoned it up.

He eyed himself in the bathroom mirror. Was this something Claude Amos would wear? Carrera had money and he dressed like this... but what about Claude? He changed into black dress pants with a belt and a collared white shirt. With a different sport coat slung over his shoulder, he went downstairs.

In the kitchen, he pulled out the steaks and potatoes, set the air fryer on the counter. Working quickly, he made a small salad, then opened a bottle of Santini Chianti.

This *wasn't* a date. Slash was his work partner, but he'd never invited a woman from the office or an employee from his company over for dinner.

Small steps.

The doorbell rang. Muscles running along his shoulders

went taut. Women didn't make him nervous, ever, so what the hell was happening to him now?

As he padded to the front door, he inhaled deep.

He opened the door and his brain went into slow motion. Slash stood there, wearing a tight blue top and white pants. She'd worn a little makeup, pulled her hair into a twist but left her long bangs framing her face.

"I'm here to work," she said.

Though she wore no smile, he wasn't put off. She was more than worth all his effort to prove he wasn't the bad guy... anymore.

He opened the door wide. "C'mon in."

He wanted to tell her she looked gorgeous, but that wasn't appropriate work talk, so he shut the door behind her.

She slipped off her sandals.

"You can keep your shoes on," he said.

"Barefoot works."

Normally good with small talk, he couldn't do that with her. Small talk was used to fill the gaps or get to know someone.

He led her into the kitchen. If she liked his home, she didn't show it, didn't comment either.

"Can I get you a drink?"

She eyed the wine bottle on his kitchen island. "Santini Chianti."

He poured, handed her the glass.

"Are you hungry?" he asked. "You want to eat, then talk shop or—"

"I can tell you're nervous." She placed her palm on his chest sending a jolt of electricity streaming through him. "We've got history. I need help with this case, a case I don't actually have. You agreed to work with me and that could involve sex. I don't know if there are cameras in the VIP rooms, but even if there are, we don't have to get physical. Sometimes, people just talk."

He took the wine glass from her, set it on the counter. With both hands on her shoulders, he peered into her eyes. "I don't do strip clubs, never been in a VIP room. If I go into one with you, we ain't gonna be talking."

She arched an eyebrow at him. "You are cocky, you know that?"

"Sex with us was good. We were awkward, then we figured it out. Together."

A whisper of a smile danced in her eyes. "Then, we got good at it. Real good."

"But it wasn't just sex. It was love."

Her expression dipped, her shoulders fell. His heart broke for the pain he'd caused her, for the pain he'd caused himself.

"Not love," she murmured. "We were just kids finding our way."

Was she lying to herself? Was this how she'd changed the narrative in order to move on?

"It was love for me, Amanda May."

"Amanda May was a project for Elsa," she said. "Don't get me wrong, I adore her, but that teen is long gone. I'm Slash now."

"Okay, *Slash*. When we go into Blue Suit, I own you."

"Free use."

"Lots and lots of sex."

"Then, you'll have it."

"Not for me," he rasped. "For you. I can't wait to watch you unravel while I pleasure you over and over again."

Like an eclipse, her pupils darkened her piercing blue eyes.

"Whatever," she said, but her body did not lie. Her body never lied. At least, not to him.

He stared into her eyes while the tension swirled around them, like an angry tornado tearing up every damn thing in its path. An overwhelming need to bury himself inside her had a growl ripping from his throat.

"I'm out of control around you," he said just before he kissed her.

Her low, raspy moan had him thrusting his tongue into her mouth. She pressed herself against him while the kiss continued.

He explored her mouth with relentless desire while she snaked her arms around him and grabbed his ass.

"I need you," he murmured.

She broke away from him. Her eyes were wild with lust, her breathing coming fast. "I want you to be out of your mind for me, so when we fuck, you'll know what you can never, ever have."

She fisted her hands on her hips, but she *didn't* wipe the wetness from her mouth. "Let's make dinner. We've got a lot to strategize."

His damn balls ached, but he bit back a smile as he walked onto his deck and fired up the grill. He left the French doors open, returned to the kitchen, pulled up a playlist of classic rock. Music flowed through the house while he seasoned the steaks.

"Medium rare?" he asked.

"That'll work," she replied as she pulled a knife from its block and began slicing the potatoes.

He fired up the air fryer, then set the olive oil on the island in front of her.

"Spices?" Instead of waiting for an answer, she began searching, finding them on her own.

He loved having her in his kitchen, loved that they were cooking dinner together. Not long ago, she couldn't even be in the same room with him.

When the grill heated up, he placed the seasoned steaks on the tray.

After wiping down the patio table and setting it, she asked, "Do you have matches or a lighter?"

He went inside, pulled the long lighter from a drawer. While she lit his mosquito candles, he flipped the steaks.

Despite the simplicity of their activities, this moment felt special. Every few seconds, he'd sneak a glance. In part, because he couldn't get enough of her, but more so because her being there was like a dream. A dream he never wanted to wake from.

Minutes later, they were seated outside, the dusky sky a stunning array of dark pink, bright orange, and light purple. As he slid his gaze from the backdrop to Slash, Mother Nature's beauty paled in comparison.

He raised his glass. "To you."

"To me," she replied and tapped his wine glass with hers.

He chuffed out a laugh.

She was staring so intently at him.

"You doin' okay over there?" he asked.

"I... um... yeah, so I've got a thing for your smile."

Progress.

"I'll take that."

"I've always loved it," she said as she sliced into the steak. "Grilled to perfection." She slid the fork into her mouth, slowly pulled it out. He sat there, mesmerized by her every move. When she swallowed it down, she ran her tongue over her lower lip.

Jesus, I'm getting hard.

"Your eye teeth jut out. It's sexy." She dragged the edge of the French fry through the dollop of ketchup, slipped it into her mouth and bit it off. After swallowing, she said, "I never told you that. I wished I had."

"Our regrets are so different when it comes to us."

"Don't you like dinner?" she asked.

He hadn't taken a bite.

"I don't want the food," he said. "I want you."

"You wanna fuck? Get the first one out of your system?"

A shock of energy jolted through him.

She smiled. "I'm just messin' with you."

"I'm not *fucking* you," he said. "Claude Amos is looking for free use, not me."

"You always took good care of me, even when we didn't know what we were doing."

That memory made her smile and he took a mental snapshot of the joy on her beautiful face.

They stared into each other's eyes. The pull to kiss her, to touch her was too strong to ignore.

"I've missed you," he said.

She steeled her spine.

Go easy.

"Let's talk about the case," she said. "Specifically, this guy named Greg. I don't know if he's a regular, so I'm gonna ask the dancers about him."

"We know he used a VIP room."

She stabbed a cherry tomato with precision before popping the fruit in her mouth. "From what I can tell, the Management Only door leads to the private rooms. There're no cameras in that hallway to hack into—"

"You can hack?" Carrera asked.

"Basic stuff, but Danielle Fox, Cooper's fiancée, is the bomb."

"Same with Stryker."

"If we can add a micro-camera in that hallway, we can monitor who goes in and out."

All he heard was *in and out.* His thoughts turned primal, a growl shot out of him before he could check himself.

She leaned back, pinned him with a steely gaze. "When was the last time you got laid?"

"It's been a while," he replied. "You?"

"An hour ago. I squeezed in a quickie after our run."

He chuckled. "Nice."

"I stopped hooking up years ago," she said. "I haven't had a boyfriend since college." She sliced off a piece of meat. "What about you? I'm kinda surprised you're not married with kids."

"Why's that?" he asked.

She shrugged. "I always thought we'd—*you*, I mean *you*—would find someone and start a family."

"I dated in college, but never got serious with anyone. Now, with the business and the undercover gigs, I work all the time."

Tell her.

"The last person who mattered was you."

"Yeah, right," she said. "You haven't had a meaningful relationship in fifteen years?"

"It is what it is," he said.

Her gaze softened as they stared into each other's eyes.

"I want to kiss you so damn badly," he murmured.

"Carrera, this is work. That's all."

He felt that zing in his chest. But he wasn't deterred.

He sliced off a piece of steak, chewed, and swallowed it down.

She's right. This is work... until it isn't just work.

"I can put a micro camera on the wall at the club," he said.

"There's one more thing," Slash said before sipping her wine. "We can't tell anyone at ALPHA we hooked up."

"Yeah, no problem there."

"They'll pull me from the gig and give me a ration of shit."

He topped off their wine. "Are you more interested in the possible prostitution or the missing women?"

She leaned back. "I want to nail Karen Woodside, and I want to find out what happened to those women." After a beat, she said, "I want it all."

"Then, I'll make sure you get it," he replied.

∽

Slash

AN IDEA HAD TAKEN hold during dinner that she couldn't shake. She wanted to have sex with Carrera *before* she got to Blue Suit.

No overthinking, no chastising, and no regret. Just sex.

There was a chance they wouldn't hook up at the club. She wasn't sure what to expect, but if Karen Woodside was involved, she was confident she'd hate it. Fucking hate it.

So, why not have a little fun on *her* terms?

"Talk to me about the twenty grand for Karen Woodside," she said as she studied his face.

"It's ten," he said. "I'm telling Karen I paid you your cut."

"Why?"

"The money is from Luciano. It's counterfeit."

Her eyes widened. "Didn't expect that."

"Anything we discuss—"

"Stays with us." After a beat, she said, "Let's get clear about free use."

"That was for Karen's benefit."

"Are you into that?"

"No, darlin', I'm not. What about you?"

She opened her mouth, closed it. "Should we be having this convo?"

"Might be good to tell me now, especially if the rooms have cameras."

"Right. I'm into CNC, consent non-consent. Sensory deprivation, like blindfolds and tying up a partner, but I've never trusted anyone enough to be tied up. Sometimes, edging is fun."

She loved the effect this was having on him. Though he looked chill, his breathing had changed, and his eyes were black as coal.

"I've never had anal, Mr. Anus," she said. "You?"

"Not a back-door guy."

That made her smile. "Whatever we do, we've got to make it look real."

"No problem there," he said.

"No stepping out of character or having a conversation about why we're *really* there."

"You do know I'm not an idiot, right?"

"I *don't* know that. In fact, I think you might be the biggest idiot on the planet."

He scooped her up and walked down the deck stairs. When she saw his swimming pool, she said, "You are *not* putting me in the water."

"Only an *idiot* would do that." She couldn't miss the playfulness in his voice.

His tone, paired with the gleam in his eyes, reminded her how he'd tease her, make her laugh, then love her with his entire being.

He walked over to the deep end and held her over the water.

"You would not," she said.

"You want to count me down."

"Go fuck yourself, Carrera Santini."

"Not when I have you to do it," he said before releasing her.

SPLASH!

The warm water felt great as she crashed into the pool. Rather than swim toward the surface, she went limp and allowed herself to sink to the bottom. Once there, she started counting.

One... two... three...

She got to fifteen before Carrera dove in, scooped her up, and swam toward the surface. When they emerged, she breathed deep.

"That took you way too long," she said as she wiped the water from her eyes.

"You scared the fuck out of me," he ground out as he swam to the shallow end, his arm still secured around her.

Fear filled his eyes.

For a split second, she wanted to pull him close, assure him she was okay. But he didn't deserve her compassion. She was going to make him work for every damn thing in this partnership.

Nothing was a given. *Nothing.*

"Can you stand?"

"Yes."

He released his vice grip.

"You play with fire, you'll get burned." She pulled off her shirt and tossed it on the tile. Off came her pants next. Now in her bra and thong, she dove below the water, swam the length, and surfaced at the far end.

He hadn't moved, his lips slashed in a thin line. She'd pissed him off.

Bring it on.

She swam over to him, rose out of the water, and glared at him. "I'm not the sweet, innocent girl you loved and dumped. I've been trained to kill, and I've been trained to rescue. I could go either way with you."

A growl so deep rumbled from him. "You are making me madder than hell."

"Now you know how I feel." She swam away.

The more laps she swam, the better she felt. Water always had a soothing effect on her. As she swam in his direction, he removed his pants, his massive boner stretching against the soft cotton of his boxer briefs. Desire made her insides tighten with delight while her nipples turned to steel inside her bra.

When a shirtless Carrera swam alongside her, he brought an intensity that couldn't be ignored... or denied.

And she loved it. Absolutely loved it.

He was part man, part beast, and turning her wild with lust.

She continued swimming, gently stretching her taut muscles as she glided through the silky water. When she ran out of energy, she pulled to a stop in the deep end. There, she rested her arms over the edge and caught her breath.

Several laps later, he joined her.

"I'm not ready to call a truce," she murmured.

"I can go for as long as you can."

"I'm gonna take off." She pushed out of the pool, wrung out her drenched clothes. "We can meet at Blue Suit later tonight."

Seconds later, he leapt out of the water, a massive man soaked to the bones, water falling like rain around him.

He stalked over to her and held out his hand. "Don't leave."

She was at a crossroads. Should she stay or should she go?

Stay, and sex him up.

She would give him a sample of what she brought as a lover. As she stared into his eyes, she knew her answer.

Let the torture begin.

She placed her hand in his. The feeling that came from his touch, the way he folded his large fingers around hers, and the power in his grip, sent anticipation racing through her.

Into the house they went.

His home was to die for. High ceilings and natural light filled the living room. Her eye gravitated to a massive black and white abstract painting on the side wall. A big screen TV hung across from the black sofa, while two white chairs—separated by a small, mahogany table—finished out the space. His uncluttered kitchen boasted more cabinets than she'd ever seen. Four cushioned barstools stood flush against the white quartz center island, and a sleek black table with six matching chairs waited nearby. As impressive as it was, she was only interested in its occupant.

The cold air from the air conditioner sent a shiver through her.

After tossing their clothes in the dryer, he said, "Let's warm you up."

A zing of electricity charged through her. That one sentence was filled with so much promise.

He stopped at the bottom of the staircase. "I can bring you something to wear or you can come upstairs with me and tell me what you want."

The way he peered into her eyes seared her soul. Those words had nothing to do with clothing whatsoever. How she answered him would direct the next several hours of their lives.

The magnetism radiating off him unleashed her inner wild. Despite her hatred of him, she wanted him more... and she wanted him now.

"Tell me what you want, Slash."

Her heart was pounding out of her chest, her insides thrumming with a need so intense, she'd stopped breathing. She wanted him to fuck her. She wanted him for her own selfish needs. She wanted to ravage him.

"You know what I want," she hissed.

He snaked his arms around her, pulled her close. "Say it."

"Raw, dirty fucking," she bit out. "Like animals."

A groan shot out of him while he scooped her into his arms, climbed the stairs, and strode into his bedroom. Another perfect room with beautiful, dark gray furniture. His large bed was covered with a black comforter and black pillows.

The second he set her down, they were on each other, lips crushing, tongues thrusting. She raked her fingernails across his back. If she drew blood, so be it. This wasn't lovemaking. This was raw and feral. This was a hate-fuck of the absolute best kind.

Revenge unleashed.

He penetrated her mouth with his tongue, lashing again and again while he held her captive in his arms. Too close, yet not close enough. The energy in his touch, his kiss was just shy of an assault. And she could *not* get enough of him.

The harder he kissed her, the louder she moaned. She was unhinged, going with every damn thing he did to her. She broke away, jumped into his arms and wrapped herself around him.

"You're ravaging me," he said. "And I fucking love it."

She kissed his neck, nibbled his earlobe, then bit it. Another growl from Carrera and her panties were soaked.

She started moving on him, arching forward and gliding away. Back and forth like a violent wave in a wicked storm. Her insides were on fire, her clit throbbing with a relentlessness that stole her breath... and her mind.

She dug her fingers into his hair, grabbed a handful and pulled. Her moans felt like sandpaper in the back of her throat. Raw, raspy, and desperate.

He bit her lip.

"Ouch, you son of a bitch," she said.

He dropped her on the bed. "Naked. Now."

The greed in his eyes sent a rush through her. He was going to take her, make her bend to his desire. Truth was, anything he would do to her, she'd fantasized about dozens of times.

Fucking dozens.

After pulling off her thong and tossing it aside, she sat up and slowly unhooked her bra letting the straps fall from her shoulders.

"Perfect tits," he said. "Perfect everything."

Her insides quivered in anticipation. Heat rose from her chest, spreading up her neck to her cheeks. A sex flush *before* sex.

Definitely a first.

She threw the pillows off the bed, pulled back the black comforter, revealing dark gray sheets. He was on her like a tsunami, crushing her with his full weight. He was all she could see, all she could feel, all she could breathe.

And she fucking loved it.

Instead of entering her, he rose over her, stared into her eyes. "You have all the power."

His gentle kiss touched the deepest part of her heart, the part she'd walled off from the world to protect herself from the constant hurt and never-ending pain.

She shoved her tongue in his mouth, raked it over his teeth. Feeling his eye teeth with her tongue sent a thrill racing through her.

Instead of going with the kiss, he ended it. One kiss to her cheek, then her chin. Down he went, dropping kisses on her chest, the swell of her breast, slowly, slowly working his way to her nipple. When he placed his mouth over it and sucked, she released an ardent moan. Her eyes fluttered closed.

He stopped.

Her eyes popped open.

"Watch me fuck you with my mouth." He placed a pillow under her head, then found her other nipple and sucked.

The harder he sucked, the more she moved beneath him, her mewls ripping from her throat. She reached down, sunk her fingers through his luscious, brown hair.

Pleasure and euphoria spun through her, holding her captive to everything Carrera. While sucking, he teased her other nipple with his thumb, then pinched it.

She yelped at the sudden shock of pain. "That felt great."

Then, his exploration continued. Over the past fifteen years, her body had changed. Stronger, more defined muscles.

He kissed her mid-section, licked her inner thighs, but his journey came to an end with his face between her legs. With a wicked gaze, he ran his tongue the length of her opening, pausing to circle the hood of her clit.

Jolt after jolt of pleasure pounded through her while she

took in the sight of him. His defined shoulders, his broad back, but her attention kept returning to his face.

Always that handsome, handsome face.

"I know what you like," he rasped. "I know that one finger is good, two are better, but three is what sends you to the moon. Get ready to fly, baby."

He slid one finger inside her, gently thrusting while he licked and flicked her clit with his talented tongue. Two fingers had a new wave of juices flooding her core.

"You taste good," he said before returning to feast on her.

In and out he thrust. Again and again, sending her higher and higher until her eyes fluttered closed.

When he added the third finger, he widened her spread legs with his broad shoulders. Now, completely open to him, she was gyrating hard on the bed. Her moans turned guttural, the orgasm starting deep inside her. And then...

Ecstasy.

Crying out, she pushed her pussy into his mouth, and shook through the extended climax.

Boneless, she just lay there. No words, no thought. Just peace.

He wiped his mouth on the sheet, inched his way toward her, dropping more kisses on her heated skin until their lips connected. And he slayed her with another torrid kiss.

She wrapped her arms and legs around him, his hard shaft pushing against her abs. She could walk, leave him with blue balls. Let him finish the job himself, but that wasn't a part of her plan.

She slowed their kiss until it ended. Had they been in a relationship, she would have kissed him again and again. Then, she would have told him how talented he was.

That's not happening.

"Time to fuck," was all she said.

12

BREAKFAST

Carrera

C overed in a condom, he planked over her, positioning himself at her opening. She pushed her ass off the bed so that the head of his cock pressed inside her.

Fuck, she feels good.

His gaze never left hers as he worked his way inside her. She was tight from her orgasm, so he took his time.

"Talk to me," he said. "Feel okay?"

"Meh." She raised her ass off the bed again, and he thrust to her end.

"You got a mouth on you," he said.

"Shut me up."

He withdrew, thrust. Her bright eyes were black with desire. He pumped her again and again, while she bucked and moaned beneath him.

Her lids were heavy, her cheeks flushed. The most beautiful girl he'd ever known had turned into a beast, unleashed. He kissed her hard. She raked her tongue over his teeth, thrust her tongue against his.

"Fuck me," she commanded, her raspy voice and slick pussy hurtling him toward a fast-coming release.

His fast, deep thrusting had her crying out.

"So good." Her kisses turned brutal, her body bowing to his.

In and out, he was pumping her good... too good. She met his thrusts with her own, her lips and teeth, fingers and nails biting and clawing at his skin.

"Harder," she urged him.

Her near-brutal attack turned him into a mad man.

"Coming," she cried out.

Her pussy clamped down on his cock, triggering his orgasm. "Here I go," he roared as he unloaded into her.

Breathing hard, he slowed his thrusts until he stilled inside her. She calmed beneath him. All that was left was the sound of their breathing thundering in his ears.

That, and the overwhelming feeling that his heart had found its home.

He shifted his weight off her.

"We never did *that* before," she murmured.

"That definitely wasn't lovemaking."

Her eyes widened. "Hell, no."

He made no move to withdraw, so she nudged him out.

Damn.

She exited the bed, and with a sexy sway, padded into his bathroom. He pushed out of bed and followed. She entered the water closet, but left the door open. While she peed, he cleaned himself up. A sense of familiarity had him glancing in her direction. She exited, sauntered over.

Soft fingers trailed his shoulders. "I got you pretty good."

He eyed his back in the mirror. Red streaks from her fingernails trailed across his shoulders and upper back, some drawing blood.

He smiled. "You got your hooks in me."

As she turned away from him, he caught her smile, the one she was fighting against.

Back in the bedroom, she scooped up her panties. "I'm gonna take off."

"No."

"What do you mean *no*?"

He sat on the edge of the bed, pulled her close, and peered into her eyes. "You don't want to leave."

Staying silent, she stared into his eyes for the longest time. "No, I don't. But this is fucking for the sake of it. Raw, dirty, screwing until I wear you out."

"I can go all night," he said.

I can go all night because it's you.

"Let's see what you got," she replied.

He pulled her onto the bed. Now, she was laying on top of him. "You fuck me," he said.

She tossed the remaining condom packets onto the bed. "I'll go until we run out. I hope you can keep up."

She sat up and straddled him, stroking his semi while he feasted on her beauty. Tousled hair, bright blue eyes that never left his. Pillowy lips he imagined around his cock.

He teased her nipple with his thumb, turning the soft nib hard in seconds. "You're so sexy."

Years ago, they'd have sex, then minutes later, have more. They had to sneak around so G-ma wouldn't catch them, which meant they'd wait for her to go out. And then, they go at it like rabbits.

Truth was, it was his supercharged attraction to her that had him on full-tilt for hours. Nothing had changed. He was hard in seconds, his shaft shooting to the moon. When his wetness oozed out, she ran her fingers over it and slipped them into her mouth, sucking on her index finger like it was his cock.

"Suck me," he bit out.

She kissed him with an intensity that stole his breath, sending streaks of white-hot desire pounding through him.

"Fuck," she rasped as she stroked his rod. "You're making me crazy."

That's exactly how he wanted her. Ravenous with desire.

"You don't deserve a blowjob," she said.

"I don't, but you want to give me one anyway."

"I hate you," she murmured. "So fucking much."

"I know."

She nudged him back onto the pillow, knelt between his thighs. He was on fire, desperate for her to take him into her mouth. She licked the head, swirling her tongue around and around while stroking his shaft. More excitement oozed out of him and she lapped it up.

"Fuck, you feel so good," he ground out.

His voice was low, the pleasure pulsing through him so hard, he thought he'd lose his mind.

When she took him in her mouth, he groaned through the explosion of euphoria. She glared at him as she took him in farther and farther. Then, her eyes fluttered closed while soft fingers curled around his shaft.

Sucking faster and faster, she massaged his balls while her cascading hair brushed against his thighs. Higher and higher he flew until he growled, "I'm gonna come."

To his surprise, she did not pull off.

The rush of euphoria sent the orgasm erupting out of him. Spasm after spasm of pleasure shot into her mouth.

When he finished, she opened her eyes. Slowly, she pulled off, disappearing into the bathroom. Seconds later, she returned. With a fiery look in her eyes, she climbed onto the bed. On all fours, she stalked up to him, kissed him long and hard and so damn good.

He folded her in his arms, kissed her back, letting his lustful energy take hold again. He was a prisoner, trapped in a sexual haze. He couldn't stop touching her, couldn't stop drinking up her beauty, taking her anger, her everything.

If tonight was going to be a series of revenge fucks, he was all in.

She ended the kiss, knelt over him, putting her pussy in his face. "I want to ride your face."

Desire flooded him.

"Hold onto the bed frame," he commanded.

With his hands under her ass, he pulled her wet snatch to him and tasted her again. As he licked and stroked her sex, she started moving over him.

"You feel so good," she groaned out.

He stroked the soft skin behind her pussy as he plunged his tongue inside her.

Over and over, faster and faster, her moans morphing into gritty growls.

"I'm gonna come again." Crying through another orgasm, she shook over him until she slowly stilled.

A sigh floated from her lips before she lay on him.

"Dumping me was the biggest mistake of your life," she murmured.

"I know," he replied. "Losing you is my biggest regret."

IT WAS SIX-THIRTY in the morning when he rolled off her... for the last time. He was dry. Bone dry. His cock had been worked and worked and worked some more. He wanted to keep going, but he was out of gas.

Rolling toward her, he said, "My god, you are beautiful."

Wild hair, flushed cheeks, the anger in her eyes long gone. If he could cajole a smile out of her, he'd be golden.

"We burned up the sheets," he said.

"Once we started—."

"We couldn't stop." He patted his chest. "Lay on me."

"Hell, no," she said.

"Breakfast?" he asked.

"I have breakfast with Elsa on Saturdays." She sat up. His focus shifted to her breasts. Perfect mounds of flesh with nipples that had gotten a *lot* of attention over the past ten hours. He still hadn't had his fill of her, but the hours apart would let him recharge.

"You've got a tit fetish," she said.

"I like yours. Always have."

"I lost track of time," she said. "We were supposed to go to the club last night."

"We got sidetracked." After a beat he said, "I'll pick you up tonight at seven."

"We can't arrive together," she said. "I'll meet you there."

"Meet me at Carole Jean's."

"For dinner?"

"Yeah."

She laughed. "First, it books up months in advance. Second, you bought me. You have free use of me at the club. *The club, Carrera.* We aren't dating in the real world and we aren't dating in the Bizarro world either."

"One call to Jericho and he'll make it happen for us."

His close friend, Jericho Savage, owned the Michelin-starred restaurant.

Slash shook her head. "No way."

To prove a point, he sent a text to Jericho.

> If I needed a res for Carole Jean's tonight, can you make that happen?

To his surprise dots appeared, then a response.

> Whatever you need brother

He showed Slash his phone before responding to Jericho.

> No to res, but appreciate the help. What are you doing up so early?

> Liam and I have father-son time on Sat so Liv can sleep in

Seconds later, Jericho sent a selfie of him and Liam eating breakfast together on the screened porch.

After liking the pic, Carrera showed it to Slash.

"So cute," she said, before pushing out of bed.

He wasn't surprised she'd turned him down for dinner, but he had the rest of his life to get a yes from her.

She pulled on her thong and bra, left the room. After a quick clean up in the bathroom, he threw on a shirt and shorts before finding her getting dressed in his laundry room.

"I'm out," she said. "Thanks for the sex-a-thon." She stepped close, ran the back of her fingers over his bearded cheek. "You fuck good. Can you bring a micro-camera?"

She'd breezed right over the best part. He pulled her close, kissed her gently, letting his lips linger on hers. "I fuck good because it's you."

Her lips tugged up in that smile he was eager to see, but she shut it down fast. "We're partners, that's it, so save the flattery. It doesn't work on me."

Yes, it does, and I meant every word.

"Micro-camera," she repeated.

"I'll bring one."

She slipped into her shoes, he unalarmed, then she left without a backwards glance.

Going forward, he would do everything possible to win her back.

Or I'll die trying.

~

Slash

SLASH FELT MORE alive than she had in years. Carrera had awakened her libido, set her insides on fire, and taken care of her, repeatedly, all night long.

One night of explosive passion and she'd gotten him out of her system. The added perk? She'd gotten her revenge on him too. Nothing like a good fuck—or several—to show him what he could have had in the future, but wasn't getting.

Now, it was time to focus up and get to work. She would use him, like he was using her. He was using her for sex and she was using him to get answers to her cases. Life is about give and take. In this case, she was giving as good as she was getting.

Sex was sex. Love was love. And then there was Carrera.

Back at home, she showered. Though she didn't want to wash off his scent, she couldn't go to Elsa's smelling of sex. She tugged on a shirt and shorts.

After stopping for Canadian bacon, eggs, a loaf of 12-grain bread, and a bouquet of flowers she parked in Elsa's driveway at eight-thirty.

She keyed her way inside, called from the entryway, "Elsa, it's Amanda May."

Then, she heard voices coming from the kitchen. When she entered the room, Elsa was sitting at the kitchen table talking with Jazz, her granddaughter.

Jazz whipped her head in Slash's direction and narrowed her gaze. "What's *she* doing here and how did she get in?"

"Good morning, Elsa." Slash dropped a kiss on her cheek before offering her the flowers.

Elsa beamed at her. "This is a beautiful summer bouquet. I still have the one from last weekend. Maybe you should go back to every other week."

"Ass kisser," Jazz mumbled under her breath.

Elsa addressed her. "Jasmine, that's not nice. Amanda May hasn't done a single thing to you."

Jazz glared at Slash. "If ruining our entire family is *nothing*—"

"Enough!" Elsa barked at her. "No more, do you hear me?"

Jazz slammed her fist on the table "Why do you always take her side! She's not even your real granddaughter!"

A stab of pain shot through Slash's chest.

Ignoring Jazz, Slash set the groceries on the counter. "How's French Toast with Canadian bacon?"

"That sounds delicious, dear," Elsa replied. "Do you want my help?"

"I got this." Slash pulled a vase from the dining room, filled it with water, and arranged the fresh flowers.

"Jasmine," Elsa said, "I'm sorry that you lost your job, but I don't think Carrera would fire you for no reason."

"I swear, G-ma, it was total BS," Jazz protested.

"Did you skip work again?" Elsa asked.

"Of course not," Jazz replied. "I took my employees out for an appreciation lunch. I mean, what is the big deal?"

"The big deal," Carrera said, standing in the kitchen doorway, "is that you got drunk, then you took the employees out for a spa day. That's why you got fired."

With a smile that made Slash's heart sing, Carrera said, "Good morning, Slash. I didn't expect to see you here."

He kissed Elsa, then set a large container of strawberries on the counter next to Slash. "I worked up a hella appetite."

After he pulled out the wooden cutting board and a sharp knife, he started cutting the ripe, red berries. Working side by side, the thunderous energy rolling off him had her heart pumping, her blood whooshing, and her insides warming.

Focus up.

She pulled out the griddle, turned on the stovetop, and cracked several eggs in a bowl.

"G-ma," Jazz continued, "Can I borrow some money, pleeeease?"

Slash glanced over before dipping the bread in the whisked eggs. To ensure all the toast would get cooked at the same time, she piled up the egg-soaked bread in a different bowl.

"I loaned you five thousand last month," Elsa said, "on top of many other thousands before that. You've never once even mentioned paying me back."

"I thought they were gifts," Jazz whined.

Gimme a break.

Carrera's ran his hand down Slash's back, stopping just above her ass. Jolts of excitement fluttered through her, but she reached behind and removed his hand. "Nice try."

He held up a strawberry. "These are good. Very moist. Sweet too. Reminds me of something…" He flashed a smile, then held the fruit in front of her mouth.

As she stared into his eyes, the air crackled with energy. She *wanted* him to place that piece of fruit in her mouth, but wouldn't that be sending the wrong message? And what the hell happened to hating him?

She plucked it from his fingers, slid it slowly into her mouth.

"Mmm," he murmured.

Jazz flicked her gaze in his direction. "Carrera, I'm broke. Maybe you could hire me back?"

Slash set a few pats of butter on the heated griddle and watched it melt into little yellow puddles. In went the soaked bread. She pulled a different pan, set it on the stovetop, and turned on the burner.

"Your position's filled," Carrera said matter-of-factly.

This time, Jazz slammed both fists on the table and shoved out of the chair so hard it crashed against the wall. "If Mom were here, she would give me money! You guys are so selfish!"

As if that immature outburst hadn't just happened, G-ma said, "Are you staying for breakfast, Jasmine?"

"No, I have to return two pairs of designer shoes and a new outfit. I have a party to go to today and *nothing* to wear!" She stormed out of the kitchen. Seconds later, the front door slammed shut.

Silence.

Blessed silence.

Carrera placed the bowl of cut strawberries on the table. "How 'bout a strawberry, G-ma?"

He pulled three forks and three knives from the drawer, along with three dinner plates. After scooping a few pieces of fruit onto her plate, he returned to pour himself coffee.

Elsa sat there like a statue, just staring out the kitchen window.

Slash's heart broke for her.

"You okay, Elsa?" Slash asked before placing the Canadian bacon on the heated pan to warm.

"I'm fine," Elsa replied, but she wasn't fine.

Her voice was tight. Any time there was family tension or drama, it always saddened her.

Angst crept into Slash's soul.

Truth was, Slash had played a part in this horrific family tragedy. The sex high that had carried her over on a magic carpet fell crashing back to earth.

But... Slash had nothing to do with Jazz's inability to save or with her incessant spending. Even so, there were many times when Slash wondered how the Santini family would have turned out if her dad had never gone to her travel soccer game.

She pulled the French toast off the griddle, the Canadian bacon from the pan. After filling two serving plates, she set them on the table, then fetched the maple syrup, and the pot of coffee for Elsa.

After topping off Elsa's mug, she was surprised to see that Carrera had poured her a mug of coffee.

"Thanks for the coffee," she said to him.

Elsa glanced up at her, then over at Carrera. "That was civil." Then, after a deep breath, she said, "Let's say grace."

Slash returned the coffeepot, sat across from Carrera, while Elsa sat at the head.

Elsa held out her palms, and on auto-pilot both she and Carrera placed their hands over hers. Then, Carrera set his hand, palm up, on the table.

Slash stared at his hand, then at him.

"Go on," Elsa said. "He won't bite you."

"Yes, I will, G-ma," Carrera said. "I'm gonna bite her real good." He winked at Slash.

Over the years, Carrera had laid his hand on the table before, but she'd refused to touch him. This morning, she didn't want to upset Elsa. Jazz had already done that. So... to keep the peace, she laid her hand over his, and his fingers folded over hers.

His heat spread up her arms and straight to her heart.

"Thank you, Lord, for this meal, prepared with love. Bless my family as they make their way today, and bless those who seek you. In the name of the Father, and of the Son, and of the Holy Spirit, Amen."

"Amen," she and Carrera said in unison.

Elsa pulled a piece of French toast off the top of the pile.

"Elsa, that one's cold," Slash said. "Give it to Carrera."

On a chuckle, Carrera took it, then two more.

Slash served Elsa the next one. "This is still hot."

A few bites in, Elsa said, "You both look so tired, like you didn't sleep a wink."

Slash could feel Carrera's gaze drilling into her. If she so much as glanced in his direction, she'd give herself away.

"Been busy with work," Slash said.

"Same," Carrera added. "I got a new assignment."

Elsa's expression fell. "Are you going out of town again?"

"No," Carrera said between bites. "I'm in town working a possible prostitution syndicate and several missing persons cases. I've got a new partner."

"I'm happy you're in town," Elsa said. "I hope you find time to visit me."

"Every Saturday morning, G-ma," Carrera said. "I know Amanda May would love that, wouldn't you, Slash?"

"I'd love it like poison," Slash replied, biting back a smile.

～

Carrera

THAT EVENING, just after nine, Carrera parked in a dark corner of the lot. He coated his fingertips with the silicone spray, collected the duffle, and walked into the Blue Suit club.

Music pulsed through him as he made his way toward the back.

The club was already busy, filled with men looking for a good time. While topless dancers slinked around the poles or shook their booties on tables, Carrera kept his gaze trained straight ahead. There was only one woman who interested him, and she wasn't arriving for another fifteen minutes.

He stopped outside the GM's closed office door.

Knock-knock.

"Just a minute," Karen called out.

After what felt like fucking forever, the door opened. A red-faced Karen lit up when she saw him. "Mr. Amos, sorry for the wait." She stepped aside.

He walked in, and his attention jumped to the bearded guy on the sofa, his wild hair covering one of his eyes. He wore a black shirt, black pants. Karen got busy smoothing her mussed hair.

Were they screwing?

"I'll come back," Carrera said.

The man left her office without saying a word. Karen shut the door as Carrera set the bag on her desk.

She hurried over, unzipped it, and pulled out wads of cash. "Do I need to count it?"

He didn't give a fuck what she did. "Ten grand."

"Wait, what? We agreed to twenty."

"Your cut is ten," Carrera said.

"But *I* pay the dancers."

He said nothing.

After a few seconds, she said, "One less thing for me to do."

He turned to leave.

"Did you want to chat for a bit? I mean, you are my highest paying client."

Her cheesy grin wasn't sweetening the offer, but he wanted to gain her trust, so he eased into the guest chair. She dropped into her chair, pulled a bottle of whiskey from the desk drawer, along with two shot glasses, neither looking clean.

Jesus, that's nasty.

"Can I offer you a nip?" she asked.

"I fuck sober," he replied.

An audible sigh floated from her lips. "So, Mr. Amos, what do you do when you're not here?"

Refusing to answer her questions, he crossed his legs, flashed a smile. "A beautiful woman like you should be on stage. Why hide back here?"

Her face went tomato red. "Oh gosh, thank you. I'm not a dancer, plus, my skills are better used behind the scenes."

"How long have you run the club? Or do you own it?"

"I'm very tight with the owner, so I run everything. I've been here almost six months." She glanced at his clothes. "Your clothing is very nice. I'd love to buy my boyfriend a sport coat like yours. Where do you shop?"

"My clothing is tailored in Italy," he said. "I fly over twice a year for fittings."

"Wow," she murmured.

"How do I access the VIP rooms?"

"I let you in."

"You're here seven days a week?"

She nodded. "I love my job."

"Karen, I prefer privacy and anonymity. Isn't that what the private rooms are for? I'll need a keycard."

She shook her head.

He stood, zipped and lifted the duffle off her desk. "I'll take my business elsewhere."

"What about Slash?" Karen asked.

He shrugged. "She's a means to an end, nothing more."

His guts churned. Uttering those words make him sick. Prepared to play chicken with Karen, he gripped the doorknob.

"Wait," she blurted, and he bit back a smile. "I can issue you a keycard."

His smile made her blush.

"*Now* I feel like I'm your most important customer," he cooed.

He set the bag down, waited while she programmed a card.

The pads of his fingers were tingling. Whatever the hell was in that spray bottle was numbing them pretty good.

She handed him a plain, black card with a chip on one side. He plucked it from her fingers and left. After stopping in the restroom to wash off the chemicals, he headed back toward the bar.

And that's when he spotted *her*.

Heat slammed his chest.

Slash, seated at a high top near the bar, was surrounded by four men. Two were seated, two stood. Her beauty stole his breath, but it was the confident way she carried herself that he loved the most.

She wore a low-cut black dress, the swell of her breasts snagging his attention. She'd worn her hair in a ponytail, her eyes darkened by makeup, and her lips slicked with clear gloss.

He didn't just want sex with her, he wanted *all* of her.

Stopping at the table, he towered over the men ogling her. The men talking stopped, all four flashed him dirty looks. When she peered into his eyes, everything fell into place. They were hunting down evil, they were doing it together, and they were about to go a little crazy in a private room.

She stood, her attention still glued on him.

The guy who'd been talking said, "Where are you going, doll? I thought we were having a good time."

"I told you I have plans." Slash walked over to Carrera.

Everyone faded away. The guys didn't matter, the pulsing music vanished, the chatter turned into white noise. Slash was all he cared about. Doing right by her was his priority over everything and everyone.

The energy that passed between them surged through him. In those few seconds, she became his entire world. He would walk through fire and slay every dragon to make her happy.

And then, he would love her fiercely for the rest of his life.

He followed as she made her way around the groups mingling at the bar. Once in the darkened hallway that lead to the VIP rooms, he pulled her into his arms, pinned her against the wall, and kissed her. Then, he fished out the micro-camera from his pocket and pressed it on the wall over the doorframe. The tiny black device blended into the dark blue walls.

With a gravelly groan, she pressed into him, and kissed him back with such ferocity, he turned hard. When he ended the kiss, he didn't move.

"You're smooth," she murmured. Pushing up on her toes, she whispered in his ear, "Nice job with the camera."

"If you liked that, you're gonna love my next surprise," he murmured as he peered into her eyes.

"I can't wait." She nudged him back. "We need to tell Karen we're here, so she can let us in."

He clasped her hand, led her to the Management Only door, and inserted the keycard. The light flashed green, he withdrew the card, and opened the door.

"I'm impressed," she whispered, before stepping inside.

After crossing the threshold, he murmured, "What the fucking fuck."

13

THE REAL BLUE SUIT CLUB

Slash

Instead of standing in a hallway lined with private rooms, they stood in one large, open space.

An orgy playroom.

She peered up at Carrera. He met her gaze.

"Surprise," he murmured.

An eerie glow from the red bulbs in the wall sconces and the recessed lighting kept the room cloaked in shadow. Naked and semi-nude couples and small groups were playing on couches, futons, tantra chairs, and the St. Andrew's Cross.

Nearby, a long counter offered small whips, feather floggers, and nipple clamps. There were several varieties of condoms, and two baskets of black eye masks. One marked "Clean", the second labeled, "Used".

Carrera pulled two masks, offered one to Slash. They pulled them on, adjusted to fit.

Instead of blaring club music, classical music floated from wall speakers.

He pressed his mouth to her ear and whispered, "We got this."

Curious by nature, Slash clasped Carrera's hand, and started moseying around. They passed a foursome—two men and two women—playing on a sheet-covered mattress. Both women danced at the club. One of the women was on all fours. She wore a thong, a collared leash around her neck. A man wearing nothing but a black eye mask held the leash while she gave the other man a blowjob. The second woman was using a mini-whip on his ass, smacking him repeatedly.

She and Carrera had entered an erotic underworld of kink play.

Just ahead, a man and a woman were sitting on a sofa. He wore leather pants, she a leather bra and shorty shorts. He was licking and sucking her toes.

Sexy.

As they approached the far corner and the dim red lighting brought everything into focus, Slash stopped. Seven masked people were playing on thick black gym mats. Most wore black eye masks, but one woman hid her face behind an elaborate feather mask, and one of the men wore a devil mask.

She leaned up toward Carrera, and he lowered his head, so she could whisper, "Welcome to hell."

He smiled, sending a white-hot streak of desire thrilling through her.

This group was so entwined, it was hard to tell who was doing what to whom, but Slash spotted a man screwing a woman in her ass while another fucked her pussy. Two women were blowing a man, and three women were busy climaxing together.

"Wow," she murmured.

The man who was butt-fucking the woman waved them over. Slash refused him with a simple shake of her head.

Next stop, a naked man was tied to the St. Andrews Cross. A dancer wearing only a G-string smacked him with her small leather whip while a man dressed in only a bra tickled him with a feather. He was yelping, then laughing.

Black gym mats took up floor space where a dancer from the club was performing an impressive yoga pose while a man feasted on her pussy.

Though the scenes were eye-catching and provocative, Slash was too surprised to feel aroused.

On another sofa, a bearded man wearing an eye mask sat with beside an unmasked woman. Both were clothed. He was caressing her hand while she spoke.

Slash spotted a tantra chair tucked into the corner, so she urged Carrera in that direction.

"I saw that bearded guy in Karen's office," Carrera murmured. "They might have been screwing."

"She's fucking the customers?" Slash murmured.

"Maybe."

Slash stopped in front of the sex chair. "The woman he's with dances here. Her name is Deb."

"What about the other women?"

"I recognize a few," Slash replied.

While the kink play was unexpected, she could roll with it. Her concern? She had no idea if the place was filled with cameras and mics.

As if Carrera could sense her discomfort, he eased onto the tantra chair, pulled her close. "Talk to me."

"There could be cameras and mics everywhere. Karen could be selling videos on the dark web or blackmailing customers."

"This *isn't* a sex club. It's a strip club. Sex *shouldn't* be happening."

"I don't want to get you in trouble," she whispered.

"You *do* care."

"No, I don't, but you work for an organization with way more rules than mine. I don't want to ruin your career. You're good at your job."

He slipped his hand behind her neck, pulled her down, and kissed her.

"Don't get the wrong idea," she murmured. "I don't like you and don't care about your career, but I don't want to be the reason you lose it."

"I'm flattered."

Fighting against a smile, she shook her head at him. "I know people who could fix this situation for me in a matter of minutes."

Staring into his eyes excited her and also grounded her.

Stop. You hate him.

"I know what will take your mind off everything." He kissed her again, placed his hands on her ass and gently squeezed.

Her insides came alive. He stroked her ass, his large hands claiming her for his own. The passion in his kiss made her panties wet, while she turned her focus on the glorious man before her. She wanted him, wanted him naked, wanted him inside her, fucking her like no other man ever could.

If Karen was watching, she'd have no doubt Slash was doing her job. She'd never question the reason they were at the club. She'd never suspect a thing.

Breaking away, Slash started dancing to the rhythmic beat of the music. Slowly, she removed her dress revealing her nude body.

His reaction was instant and intense. A growl shot out of him, his eyes bled black, and he raked his hungry gaze over every inch of her. She raised her arms, continued her seductive sway, massaging her breasts and pinching her nipples. Then, she ran her hand over her pussy and touched herself.

"Fuck," he bit out.

She sashayed over, placed her hands on his sculpted face, and kissed him. Not like a stranger he'd bought for free use, but like the girl who'd once loved him fiercely.

Then, she ended the kiss to unbutton his shirt. When finished, she helped him out of it. Seconds later, he too stood naked. He reached into his pants—discarded on the floor—and extracted a packet of condoms.

As he opened it, she knelt, took his hardness into her mouth, and teased him with her tongue, raked his shaft with her teeth. His moans grew gritty, his fingers sunk into her hair. She was turning wild with desire, like a lioness on the prowl for her next meal.

She licked and sucked, never increasing her speed. When his balls tightened, she pulled off and led him to the tantra chair.

After rolling on the condom, he straddled the black leather. She climbed on facing away, positioned him at her core, and slid down. One delicious, pleasure-filled slide until he was rooted deep, deep inside her.

And then, she laid back, resting her shoulders on his, and she started moving. His throaty groans filled her ears with sounds she'd once loved, sounds that reminded her how much pleasure she could bring him. He ran his hands over her breasts and abs, down to her pussy to tease her clit.

Groaning through the onslaught of pleasure, she wanted to slow, wanted to take her time, but she couldn't. Desire pounded through her at a frenetic pace while she pumped his cock again and again.

Faster and faster.

He pinched her nipples, squeezed her tits. The build was insanely quick, like a race car whizzing around a track.

She climaxed, her orgasm rocking her with ecstasy while she ground against his shaft, shoving him clear to her end.

"Fuck," he roared in her ear. "Coming so hard."

They climaxed together while he wrapped his arms around her and held her tight. Spasm after spasm of ecstasy shot through her as she unraveled around his hardness.

Breathing hard, she relaxed against him.

"What the hell just happened?" she asked.

"Round one," he replied.

She pulled off him. On the table nearby, she collected a few tissues. He cleaned himself up, wrapped his arms around her and kissed her breathless. His tongue swept inside her mouth and she welcomed him with a hard thrashing of hers. Still kissing her, he lifted her into his arms and set her in the middle of the chair, then ended their sexy embrace.

With another condom packet in hand, he straddled the chair, facing her, and slithered his arms around her back. "I can't get enough of you. You fuck like a goddess. I'm addicted to you, so if this is your revenge, it's perfect. Absolutely perfect."

Was she punishing him or punishing herself? This was work, work that could get her fired, work that could break her heart when the assignment came to an end.

"Lay down, drape your legs over the lower half," he said. "I'm going to eat you."

She did as he ordered and he dropped to a knee, so he was eye level with her pussy. With a ravenous gaze, he said, "I'm hungry."

He placed his mouth on her sex, his hands on her tits, and he unleashed a maelstrom of energy into her. This was an assault to her erogenous zones. She started gyrating her hips... up and down, up and down. She covered his hands with her own while he teased and aroused her tender nipples.

When he slipped fingers inside her, she rose off the leather, her groans coming fast, her thoughts focused on the pleasure he was bringing her. In and out he thrust, but when he added a third finger and rubbed her clit, the orgasm overwhelmed her.

She shook and convulsed through her ecstasy until she stilled on the chair.

He stood, she sat up. Their eyes met. His lips were wet with her juices. But it was the look in his eyes that had her pushing to her feet. To her surprise, it wasn't lust.

It was love.

I'm seeing things. The red lights are messing with me.

His jutting erection reminded her that she was in a hidden orgy room and her job was that of free-use sex worker. As he rolled on another condom, she ran her fingers down his shoulders, his back, and over his hard-muscled ass.

He's got it goin' on, that's for sure.

"Sit facing me," he ordered, his voice commanding obedience.

She straddled the chair, he did the same, facing her. Instead of entering her, he pulled her close and kissed her. An Adonis of a man who claimed her with his touch and the possessive way he held her in his striated arms. It felt like she was his, trapped in a cocoon he'd created to protect her and keep her safe.

He ended the kiss, dipped down, and sucked her nipple. Hard sucking with a firm tongue lashing. Sounds were escaping her that sounded foreign. Deep mewls paired with whimpers. When he'd had his share of one breast, he ran his tongue around her nipple while he squeezed the other.

His bobbing cock screamed for attention, so she ended the kiss and spread her legs wide. "Fuck me," she instructed.

He was a big boy, but as he entered her, her insides expanded to accommodate his girth. They started moving as one, and he kissed her again.

Her body flooded with dopamine while she stared into his eyes. She ran her fingers over his face, sunk them into his thick hair. The more she had him, the more she wanted him. And there was nothing she could do to stop herself.

This time, he thrusted slowly. Very, very slowly.

"You're so sexy," he said. "I'm addicted to you, to our hard, wild fucking. Do you like this?"

He thrust to her end, stilled.

"I plead the fifth," she replied between breaths.

His sexy smile wasn't helping her hate him.

On a gritty groan, he said, "I'm gonna fuck you hard and fast."

"Yessss," she ground out.

He moved inside her at a maddening pace, her insides humming with euphoria that spread over her like melted butter.

Another orgasm, and she cried out through this one while he moaned, "Fuck, coming."

She was shattered, drained, yet more alive than she'd felt in years.

The more they fucked, the more addicted she became. He'd been her naughty addiction all those years ago, and he still was. She could pull another all-nighter with him. No problem.

They came together in another panty-searing kiss. When they finally broke away, they were breathless.

His beautiful chest rose and fell, glistening in sweat. She slid her fingers over his biceps, then she dropped her hands by her side. They were partners, not lovers. This wasn't the tender afterglow. This was work.

Plain and simple.

Her job there was done. She could report back to Providence and let them move in to make an arrest. The club would get shut down. Karen and the owner charged with running a prostitution syndicate.

Would Carrera work the missing persons case with her? He had his own caseload, so she'd go it alone. An overwhelming sadness slithered into her soul. She was used to being alone.

This is crazy.

I hate him. Let him go and move on.

But if she *didn't* tell Providence, and they had to return again and again, until they learned who *owned* the club, she'd have more information to provide when it was time to make an arrest.

That's a better plan.

Truth was, she liked hooking up with Carrera at the club. It gave her a legit excuse to see him. Screwing him was an added perk. She couldn't trust her heart to him. He would only break it again. She'd barely survived their first break up. No way would she get over another.

Carrera Santini had wrecked her for any other man.

She felt eyes on her and looked over. The bearded man— the one who'd been talking with Deb—sat alone on the sofa, watching them.

A chill streaked down her spine.

Carrera

LIKE YESTERDAY, Carrera's mind was blown. He needed to move Slash out of the club and into a more intimate setting. He had no off-switch around her, had no intention of slowing down. But she wasn't a booty call. He needed to take this—whatever this was—to the next level.

While cleaning himself off, he spotted the guy on the sofa watching them. Even in the glow of red lights, Carrera couldn't miss it. The man was locked on them.

Carrera glanced around. New people had arrived, others had left. The aroma of sex hung thick in the air. Since they'd gotten there, the smack of a whip or the cries of ecstasy had caught his ear, but his attention had stayed on Slash.

That was the easy part.

The challenge? How did she want to work this case?

"Hey," she whispered after slipping into her dress. "You see the bearded, masked guy?"

"Yeah."

"How long has he been watching us?"

"No idea. I was focused on you."

"You ready to call it?" she asked.

"No."

She started to remove her dress, but he stopped her. "I'm ready to leave, but I'm not ready to say goodnight."

He couldn't read her. Did she like what he'd just said? Was her mind on work? He'd wait until they could talk in private.

They left the kink room. Saturday at one in the morning and the club was wall-to-wall with members. He clasped her hand, led her through the crowd, and out into the night.

The balmy breeze cooled his heated skin.

"I thought I was in shape, but I'm not," he said. "You're wearing me out."

"You gotta get out there and prime the pump," she said.

He laughed. "I don't want what's out there."

"Now that you're back in the area, jump in the dating pool."

He walked her to her SUV. "No."

She opened the door. "We gotta talk about tonight. Meet for coffee tomorrow?"

What? Hell, no.

"No, we should talk *tonight*," he insisted. "I'll swing by."

"Is your pool open?"

"For you, it is. Did you bring a bathing suit?"

With a hint of a smile, she climbed into her vehicle, shut the door. Seconds later, she drove away.

He strode to his truck and hopped in. As he pulled out of the parking spot, the bearded guy exited the club, head down. Instead of walking into the lot, he vanished around the side of the building and disappeared into the night.

What's up with that?

Carrera drove home, his thoughts filled with Slash. When he drove down his street, she was waiting in front of his house. Excitement pounded through him.

He parked in his garage, headed down the driveway as she pulled an overnight back from her vehicle.

"Someone came prepared," he said.

"I'm using you for your body and your swimming pool," she said, but he caught the playful gleam in her eyes.

In the kitchen, he offered her a glass of wine.

"Swim first," she replied.

"Make yourself at home," he said and poured himself a whiskey.

"Spare bedroom?" she asked.

"Upstairs," he replied.

"I'm changing." With her leather bag in hand, she headed toward his stairs.

He was flat-out thrilled she was there, but he didn't want to get ahead of himself. Better to stay chill, not give off exuberant puppy vibes.

He ventured outside, relaxed into a chaise lounge chair by the pool, and sipped the top-shelf drink. As the liquor rolled down his throat, the reflection of light dancing on the water caught his eye.

A few moments later, Slash moved into view, and his gaze stilled on hers. So much beauty stared back. The need to go to her, wrap her in his arms, and never, ever let her go urged him forward.

But he did *not* move.

Looking sexy in a sleek, black one-piece, she kept her hair tied in a ponytail. Like yesterday, she was barefoot. He wanted to tell her she belonged in his home with him, but he didn't do that either.

He hated having to censor his words, his actions, but if he told her the truth, she'd bolt.

After padding over to the diving board, she dove in. He kept his attention trained on her as she glided effortlessly through the water to the pool's edge and back.

He wondered how their lives would have turned out if he hadn't broken up with her. Would they have married years ago? Would there be children?

She swam the breast stroke before switching to freestyle, and then sidestroke. Back and forth with a grace that had him glued to her every move. So much elegance, so much beauty. Yet there was a strength and a purpose to everything she did.

A sadness curled itself around his heart.

He'd treated her so badly.

She deserves so much better.

When she finished, she floated on her back. Watching her helped assuage the fury he carried around day in and day out. As she exited, he was waiting with a towel.

She went to take it from him, but he said, "I got you."

Standing behind her, he blanketed her in warmth, then wrapped his arms around her and held her close. Their breathing fell in line while the mating songs of tree frogs filled his ears, and dancing fireflies lit up the night.

She broke away, turned to face him. "I'll rinse off and meet you back here."

"I'll be in the kitchen."

They went inside together. She continued upstairs, he opened his laptop, checked work email at the Bureau.

Too many unread ones to get through in an evening, but he clicked on a few, scanned their contents. Then, he rose to make them a late-night snack. Two turkey sandwiches with lettuce and tomato, and a freshly popped bag of popcorn.

"Computer, turn *off* the recessed lights on the first floor. Turn *on* the floor lamp in the family room."

The kitchen went dark, save for the stovetop light, the soft light from the floor lamp illuminated the family room.

Minutes later, she returned.

After eyeing the sandwiches, she said, "Good call."

"Wine?" he asked.

She pulled a glass from his cupboard. "Water."

They sat at the kitchen island, munching down the sandwiches.

"I like that pool," she said.

"I'll add you to my security system and scan your retina. You can use it whenever—"

"No," she said.

"Why not?"

She drank down some water, then said, "Let's talk shop. I agreed to find out if the club was running a prostitution ring. We learned that Karen is running—"

"We *don't* know what the owner knows."

"Or who the owner is," she said. "If I tell Providence about the playroom, they'll plan a raid, make their arrests, and shut the club down."

"The owner could walk."

"I don't want that," she said.

"What about the missing person cases?" Carrera asked. "How will you work those if the club is closed? If you want to interview any of the dancers, it'll be impossible to track them."

"So I say nothing until I—"

"We," he interjected. "We say nothing."

She peered at him for an extra beat. "Okay, so you're still working these cases with me?"

"Hell, yeah. Why wouldn't I?"

"Because you have forty-three unread work emails and a lot on your plate, especially with your cruise line."

He could utter some bullshit, he could man up and say something significant... or he could grovel.

"Let's go sit by the pool," he said.

"I should take off."

"Five minutes."

Poolside, she eased onto a chaise lounge, he sat in a chair beside her.

"I'm working these cases with you," he said. "Whatever you need. Okay?"

"Got it."

"I fucked up," he said.

She glanced over. "Did you tell someone about the orgy room?"

"Hell, no." He peered over at her. "I fucked up with you, with us. I apologized yesterday, but apologizing isn't enough."

"Carrera, please—

"If it takes the rest of my life, I will make it up to you."

"So, this is payback. You shredded my heart, so you're gonna help me work some cases, all while screwing me? I'm not sure you're doing a whole lotta suffering here."

"I messed up," he said. "I regretted it, but I was too angry to act like an adult."

"You got that right." She huffed. "I don't think it's a good idea to dredge this up. Let's just agree that we can't stand each other, do our jobs, and then go back to flinging obscenities. I liked those times, especially when Elsa says, "*Language.*" She laughed.

The light from the swimming pool captured the smile in her eyes. He would do whatever it took to be the one who made her smile like that.

Every. Single. Day. For the rest of their lives.

"I regret being an ass. I regret dumping you. I regret not apologizing sooner. I would never treat you that way now. I loved you more than anyone in the world and I treated you the worst."

That got her attention.

"I'm not working with you because I owe you," he continued. "I'm partnering with you because my life is better when you're in it. I will do whatever it takes, for as long as it takes, to earn back your trust."

After what felt like an eternity, she asked, "Why do you care if I trust you?"

"Because I never stopped loving you."

14

ANOTHER WOMAN GOES MISSING

Slash

Slash needed to leave.

Now. Right now.

It was bad enough that they were hooking up, but love?

"I gotta go." She snatched her plate and pushed out of the chaise. "I'm gonna cut you a break. Your brain is mush. We've had a *lot* of sex in the past two days."

"You hold *all* the power."

She snickered. "You've lost it."

He stood, draped his arms over her shoulders, peered down at her. "I know exactly what I'm saying, and I mean every word. But I gotta know... if there is zero chance you'll take me back, I will back off. We'll work together, that's it."

She could tell him the truth, but that would give him all the power. Earning her trust would take time. But... she didn't want to push him away for good.

"One," she said after a beat. "One percent chance."

A smile so big and so breathtaking filled his face. "The odds are in my favor."

Biting back a smile, she returned to the kitchen, set her plate in the sink, grabbed her leather overnight bag, and headed toward the front door. She was moving, but he was faster, and he caught up with her before she left.

"Let me add you to the security system," he said. "Two minutes."

"Why?"

He ran his long fingers down his beard, and she tracked his movement like a hungry fox tracks a rabbit.

"Which answer do you want?" he asked.

"The honest one."

"Here, we can work the missing persons cases in total privacy."

"Makes sense."

"And I love having you here with me."

Hmm...

"And if I stopped having sex with you?" she asked.

He caressed her cheek with the back of his fingers. "I'm all in. Sex or no sex."

She wanted to wrap her arms around his muscled torso and hide from the world. A few precious moments of much-needed escape. Instead, she crossed her arms to thwart her true feelings.

"Okay. I'll do it," she said.

He took a few voice recordings for the computer, then scanned her retinas.

"Test the computer," he instructed her.

"Computer, lock the external doors," she said.

"Welcome to Carrera's home, Slash," the computer replied. "The house is secure."

He couldn't hide his surprise. "Are you staying?"

"Hell, no," she said. "I was testing the computer. Computer, unlock the front door for me."

"Unlocked," the computer replied.

"I have a self-adhesive white board to track our clues," she said. "It's not permanent—"

"Permanent's okay too," he said.

He's lost it.

There was no other rationale for his behavior.

"I'm working on the case tomorrow," she said. "I can set up at my house if you're busy."

"I just gave you access to my home. Come over whenever you want."

"What if you have, you know, someone over?"

He looked confused. "You mean, like a woman?"

"Yeah."

"I'm off the market."

"Clearly, you don't know how odds work."

"I heard one percent and I'm running with that."

"Your call," she said, "but if the right man comes along—"

"I am that right man."

Words are shit if he doesn't show me.

"I'm taking the fam on a brunch cruise tomorrow," he said. "Come with us. You're family."

She shook her head. "No way. They hate me."

"G-ma says you're her number one," Carrera pushed back. "Luciano adores you."

"I'll work here in the afternoon, then I'm having an old friend over for dinner."

"Should I be jealous?"

She placed her palm on his forehead. "No fever, but you're delirious. There's a dancer at Blue Suit. Her name is Jilly. We were in foster care together. I tried to find her, but never could. Anyway, she's coming over."

His brows knitted together. "You were in foster care?"

She opened the front door, turned back. "There's a lot about me you don't know, Carrera Santini."

When she drove away, a car parked at the curb a few houses down pulled onto the quiet residential street. At three in the morning, she couldn't help but wonder if she was being tailed. She extracted her switchblade from her bag.

Into the garage she went, but instead of heading inside, she walked into her driveway.

She should have been afraid, but she wasn't. There had been a time in her life when her only friend in the world had been this switchblade.

Instead of driving past her house, the car stopped up the street. Without binos, she couldn't see the plate. She waited, but no one exited the vehicle.

Am I being paranoid?

In the garage, she watched the door close before walking inside and flipping the bolt. At the moment, she had bigger problems than someone following her home. Carrera had groveled, admitted he still loved her, and was willing to do whatever it took to win her back.

While her heart rejoiced, she was a realist. She would guard her heart, enjoy the hell out of the sex, and work these cases like the pro she was.

Carrera and his profession of love would have to wait.

Her phone buzzed with a text from Carrera.

Make it home okay?

She was surprised he hadn't driven by to check, but if he had, she probably would have waved him in.

If she told him she thought she'd been followed, he'd attach himself like a leech. Better to keep this to herself, watch her six, and see if it was a one-off.

All good

> I'll miss you tomorrow

Ohmygod, he's become unhinged.
As she walked upstairs, she couldn't help but crack a smile.
She'd never stopped loving him either.

~

Carrera

CARRERA ALMOST CANCELED the family outing, but he didn't want Jazz's outburst at G-ma's to ruin a fun time. Twice a year, he took his family on a Carrera river cruise. Once in the warmer months, and a second time before Christmas.

This was the first time they'd boated together since Mara's death.

Sunday morning, he arrived at the marina, boarded the yacht, and checked in with his staff. The chef was prepping for brunch along with a few lunch options. The bar was open, but limited to champagne or mimosas, a white wine, a wine spritzer, and beer on draft. This was a family event, not a booze cruise.

Of all his vessels, this one was the smallest. It capped out at twenty-five guests versus his largest, which could accommodate well over a hundred.

He fished his phone from his pocket, texted Slash.

> House is clear if you want to work

Dots appeared.

> Just got here. Raiding your fridge. You've got a lot of eggs

He smiled as his fingers flew over the keys.

> Text me anything you want, and I'll grab it from
> the store

When she didn't reply, he spotted G-ma and walked onto the stern to help her aboard. To his surprise, Jazz was right there by G-ma's side, offering an assist.

"Be careful, G-ma," Jazz said as she helped her into the craft.

Once aboard, Carrera pulled his grandmother in for a hug. Over the years, she'd shrunk a little, but she was still a formidable force.

"Thank you, Jazz," G-ma said. "Check on the food options for me."

When Jazz disappeared inside, G-ma blew out an exhale. "She's driving me crazy."

Carrera chuckled. "Laying it on thick, huh?"

"Now, she wants $10,000, and she thinks I'm going to fork it over." She shuddered. "Get a damn job."

His dad appeared, dressed to captain the vessel. After he hugged his mom, he slapped Carrera on the back. "It's a beautiful day to be on the water. How's everyone doing?"

"Jazz wants more money," G-ma mumbled.

"Got it," his dad replied. "How are you feeling, Ma?"

"Me? I'm doing great," she replied.

"I'll check in with the staff."

After his dad retreated inside, Carrera regarded G-ma. "Let's talk before things get crazy."

Rather than venture inside, G-ma sat on the white leather sofa on the stern.

"I invited Amanda May," Carrera said.

Her face lit up. "That's wonderful. Where is she?"

"She declined."

G-ma's smile fell away. "I'm not surprised. That was a very

nice thing to do, Carrera." She patted his thigh. "I'm proud of you."

"I need to confide something," he said.

"Are you confessing your sins?"

He smiled, then moved right next to her. "I'm working with her on two cases," he murmured.

"Oh, my."

"And I told her how I feel."

"How is telling her you can't stand her a smart thing to do?"

"How I *really* feel. That I never fell out of love with her."

"And?" G-ma asked.

"She thinks I'm delirious," Carrera said, and she laughed.

She patted his hand. "You're a grown man, so I'm not going to give you my advice."

"Bring it on."

"She'd got a tough exterior, but she is the *exact* same sweet, vulnerable girl from all those years ago."

"Yeah, about that, she said something about foster—"

"Surprise!" called a familiar voice from the pier.

His childhood friend, Russell Fitzpatrick, stepped onto the boat wearing a striped shirt, white pants, and soft-soled shoes.

"Good to see you," Carrera said. "What are you doing here?"

Russell mimed a dagger to his heart. "I'm crushed. And here I thought I was family." He plopped down next to G-ma and kissed her cheek. Then, he leaned back, crossed his ankle over his thigh and shot Carrera a cheesy grin. "I ran into Jazz, and she invited me. We've been hangin' out."

Oh, boy.

Jazz rushed outside, sat on Russell's lap, and hugged him. "You made it!"

"I hope it's okay that I crashed your family event," Russell said. "Jazz said you haven't done a family cruise since Mara died."

All the joy in that moment got sucked into a black hole.

No one spoke, the impact of Russell's words sending everyone spiraling into thoughts of pain and loss and despair.

"Sorry," Russell said. "I should go."

Jazz jumped off him. "They'll be okay. Come inside and we'll have a drink." Jazz and Russell hurried inside.

A low, raspy growl shot out of Carrera while fury jumped to the surface. "I could put my fist—"

"Let it go," G-ma said.

Carrera regarded his grandmother while the fury swirled in a vortex all around him, threatening to take control of his judgment.

She patted his hand. "I feel the same way, but now isn't the time."

She was right. He had to shake it off, so he clasped her hand and kissed her soft, wrinkled skin. "Love you, G-ma."

Her rueful smile tore through him. "I love you too."

His dad returned to the stern.

"I didn't know you invited Russell," his dad said. "It's always good to see one of your childhood friends."

"Jazz invited him," Carrera said.

"Paolo, I'll sit with you in the helm," G-ma said.

Though his dad went by Paul, G-ma never stopped calling her son Paolo.

After G-ma vanished inside with his dad, boisterous laughter snagged his attention. Luciano, Teddy, and Gabriel made their way down the pier. Three cousins who were more like brothers than his real one.

His anger stood down as his cousins climbed aboard.

After hearty hugs, Carrera excused himself, found his dad at the helm, G-ma by his side. "We're ready, Captain."

Pride shone in his dad's eyes. Once he instructed the crew to cast off, Carrera joined his cousins at the bar.

"Excuse me, Mr. Santini," said the bartender.

All four men looked over.

The bartender laughed. "That was easy." He rattled off the beverage options.

Champagne all around, so the bartender got busy filling flutes.

"Gabriel, when did you get back?" Carrera asked.

Gabriel Santini was sandwiched between Teddy and Luciano. His dark hair rested in layers on the collar of his white shirt, his light brown eyes as intense as Carrera remembered. Normally clean-shaven, he'd grown a mustache and goatee, with a light dusting of whiskers covering his cheeks.

Luciano and Gabriel were both dark haired with olive skin. Teddy had blond hair, always looked tanned, and had a meatier build.

"I'm not back," Gabriel replied. "Luciano told me it was cruise time, so I flew in last night." He slung his arm around his older brother's shoulder. "And I stayed in the mansion with Dracula himself."

Teddy started laughing.

The bartender set the flutes on the bar and Carrera passed out the drinks.

Luciano raised his glass. "Santini."

"Love you, brothers," Carrera said to his cousins.

To Carrera's surprise, Jazz didn't badger G-ma for money all afternoon. She didn't even bring up her financial woes. It was a relief that the family could spend an afternoon together without some argument breaking out. When there were this many strong-willed Santinis in a confined space, it was inevitable.

But the sun was shining and the weather was perfect. Nothing but clear sailing. After a sit-down lunch, everyone chilled. A few inside, most out.

While Carrera was talking with Gabriel on the back stern, his cousin's phone rang. "Excuse me," Gabriel said before stepping away to answer.

The sliding door opened and Russell stepped outside. "How've you been?"

"There's the future Congressman Fitzpatrick from the great state of Virginia," Carrera said. "How's the campaign going?"

"Fantastic. Being that it's a special election, things move fast," Russell explained. "I've been working non-stop, and I've got a great staff, along with energetic volunteers. *They* want me to win more than *I* want me to win." He puffed out his chest and laughed.

"Good for you," Carrera replied. "So, you and Jazz, huh?"

"She's great." Russell finished the wine spritzer.

"Has she hit you up for money yet?" Carrera asked.

"She's been spending a lot of time at my campaign headquarters. She's a big help and a hard worker."

That didn't sound like the Jazz Carrera knew.

"So, are you seeing anyone?" Russell asked.

Slash crashed into his thoughts.

Russell chuffed out a laugh. "The Magic 8 Ball points to *definitely*."

"I haven't said anything," Carrera said.

"You don't have to. I've known you since we were six." He shrugged. "I can just tell."

Carrera shook his head. "There's no one."

"Maybe you can squeeze in a little campaigning for me. You know, ring doorbells, chat it up with the good folks in your district."

Carrera was starting a new position at the Bureau tomorrow, plus he was still working the cases with Slash.

"Sorry, Russell. I'm short on time."

Russell stood. "No problem."

When the yacht docked back at the marina, the fam thanked him for a great afternoon, said their goodbyes, and took off.

Last to exit, Luciano extended his hand. "Today was good.

No family drama."

"It's a first," Carrera replied.

"Speaking of firsts," Luciano murmured, "Tomorrow's a big day for you."

"First day of my new job."

"First day of having real power," Luciano said. "You deserve it."

"Thank you, brother."

"Expect pushback," Luciano warned.

"I always do," Carrera replied. "I always do."

Slash

SLASH HAD SPENT the afternoon in Carrera's beautiful home. After taking herself on a self-guided tour, she had to admit, he had fantastic taste. In his home office, she unrolled the white board, removed the protective layer from the adhesive back, and attempted to stick it onto his wall.

First time, crooked. The second time, too low. The third attempt was the winner. Next, she listed each missing person, along with the clues she'd gathered on Terri and Kim Billiawitz.

Even though Karen had accepted cash for sex trafficking, she added the prostitution case. Next steps? Speak to dancers about this Greg guy, and find the owner.

When she finished, she instructed the computer to activate the home security system, then left through the front door.

Sunday brought more activity in Carrera's neighborhood. A family walked by with a stroller, their dog leading the way. A group of kids played ball a few houses down. A carload of teenage girls drove by, their windows open, tunes blaring. Her life, at that age, had been a living nightmare.

Shoving out the painful memory, she eyed the parked cars

that lined the curb. No sign of the car from last night, so she jumped in her SUV and headed to the grocery store.

Back at home, she prepped for dinner.

Thirty minutes later, the doorbell rang. Jilly stood on her front stoop with a six-pack, a bottle of wine, and a big smile.

"Love your home," Jilly said after stepping inside and offering the wine.

"Thank you, but you didn't have to." Slash brought Jilly into her kitchen, placed the chardonnay in the fridge to chill.

"I'm not much of a drinker," Jilly said, "and I didn't know if you liked beer more than wine." She set the six-pack of bottles on the kitchen counter.

"I've got iced tea, I can make a pot of coffee, I've got Pom juice, sparkling water."

"I'd love sparkling water with a splash of Pom," Jilly said.

Slash made her the drink, popped open a beer for herself. "Dinner is chicken thighs in the air fryer, I've got kale to steam. I made a dinner salad if you hate kale, and either sweet or baked potatoes."

Jilly laughed. "You do know there's only two of us."

Slash smiled. "I went a little crazy, plus I got us a chocolate cake with chocolate icing from the bakery. I never go in there, but this is a special occasion."

Jilly nodded. "I've thought about you over the years and wondered what happened."

"Same," Slash said. "Those were some crazy times, and not good crazy." She drank down a mouthful of beer. "Are you hungry?"

Jilly hesitated.

"You can be honest with me," Slash said.

"I'm starving. I ate a quick breakfast hours ago, then got busy studying."

"Let's get you some food."

While Slash brushed the chicken thighs with her homemade olive oil spice mix, Jilly ate a salad.

"Catch me up on your life," Slash said.

"I toughed it out at the foster home for the last few weeks, then got the hell out," Jilly said between bites. "I got a job in a department store for a while, then worked other retail jobs before finally landing an office job. I started as receptionist, worked my way up to office manager. After the owner sold the company, it fell apart. He was paying for my college courses, but the new owners weren't offering that. "Deb from the club is a close friend of mine. She told me how much she made dancing, so I got a job at Blue Suit. I'm close to getting my degree, and I want to land a job that I can turn into an actual career. Then, adios to dancing."

"What are you studying?"

"Marketing."

"If I hear of anything, I'll let you know," Slash said.

With dinner ready, they filled their plates, sat at the kitchen table.

After trying the chicken, Jilly said, "Delicious. Love the coating."

"The magic of the air fryer. Do you have one?"

"No, all my money goes to rent, food, and college. A lot of the girls at the club are always buying new dance outfits, getting mani-pedis, facial fillers, tanning. I'm sure it makes a difference with tips, but I'm all about getting this degree."

"How many more classes?" Slash asked.

Jilly beamed. "Two. I'm taking them this summer, then I'm throwing the biggest party."

"And I will be there to cheer you on." After stabbing a kale leaf, Slash said, "Let me pay for those classes for you."

Jilly laughed. "I know you're totally slaying it at the club, but that's crazy. I can't—"

"When we lived together in the foster home, I heard that monster assaulting you," Slash said. "It was terrifying, but I was too scared to save you from him."

"We were children." After a beat, Jilly continued. "Not gonna lie, it messed me up for a while, but I'm strong. I'm a survivor." Jilly forked the kale. "What happened to you after you left?"

"It was rough. I didn't want social services to find me, so I moved to Alexandria and slept in my car. I got good with a knife and that saved me a bunch of times. I danced at a seedy club for several months. Then, I met a woman who turned out to be my guardian angel."

"Wow, that's intense," Jilly said. "We're both survivors and we're trying to live our best lives."

"Can I cut you a check or pay your bill when it comes?" Slash asked. "Let me do this for you."

"Are you serious?"

"Totally, and you can't talk me out of it."

"We can go online," Jilly said. "Classes start next week and I haven't paid yet."

Fifteen minutes later, she'd paid Jilly's last two college courses and bought all her books.

Jilly hugged her. "Thank you so much. This means the world to me."

"There's no way I can ever repay you for what you did to protect me, but this is a good start."

"We've come a long way since we first met," Jilly said while Slash made a pot of decaf.

There were times that Slash wished she could confide the truth about her career. She was so proud of what she'd accomplished, so grateful to be part of ALPHA. But she wasn't bigmouth Karen Woodside. Instead, she opened the bakery box with chocolate cake and breathed deep.

"So good," Slash said with a smile.

"Are you seeing anyone?" Jilly asked while they ate the sweet treat.

Carrera's handsome face and dope body popped into her thoughts. "An old boyfriend came back into my life. Weird how my past has caught up with me."

"How's that going?"

"He lost my trust, so I'm taking things slow. Very slow."

"Did he step out on you?"

"No, he dumped me, then stopped talking to me. It doesn't sound bad, but it was brutal."

"Do you still love him?"

"There's a fine line between love and hate," Slash said.

Jilly laughed. "Amen to that."

Jilly's phone started ringing. She glanced at it. "Hmm, it's Deb's roommate. I'll be quick."

"Take your time." Slash started clearing the dinner dishes.

"Hey, girl, what's up?" Jilly listened. "Do you think you just missed her and she's back at the club? I'll swing by and see if she's there. No worries. I'm sure she's okay."

Jilly hung up. "My friend Deb, from the club, didn't come home last night."

Slash's stomach dropped. Deb was in the orgy room with the bearded man. "I saw her there last night."

"I saw her too," Jilly said.

"Is she seeing anyone?"

"No."

"Has she ever gone home with a customer?"

"Not that I know of." Jilly rose. "I'm sorry to bolt, especially since you've been so generous—"

"Are you going to the club?" Slash asked.

"Yeah."

"I'll follow you there," Slash said.

Twenty minutes later, they entered Blue Suit. Sunday night brought the least number of customers, but there were asses in the seats and dancers on all four stages. They made their way toward the back, entered the dressing room. Deb's station was dark.

"I'm gonna check with Karen," Jilly said.

"I'll ask the bartenders."

As Slash made her way toward the front of the club, she scanned for the bearded man. When she didn't see him, she walked over to the bar. Bradley acknowledged her, finished serving a customer, and came over.

"Hey, how's it going?" Bradley asked.

"I'm Slash, one of the new dancers."

"Whatcha need?"

"I might be looking to pick up a few shifts," she said. "Karen said you need fillers."

"Have you bartended?"

"Yeah, but it's been a while."

He pulled out his phone. "I'm doing the July schedule. How often can you work?"

She didn't need the money, she needed access to the employees without looking like she was pounding them with questions. If Karen got wind of that, she'd know Slash was up to something.

"Once or twice a week." Slash gave him her phone number.

"That's pretty barebones."

"My schedule's a little crazy right now."

"Got it," he replied.

"Have you seen Deb?" Slash asked.

"Not tonight. Seasoned dancers don't work Sundays, unless their regulars come in."

Jilly appeared beside Slash.

"Hey, Jilly," Bradley said. "Sunday's not your normal night."

"Deb's roommate was looking for her, so I thought I'd check here," Jilly said.

"Yeah, I was telling Slash I haven't seen her." Bradley tossed a nod toward a group of guys. "I gotta take care of the customers." Bradley moved on.

"What did Karen say?" Slash asked.

"No help."

"Does Deb have family in the area?"

"No."

"Did you check with other dancers?" Slash asked.

"A few girls saw her last night, but not today."

Striking out, they left the club.

In the parking lot, Slash suggested she call Deb's roommate. Jilly put the call on speaker.

"Hey, Jilly," the roommate answered. "Did you find her?"

"She's not at the club."

"I'm kinda freaking out here," said the roommate.

"Hey," Slash said. "I'm Slash, a friend of Jilly's. You need to file a missing person's report. Where do you live?"

"Arlington," the roommate replied.

"Call your local police station," Slash instructed. "They'll take the information and they might send an officer over."

"This isn't like her," the roommate's voice broke. "I'm scared for her."

"What's Deb's last name?" Slash asked.

"Weaver," the roommate replied. "Deb Weaver."

Slash knew that the first twenty-four hours were critical with missing persons.

"Do you want me to come over?" Jilly asked.

"Please," the roommate replied.

"Be over soon." Jilly hung up, regarded Slash. "Sorry to run."

"Hopefully Deb will turn up."

After Jilly took off, Slash climbed into her vehicle. As she pulled out of the parking lot, she made a call.

"Hey," Carrera answered. "I'm glad you called."

"I need your help," she replied.

15

POWER

Carrera

arrera listened as Slash explained the situation. While there was legit reason for concern, she remained calm.

After presenting the facts, along with the timeline, she said, "Is it too late to swing by?"

"Come on over."

First time she'd turned to him for help. Another opportunity to do right by her. He returned to lifting, straining against the weights helped diffuse his anger. Anger that haunted his dreams, that clung like a cancer. It had taken hold years ago, when their family had been torn to shreds. Then, when Mara had been murdered, that anger had morphed into fury. Fury that wouldn't abate, no matter how many monsters he took out.

He lay on the bench, pressed the bar, fighting against the massive weight. He should have a spotter, shouldn't swim alone either. If he were being honest, he shouldn't be an assassin. Lots of shouldn'ts that he dismissed because he played by his own set of rules.

Grunting through the lift, he finished the set, rested, and repeated. His workout always ended with biceps. He upped the weights and started curling up and down, alternating left, right, left, right.

Soaked in sweat, he traipsed up the stairs as his computer interrupted his fury-filled thoughts.

"Slash is approaching the front door," said the security system.

He waited to see if she'd ring the bell.

The door opened. "Carrera, it's Slash," she called out.

A jolt of energy powered through him. She felt comfortable enough to let herself in.

"Kitchen," he called out.

He thought he heard a whisper-soft moan as she gave him a very obvious, very slow once-over.

"Hey," she said.

While she was eye-fucking him pretty damn good, he checked her out.

Her black tank top and black yoga pants accentuated her womanly curves. And his thoughts jumped to slowly peeling everything off her.

"Hey," he replied as he filled a glass with water. "Want a drink?"

"I'm good." She sat at the island. "Do you mind if I review the club video from last night?"

After gulping down the water, he pulled a barstool close, sat next to her, and queued up the surveillance from Blue Suit.

A peace settled into his soul while his pulse kicked up speed. Having her in his home was surreal enough, but part-nering with her was mind blowing. He knew she was good, heard it plenty of times from the guys. While everything was happening fast, being with her felt right.

Determination shone from her eyes as she reviewed the

surveillance. She flicked her long bangs off her face, rewound. "Check this out."

He leaned close. Inches away, her fragrance had him breathing deep, her energy seeped into his bones.

"Karen is escorting Deb into the playroom."

"Makes sense," he said. "She's the only one with a keycard."

Minutes later, Karen escorted the bearded man in. Slash continued to speed through the footage until Karen brought someone new into the room.

"Here's something," Slash said. "Karen escorts the dancers *and* their customers at the same time," Slash rewound the video. "Here, it's a threesome. A little later, a couple." She stopped the video, turned toward him.

Electric blue eyes bore into his. The energy swirled around them, her intense gaze turning up the heat. But she wasn't there to soothe his desires, she was there because he'd agreed to work with her. This was the first solid lead they had. No way would he screw that up by letting his super-charged attraction get in the way.

"Karen knows him," Carrera said. "He was the guy in her office when I dropped off the money. He was chillin' on the sofa."

"Right," she said. "You thought they were screwing, but he and Deb were just talking in the orgy room. As we were leaving, I saw him alone on the sofa, watching us."

"I can't fault him for ogling you," he said. "You're every man's fantasy. Maybe he's screwing Karen, talking to the dancers in the orgy room, *and* he's a voyeur."

She nibbled her lip for a quick second. "He's not adding up for me. Why not have sex with Deb?"

"Maybe he doesn't want to screw in an open room. Maybe she said no."

"Karen is unreasonable, narcissistic, and out of touch with reality. Trust me, I worked with her. I can see her firing a dancer for *not* doing something." Slash forwarded the video sixty minutes, then stopped. "Deb's exiting the room alone."

"She doesn't look scared," Carrera said.

"No, she doesn't," Slash agreed. "We don't know if they left together."

"They didn't," Carrera said.

Her eyebrows jutted up. "How do you know?"

"When we drove out, I saw him leaving alone."

She fast-forwarded the video until the guy left. He kept his head down as he made his way down the low-lit hallway.

Slash pushed off the stool. "I think we've got something." She wrapped her fingers around his biceps and led him into his office.

The second she touched him, heat spread through him like a raging wildfire. In the office, she let go, leaving him wanting more.

So much more.

She tapped the white board next to the name Kim Billiawitz. "Kim journaled about Greg. She said he was shy and sweet, and he tipped her $500 after talking to her in the VIP room. Then, they ran into each other outside the club."

"You told me he said he worked for the CIA. Easy excuse for not being able to talk about himself."

"Exactly," Slash said. "Kim wrote that he fumbled his way through asking her out, which she found adorable."

"Would you like that?" he asked.

"Like what?"

"A man who's shy and awkward."

Her gaze stilled on his. "Shy and awkward are definitely *not* my hot buttons."

"What is your hot button?"

"You find it, you can push it."

"Challenge accepted," he said.

Her gaze darkened, she ran her tongue over her lower lip.

She liked that.

"Have dinner with me on my boat," he said.

Silence.

"What?" she murmured.

"Dinner, my boat."

"Aren't we supposed to be screwing at the club?" she asked.

He raked his hand through his hair. "Dinner first, then the club. You can dance for me, then we'll look for Greg in the back room."

"You love having all the power, don't you?"

He cupped her face with his hands. "I love watching you strip, love how you use your power to manipulate the customers. I fucking love that I own you there. You're mine and only mine."

Her raspy moan sliced through the sexual tension. She gripped his shoulders, pulled him to her, and kissed him with a wildness that had him growling from sheer need.

She flicked her tongue against his, ground against him, turning him rock hard in seconds.

In truth, *she* had all the power. Not just over the men at the club, but over him too. All the damn time. And she knew it. She was too smart, too cunning, to let anyone—him included— have the upper hand.

She ended the kiss, pushed him away. "I hate you," she whispered.

He wasn't buying that.

Slash picked up a black marker, added the name Deb Weaver to the list of missing women.

"That makes seven," he said.

"You can count," she said, her sarcasm front and center.

"Only up to ten," he replied.

Her smile felt like a burst of sunshine on a cloudy day. Brilliant, beautiful, and just for him.

Slash's phone rang. "It's Jilly." She answered, put the call on speaker. "Hey, Jilly, what's going on?"

"We called the police, they sent an officer over," Jilly said. "She was very thorough. She said she'd keep Deb's roommate posted. I'm worried. Do you think the dancers are being targeted?"

Slash lifted her gaze to Carrera. "I think we should be careful at the club."

"When are you working next?" Jilly asked.

"I'm not sure dancing is for me," Slash said, her gaze on Carrera. "I might pick up a few bartending shifts. I'll let you know when I'm there."

"It was good catching up," Jilly said. "Your gift was so generous. Seriously, I can't even believe what you did."

"You deserved it," Slash said. "Now, you've gotta stay safe so you can graduate."

After saying goodbye, Slash hung up.

"What did you do?" Carrera asked.

"It was nothing," Slash replied.

He clasped her hand, brought it to his lips, kissed her finger, letting his lips linger on her warm skin. In that instant, their connection changed from partners to something more. Something that made her breath hitch, something that softened her gaze.

Is romance her hot button?

"It must've been something if your friend mentioned it," he murmured.

She could have tugged her hand away, but she didn't.

"She's two classes away from a college degree, but she was strapped for money." Slash jumped her gaze from his mouth back into his eyes. "I paid for her courses."

"Wow."

"It was a small price to pay. Because of her, I got away from a predator who was sexually assaulting the foster kids."

A growl shot out of him. "If there's anything I fucking hate, it's the monsters who prey on the innocent."

"You and me both, honey."

He cracked a smile. "I'm your honey. Love that, *babe.*"

"Yeah, uh-huh." Even though she tugged her hand away, her gaze stayed anchored on his.

G-ma's right. Hard outer shell, but if I can get past that, she's the same amazing girl I fell in love with.

Slash

SLASH WANTED TO HATE HIM. She'd gotten used to hating him. It felt odd having adult conversations with him. It felt flat-out foreign they were working together. And the sex? That was the best. Always had been. Crazy, how some things never change.

"I want to kiss you," he murmured.

Her pulse kicked up.

She *wanted* him to kiss her. So. Damn. Badly.

He dipped down, she lifted her chin. Their lips came together in a gentle kiss. He cupped her cheek, kissed her again. On the third kiss, he slinked his arm around her waist.

She melted from the tenderness of his touch. When the romantic kiss ended, he dropped his hand and gave her ass a gentle squeeze.

Then, he kissed her forehead, and let her go.

Whoa.

"I'll follow you home," he murmured.

She blinked back to reality. "You didn't do that the last time I was here."

"Yes I did," he replied. "When I texted you asking if you got home okay, I was on my way over."

"Did you see a car out front?"

His brows slashed down. "Were you tailed?"

"Did you or didn't you?"

"No," he replied. "Were you followed?"

She didn't want to lie, didn't want to make a big deal out of it either. "Maybe."

"Jesus, why didn't you tell me?"

"I can take care of myself."

"I'm not letting you out of my sight," he said.

In a flash, she pulled the switchblade from her ankle sheath, wrapped one hand around his throat, and pressed the tip of the knife against the fabric, directly over his heart.

"I got this," she said.

After a beat, she backed off, tucked the knife away.

He stared at her. "You should be protecting me."

"I'm gonna pick up a bartender shift or two this week," she said.

"I don't want you going to the club alone—"

She barked out a laugh. "Why not?"

"We're partners."

"I'm out." She headed toward the front door. "Thanks for letting me swing by."

He grabbed his key, pulled up alongside her.

"Where are you going?" she asked.

"I'm following you home," he replied. "If I can lift a clear pic of Greg, I'll run it through Stryker's IDware."

"He's keeping his head down for a reason," she replied before stopping at his front door. "Over the next coupla days, I'm working the missing persons cases. We should sync up once I know more."

"Dinner, my cruise ship."

Outside, the night was still, the chirping crickets reminding her of summers gone by. Of a happy childhood and two loving parents.

A sadness fell over her.

He followed her home. In her driveway, she flipped him off. Even in his darkened truck cab, she couldn't miss his smile.

Despite everything, his smile still turned her inside out.

Once inside, she watched from the front window as he drove away. For the first time in fifteen years, he took her heart with him. And like all those years ago, there was nothing she could do about it.

Absolutely nothing.

Carrera

AT JUST AFTER eight in the morning, Carrera rode the elevator to the top floor of the J. Edgar Hoover building. He had no idea how the first day in his new position was gonna work, exactly. He hadn't resigned as a Special Agent, hadn't told his boss either.

Of one thing he was certain. Scant few would like the power he now wielded.

Too fuckin' bad.

Years earlier, when he and Rebel had first met at Quantico, they'd formed a fast friendship. Through the ranks at the Bureau they rose. After Rebel went undercover, he encouraged Carrera to give it a try.

Carrera had taken Rebel's suggestion, and he loved it. When Dakota had talked to him about joining ALPHA, he wasn't ready to leave the Bureau. Playing the bad guy intrigued him.

In the last year, the jobs he did for his cousin were his hot button. Playing both sides of the law was risky, but he loved every damn minute of it.

My Jekyll and Hyde life.

Upon exiting the elevator, he held his card against the reader by the locked glass doors. The light stayed red.

That's great.

He caught the eye of the receptionist. She hurried over. "Deputy Director Santini, good morning. ID not working?"

"Tina, right?"

"That's me."

He held it out. "Can you reprogram it?"

Peter Hirzog sauntered out of the office Carrera was supposed to occupy. As the receptionist made introductions, Peter's smile dropped away. His vice grip was an indication he viewed Carrera as an adversary.

Carrera didn't give a fuck and he wasn't intimidated.

"I'm not leaving my office," Peter said.

"Tina," Carrera said, "where is Peter setting up?"

Tina glanced furtively at Peter, then back at him. "Deputy Director Hirzog, we've got a great office for you down the hall."

"I'll take a look at that office," Carrera said.

"There we go," Peter said with a smile. "Cooperation. That's how we do things around here."

Tina led Carrera down the hallway to the last door on the right. He poked his head inside, then shot Tina a smile. "This'll be perfect for Deputy Director Hirzog."

"Oh, boy," Tina murmured. "You are definitely going to ruffle some feathers."

Movement caught Carrera's eye.

Sin joined them. "What's going on?"

"Hirzog hasn't moved out of my office, so I'm checking out his options," Carrera said.

"We've got a packed schedule today," Sin said before sliding his gaze to Tina. "Let's get security up here."

While Tina called security, Carrera and Sin paid Hirzog a

visit. He was on his computer when Sin walked in without knocking.

"Peter, it's been a while," Sin said. "Did you meet Deputy Director Santini?" Before Hirzog could answer, Sin continued. "Be a good team player, or I'll make your life a living hell."

Carrera bit back a smile.

"Fuck you, Develin. I don't take orders from you."

Z appeared in the doorway.

Small in stature, he glared at Hirzog. "No, you don't take orders from Develin. You don't even take orders from me. You take orders from the Director, but since he's not here, I'm calling the shots. Out, or we'll roll you down the hall in your goddamn chair."

Z spoke quietly, but the bite in his words reminded Carrera that he was playing in the big leagues now.

For the first time in his life, he acknowledged that he had power. A lot of power.

A red-faced Hirzog narrowed his gaze. "You can't bully me. I refuse to leave this space."

Tina popped her head in. "Security is here."

"Do you like your job?" Z asked.

"What kind of a stupid question is that?" Hirzog bit out.

"One minute, Tina." Sin shut the door. "Answer his question."

"Of course I do," Hirzog replied.

"And you like your beautiful house and your loving wife too, right?" Sin continued.

"Ah, fuck," Hirzog bit out. "Fuck me."

"Two years ago, you had a year-long affair with a Special Agent in Charge," Sin said. "You ended it, then you had your attorney pay her to stay silent. Conveniently, she got transferred out west." Sin laid his hands, palm down, on the desk. "If you think for one fucking minute that I don't know every goddamn thing that goes on in this cock-sucking town, you mistake me for an idiot."

"Shit," Hirzog groaned.

"Z, am I an idiot?" Sin asked.

"No," Z replied.

"All we're asking is that you give Deputy Director Santini your office," Sin continued. "It's a small request in exchange for our silence. I knew what you did, but I kept my mouth shut. Now, they know. You've got all the power, Hirzog. How do you want to play this?"

Hirzog slapped his laptop shut, yanked the cord out of the monitor. "Go to hell. All of you." With his laptop under his arm, he stormed out.

With a smile, Sin said, "That's how we get things done in DC."

Z chuckled. "That's how *you* get things done in DC."

"I have dirt on everyone who's anyone, and I have a team who can dig up dirt on anyone else," Sin said to Carrera. "You need anything, you call me."

Carrera smiled. "Understood."

"We're heading to ALPHA," Sin said to Z.

"I came up to check on Carrera," Z said. "We'll meet tomorrow. My office." He slid his gaze to Sin. "I'm gonna miss that."

"Miss what?" Sin asked.

"You, being you," Z replied.

"We see each other every month," Sin said.

"We play poker," Z replied. "You have a terrible poker face and we never talk shop."

"I have a fantastic poker face," Sin said. "I smile, no matter what my hand."

Z paused. "Hmm, that is a strategy." He shook Carrera's hand. "Tomorrow."

On the way out, Carrera stopped at Tina's station. "Thanks for the help. I'll need the office first thing tomorrow."

Tina glanced from him to Sin, then back to him. She walked around her desk, right up to them. "Do either of you have friends, you know, who are on the market?"

"I know a few men who would be lucky to date you," Sin said. "I'll let them know you're available."

With a satisfied smile, she sat back down.

"Deputy Director Santini, your office will be ready for you in the morning," Tina said, a definite pep in her tone.

As he and Sin headed toward the elevator bank, Carrera said, "You're ruthless *and* charming."

"It's about knowing how to take the power and when to use it," Sin said. "It's something I had to learn... most of it from Z."

"I have big shoes to fill," Carrera said.

"No, you have to get comfortable in your own shoes," Sin corrected. "You are the perfect person for this position. Over time, you'll come to know that."

"How does Evangeline deal with you?"

Sin's sincere smile touched his eyes. "She holds *all* the power, mine especially."

In that moment, Carrera knew what he wanted. A love so pure and so true that it would withstand any challenge, any obstacle, any setback. A partnership that would last a lifetime.

Slash.

She's the one. She's always been the one.

Sin drove them to ALPHA HQ in Tysons. First time for Carrera, and he chuffed out a chuckle as he eyed the ALPHA MEAT PACKING sign over the front door.

After Sin parked out back, Cooper let them in. Another windowless building with nothing in the offices to identify the occupants. During their morning meeting with Providence and Cooper, they went into detail about an organization few knew existed. After a thorough briefing, Cooper asked Carrera if he had questions.

"What's the deciding factor in ALPHA making an arrest versus a kill mission?" Carrera asked.

"Z," Sin replied. "He bases it on the rap sheet, on the number of arrests, DNA—"

"If the perp escaped from prison," Providence added.

"A lot of it depends on the actual mission," Cooper clarified. "Some start out as an arrest, but if they open fire, it's all over."

When the meeting ended, Carrera and Sin said their good-byes and left.

On the fifteen-minute ride to Great Falls, Carrera asked Sin, "When does Luciano get involved?"

"That's where things get interesting," Sin explained. "Luciano has a lot of connections in the underworld. He's plugged in to the dark web, knows where to look, who to ask. He loves the thrill of the hunt, so the more dangerous the monster, the happier he is."

"That, I knew," Carrera said.

They'd ordered lunch from Carole Jean's, Jericho's Michelin-starred restaurant. When they arrived, the maître d' hurried outside with their order. "Good to see you, Mr. Develin. Bon appétit." He tucked the bag behind the back seat of Sin's Mercedes-Maybach sedan.

Back on the road, Sin continued. "Luciano focuses on the monsters who harm women and children, so when he's tracking someone, he'll run the name by me. Sometimes we get a hit that law enforcement is after him, sometimes not. More guys get away with murder, rape, trafficking than are caught. If he finds them, he eliminates them."

"He doesn't believe in second chances," Carrera added.

"No, he doesn't." A sinister smile filled Sin's face. "That's what makes him so deadly."

Sin drove off a main road, made a few turns before he entered a wooded area. Just before the road dead-ended, he turned onto a dirt road, passing a large sign.

Private Property
NO TRESSPASSING

Sin drove to the end. In a clearing stood a windowless warehouse, similar to ALPHA, though this building didn't have a front entrance or visible signage. After driving around back, he tapped a button on his console, and an oversized door lifted, revealing a large garage with several identical black SUVs parked in neat rows.

After parking, he tapped the button, and the door lowered.

"Welcome to BLACK OPS," Sin said before exiting the vehicle. He grabbed the food, and the men walked toward a glass door.

Sin made a call. "We're here."

A moment later, his identical twin, Dakota Luck, opened the door. Carrera could tell them apart by how they styled their hair. Sin wore his combed back, whereas Dakota's was wild and unruly.

Otherwise, they were identical. Same height, same build, same eye color. Both had light beards and mustaches. Both wore dark suits, white collared shirts. Sin wore a black tie, Dakota a pink one.

"Hey," Dakota said to his brother before shooting Carrera a smile. "Let's get you set up on the system."

They scanned his retina, took his picture and his fingerprints. Minutes later, he had full access to a building he didn't know existed ten minutes ago.

The building was drab, both inside and out. Concrete exterior. Gray paint on the walls, the flooring was concrete covered with luxury vinyl tile.

"I'll meet you in the small conference room," Sin said.

Dakota showed him the individual offices. No art, no family pics, no plants, not even a fake one. Desks, chairs, a few had a sofa tucked against the wall. The large conference room had six monitors affixed to the wall.

In Dakota's office, a laptop the only indication anyone even worked there.

As Dakota brought Carrera around the corner, he said, "This doubles as ALPHA's safe house. We've got a stocked kitchen, a family room, several bedrooms with private bathrooms." He stopped in front of an open door. "This is our surgery center."

Carrera was taking everything in stride, rolling with all the new information.

They finished the tour in the conference room. Sin had set out utensils, plates, serving spoons.

"Fancy setup," Carrera said as he eased into a chair.

"I don't use plastic utensils or paper plates," Sin said. "Bad for the environment."

"At parties, I've seen him searching a kitchen for a glass," Dakota said. "He won't use plastic cups."

"Those are the worst," Sin said.

Dakota shook his head, and Carrera chuckled.

During lunch Dakota offered up a deep dive on BLACK OPS' first international rescue mission, in the Middle East.

After they finished eating, Dakota said, "We've got some leaks in the Bureau. No idea how many or how long it's been going on."

"That's why ALPHA has always been in its own building," Sin added. "People can't keep their mouths shut, so at least at ALPHA, it stays within ALPHA."

"How did you find out about the leaks?" Carrera asked.

"Luciano," Dakota replied.

By the end of their briefing, Carrera was convinced there was more evil in the world than good.

Sin rose. "I'm taking off."

"Help clean up," Dakota said.

"You clean up," Sin pushed back. "I picked up lunch."

Dakota laughed. "You didn't *make* it."

"Fuck you," Sin said, and the brothers laughed.

After the guys cleaned up, Sin extended his hand to Carrera. "If you get pushback—from *anyone*—call me immediately."

"I could use a ride back," Carrera said.

The brothers laughed.

"You're getting a specialized vehicle," Dakota explained.

After Sin left, Dakota escorted him back to his office and sat behind his desk. Carrera eased onto the sofa.

"You've been brought into the inner circle for several reasons," Dakota began.

Here it comes.

"You're very smart, well-connected, and well-liked at the Bureau and at ALPHA," Dakota said. "You're also a solid team player. We know Luciano will listen to you. His demons have turned him into a ruthless killer, but there has to be some balance. He can't be killing men who've pissed him off. We're chasing the guilty, not the ones we have personal grudges against."

Carrera released a growl. "I thought this was an earned promotion, but if I'm being used to get to Luciano, I'm out."

"We have a direct line to Luciano," Dakota said. "He and Sin have become good friends. They work well together. Everyone wants to take out the bad actors. The problem is, we don't want to make mistakes."

Carrera's anger settled back down.

"I know Luciano is intense," Carrera said. "He's also fiercely loyal, and he lives by a set of rules in a world he's built from nothing."

"A dark underworld."

"If he's going to find the worst of the worst, he needs a long leash," Carrera said.

"Agreed," Dakota replied.

This *could* have been when Carrera shared how close he and Luciano really were. That Luciano had brought him into his inner circle. That Carrera was a Santini Assassin. But this was *not* that moment. No matter how far off course Luciano went, or how many murderers, rapists, or monsters Luciano tracked and killed, Carrera would not stop him.

Luciano had his reasons, and Carrera understood them.

Dakota rose. "Let's put you in a fleet vehicle." En route to the hangar, he said, "The vehicles are bulletproof. The license plates and the VIN number can't be traced back to ALPHA."

After they rounded the corner, a handful of people dressed in combat fatigues headed in their direction.

"Perfect timing," Dakota said. "It's the rescue team."

Rebel, Brit, Addison, Hawk, and Prescott loomed into view.

"Hey," Rebel said pulling Carrera in for a bro-hug. "What's this guy doing here?"

"Are you coming on board?" Hawk asked.

"He's Z's replacement," Brit said.

Carrera broke into a smile, but said nothing.

"He's on special assignment," Dakota said, and the team laughed. "We have no secrets, do we?"

"No, brother, we don't." Prescott extended his hand to Carrera. "It's great to have you here."

"Where's Slash?" Dakota asked.

"Outside, on the phone," Rebel replied. "She's on an under-cover job, but she's still training with us."

Slash turned the corner, and her beauty stole Carrera's breath. Like the others, she'd dressed in camouflage fatigues, pulled her hair into a ponytail, sunglasses shading her eyes.

"Why is everyone standing around?" she called out.

"We're waiting for you," Brit replied.

As she got closer, her gaze found Carrera's, and she pulled off her sunglasses. "Hey, Carrera."

"Slash," he said.

"What are you doing here?" she asked.

"Special assignment," Dakota replied, and the team laughed.

Slash swept her gaze over the group, settling on Carrera's. "I'm missing something here."

"I'll fill you in," Addison said, looping her arm through Slash's. "We're rope dropping from the helo today."

"We're also climbing up," Rebel said. "Carrera, if you've got time, stick around."

As the team hurried toward the locker rooms, Slash said, "Hey, Carrera." She flipped him off before vanishing into the women's locker room.

"She either loves you or she hates you," Dakota said.

Carrera couldn't contain his smile.

"Let's get you that SUV." Dakota led him over to one, handed him the key fob. "Welcome aboard. You're in an enviable position."

Carrera shook his hand. "Thanks for today."

"I've gotta change for training." Dakota retreated back inside.

Leaving his SUV in the hangar, Carrera went in search of the team. The bright afternoon sun had him pulling on his shades.

As liaison between the Bureau and ALPHA, he wanted to know every aspect of the organization. His interest in sticking around had absolutely nothing to do with the beautiful, badass blonde who'd just flipped him off.

Nothing at all.

Hawk was on the helipad doing his preflight check while the team warmed up.

Slash was doing push-ups, Prescott on one side of her, Brit on the other. They were counting and dropping in sync. At fifty, they stopped, then started doing sit-ups.

She was a beast. After sit-ups, they moved to pull-ups. From what he could tell, she was having a blast. When they finished, Rebel instructed the team to gear up. Helmets went on, followed by gloves, then their rucksacks. Despite the summer sun, they ran in formation toward the chopper. They boarded, and the helicopter rose into the bright, afternoon sky.

Hovering overhead, someone threw out a rope. One by one, they rappelled down, their rucksacks still on their backs. Then, Rebel called them over. Carrera couldn't hear over the roar of the helo, so he strode over to listen.

"Addison has climbed up the rope before. Addison, you want to demonstrate?"

"Sure." She pulled off the forty-pound backpack, set it on the ground, and jogged toward the dangling rope.

She waited at the base until Rebel gave her a thumbs-up. Then, she grabbed on with gloved hands, wound the rope around her leg and ankle, and started pulling herself up. It was slow going until she found her rhythm.

Everyone shielded their eyes from the sun as Addison climbed higher and higher, then vanished inside the bird. A minute later, she slid back down and re-joined the group.

Impressive.

"Who's next?" Rebel asked.

"I'll go." Slash took off toward the dangling rope.

She did exactly what Addison had done, except she didn't remove her rucksack. After securing her foot around the rope, she started climbing. It was slow going. Even from the ground, Carrera could see her straining against the weight of the pack. She got halfway up and stopped.

"C'mon," he murmured. "You can do it."

Then, she slowly slid down, dropped the pack off her shoulders, and re-looped the rope around her leg.

"Slash is on her way back up," Rebel said to Hawk through the comms.

Moving much faster without the added weight, Slash climbed up the rope, vanishing inside the chopper. After a brief moment, she slid back down, then jogged over.

"Too hard with the pack," she said, breathing hard.

"Nice job," Rebel said. "We'll work up to that."

After everyone had their turn, Carrera said goodbye to the team, his gaze cemented on Slash. "I'm super impressed. You guys are the true beasts of ALPHA." He tossed Slash a nod. "I'll talk to you." Then, he made his way to the hanger to pick up his ALPHA SUV.

First stop, home. After he dropped his vehicle in the garage, he took a rideshare back to the Bureau to pick up his truck.

On his drive home, he called Luciano.

"How'd it go?" Luciano asked.

"I'm in," Carrera said.

"This ought to be interesting," Luciano said.

"Why's that?"

"They don't trust me."

"Doesn't matter," Carrera said. "They trust me."

"Where does your loyalty lie?"

Wasn't the first time Luciano had asked him that question. Wouldn't be the last.

"My loyalty lies with all the vics and their families," Carrera said. "My loyalty is to the innocent, the stolen, the raped, the survivors. My loyalty is to Mara. My promise to you is that I will help you take out the evil in the world, whether it's with you or through ALPHA."

"Justice is so civil. The guilty are arrested, they're treated decent, they say they're reformed, they get released."

Carrera chuckled. "No, Luciano. Sometimes the innocent get wrongly imprisoned. The guilty aren't always released, and sometimes reform doesn't work. You know that better than anyone."

Luciano mumbled something in Italian that Carrera didn't pick up.

"I like my way of justice better," Luciano said.

"Most of the time, I do too," Carrera replied.

Minutes later, he pulled into his neighborhood. Instead of driving straight home, he drove past Slash's.

For the first time in my life, my loyalty is to a woman.

One woman, and only one woman.

After parking in his garage, he entered his home, and strode into his office. There, he connected his laptop to his large monitor, and logged in to ALPHA. His new position gave him access to a wide variety of cases, on the local and the national level. He could see which agents were working what cases, and which local law enforcement were working in tandem with federal agents.

His first task as Deputy Director was easy. He didn't have to check with anyone, didn't need approval from his superior either.

Determination, paired with a newfound confidence, coursed through his veins. People in power trusted him to get the job done with charm, finesse, and a can-do attitude. Without a doubt, he was the right man for the job.

One by one, he pulled up each of the missing persons cases, and assigned them to ALPHA Operative, Amanda Maynard.

Then, he read her file. Graduated at the top of her class at Quantico, worked for the Bureau in Atlanta and Miami before returning to the DC area. She'd received several internal commendations and awards. She was the first female agent asked to join ALPHA, then recently accepted into BLACK OPS rescue team. It had been noted that she was a committed team player, an excellent markswoman, and fearless when rappelling from the helo. Her top ranking came from her ability to use a knife.

She isn't just a badass. She's a rock star.

Shame washed over him. He'd been a total heel, an immature prick.

Never again.

Now, the cases were officially hers to work and hers to solve. One step at a time, he would earn back her trust, and make her his.

Forever.

16

SLASH'S GUARDIAN ANGEL

Slash

Slash woke to the annoying buzzing of her phone. *This better be a damn emergency...*

It was Carrera. Her heart skipped a beat.

Calm the hell down. It's probably nothing.

"Hey," she answered, her voice groggy.

"Sorry to wake you."

"What's going on?"

"I've got a surprise for you."

"Is that code for sex?"

He chuckled. "I always want you, but no, it's not."

"It's after one in the morning. Free use doesn't extend to outside the club, bud."

"I need to talk to you in person."

"Ugh. Fine. Whatever."

She hung up, pushed out of bed, and groaned. After spending the morning talking to three detectives working the missing persons cases, she'd trained with BLACK OPS.

Working with the team was one of her favorite things, but she'd pushed herself hard.

Too damn hard.

She was halfway down the stairs when she realized she was naked. Back in her bedroom, she shrugged into her plush cotton bathrobe. A gift from Elsa.

Down into the kitchen she went, flipped on the light. Her arms were aching from the rope climb, her back muscles screaming from her efforts. Resting her head in her hands, she tried shaking away the cobwebs.

Her doorbell rang.

She opened the door and zing after zing of attraction zipped through her. At least if he was gonna wake her from a sound sleep, there were definite perks. Turning on her heel, she made her way back to the kitchen, sat at the table.

He followed, but he didn't sit. He opened her fridge. "I'm starving."

"Seriously? You're here for food?"

He pulled out a few containers. "What's in here?"

"Chicken, pasta."

An adorable smile spread slowly across his face. "Me?"

"Go ahead. There's a jar of sauce in there too."

He filled a plate, heated it, then sat beside her.

"Look at you," she said. "You know how to use a microwave."

He nodded as he cut a large piece of chicken, forked it in, and sighed. "I haven't eaten all day."

"Free use *and* free food. What's in it for me?"

"All seven missing person cases," he replied. "Legit, they're yours."

She sat ramrod straight. "What does that mean?"

"Check."

Slash beelined upstairs to her home office, returned with

her laptop. She logged in to ALPHA, then hopped over to her cases.

"Whoa."

All seven missing person cases had been reassigned to her.

"Now, they're yours," he said. "You're primary. I'm available as your partner, but I didn't list myself."

"You didn't *list* yourself? How does that even work? You hacked into local law enforcement—"

He stopped her with a kiss. And her body hummed with joy. A soft tender kiss, then several more.

"That's better," he said. "Going forward, kissing first, talking next."

"I love that," she said. "I'm going to take that message with me when I train with BLACK OPS. We kiss first, then we fire off a round or two for target practice."

He smiled. "Seriously, maybe the world would be less violent if everyone started off with a kiss."

"Hello? Ever heard of the kiss of death?"

"There is that."

"Okay, so you've got friends in high places." She pushed out of the chair, pulled two glasses. "Water?"

"Thanks," he replied.

After filling them, she sat back down, and she waited for him to tell her how in the hell he'd pulled this off.

"I'm the friend in high places," he said.

He looked so sincere, she wasn't sure how to respond, so she said nothing.

"I'm going to confide in you," he said. "I'm doing everything right this time 'round."

"This time around?"

"I'm trying to move my chances from one to two percent," he said.

"Yeah, that'll win me back," she said, her voice thick with sarcasm.

"That's a one-hundred percent increase." His adorable smile made her heart pitter-patter in her chest.

"You go girl," she said, and he laughed.

"I have a new position at the Bureau. Deputy Director Special Projects."

She started laughing, hard. So hard, she flinched from the pain. Gales of laughter had her holding her midsection. This was one of the funniest things she'd ever heard.

When she finally got herself under control, she said, "I'm in pain from training, but that was worth it. I can't remember the last time I laughed that hard." She chuckled. "You're Deputy Director, and I'm a princess from a faraway land."

He put his dish in the dishwasher, then held out his hand. She stared at it.

A devilish smile spread across his face. "C'mon, you can do it."

The temptation to touch him was impossible to ignore, so she placed her hand in his and stood. Together, they walked into the living room and sat on the sofa.

She *should* have pulled her hand away, but she didn't. She could tell herself it's because she didn't have the strength... but that was total BS. She liked it.

Ugh.

"Z is retiring," he said while caressing her hand with his thumb.

Soft, delicate strokes that soothed her inner beast.

"Brit had mentioned he was thinking about it," she replied.

She loved looking into his eyes.

"He's out at the end of July, and I'm his replacement."

"You are not."

"Z and another man, Luther Warschak—"

"Luther brought me into ALPHA," Slash said. "I adore him, his wife too."

"He and Z picked their replacement. Well, actually, Sin and Luciano chose me—"

"Whoa. Back up."

"Yeah, so I'm not supposed to tell you any of this."

"Clearly," she said.

"Luther was good with their decision. Z was not, but Luther and Sin changed his mind."

"I can't believe this. What does Luciano have to do with this?"

Carrera broke eye contact.

"Let's leave him out of this," she said.

"After spending yesterday morning at ALPHA and part of the afternoon at BLACK OPS, I spent the evening transferring the cases to you," he explained. "You're officially working them as FBI Agent O'Reilly."

A sudden feeling of gratitude washed over her. Leaning close, she kissed him. "Thank you."

He smiled. "I'm still your partner, so we'll work them together."

"You don't have time—"

"For you, I do."

"This is crazy," she murmured.

"But there's a catch."

She yanked her hand away. "Dammit, Carrera. Why do you always—"

"I just want to know why these cases are so important to you," he said.

Oh, boy.

She heaved in a slow, lung-filling breath. She could answer his question or not. It's not like he'd take the cases away from her if she didn't.

Do I want him to know?

She pushed off the sofa, pulled a bottle of Santini Brandy

from her kitchen cabinet, along with two snifters. A finger's worth in one, two in the other. Back in the family room, she handed him the fuller glass, sat beside him, and sipped the top-shelf liquor. The sweet flavor ignited her taste buds, and she savored it before swallowing it down.

Turning toward him, she crossed her legs. "You sure?"

After sipping the brandy, he cemented his gaze on hers. "One-hundred percent."

"There's a part of my past you never knew about," she said. "This is hard for me to talk about, but I have no expectations when it comes to you. None. If this dredges up why you dumped me, it's on you this time."

"Got it," he said.

Pausing, she questioned how far back she needed to go.

Tell him... everything.

"After my mom's killing spree, I was left an orphan. One set of grandparents and a grandmother were deceased. My other grandfather lived in Montana, but he couldn't take me. I was sixteen, so I went into the foster care system. The first home was fine, but I was a total mess over the loss of my parents. One minute, we're normal. The next, my parents were dead, along with your mom. She was my travel soccer coach, and I adored her. She was a terrific coach and mentor to all the girls on the team."

Slash had never told anyone the full story, not even Elsa. She'd pushed it from her mind. Looking back, it was her survival mechanism kicking in. Heaving in a breath, she hugged herself.

To her surprise, Carrera took her hands and held them in his. His warm hands made her feel safe.

"The first foster mom sent me back when her time ended. The next home started okay. The man and woman—I thought they were married, but they weren't—had three foster kids living there. Two boys and a girl. Jilly, the dancer from Blue Suit."

He nodded.

"After a few weeks there, I heard weird noises in the middle of the night. I wasn't sure what it was. Sounded like whimpering and muffled voices. That monster was raping Jilly."

"Ohgod," he bit out.

"It went on like that for a while. I found out he was molesting all three of them. I tried talking to Jilly, but she shut me down. One day, on the way home from school, she warned me that he was coming into my room that night. She told me to run. I wanted her to come, but she had two weeks until she turned eighteen. She said she'd been on the streets, and she wasn't going back."

"Where was the woman who lived there?"

"She worked nights at the hospital. On the nights she was home, he wouldn't do anything, or he'd bring one of them into the basement."

"Jesus," he murmured.

"After Jilly warned me, I took off. I had my car, so I slept in that. My mistake was that I continued going to school, showering after gym class. It didn't take long for social services to catch up with me, so I bolted. I drove from Winchester to Alexandria. I was homeless, sleeping in my car. I needed a job, so I went into DC, got a job stripping. I had a fake ID. I figured the owner knew I was young, but he didn't care. The men liked me, and they spent more money whenever I danced."

Normally rock solid, she started trembling. She tossed back a mouthful of brandy before covering her shoulders with the throw blanket.

He stroked her back. Tender caresses that helped settle her down. "Do you want to take a break?"

"Let me get this out," she said. "One night, I was propositioned. Not a hand job, not a blowjob. Fucking. I said no. The owner encouraged me to help out one of his regulars. I told him I'd think about it. I didn't want to have sex with him. Plus, I was a virgin." She paused. "Well, you know that."

He dipped down, dropped a kiss on her cheek. His encouraging smile spurred her on.

"One Sunday, I was supposed to work the lunch crowd at the strip club. I couldn't go in. I knew if I did, that customer—or some other creep—would expect sex. I was walking down a beautiful residential street in Alexandria, thinking about my messed-up life. How I'd planned to get a soccer scholarship, and how my dreams had gone to shit, all because I asked my dad to watch me play soccer with my travel team."

On a huff, she threw the blanket off her shoulders and steeled her spine. "When I passed this pretty chapel on the corner, I heard singing. It was lovely." She smiled at the memory. "Like the angels were beckoning me inside. I remembered that after church, people usually gathered, and there was food. I was starving."

"Did you go in?" he asked.

"I did." Tears filled her eyes. Unexpected, unwelcome emotion that she couldn't stop. "Elsa was helping to set up lunch. She lit up when she saw me and asked me to help. After I did, she made me this huge plate of food. And I'm not talking cookies. It was a meal. I wolfed it down while she sat with me."

Tears rolled freely down her cheeks, and Carrera gently brushed them away with his thumb.

"The next thing I know, Elsa invited me home with her," Slash said. "I spent the night and slept so good, the best sleep since before my parents' deaths. Elsa was an angel." Unable to stop herself, Slash started sobbing.

Gut-wrenching cries exploded from the depths of her soul. Carrera pulled her into his arms while she released all the pain, all the fear, all the anguish long buried from years ago.

When she finally got herself together, she blew her nose, wiped her eyes.

"I'm sorry," he whispered. "I'm so sorry."

She finished the brandy. "Two weeks into living with Elsa, I learned that her daughter-in-law—your mom—had been murdered. That's when I realized who Elsa was. I knew I'd have to leave because she'd kick me out when she found out."

"What happened?"

"I told her who I was and that I didn't want to go back into foster care because of what had happened at that last home. Elsa was amazing. I told her how I'd begged my dad to watch a travel game. She said that what had happened *wasn't* my fault. She explained that the problem wasn't with me, it was with the adults. Had my dad and her daughter-in-law never cheated, everyone would still be alive. She acknowledged that what my mom did was horrific, but that also had nothing to do with me." Pausing, Slash wiped her newly-spilled tears. "Then, she told me she had a dream that a girl with bright blonde hair would come into her life, someone who needed her help. She said it was a nice dream, but she never thought about it again. When she saw me that morning in church, she knew. She confided that she loved her sons, but she'd always wished for a daughter." Slash cracked a smile. "I think I became her project. We decided I needed a fresh start. She told me she'd always wanted a daughter named Amanda May. We came up with Amanda Maynard. I don't know how, but she got me a new social security number. Then, she took me for a new driver's license. After that, she enrolled me in high school. I felt like the luckiest girl in the world."

She raked her trembling hands through her hair. "God, I never talk this much."

"You got this," he said. "You're doing great."

"You met me after your dad hit rock bottom," Slash said. "Your sisters went to Texas, right?"

"They went to live with an aunt and uncle, but I wanted to stay with G-ma."

"Things were so perfect between us," she said, "until the day you learned I was Melody Donaldson."

He clasped her hands, peered into her eyes. "I'm sorry for what you went through. I'm ashamed at how I treated you, how my family treated you when they found out. I wouldn't trust me either."

"Finding those women is important to me because that could have been me," Slash said. "If Elsa hadn't come into my life, it would have turned out very differently. My friend Jilly saved me from being raped, so paying for her college courses was nothing. That monster is someone I dream about killing." She shook her head. "How sick am I?"

"Why don't you?" he asked.

"Kill him?"

"Yeah, why don't you?"

"Once I was safe with Elsa, I reported him. I found out he left the area, and I could never find him."

"What's his name?"

"He went by Elwood Tosh, but that could have been an alias." She rose from the sofa and winced.

"You okay?"

"I pulled something during my less-than-impressive rope climb."

"You're a beast," he said. "You climbed halfway up with your sack, then all the way without it. Do you know how hard that is?"

"My brain doesn't, but my body does." She checked the time. "Whoa, it's almost three. Thank you for the cases. I'll keep you posted." She started walking toward the door.

"Where are you going?" he asked.

"To walk you out."

"I'm not leaving," he replied.

She stopped, turned. "You can't just stay here whenever you feel like it."

"I'm going to rub your sore muscles, then I'm going to watch you sleep."

She snickered. "Good one."

"Where's your lotion?" he asked.

"Bathroom."

"Get naked, get in bed."

She stared at him. "You're kidding, right?"

"I want to be the man you deserve. Someone you trust and can rely on. The one you share your fears, your dreams, your dirtiest fantasies with. I'm not holding back. You're gonna hear about my goals, my dreams, and my secrets, even the illegal ones—"

That last one caught her attention. "What illegal ones?"

"Get in bed and I'll tell you." He waggled his eyebrows.

"This, I gotta hear." In her bathroom, she collected the lotion, handed it to him. "Need a sock?"

He chuffed out a laugh. "This rub isn't for me."

She dropped the robe, his gaze fell to her naked body, and a growl rumbled out of him.

"You sure you're not here for a three AM booty call?" she asked.

"No sex."

She lay on her stomach, turned to watch him strip down to his black boxer briefs.

"How is this not a role play?" she asked. "You're my massage therapist. I'm in pain, you rub me, you've got a hard on. I'm getting aroused just laying out the story."

"You get one story tonight," he said. "My illegal kills or a sexy story."

"I'll take one tonight, one tomorrow night."

"That sounds like a date," he replied.

"A massage," she said. "One now, one tomorrow."

"You got it," he replied. "Right after dinner on the Potomac." After moving her hair off her shoulders, he squirted lotion into his hand, rubbed them together, and started massaging her.

"That feels great," she said on a sigh.

Strong hands worked her muscles until they hummed. He took his time, caring for her in a way that made her soul sing. She relaxed, breathing through the pain of a knot until he massaged it away. She never envisioned they'd be decent toward each other, but a massage? Didn't seem real.

"How am I doing?" he asked.

Her eyes fluttered open and she was rewarded with his smile. "You might have jumped from one to *five* percent."

"A five percent chance of winning you back," he murmured. "Big win today."

"Yeah, you went from a Special Agent to a Deputy Director."

He leaned down, whispered in her ear, "Not that. You. I'm confident that one day you'll be mine."

This is feeling way too romantic.

Time to shut this down.

"Tell me about your illegal secrets," she said.

"I'm an assassin for Luciano," he murmured while continuing to massage her back.

She smiled. "Yeah, me too."

Silence.

She opened her eyes, rolled onto her side, and peered up at him. "For real?"

"Ma'am," he said. "You can't be flashing your fantastic breasts. I'll want to touch them, then I'll lose my massage license."

On a laugh, she rolled onto her stomach. "We can't have that, can we?"

He massaged her lower back and she flinched.

"You did a job on yourself," he said.

"I just overdid it, that's all. What kinds of hits do you go on?"

"Monsters ALPHA can't touch because they've never been captured."

"Like Mara's killer?" she murmured.

"Like Mara's killer." He moved to her glutes and she released a long sigh.

"I would work that case with you," she said.

He placed his lips on her back, kissed her. "Let's find these missing women first. At least, with them, there's a chance they're still alive."

"Will you continue to work for Luciano?"

"Yes, but even Sin doesn't know that."

"You're really putting yourself out there with me."

He gave her ass a gentle squeeze before moving on to her thighs. "I'm trusting you with things that could land me in prison. If I hold back, keep anything from you, this will never work."

She grew quiet while he massaged the backs of her legs. He had a point. If they were going to try again, it would be eyes wide open. She would keep his secrets and, in exchange, she would have to trust him not to hurt her again.

"Babe," he murmured, "turn over so I can massage your arms."

When she rolled over, he covered her with the sheet, then set her arms on top. With tender strokes he began.

She studied his face, letting her gaze roam over every feature. Things were moving so fast, yet—in her innermost heart—she loved having him in her life again.

"This might not work," she said.

"The massage? Sure it will."

She smiled. "Us."

"Yes, it will," he said, his confidence front and center.

"You don't know that. Maybe we were meant to be each other's first loves only."

His gaze found hers as he massaged her triceps. "First *and* last. I wouldn't have told you something that would get me fired *and* put me in prison if I wasn't confident about winning you back."

She wasn't going to argue. What would be the point? He was right. It was just a matter of time before her heart would lead her, and she'd go tumbling back down the rabbit hole. Her only question...

When she landed in Wonderland, would he catch her or would he let her fall?

$\sim$

Carrera

CARRERA FINISHED MASSAGING HER, then dropped a worshipful kiss on her lips. "Sleep, my angel." Then, he walked around her bed and crawled in beside her.

"Smooth move."

"I do this with all my massage clients." He pulled her onto him, so her head rested on his chest, and he folded his arms around her.

"Thank you for the massage," she murmured as she relaxed onto him.

Within seconds, she was asleep.

A sadness washed over him. He had no idea what she'd been through. She never talked about it. G-ma hadn't either. Once, in the middle of their senior year of high school, he asked her how she ended up living with his grandmother.

"She's my guardian angel," Amanda May had replied.

Since she didn't answer his question, he asked G-ma. Her answer was just as vague. "God's plan."

He'd been looking for an answer he hadn't been mature enough to hear.

But he could handle it now. He could be the man Slash needed. The one who had her back and put her first.

His heart broke for what she'd had to endure on her own. At the very least, he owed his grandmother a thank you. But he could do much, much better than that.

He could show them *both* he was worthy of Amanda May's love.

~

Slash

SLASH WOKE FEELING FANTASTIC, thanks to the very sexy man snuggling behind her. She was at a crossroads. Limp along, terrified he'd hurt her again, or throw aside her fears, live like the boss she was, and give him a legit second chance.

Before she said anything to him, there was one person's advice she revered above all else.

Until then... a little early morning fun wouldn't hurt. She rolled toward him and was met with large brown eyes and a sleepy smile.

"Why, it's my uber-talented massage therapist," she said. "What are you doing here?"

"I couldn't leave," he murmured.

"Well, now you're my prisoner," she said climbing on top of him. "And I can't let you escape without sealing your secrets with a kiss."

She married her lips to his and kissed him good. Real good. So good, Mr. Woody woke up, and was pressing against her bladder.

"Romance takes a back seat to peeing," she said before stealing one more kiss.

Into the bathroom she went. Seconds later, Carrera walked in. After she peed, she went in search of a toothbrush. She found a new one from her dentist's office. He brushed beside her, their gazes cemented on their reflections in the mirror.

When they finished, she asked, "What are you plans today?"

"I gotta meet with Z, so he can start handing off his responsibilities to me, then I can help you with the cases."

"Don't sweat it," she said. "I'm following up with the detectives I didn't talk to yesterday, and have more family members to question. It'll take me a few days, at least."

She clasped his hand, led him out of the bathroom, and over to the bed. "We have unfinished business."

He swept her into his arms and they fell into bed.

She pulled a condom box from her night table, opened the sealed box, and tore off a packet. "Where were we?"

"You were thanking your massage therapist."

She pressed her mouth to his and kissed him. Delicious tingles spread through her while he deepened the kiss and palmed her ass. Like a struck match, her insides ignited.

As the kiss continued to build, she planked over him and stroked his shaft and head.

"I love your touch," he murmured before tucking her hair behind her ears.

He raked his teeth over her tongue, she moaned through the pleasure while her pussy turned slick with need. When she started moving over him, his urgent groans had her biting his earlobe, his chin, his shoulder.

She tore open the packet with her teeth, rolled it on. Then, she rose over him, fisted his hardness, and took him inside her.

Pleasure exploded through her and she released an ardent groan, but it was his gritty moan had her peering into his eyes. So much passion and lust stared back. She glided over his shaft, back and forth, each time taking in more of its length, letting it stretch her small space to accommodate its thickness.

Their mouths came together in a fiery kiss. He dragged his fingers down her back, grabbed her hips, and drove himself inside her.

"Ohgod," she gasped. "So deep."

She sat up and started moving on him. Up and down, letting the passion carry her away. He fondled her breasts, tweaked her nipples, now hard, sensitive nibs. She glided faster and faster, the euphoria taking her higher and higher.

"You are so damn sexy," he said, his voice gritty. "Kiss me."

She covered him with her body, pressed her lips to his.

In one easy move, he flipped them over, and he did what Carrera Santini did best. He took control.

Complete and total control.

He withdrew, she whimpered. He took her nipple into her mouth and sucked before he tugged with his teeth. She cried out, the painful pleasure numbing her mind, drawing her attention to him. The passion in his eyes, the ferocity in his touch kept her begging for more.

She spread her legs. "In me."

"You are mine," he growled. "And I am yours."

He slid back inside her. She raised her ass off the bed. And they unleashed their fury, their energy, and their passion with an intensity that had her gasping for air.

The harder he fucked her, the harder she fucked him back. His groans were long and deep, and so damn satisfying. As she passed the point of no return, she told him she was about to come.

"Give it to me," he growled. "We'll come together."

She started shaking, the orgasm starting deep inside, exploding out of her with so much power. She released a cry from the depths of her soul. He roared through his release, then kissed her, sinking his tongue into her mouth. When they calmed down, he rolled them back over, and she collapsed on his chest.

"Damn," she murmured.

"Yeah."

She ran her fingertips over his shoulder. He held her close, caressed her heated skin.

"You fuck good," she whispered.

"Only 'cause it's you," he replied.

17

THE WHITE HOUSE

Slash

Wearing her brunette wig, non-prescription glasses, and forgettable clothes—a black collared shirt and black pants—Slash entered the Alexandria police station and flashed her FBI badge at the front desk officer. "Special Agent O'Reilly for Detective Flickinger."

Not long after, a heavyset man with short hair and graying temples walked over, shook her hand. "I'm Flickinger. Come on back."

At his desk, he pulled up the case file. "Wish I had more to tell ya. The first case—Julie Darden—she went missing five months ago. She danced at The Blue Suit club. Her sister, who lives in Dayton, called to report her missing. Said she wasn't returning texts or answering her phone. Ms. Darden had no relatives in the area. I talked to two outta three roommates." He paused to read his notes. "One said Miss Darden had been looking for a different job. The second hadn't seen her in a coupla days, but they weren't concerned."

"Why's that?" Slash asked.

"Their schedules were varied, plus two had boyfriends, and stayed with them. I checked with her employer, Karen—" he paused. "I can't find her last name."

"Woodside," Slash said. "What did she say?"

"She hadn't worked there long and she was still figuring things out."

"What about Ms. Darden's mom and dad?"

"Mom said she saw her at Christmas. Her daughter mentioned wanting to move to Hawaii. Dad took forever to return my call. Didn't know anything."

"Foul play?" Slash asked.

"If she had a boyfriend, no one knew about him," the detective replied. "I checked with a couple of dancers at the club. They didn't know who her regulars were. I asked one of the bartenders, but he said she was quiet. Did her job, didn't hang around the bar. I can forward everything I have to you. I could use fresh eyes on this."

Slash nodded. "You said Ms. Darden was your first missing person case at Blue Suit. Who else do you have?"

The detective pulled a different folder from his desk. "Felicia Jones, also a dancer, vanished four months ago."

The detective had followed up with family, a few friends, and Karen Woodside. He had no leads for that case either.

"I've got nothing," he said. "No signs of foul play, no boyfriends. I've got two women who work as exotic dancers at a club where the GM tells me turnover is high."

"Did your crime scene dust for prints?" Slash asked.

"Yup. Nothing." He leaned back. "You new to the area?"

"There are cameras in the club," Slash replied, sticking with the cases. "Did you ask the GM if you could review the videos?"

"A lot of the guys at these clubs aren't from around here," Flickinger said. "They're on business, looking for a little fun."

"So, is that a *no* to the video surveillance?"

Flickinger's eyes went flat. He reviewed his notes. "I didn't ask on the first case, but I did on the second."

Slash waited, but the detective didn't say anything.

Ohmygod, really?

"Who did you ask about the cameras?" Slash asked, her patience growing thin.

"That woman, the manager."

"And?"

"And what?"

"Did she give you access to them?"

"She said they don't work," Flickinger replied.

That was information Slash didn't have. "I need a copy of your reports."

He made copies, walked her to the lobby. "I've got six months until I retire. If these women were gonna turn up, they'd have turned up."

What the hell?

She wanted to tell him it was his fucking job to find them. That's why he had the title "detective" in front of his name, but with six months left, he was counting down the days.

Slash left.

In the parking lot, she pulled on her sunglasses, muttered several obscenities, jumped in her ALPHA SUV, and drove out.

Next stop, the courthouse in Arlington. After searching for street parking for too damn long, she pulled into a paid lot. Once inside the building, she asked to speak with Detective Rosario.

A few moments later, a woman approached. "Agent O'Reilly, I'm Detective Rosario. I'm gonna grab a sandwich. Can we walk and talk?"

"Works for me," Slash replied.

Once outside, the detective said, "Missing persons cases are always a challenge. Time is against us from the beginning. I try to stay positive, but most times the outcome isn't what anyone wants.'"

The detective led her to a small sandwich shop. After Rosario grabbed something to eat, she suggested they sit in the courtyard.

"Thanks for sending over the reports," Slash said.

"Both these cases went cold fast, which is frustrating," the detective said. "Kim and Terri Billiawitz both worked at the Blue Suit for years. I talked to several dancers. They said the sisters were there almost daily and both had regulars. I spoke with as many clients as I could, but most of these men are married or in a relationship, so they didn't say much." She drank down some of her iced tea. "Their memories get foggy. They can't remember shit."

"No surprise there," Slash said. "Anything stand out to you as unusual?"

"The dancers had great things to say about both women, but the GM trashed them pretty good."

"Did she call them unreliable?" Slash asked.

"Yeah, did she tell you that too?"

"There are seven women who've gone missing from the club in the past five months." Slash sipped her water.

"That's a lot."

"The GM, Karen Woodside, said they *all* ghosted on her. I don't believe that," Slash said.

"I didn't realize seven had gone missing."

"I spoke with Detective Flickinger over at Alexandria," Slash continued.

"I know him," Detective Rosario said. "He's good, but he's about to retire, so I think he might be—"

"Clocked out?" Slash asked.

Rosario nodded. "Between you and me."

"I just want to find these women," Slash said. "I spoke with Kim and Terri's mom. Kim kept a journal and talked about a customer at the club who tipped her five hundred, then she ran into him at a store. Invited her to dinner—"

"Where?" Rosario interrupted.

"No idea," Slash replied.

"I spoke with the mom. She didn't mention that."

"She didn't know. We read Kim's journal together and found the entries. POI calls himself Greg. No physical description, but he comes across as shy and awkward. I think he's kidnapping these women, but I have nothing to go on."

Rosario finished her sandwich. "No fingerprints, no foul play. No one saw anything. I wonder if this Greg guy actually takes them out or he's just kidnapping them and killing them."

"Same. The pressure to solve these—"

"My insomnia is through the roof," Rosario said. "With this many women going missing, do you think we should let the dancers there know?"

"I'm undercover at the club, so I can't say anything too obvious," Slash said.

"Gotcha," Rosario replied.

"I gonna ask around about Greg but I need to keep things chill. If he finds out, he might bolt."

Rosario nodded. "Are you working the case alone?"

Carrera's handsome face popped into her thoughts.

"Who is he?" Rosario asked.

"Who?"

"The reason you're smiling," the detective replied.

"My partner's got my back," Slash said.

Rosario drained her iced tea. "Makes a big difference."

Having Carrera in her corner made *all* the difference. For the first time in fifteen years, he brought a smile to her face.

And she liked that... she liked that a lot.

Carrera

CARRERA TOOK the stairs to the basement in the FBI building. As he rounded the corner, a mouse scurried away.

Why in the hell would anyone work down here?

He stopped in front of Z's office. Though the door was shut, he could hear him on the phone. "That'll get assigned to a Special Agent." Silence. "I disagree. Why would ALPHA take that case? How do you know about that? You can't *reveal* your source? Are you shitting me, Sinclair? When have we ever kept secrets?"

Knock-knock.

"Carrera's here," Z said. "I'll let him decide." After a second, Z said, "Come in."

Carrera opened the door. "Now a good time?"

Z had ended his call with Sin.

"I'm gonna throw you in the deep end, starting with a very unusual case." Z typed in a few keystrokes and all four monitors on his wall came to life. Each had different information on them.

Carrera eased onto the worn office chair.

"These are all the cases assigned to Special Agents," Z began. "They're by state, county, office." Z scrolled and scrolled and scrolled, then jumped the cursor to the next screen. "These are ALPHA's cases. The next screen are BLACK OPS missions. Cold cases for the Bureau are on this last screen. If you need to look up any case—active, closed, or cold—you can." He showed Carrera how to search.

"Got it," Carrera replied.

"Most cases are handled by the Bureau," Z said. "I move some to ALPHA before they're assigned, but occasionally I reassign after the fact. It's risky since the case just disappears."

"Understood."

"If you move a case to ALPHA, *you* decide if the team will arrest, make a partial arrest partial elimination, or do a total elimination." Z leaned back. "A kill mission should never be taken lightly." He clicked on his computer and a case appeared on one of the screens. "Here's a closed case. The Midnight Raper was a kill mission. A serial rapist who preyed on his victims for decades while continuing to outrun and outsmart law enforcement. When we got confirmation we found him, I executed the order."

"Tell me about the kill missions."

"Those are handled by a select few whose names will never appear on any report. How's your memory?"

"Good."

"You'll have to retain information that can't be written down."

Carrera nodded. "Who took out The Midnight Raper?"

"Dakota took the job, and brought Sin and Stryker," Z replied. "They found a woman being held captive, then the rapist came home with a second vic. We had no indication there would be prisoners."

"How'd they handle that?"

"They took out the rapist, called 911 for the women, and got the hell out of town."

"Why no BLACK OPS?" Carrera asked.

"We didn't have BLACK OPS back then and the hostage situation was unexpected." Z typed a few keystrokes, and a photo of Luciano on his yacht appeared on the screen.

Here we go.

"How much do you know about your cousin?" Z asked.

Carrera leaned back, crossed his leg. "What do you mean?"

"While I have no proof, I have reason to believe there's more to him than his company."

"Like what?" Carrera asked.

"Syndicated crime."

Carrera chuckled. "My cousin runs Santini International. He's not a crime boss."

"Luciano and Sin have become close friends."

"You've got tails on them?"

"I've had tails on all three of you," Z disclosed. "I had my watcher watching you."

What the hell?

"Your watcher?"

"Do you understand the power of this position?" Z asked.

"How am I supposed to do this job if you keep secrets from me, and who the hell is your watcher?"

Z studied him for several seconds. "How do I know you're not keeping secrets from me?"

This question-for-a-question tactic felt like a cat chasing its damn tail. Carrera wasn't intimidated and he wasn't concerned. Luciano's real business was well hidden and beyond the scope of anything Z could imagine.

Silence.

Carrera refused to speak first. As the two men eyed each other, the air swirled with angry energy.

"My watcher is Liv Savage," Z said after a tense moment. "She works directly for me and vets certain hires."

"Thank you," Carrera replied.

"You and Sin both checked out or you wouldn't be my replacement, but your connection to Luciano is a concern."

Carrera shot him a relaxed smile. "You have nothing to worry about, Philip."

Z checked his watch. "Time to go."

"Where?"

"The White House."

As they made their way upstairs to the lobby, Carrera texted Sin.

WH

Thanks for the heads up

They exited the building, Z gestured to a waiting sedan. The ten-minute drive was filled with silence. Despite the privacy shield, they would never discuss work in the presence of others.

Carrera needed to give Luciano a heads-up. Neither Carrera, Sin, or Luciano suspected anyone in law enforcement —Z included—knew about Luciano's *other* business.

Running a highly-skilled, highly lethal team of assassins.

If Z had a confidential informant, had that person told anyone besides Z? And if there were eyes on Luciano's home, would they see that he and Sin were regular visitors?

Well, there's no crime in stopping by to see my cousin.

But their hits *were* criminal.

Carrera snapped back to the moment as the guard cleared them to enter the gates at the White House West Wing. The driver pulled around the circular driveway. Despite the building's age, the mansion looked like it had a fresh coat of white paint. The surrounding grounds were pristine. A well-maintained manicured lawn filled with gardens of brightly-colored flowers and perfectly clipped bushes.

When Carrera was a kid, his parents had taken him, his older brother and two sisters to the White House for a public tour. He was more intrigued with the armed guards than with the old furniture. But today's meeting didn't include a tour of the public rooms. It was a secure meeting where he had one chance to make a strong first impression.

Once inside, they were brought into a small room where Carrera could store his weapon. Next, they passed through security. Despite *not* setting off the alarm, a guard waved a wand over them and a second one patted them down. Two armed guards escorted them to an office and handed them off to an assistant who showed them into a small sitting area.

"How have you been, Z?" the assistant asked.

"Very good, Betty. You?"

"Fine, thanks." With a warm smile, Betty introduced herself to Carrera.

"Carrera Santini."

"This is my replacement," Z said.

With a gleam in her eyes, she said, "Z, I don't believe you're retiring for *real*."

"That's what it says on paper," Z replied.

"Welcome to The White House," Betty said to Carrera. "You'll go through me to set up any meetings with the President."

She gave him her direct number and he added it to his phone.

"Can I get either of you a beverage?" she asked.

Both men declined, the assistant returned to her desk, and the men waited on the sofa.

"First time?" Z asked.

"Yeah," Carrera replied.

Z smiled. "Even after three decades, it doesn't lose its panache. I never forget with whom I'm meeting."

The assistant's phone buzzed. She answered, spoke quietly. "Gentleman, the President will see you now."

With a polite smile, she escorted them into the Oval office.

Despite the grandness of the room, Carrera's attention was fixed on the man rising from the world-famous desk. Tall and lean with a pleasant smile and warm eyes, he kept his dark hair short, his face clean-shaven.

"Mr. President," said the assistant. "Deputy Director Philip Skye and Deputy Director Carrera Santini."

"Thank you, Betty," said the President.

She closed the door behind her.

The President extended his hand to Z. "Who am I going to argue with now that you're leaving us?" Both men chuckled. "I'm going to miss you, Philip, but maybe now, we can finally do some of that fishing we've been talking about."

"That would be great, Mr. President," Z said. "This is Carrera Santini, my replacement."

Carrera shook the President's hand. "It's an honor, Mr. President."

"The torch is being passed," the President said as he gestured toward the sitting area.

Carrera waited for both men to sit before he eased onto the upholstered chair.

"Carrera, tell me about yourself," the President said.

"I'm here to serve, Mr. President," Carrera said.

Both Z and the President smiled, and the angst in Z's eyes disappeared.

"You have an exemplary record with Justice," said the President.

"Thank you."

"Finding Philip and Luther's replacements was a long process," said the President. "Consider yourself amongst the most trusted and the most elite."

"Thank you, Mr. President," Carrera replied with a smile.

Carrera's goal for the meeting?

Charm and brevity.

Z brought the President up to speed as Carrera glanced around the historic office. Photos of the President, First Lady, and their large family peppered the room. Two porcelain vases, along with several books, filled the built-in bookshelves.

On the President's desk sat a computer and three phones.

"I ordered lunch for us," the President said. "Maybe we can get Carrera to say more than ten words."

Carrera smiled.

Knock-knock.

"Come in," said the President.

The door opened and in walked Sin.

Carrera slid his gaze to Z. A flicker of surprise flashed in his eyes before he masked it with a friendly smile.

"There he is," the President said as he stood. "Good to see you, Sin. I wondered if you were detained in some high-ranking meeting of your own."

Sin shook the President's hand, then Z's, and finally his. "There was a bit of a snafu with the meeting time, but Carrera had my back."

"Excellent," the President said. "Teamwork in your position is extremely important. You're dealing with the nation's most violent criminals. If you don't work as a cohesive team, we don't stand a chance. While I love to tout that I run my administration in an upside-down hierarchy, we all know that's bullshit."

The men chuckled.

"I have the other branches of government and my opponents keeping me in check," said the President. "All you have is each other."

And Luciano. But he's operating so far below the radar, he might as well be in hell.

The President's assistant escorted them to a private dining room where lunch was served.

Carrera was eating filet mignon tips, roasted fingerling potatoes, and a blend of perfectly steamed vegetables with three of the most powerful men in the world.

And he was acting like it was a regular Monday. The three men had a comfortable rapport from years of working together. Mutual respect flowed between them as they discussed the top political situations of the day.

"Carrera, what are your thoughts on ALPHA?" the President asked.

"It's an elite group run by highly-skilled individuals," Carrera replied. "Where it falls short is the size. It needs to be significantly scaled up, both personnel and facilities. We could double the size of the Operatives and still not close the gap between law-abiding citizens and the country's most lethal criminals."

"Well said," the President answered, "and it's good to hear your opinion. I appreciate brevity and humility, but let's be honest. We wouldn't be in the positions we're in if we didn't have healthy egos."

"Yes, sir," Carrera said.

The conversation continued until their luncheon ended and the assistant whisked the President away to another meeting.

Minutes later, Secret Service escorted him, Sin, and Z out of the building.

"What the hell was that?" Sin bit out once they were outside.

"What?" Z asked.

"You introduce Carrera to the President and you *don't* include me," Sin said. "How does that make us look?"

"It was a simple introduction," Z said. "You've got direct access to the President, and I'm certain, his *personal* cell phone number."

"That's not the point," Sin said. "Carrera and I are a team."

"Duly noted," Z said, "but I think you're overthinking this one."

Sin extended his hand, and Z shook it. "Is the Bureau throwing you a retirement luncheon?"

Z gasped. "God, I hope not!"

Carrera and Sin laughed.

"Difficult to the end, aren't you, Philip?" Sin asked with a smile.

Z laughed before addressing Carrera. "Let's go."

"I need a few minutes with Sin," Carrera said.

"I'll drive him back," Sin said.

Carrera shook Z's hand. "Thanks for your guidance and expertise. Very valuable."

"Same time, tomorrow?" Z asked.

"I need a few days to review everything. How's Friday?"

"It's a short week. Saturday is the Fourth of July. We're off Friday."

"Monday, then."

"You're in the fray upstairs," Z warned. "Too many people want to take your power or shove their head up your ass so they can learn things they have no business knowing."

Carrera chuffed out a laugh. "That's a visual I don't need."

"Relax, Philip," Sin said. "Carrera knows what he's doing."

"I won't be intimidated, and they can't take my power," Carrera said.

"With power comes great responsibility," Z said.

"I got this," Carrera said before he and Sin made their way to his car, parked nearby.

After Sin drove out of the White House grounds, he asked, "What's going on?"

"Z had tails on us," Carrera said.

"Liv Savage, Jericho's wife," Sin said. "I saw her following me a few times. I expected Z would vet us."

"He's concerned we're close to Luciano."

Sin chuffed out a laugh. "We *are* close to Luciano. I'm sure Z tried to find out what we're doing, but even he can't. Luciano's good at covering his tracks."

After a beat, Sin said, "Watch your back at work. Peter Hirzog was gunning for Luther's job from the moment he retired."

"What's his story?" Carrera asked.

"He's been with the Bureau for decades," Sin said. "Luciano can't stand him, but I never asked why. There are some problems I don't need to know about... until I need to fix them."

Sin's phone rang. "It's my wife." He tapped the button on the steering wheel. "Hey, babe, I've got Carrera with me."

"Hi, honey," Evangeline said. "Carrera, congrats on the new gig."

"Thanks, Evangeline. I'm looking forward to seeing you this weekend."

"Me, too," she replied. "What can I bring?"

"Your husband," Carrera replied.

She laughed. "Of course my husband. Do you need me to bring dessert?"

"I've got staff working the event."

"On the fourth?" Sin asked. "You're a tough boss."

"They volunteered," Carrera replied. "Being on the water for the fireworks is a great gig."

"Babe, we've got a graduation ceremony tonight," Evangeline said.

Sin and Evangeline founded and ran The Develin Home for Runaway Children.

"I'll be at the office in thirty," he said.

"I'm not there, so I'll see you at the event. Love you, baby. See you Saturday, Carrera." Evangeline hung up.

"You do great things for those kids," Carrera said.

"Evangeline and I love working with them," Sin said as he pulled up to the curb at FBI headquarters. "What's the plan for Saturday?"

"Cocktails at five," Carrera said. "We cruise at six."

"Thanks for the text earlier," Sin said. "Z might have been testing you."

On a chuckle, Carrera opened the door. "Too many damn mind games for me."

"Ah, my friend, the mind fucks have just begun," Sin said. "Welcome to the *real* show."

Carrera entered the building, but instead of heading upstairs to his office, he took the elevator to the parking garage.

Once in his ALPHA SUV, he headed toward Carrera Cruises, stopping to pick up a surprise for Slash before continuing on to his offices.

To his relief, he found his employees hard at work. They greeted him with a friendly smile, or a wave if they were on the phone. His dad was in a meeting with the accounting team, so Carrera checked his texts.

He had two. The one from Slash sent a hit of adrenaline through him. He clicked on it.

Gotta cancel tonight

Hell, no.

Rather than text her, he called.

"Hey," she answered, "you got my text."

"What's going on?"

"I'm so damn frustrated."

"Tell me."

"Providence texted me for an update. I told her I need more time, but they want to move in for an arrest."

"You still don't know who the owner is. I'll work my charm on Karen tonight."

"You call that charm?" He could hear the smile in her voice. Loved that he could do that for her. She was under a lot of pressure.

"I'll pick you up in an hour," he said.

"I should get to the club, pick up a bartender shift before you show up."

Dammit.

"Babe. One hour on my boat." Silence, so he pressed on. "You have to eat. Being out on the water is your happy place."

"You remembered," she murmured.

If he didn't get off the phone, she'd change her mind again. "I'll see you in an hour."

He hung up, found his dad in his office.

"Hey, Carrera," his dad said. "How's your search going?"

How does he know about the missing persons cases?

"Have you started interviewing anyone for my position?" his dad asked. "I'd really love to get back on the water."

Carrera had been so busy, he hadn't even contacted a search firm. "Dad, you gotta handle it."

"I've been working with Gracie," he said. "She'd be great. Spend ten minutes talking to her.

"I'll talk to her now."

"I'm headed to the pier," his dad said. "I'm stepping in to captain a private gig."

"Is the cruise a romantic dinner for two?" Carrera asked.

"Yeah."

"That's me," Carrera said.

His dad grinned. "That's great, son. I look forward to meeting her."

He could say nothing, or he could talk to his dad now, and possibly avoid a total disaster later. Carrera shut the office door. "I've been seeing someone and she's very special to me."

"Do you want me to pretend I'm not your dad?"

"What? No. It's someone I used to know."

"Rekindling an old flame?"

"It's Amanda Maynard," Carrera said.

The air got sucked out of the room. His dad's smile fell away, anger flashed in his eyes. "Again? She was enough of a wrecking ball the first time. What the hell is she going to do this time 'round?"

Fury jumped to the surface, but Carrera needed to keep himself in check. "Have you ever talked to G-ma about what happened?"

"I've talked to your grandmother a million times. That girl was the reason our family—"

"That *girl* asked her dad to go to a soccer game. That was all she did. She was sixteen and she had *nothing* to do with his affair with Mom. She didn't introduce them, she didn't even know they were seeing each other! I was in love with her then, and I ended up being a total shit to her. She is very important to me, but if you won't act civil toward her this evening, don't captain my ship."

Carrera's gaze ripped through his dad while the air turned turbulent.

Silence.

Deafening silence.

"Do you love her?" his dad asked.

"I never fucking stopped, but I was too immature to see past my own pain. Her life got wrecked, but she turned it around. She's an amazing woman. G-ma adores her, and so do I."

"Her life wasn't the only one that got ruined."

"But not by her, Dad." Carrera raked his hand through his hair, trying to diffuse the anger. "Not by her."

~

Slash

SLASH'S WORKDAY had been one big pile of stank. She hadn't made any progress on the cases, and based on everyone she spoke with, she knew more than they did.

How do seven women from the same nightclub vanish without a trace? No leads. No bodies. Nothing.

"C'mon, Greg, where are you? Show me your ugly fucking face so I can wipe that sick smile right off it."

Slash showered, dressed in a bright pink, form-fitting halter dress and sandals. Normally rock solid, her guts churned as she put on her makeup. Was this a date? It felt like a date. Or were they just two partners taking a break from a stressful case?

It's a date.

She pulled her hair into a ponytail, leaving her bangs to frame her face.

I don't do dates.

Stepping back, she checked herself in the bathroom mirror. "Well, you're doing this date, so get it together."

The doorbell rang and she went downstairs.

She opened the door and her heart skipped a beat. Carrera looked like he'd stepped out of a fashion magazine. From his perfectly styled hair, to his shiny black shoes, he was the epitome of power, sex appeal, and charisma.

Time stopped while she stared into his eyes.

"You look stunning." He stepped inside, pulled her close, and kissed her cheek. "You smell good too."

Then, he gave her a very slow, very deliberate once-over. "Gorgeous."

She smiled. "You clean up well."

He looked freakin' amazing in a white collared shirt, black pants, and black sport coat. She picked up the backpack next to the door. He took it from her, and they left. Once in his ALPHA SUV, he drove out.

"Who'd you talk to today?" he asked.

"Two detectives, and I made some calls about the missing women who didn't have reports filed on them."

"How'd that go?"

"The detectives didn't have much. I spoke with a landlord for one of the women who'd gone missing three months ago. He ended up selling her things and renting her apartment."

"He never called the police?"

"He said he did, but there was no record that law enforcement talked to him. I spoke with her neighbors. Most had no idea who she was." She glanced over at him. "What kind of world are we living in? People just don't give a damn."

He clasped her hand. "I give a damn."

She smiled. "Good for you, Superman." Then, she pulled

out her phone. "I check in with Elsa every day. She dialed, put the call on speaker.

"Hello, angel," Elsa answered.

"Elsa, hi, how are you?"

"I'm reorganizing my kitchen drawers," Elsa said.

"Have you eaten?"

"Not yet. Are you stopping by?"

"I can't tonight," Slash said. "How 'bout tomorrow?"

"I'd love that."

"I can pick up something."

"Sushi is good. Or that dish I like from the Mexican restaurant."

"What about the fusion restaurant?'

"Any of those work. Can you pick up a few things for me at the store?"

"Text me whatever you need," Slash said.

Elsa started coughing.

When she finished, Slash asked. "You okay?"

"I'm fine, honey." After a pause, Elsa said, "Jasmine stopped by with Russell today."

"Oh, yeah. How was that?" Slash asked.

"They brought cupcakes and stayed for about an hour."

"Did she ask you for money again, G-ma?" Carrera asked.

Slash glanced over at him.

"Carrera, is that you?" Elsa asked.

"Yeah, G-ma," Carrera replied.

"Russel hired Jasmine to run his campaign, so she didn't even mention money." Elsa started coughing again.

When she stopped, Slash asked, "Do I need to bring you some cough medicine?"

"It's just one of my tickles. Hold on, I'll have a sip of water." A few seconds later, Elsa said, "Carrera, don't give Amanda May a hard time."

Slash raised her eyebrows at him.

"I invited her for dinner on the river," Carrera said.

"That's wonderful," Elsa said. "I hope you have a good time. Be nice to her. Do you hear me?"

"I promise G-ma. I'll be very, very nice to her."

"You're a good boy. Put Amanda May back on please."

"I'm here, Elsa. Text me whatever you need, and I'll see you tomorrow for dinner. Love you."

"I love you both," Elsa said.

Slash hung up.

"Well, so much for keeping this *business* arrangement under wraps," she said.

"We're way past the business," he said pulling into the marina parking lot.

They exited his truck. He grasped her hand and they made their way down the pier to the forty-foot yacht.

"This is beautiful," she murmured.

He climbed aboard, offered her a hand. The evening was perfect for boating down the Potomac. Not a cloud in the sky as the summer sun scooted toward the horizon.

He was greeted by the host. "Mr. Santini, good to see you." He smiled at Slash. "Ma'am. I'll let the captain know you're aboard."

They were standing close enough that she felt Carrera's triceps tighten. She glanced his way.

"Would you like a beverage as we cast off?" asked the host.

"Water for me, please," Slash said.

"Sparkling?"

Slash nodded.

"Two," Carrera said.

"Would you prefer wild-caught salmon or free-range chicken?" the host asked.

They both selected salmon.

"Would you like wine with dinner?"

"I'd love a glass, but I've got to work," Slash said to Carrera.

"Just the sparkling waters," Carrera said.

With a nod, the host left.

"You can drink," Slash said.

He leaned close and pressed his mouth to her ear. "I don't need alcohol. I need you."

The energy shifted. He pulled her close, kissed her. "I've got your back, especially at Blue Suit. Those men are piranhas."

"I'm not afraid of them." Then, she shot him a smile. "But I appreciate that you're there with me."

"Let's head to the bow." He clasped her hand.

She loved that he took her hand. Loved that he insisted that she take a quick break from the stress of the cases.

They stood at the front of the vessel as the ship pulled out of the marina before gliding effortlessly down the river. He stood behind her, wrapped his arms around her, and kissed the top of her head. Tingles skittered through her.

Being with him felt incredible, a dream come true. She'd never stopped loving him, but loving him now left her feeling incredibly vulnerable.

"Thank you," he murmured as he wrapped his arms around her.

"For what?" she asked.

"For being here with me." He kissed the top of her head.

As she gazed at the buildings along the shoreline, she grasped his strong forearms. They passed another Carrera Cruises vessel, and everyone waved.

She and Carrera waved back as the host returned with their drinks. "Would you prefer to dine inside or out?"

"I'd love to sit outside," Slash replied before sliding her gaze to Carrera.

"Absolutely," he agreed.

They took the beverages, and the host disappeared inside.

"To a perfect evening," Carrera said.

After tapping his glass and sipping the icy drink, she asked, "What are we doing here?"

"We're taking a break from the mayhem," he replied.

She peered into his large brown eyes, eyes that could see into the depths of her soul. "Us," she said. "I'm talking about us."

He leaned close and whispered, "We're falling in love."

"Ohmygod," she whispered. "Oh. My. God."

18

CRUISING TO LOVE

Carrera

Carrera wasn't backing down, despite Slash's less-than-desired reaction. She stepped back, but she didn't walk away. Small victory.

"This was a mistake," she murmured.

He kissed her. Once. "Let this happen." Still inches away, he smiled.

She tried not to smile. He watched as she struggled against the joy. He understood her conflict. If she trusted him, if she let herself love him, he could rip her to shreds all over again.

But that wasn't going to happen. Not this time.

"You want to smile," he murmured. "Go ahead, be free."

Her joyful expression sent him flying to the moon.

Their server appeared with a tray of appetizers. "Good evening, Mr. Santini, ma'am." She set the small plates on a nearby table. "Enjoy," she said before retreating inside.

"Are you hungry?" Carrera asked.

"Starving."

He seated her, sat beside her, so they both faced the south-west shoreline. The water looked like cut glass, the orange sun reflecting in every direction. Rather than dig in, he sliced off a piece of Portobello mushroom stuffed with wild truffle and parmesan, and offered her a bite.

She opened her mouth, her lips closed around the utensil, and he slid it out. She smiled as the flavorful appetizer stimulated her palate. He took a bite. It was delicious.

Next, they tried the Spicy Crab Salad Tapas. Another first-class culinary delight.

"How did you start the cruise line?" she asked.

"My sister, Mara, and I decided to go into business together," he said. "We wanted everything from a tiki bar on the water to fine dining while enjoying a cruise down the river. I worked for the Bureau, so she did the majority of the work, but we worked together on the weekends. We launched with a single vessel."

Her rueful smile tugged at his heart. "I'm sorry for your loss," she said. "I know you and Mara were close."

"She would have loved you," he said.

"I don't think so," she said. "I'm not a family fave."

"You're my favorite and that's all I care about."

"You say that now, but family get-togethers aren't fun if they're always contentious."

He reached into the pocket of his sport coat, set the small box on the table. "For you."

She stared at that gift like it had horns and was baring its teeth at her. "Why?"

Leaning close, he kissed her cheek, then her lips. "Love," he replied.

When she didn't open the jewelry box, he opened it, pulled out the diamond heart necklace and held it up. The stones sparkled and twinkled in the setting sun, their brilliance a thing of beauty.

"When we were kids, I wanted to buy you a diamond necklace, but I couldn't afford it," he said as he unclasped it. "Try it on. See if you like it."

"You gotta take this down a few notches."

"I can't stop how I feel about you." He clasped the necklace on her. "It looks beautiful. Do you like it?"

She ran her fingers over the pendant, her gaze locked on his, then she kissed him. "I love it. Thank you." One more kiss before she peered out at the water. "I want to keep you at a distance. I tell myself it's just a work thing—"

"It's not." He gently moved her long bangs away from her eyes.

"No, it's not."

She wouldn't look at him, so he tipped her chin in his direction.

"I'm falling in love with you all over again," he said. "Only this time, I'll be your rock."

Her gaze softened, a smile tugged at her lips. "Let's see whatcha got, babe."

"Are you challenging me?"

"I'm just protecting my heart," she replied. "And I'm keeping things real, you know?"

The server returned with their salmon entrees served with a harvest salad of quinoa and arugula.

Slash forked off a piece of salmon, offered it to him. As he pulled the fish into his mouth, he gazed into her eyes. The woman by his side was a vision of beauty and grace. The love in her eyes gave him more hope than he deserved.

"Thank you," he murmured, "for having dinner with me."

A nod of acknowledgment before she tried the salmon. "What did you do today?"

"I had a meeting at the White House," he replied.

She hitched an eyebrow. "Oh, yeah. Who was there?"

"Z, Sin, and the President," he said.

She grew silent while she tried the quinoa. "For real?"

"Yeah, for real. We had lunch with the President in a private dining room." He leaned close. "Z suspects Luciano is working with Sin and me."

"There are spies everywhere," she whispered.

"Did you know Jericho's wife, Liv Savage, is a watcher?"

"Danielle Fox told me a while ago." She sipped her water. "Now you know why I trust very few people."

"Do you trust me?" he asked.

"Not with my heart, but as partners, you're solid."

"Do you want to trust me?"

After a beat, she said, "Yeah, I do. Do you trust me?"

"One hundred percent," he replied with conviction.

They finished the first-class dinner. When their server cleared away their plates, she asked if they were celebrating anything special.

"An anniversary," Carrera replied. "Slash and I met on July first, sixteen years ago."

"You remembered," Slash said.

The server regarded Slash. "That is just the coolest nickname. Wow."

"Not impressed with the anniversary?" Carrera asked.

"Oh, sorry, happy anniversary," said the server. "Are you married?"

"No," Slash replied.

"Not yet," Carrera said.

"Easy, cowboy," Slash said, but she couldn't kill the smile.

"Where'd you get that nickname?" the server asked.

"I'm good with knives."

The server's eyes widened. "Okaaaay." She flicked her gaze to Carrera, then back to Slash. "We have some amazing desserts. I'll bring you a sampler tray."

∾

Slash

THE SERVER LEFT, and Carrera grasped her hand while they stared out at the water.

Truth was... she liked the doting, the attention, the groveling. She liked that he was going out of his way to let her know she was important to him.

"Thanks for tonight," she said, "and for confiding about work. You're right. I did need a break."

"I've got something fun planned for later."

As she stared into his eyes, desire flamed low in her belly. "That sounds intriguing."

The boat slowed, then stopped. A moment later, the hostess, the server, the chef, a cook, and the captain appeared on deck.

"Ready?" said the captain.

They sang happy anniversary to a completely unfamiliar tune and mostly off key. Slash loved their originality. When they finished, she applauded. "You guys killed that. It was great."

"They met sixteen years ago today," said their server.

"Happy anniversary," said the chef. "I hope enjoyed dinner."

"It was fantastic," Carrera said.

"Loved everything," Slash added.

"We'll have your desserts out right away," said the chef. "Back to the kitchen, team."

Everyone retreated inside, except the captain. Slash slid her gaze from him to Carrera, and a chill slid down her back.

"This is my dad, Paul Santini," Carrera said. "Dad, this is Amanda Maynard."

Slash felt like she got punched in the gut. Was this how he had her back?

Here we go.

"Hi," Slash said.

Her dad extended his hand. She was surprised his was clammy.

"I hope you're enjoying the cruise," Paul said.

"It's been great, Dad," Carrera said.

"Congrats on the anniversary," Paul said. "I should get back to the helm."

"Sit for a minute," Slash said.

Fuck. Fuck me. Why did I do that?

"I... um—" His dad looked at Carrera.

Carrera nodded.

Paul Santini eased into the chair across from her. Despite the grief both families shared, she'd never met him. Seeing father and son, she could see where Carrera got his good looks. A fit man with short, dark hair, Paul Santini had large, brown eyes and a sad smile.

Elsa had told her that when his wife had been murdered, he tried to keep it together for his children. The oldest son had just left for college, but Carrera and his two sisters were still at home. Carrera's dad started drinking heavily, ended up losing his job. He stopped caring for himself, the house, and the kids. That's when Elsa got involved. She sent her son to rehab, Carrera's sisters went to live with their aunt and uncle, and Carrera moved in with her.

When Carrera's dad got out of rehab, Elsa spent time with him at his house, but he never came by to see her. Slash knew it was because she was there, and Elsa just wanted to protect her.

"Great night for a cruise, huh?" Paul asked.

Slash could feel his uneasiness. This was an awkward situation that Carrera had thrust them into, but she'd do her best to get them through it without things blowing up.

"Perfect," she replied. "How long have you been a ship's captain?"

"Seven years. After I got sober, I worked for Carrera as a

server, got my captain's license, and have been on the water ever since."

She smiled. "It's very comforting, isn't it?"

"Yeah, I love it. So, what kind of work do you do?"

She couldn't tell him she was with ALPHA. She wasn't telling him she was working a case undercover as an exotic dancer, so she fell back on something she hadn't used in years.

"I work at Luck Marketing," she replied.

"No kidding," his dad said. "Did Carrera tell you we're hiring? I've stepped in to help out—Son, did you talk to Gracie?"

"I did, Dad," Carrera replied. "I told her the job was hers, but she's on a thirty-day trial."

His dad's shoulders fell. "I have to manage the team for another month."

"Just a week, until she feels comfortable doing it without you."

His dad smiled. "Thank you." He slid his gaze to Slash. "Thanks for letting me crash your dinner party. I've gotta bring you back to the dock." He grew silent for an extra beat. "Amanda, I owe you an apology. I blamed you for something that wasn't your fault. I'm very sorry."

Overcome with emotion, tears pricked her eyes. "Thank you, Paul."

Carrera rose and hugged his dad. "Thanks, Dad."

"I love you, son."

When Carrera sat back down, his eyes were also wet with emotion. She leaned over, kissed his cheek. "How'd you manage that?"

"When I stopped by the office today, I threatened him within an inch of his life," he replied.

"Now, that's what I'm talking about," she said. "Maybe you do have my back."

"Damn straight I do," he replied.

~

Carrera

THE CRUISE HAD BEEN PERFECT, his dad had stepped up for him, and he was ready to get to work at Blue Suit. With their plan in place, he parked at the club. She grabbed the backpack, and left. Watching her disappear into the club had him pushing out of his vehicle.

Yes, Slash could handle herself, but he couldn't have her back if he was sitting on his ass outside. While she didn't want it to look like they were a couple, he didn't give a fuck what that GM thought.

Inside, he made his way over to the bar. The place was less crowded than the weekend, but still busy for a Monday. He glanced around for Slash, and found her talking to a bartender.

As he made his way through the club, he eyed the dancers on all four stages, he counted five women giving lap dances, and a few more dancing on the tables.

Tonight, he wanted answers from Karen Woodside about the man who'd been in her office... the last person Deb had been seen with.

He walked down the hallway, stopped in front of the GM's office.

Knock-knock.

A minute later, Karen swung open the door and painted on a smile. "Mr. Amos, hello, hello. How're things with Slash?"

"They're fine, but I like chatty women. Women who entertain me with their words. Can I interest you in a drink?"

Her face flushed so red, he thought she might keel over. She ran her fingers through her hair, flicked her head. "I'll be right out."

He glanced over her shoulder. "Are you in the middle of something?"

She opened the door wider. "I was hoping my boyfriend would be stopping by, but he can't make it."

"I'll save you a seat."

She giggled as she shut the door.

Bait cast. Bait taken.

As he made his way through the club, he spotted Slash serving drinks at the bar. He slid into an empty seat and waited while she finished up with customers.

She sidled over, set a napkin down in front of him. "Hello, Mr. Anus. Are you ready for me?"

"I'm always ready for you," he murmured.

Her gaze darkened. "I like that."

"I'm having a drink with the GM," he said.

"What's your poison?"

"You," he replied.

"Here she comes," Slash said.

"Finger's worth, top-shelf whiskey," he said.

"Just one finger?"

"I'm saving the other two for you," he murmured as Karen pulled up beside him.

Karen's lip curled when she spotted Slash behind the bar.

"Let's sit at a table," Karen said.

"I like the one in the corner," he said. "What are you drinking?"

"I can't. I'm working."

"One drink," Carrera pushed. "What's the harm in that?"

"I'm such an easy drunk."

"I'm having whiskey," Carrera said.

Karen looked down her nose at Slash. "Get me a whiskey too."

"Got it," Slash said.

He and Karen moved to the corner at a two-person high top.

"Tell me about yourself," he said.

"I'm an open book," she replied. "Ask me anything."

"What do you do when you're not here?"

"I'm here all the time so, sleep, I guess."

"What did you do before you worked here?"

"I was in law enforcement," she replied.

"That's interesting."

"Yeah, and I got fired, which still pisses me off."

"I'm sorry," he said. "What happened?"

Slash brought over their whiskeys.

"She's the reason I got fired," Karen grumbled.

"What time does your shift end?" Carrera asked Slash.

"I'm just filling in, so I'm available whenever you are, Mr. Anus."

"What did you call him?" Karen snapped.

"Amos," Slash replied. "Isn't his name Claude Amos?"

"Yes, that's correct," Carrera replied.

"You said anus," Karen insisted, her beady eyes drilling into Slash.

Carrera lifted his glass. "I look forward to getting to know you, Karen."

Karen's smug expression had him stealing a glance at Slash, who bit back a smile.

"Lemme know when you want to take advantage of that free use, Mr. Anus."

As Slash returned to the bar, Karen shouted, "There! I heard it again!"

"Karen, relax," Carrera said. "It's all good, baby."

He fought the bile that surfaced. His *baby* was twenty feet away, and she was chatting it up with a dancer who'd swung by the bar for a drink. If anyone could ask about Greg, without sounding like she was pumping them for information, it was her.

"Drink up," Carrera said before swallowing down the whiskey.

The booze was okay, but it wasn't a Santini Whisky.

Karen took a sip, then another. "I never drink at work. This is such a treat for me, Mr. Amos."

"So, Slash got you fired," Carrera said. "What went down?"

"I worked for ALPHA. She did too, but she also got fired."

What the fuck.

She was putting an entire organization at risk by her running her damn mouth.

He had to ask. "What's ALPHA?"

Karen tossed back another mouthful. "It's a top-secret organization." Then, she drank down more.

"Not so secret if you're telling me about it."

Her cackle made him grimace. "Well, I can trust you." She sat up straight. "I slouch."

Move her away from ALPHA before someone hears her.

"Tell me about your boyfriend."

"He's great. Really, really great, but sometimes he promises me he'll show up, then he can't make it. And I get bummed."

"What's his name?"

"Greg."

Jesus.

"What does he do?"

She finished the whiskey. "He's a very busy businessman." She chuckled. "That's funny. Busy businessman. Say that fast three times."

He said he liked chatty women, but he should have qualified that comment with chatty women of substance. Karen was babbling like a damn fool.

"Another drink?" he asked.

"I shouldn't," she replied. "Maybe we could get together for coffee sometime, you know, outside of here."

He leaned close. "I'm a very bad man, Karen. You wouldn't want to get caught up with me."

Her breath hitched and she stared at his mouth. "I would

kill to get caught up with you. You're so sexy I could stare at you for hours and hours."

He fisted her hair into a pony tail and tugged. "I'm evil. You should stay away from me."

"Ohgod, yes," Karen bleated.

He released his vice grip on her hair. "Make sure your boyfriend treats you right. You deserve it."

She flicked her head. "You're right. I do. I'm going to insist he come down here."

"Take a night off and let him take you out somewhere fun."

"Yeah, that's a good idea."

Carrera stood. "Thanks for your company. Always a pleasure."

"Where are you going?"

"Into the back, to fuck."

"Ohmygod," Karen blurted before Carrera made his way toward the bar.

Slash was talking with two dancers. He found an empty stool, cemented his gaze on her, and waited. Being around her, falling in love with her... these were things he would never take for granted.

The head bartender made his way over. "Sorry for the wait. What can I get you?"

"I'm waiting for Slash."

"Gotcha," he said before moving on.

Slash sauntered over. "What can I do for you, Claude?"

"I want a table dance."

She loved the lust in his eyes, loved how his deep voice rasped out his dirty desires.

"Let's get wicked," she replied.

Slash

WITH HER BACKPACK slung over her shoulder, she clasped his hand, led him to a table. Once he sat, she ran her hand over his crotch. "I'm going to change. Try not to get into too much trouble."

In the dressing room, she went to her station. Her barely-there one-piece string bikini covered the essentials. Truth was, she had no problem putting herself out there to find these women.

Jilly entered the dressing room from doing a shift, and hurried over. "Hey, I thought you were done dancing."

"My client requested a table dance," Slash replied.

"I'm concerned about Deb," Jilly said. "She hasn't come back."

Slash stepped close. "There's a guy who's been floating around the club. He's White, has a wild head of hair, a full beard and mustache. He invited Deb into the VIP room."

Jilly's eyes grew wide. "I had no idea she was going back there."

"Have you seen him around?"

"He doesn't sound like one of my regulars," Jilly whispered.

"Just be careful," Slash said.

"You too," Jilly replied.

Slash pulled on her stiletto sandals, tied her sarong around her waist, and left the dressing room. She swept her gaze over the faces in the club, searching for her target. When she found Carrera, he became the only man in the room. As she sauntered over, his eyes blackened with desire.

She stopped in front of him, leaned down, and whispered, "Good evening, Claude."

"Holy hell," he ground out.

"Hey, honey," called out a customer. "Come over my way."

Carrera stood, his massive body dwarfing hers. After helping her onto the table, he sat back down, his fiery gaze raking over every inch of her.

The intensity in his eyes made her breath hitch. His energy, his magnetism had a hold on her. She couldn't look away, didn't care who else was there. Her entire being was focused on him. Making him wild with desire, teasing him to the brink of insanity, and being the one to relieve him of his torment.

Was this revenge? Was this desire? Was this love?

Is he my past, my present, and my future?

An iconic rock song by the Black Crowes had her swaying to the seductive beat. Slash let the tune carry her away to a place of total hedonism. She started moving her hips, arching her back, snaking her arms in the air like a vine. With her gaze bolted on Carrera, she untied her sarong and draped it around his neck, then continued her erotic dance.

She ran her hands down her breasts, her abs, and caressed her sex before stroking her sides and sinking her fingers into her hair. On fire, she couldn't stop the pulsing lust as it swept her away.

"Yo, honey, dance this way," yelled the annoying customer at the table.

She snapped to attention when someone grabbed her calf. She spun around. grabbed the guys wrist, and twisted.

"Fuck!" he screamed.

She let go and glared at him. "You touch me again, you lose that hand."

Carrera had shoved out of his chair. His eyes were narrowed, his nostrils flared, and his fingers curled into fists. His "Don't fuck with her" stance turned her on... and made her feel safe.

For the first time in a long, long time, someone had her back.

One of the security guys hurried over. "Everything okay?"

"He got handsy," Carrera tossed a nod toward the guy, "but the dancer handled it."

As if that outburst hadn't just happened, Slash continued to gyrate and shake her assets in front of him. When the song ended, the men at the table erupted in applause. Several offered her money before Carrera helped her down.

"You slayed me," he growled. "Fucking slayed me."

"Sit," she commanded him, her voice thick with lust. "Time for a grind."

"Damn, woman," he ground out. "You fucking own me."

He moved his chair, she slinked close, circling her hips, arching her back, and thrusting her tits in his face.

He eyed her breasts. Lust streaked through him, and his cock firmed.

After shaking her titties, she turned around, bent over, and wiggled her ass. He caressed her bottom, his throaty growl ripping through her like wildfire.

His hands on her bare ass had her insides quivering, her core slickened with need. She couldn't deny that the boy she'd once loved fiercely had become the man of her dreams. She craved his touch, desperate to feel him claiming her, making her surrender to him... to the ecstasy.

Facing him, she lowered herself into his lap, and arched her back. With her hands over her head, she let the beat of the music sweep her away as she imagined his hard cock buried deep inside her.

On a moan, she ran her tongue over her lower lip while his ravenous gaze turned her into a wild beast, filled with a lust so powerful, she started grinding on him.

"Fuck, you are so hot," he bit out.

As the song roared to a climax, she pulled aside the material covering her nipples. His gaze jumped to her pink nibs, and he released a long, deep growl that sent jolts of adrenaline racing through her.

Leaning close, she pressed her mouth to his ear. "I can't wait for you to suck them."

"Fuck," he groaned.

When the music ended, she collected her sarong from around his neck, and stood. After tying it around her waist, she whispered, "Back room?"

"Hell, yes," he rasped.

She couldn't wait, didn't care who was in the orgy room, didn't give a fuck who watched them. She had to have him. Couldn't wait to rip off his clothes, rake her hands over his hard-muscled body, and take him inside her.

A throaty growl ripped from his throat. He stood, grasped her hand, and led her through the club. Down the dimly-lit hallway they hurried to the door at the end. He swiped his card and in they went.

Within seconds their eyes adjusted to the red room. Several couples and small groups were scattered around the space, everyone laser-focused on their carnal fun. He led her to a dark corner where a sofa, covered in a black sheet, waited. He dropped his sport coat, unbuttoned his shirt enough to yank it over his head. His pants were gone in seconds.

On went the condom. He lifted her into the air, backed her against the wall, shoved aside her thong, and drilled into her.

The rush of euphoria had her crying out, her body shaking from the onslaught of pleasure while he slammed into her again and again.

She wrapped herself around him, kissed him hard, and thrust against him. The kiss was an assault of tongues and teeth, their guttural groans unlike anything she'd ever heard. Their feral sounds and their near-brutal kissing had her grinding hard against his shaft. She couldn't slow, didn't want to stop.

The euphoria spun her higher and higher, his hard thrusting hurling her toward an orgasm. "Coming so hard," she hissed as she surrendered to the ecstasy.

He grunted through his orgasm, his kiss intensifying as he released inside her. Their wild kiss slowed as their bodies stilled. Him, nestled in her. Their breathing thundering in her ears while he kissed her softly again and again.

"I'm out of control around you," he said. "Fucking out of control."

"I love how you took me," she whispered. "Mygod, that's sexy."

"I can't get enough of you," he rasped. "I need more."

"I can go all night." Her attention was diverted when someone walked by. "Karen's watching us. She's in a black mask, but it's her."

"Let's get outta here," he murmured.

"So, you've had your way with me, and you're tossing me aside?" she teased.

He kissed her. "I want you in my bed."

You gotta do it.

They retreated into a restroom, cleaned up, and dressed. He, in his street clothes. She, into her pink dress. Before she'd even reached behind to zip herself, Carrera was right there. "I got you."

As he zipped, he paused to kiss her bare skin.

While leaving the room, Slash spotted Karen glaring at her. In her hands, she held a spray sanitizer and a rag.

"Three o'clock," Slash said.

As Carrera held open the door for her, he glanced over his shoulder. They made their way through the noisy club, the pulsing music and beehive of clubbers a far cry from the sexy ambiance of the private room.

Once outside, Carrera said, "Karen's got clean-up duty."

"She was shooting daggers at me pretty good. Did you give her another reason to hate me?"

"I was just my normal charming self." He opened the passenger door of the SUV, waited for her to climb in.

"She probably has a massive crush on you and wanted to check you out."

He kissed her, shut her car door.

As he drove out of the parking lot, he said, "Karen's boyfriend is Greg."

Whoa, that's big.

"Nice job," she said.

He flashed her a smile. "All for you, babe."

"Do you think the man in her office was Greg?"

"Yeah, and I'm thinking we should stake out the club from the parking lot. If we see him go in, we attach a tracker to his vehicle."

"I like that."

He wrapped his hand around her thigh. "We're good together."

Rather than respond to his comment, she entwined her fingers through his. In the dark car, he glanced over. She met his gaze.

This is it.

The truth was impossible to ignore. They were falling in love all over again. Joy, mixed with trepidation, had her tugging away her hand.

"I got you," he murmured.

"Thank you for saying that."

"I saw you talking to a dancer at the bar," he said.

She appreciated that he changed the subject, putting her on more solid footing.

"I spoke with two of them," she said. "They'd both been propositioned by customers, but not together. One remembered his wild hair, the other didn't remember what he looked like, but they both remembered the tip. Five-hundred bucks each."

"When?"

"One happened months ago, one recently. After he tipped them, he asked about private time in a VIP room. One refused, but the other said yes. When she went into the room with him, she said she didn't like the set up and left."

"Did they get his name?"

"They didn't remember."

"We gotta find this Greg guy."

She lifted her phone from her bag. "I'm checking on Elsa."

"Now?"

"It's only eleven-twenty. She doesn't go to sleep until after the news."

Slash put the call on speaker. It rang and rang, then rolled to voicemail. "Hmm."

"Baby, she's sleeping."

"She was coughing pretty good. Maybe she's sick."

"People cough."

"Drop me off," she said. "I'll swing by."

"We'll go together, but if she gets mad because you woke her—"

"I'll blame you," she said with a smile.

Carrera drove toward Elsa's Alexandria home. After turning onto her street, Slash smelled smoke.

What the hell...

Elsa's house was backlit in a bright orange, flames shooting into the night sky.

Carrera hit the gas as Slash blurted, "Her house is on fire!"

19

THE RESCUE

Slash

Slash grabbed her key ring as Carrera slammed on the brakes in front of Elsa's house.

"I'm calling 911," he said as Slash bolted from the SUV.

With the key in hand, she ran toward the front door.

Laser-focused, she needed to find Elsa and get her out. Despite everything she knew about fire safety, she was going into that burning building.

"Don't go in!" Carrera screamed.

Ignoring him, she tapped the handle with her fingers. It was cool, so she keyed her way inside. A swarm of black smoke billowed out the front door.

Turning away, she sucked down a breath, then turned back. "Elsa!" she screamed.

No answer.

She dropped to her knees, crawled into the foyer. The smoke was billowing down the stairs from the west side of the home. Holding her breath, she crawled into the front room. She felt around, but she couldn't find Elsa so she hurried, on hands and knees, toward the family room.

Elsa always watched TV in there.

Please, please be in there.

As she passed the staircase, it felt like she'd stepped into an oven. Glancing up, vibrant orange flames were shooting upward, engulfing the entire upper level.

Moving fast as she could in the smoky darkness, she hurried into the family room. As she was making her way toward the sofa, she bumped into something.

Elsa was lying on the carpet.

"Slash!" Carrera screamed, "I'm coming in after you!"

Slash scooped her up, then stood. It was impossible to see two feet in front of her, but she had a general idea where the front door was.

"Got her!" Slash screamed. "Coming out!"

She inhaled, started coughing, as she made her way toward the exit, bumping into Carrera.

He grabbed her, and rushed them outside.

On the front lawn, she set Elsa down and started coughing. Then, she hocked up black phlegm. Carrera was performing CPR on his grandmother as the roar of sirens grew louder.

Elsa lay lifeless on the grass. Shoving out the mounting fear, Slash held her hand as Carrera breathed life into her.

"Elsa, breathe," Slash said. "You can't leave us. Fight, fight hard."

Carrera continued with the compressions before he paused to breathe into her. "Come on G-ma, you got this."

The fire truck stopped out front, and the crew jumped into action.

Elsa breathed, opened her eyes, then started coughing. Carrera sat her up as the paramedics rushed over.

"Oh, thank God," Slash said.

As the medics moved Elsa away from the house, the fire

crew started spraying the home, dousing it with part water, part fire-retardant chemicals. The paramedic attached an oxygen mask to Elsa.

"What's her name?" asked a first responder.

"Elsa," Slash replied.

"Elsa, you're doing great," said the paramedic. "We're going to transport you to the hospital."

"I had to perform CPR," Carrera said.

One of the fire crew made her way over. "Can someone tell me what happened?"

"I'm going with Elsa," Slash said.

"I'm right behind you," Carrera said.

Elsa was loaded into the ambulance. Slash hopped in, started coughing.

"Did you enter the house?" asked the medic.

"I did," Slash said, and continued coughing.

The medic attached an oxygen mask around her face. "We'll have you checked out too."

Slash clasped Elsa's hand. Elsa squeezed her fingers. Elsa looked small and frail on that large gurney. The fear Slash had ignored rushed to the surface, the emotion welling in her eyes.

Elsa smiled. Even with the oxygen mask, Slash saw the relief in her eyes. Slash's heartbeat slowed as she inhaled a cleansing breath.

She'd gotten Elsa out, hopefully, in time.

In the emergency room, they placed both women in a triage room, but the dividing curtain made it impossible for Slash to see Elsa, so she removed her oxygen mask, opened the curtain, and sat on the edge of the bed facing Elsa.

Elsa opened her eyes and shook her head, then pointed to the bed.

A nurse entered. "We're going to take you both for chest X-rays to check your lungs. Who wants to go first?"

Elsa removed her mask. "We go together. Please don't separate me from my grandbaby."

Even though they didn't know the extent of the damage to Elsa's lungs, she was alert, talking, and dictating orders.

Like a Santini.

Slash's soaring pulse started to calm.

Wearing their oxygen masks, they were wheeled into X-ray. By the time they returned, Carrera was sitting in their triage room, along with Luciano, and Teddy.

After kissing his grandmother's forehead, Carrera said, "Close call, huh?"

Elsa started to remove her oxygen mask, but Carrera pulled her hand away from the elastic. "We'll talk later. Rest now."

Then, Carrera stepped over to Slash. Love and gratitude poured from his eyes. He leaned down, kissed her forehead, then sat in the chair by her bed, and held her hand.

Both Luciano and Teddy kissed Elsa.

"I hear we've got a hero in the group," Luciano said as he kissed Slash's forehead.

She wanted to speak, but she didn't want to remove the oxygen mask, so she pointed to Elsa.

Though Teddy was Carrera's cousin, he'd been part of the clan who'd blamed Slash. She wasn't surprised that he hadn't said anything to her. More importantly, she didn't care.

All that mattered was Elsa. She was safe, and she needed to make a full recovery.

Carrera's dad, Paul, rushed into the room, and over to Elsa. "You okay, Ma?"

Elsa nodded, then pointed to Slash.

"Are you okay, Amanda?"

Slash nodded.

"Carrera told me you ran into her house to save her," Paul said. "Very brave. Thank you. She would have died if you hadn't insisted on checking her."

"How do we know she didn't start the fire?" Teddy blurted.

Carrera jumped up, his hand curled into a fist. "I'm gonna fuckin' put this through your face."

"Whoa, whoa, I'm not the bad guy here," Teddy said. "Don't bite *my* head off."

Carrera lunged at his cousin, but Luciano and Paul held him back. "You apologize to Amanda," Carrera growled. "*Now.*"

A poisonous silence filled the hospital room.

Elsa removed her mask. "Shame on you, Theodore Santini."

"That's not nice," Paul said. "Amanda saved G-ma's life."

"I'm just sayin," Teddy said.

"You make me sick, Teddy," Carrera said. "Get the hell out."

"You know, there was a time when you would have agreed with me," Teddy said.

"*Enough,*" Carrera growled.

A doctor entered carrying a tablet, regarded the men, then eyed the patients. "Good evening, everyone. Looks like you've both been through a lot." He glanced at the tablet. "Which one of you is Amanda?"

Slash raised her hand.

The doctor reviewed the pulse oximeter attached to her finger. "Your oxygen levels have returned to normal. Your lungs are clear, but I'd like you to continue with the oxygen mask until you're discharged. I recommend a follow up with your healthcare provider if you experience any coughing, wheezing, hoarseness or dark saliva."

Slash nodded.

"Any questions?" he asked.

She shook her head.

The doctor checked Elsa's oxygen levels next. "Mrs. Santini, you're lucky to be alive. Your lungs aren't as clear as I'd like, so I'm going to admit you. We can re-evaluate in the next twenty-four."

Slash's heart dropped, but she was a realist. Elsa had been

in the house longer, and while the smoke inhalation could have been much worse, it was still a lot for her to endure.

The doctor offered a warm smile. "Do you have any questions?"

Elsa shook her head.

"I'll put through next steps for both of you." The doctor addressed the group. "There was some commotion when I walked in. It would be good if the patients rested. They've been through a lot." The doctor left the room.

"Okay, guys, you heard the doctor," Paul said before kissing Elsa's forehead. "Love you, Ma. I'll check on you tomorrow." Then Paul walked over to Slash. "Thank you."

She acknowledged him with a nod.

Luciano kissed them both on their foreheads, told them both he loved them. "Rest up," Luciano said.

Teddy said goodbye to Elsa, didn't apologize, and ignored Slash completely. Fortunately for her, she'd developed a thick outer skin, and she didn't give a damn.

While she was concerned Elsa had a longer road to recovery, she felt confident she'd make it. She was a strong, healthy woman.

Top of Slash's mind... had the fire been intentionally set?

Carrera

THE FAMILY CLEARED OUT, and Elsa fell asleep. Carrera wanted to talk to Slash, but he didn't want her to remove the oxygen mask, so he stayed silent. For now, he was grateful the two most important women in his life were safe.

Slash dozed, jerked awake, and looked over at Elsa. Carrera lifted her hand to his mouth, kissed her warm skin, shot her a loving smile.

"She's okay, babe," he murmured. "I'm right here and I'm not leaving. You can sleep—" His phone rang. "Santini," he answered.

"Mr. Santini, this is Detective Milholland, with the Alexandria Police Arson Unit. I was called to your grandmother's house fire because the Fire Marshall's investigator found an accelerant."

Fury swept through Carrera.

Who the hell would want her dead?

"Can you confirm who lives in the home?" asked the detective.

"My grandmother, Elsa Santini."

"I'd like to talk to her," said the detective.

"She's being admitted to the hospital and she's on oxygen," Carrera said. "I'll ask her to call you as soon as she can."

"Please let her know that the damage on the west side of the home is extensive. The structure isn't safe to enter."

"Understood."

The call ended and Carrera hung up. His head pounded, the anger coursing through him with lightning speed. He would go to the ends of the earth to find the person, then rip his heart out of his goddamn chest.

Both women were uber-focused on him.

"An accelerant was found," Carrera said. "Someone set the fire."

Slash's eyes widened, G-ma started to sit up. After Carrera propped her pillows, she eased back onto them.

While they waited for the hospital to discharge Slash and move G-ma to a room, Carrera paced. He couldn't stop his thoughts from firing one after the other, like a semiautomatic. Was this random or a targeted hit? Was this the work of a serial arsonist? Who would want to hurt her?

Two long hours later, Slash had been discharged. G-ma had been moved into a private room where she was sleeping soundly. Her oxygen mask had been replaced with a nasal cannula and, to his relief, she was coughing very little.

Slash's oxygen mask was also gone, but the anger in her eyes was not.

She'd been sitting next to G-ma in a chair, holding her hand while she slept.

"What do you think?" Slash asked, breaking their long silence.

He moved a chair next to Slash, sat beside her, and dropped a soft kiss on her lips. "I'm grateful you insisted on checking on her. If you hadn't—"

"Don't even say it," Slash said. "Just thinking about it makes me crazy."

"G-ma's strong," he said. "She'll recover."

"She better."

"Elsa will stay with me." He caressed her hand. "I need you by my side. G-ma would want you there too."

"Whatever you need," she replied. "As much as I'm concerned about these missing women, everything takes a back seat to Elsa. Everything."

"I'm sorry about Teddy," he said.

"No surprise."

"You risked your life for her," he said.

"You were right there with me."

They talked a little longer, then dozed for a few hours.

Carrera's dreams were dark, like the smoke-filled house. He was chasing someone, someone he could never get close to. But he was filled with unmistakable hatred for whoever he was after. He jerked awake to find Slash studying his face.

"You talk in your sleep," she whispered.

"I was chasing a bad guy," he said.

"Catch him?"

"No," he replied. "Did you sleep?"

"A little. I'm pretty keyed up. Providence is gunning for an arrest, I want to talk to this Greg guy, I feel so much pressure to find the missing women." She glanced over at Elsa. "We've got to tell her a little about these cases."

"Why?"

"If she's living with you, but you're locking her out of your home office, she'll wonder what you're hiding from her."

"I'll tell her it's my kink room."

"And I go in there with you because it's our torture chamber."

They shared a laugh.

Elsa woke up and smiled. "Seeing you like this makes me very happy."

"I was wrong about Amanda May," Carrera said. "I want to apologize to both of you. Slash, I should *never* have treated you badly and I'm deeply sorry for hurting you. G-ma, you were right. Slash is an amazing woman and I get why she's your number one."

G-ma smiled. "Thank you for saying that."

Slash's smile meant everything to him. Absolutely everything.

One step at a time.

"How did I get out of the house?" G-ma asked.

"Slash ran in and pulled you out."

"Oh, my goodness. That was so brave of you. And so dangerous. You're not supposed to run into a burning building, honey."

"I did what I had to do," Slash replied.

Elsa squeezed her hand. "Thank you."

"Carrera ran in too," Slash said. "He got us both out." She kissed G-ma's forehead. "How are you feeling?"

"Tired. My chest hurts a little. Did you say the fire was intentionally set?"

"Yeah," Carrera replied. "We'll talk more later. For now, rest."

After G-ma fell asleep, Carrera asked Slash who she thought could have done it.

"I have no idea," Slash replied. "What about you?"

Carrera raked his hands down his beard. "It makes no sense."

"What about someone trying to hurt a family member, but targeting an old woman?"

"I thought of that," he said. "But who?"

"What about someone who wants to distract me from the case," she said. "Or someone who resents your promotion at work?"

"It's messed up, but maybe. What about family?"

"Everyone loves G-ma," Slash said.

"What about money as motive?"

"They'd have to be listed as a beneficiary in her will. I've never seen her will. Have you?"

"No, but Luciano's her executor." Carrera pulled out his phone. "I'll ask him." Carrera fired off a text to his cousin.

> Fire was set. Who are G-ma's beneficiaries?

When no dots appeared, he checked the time. It was three in the morning.

"Tomorrow, I'll buy her some new clothes," Slash said. "And whatever else she needs."

"Grab what you need from your house," he said.

"Are you sure about this?"

He slid his hand behind her neck, leaned over, and kissed her. "Absolutely. I can hire a nurse if she needs help, so you don't end up taking care of her."

"I would do that for her," Slash said.

They slept on and off 'til seven. Carrera went to the cafeteria for breakfast, returning with a tray of food.

G-ma was awake and alert.

He set the tray on a table. "I got eggs, sausage, toast, and three mini boxes of cereal."

"The nurse checked on Elsa and her breakfast is on its way," Slash said.

Elsa pulled her oxygen mask off. "Don't you need to get to work?"

"Work?" Slash said. "Hell, no."

"We're not leaving you," Carrera said.

That made Elsa smile.

After breakfast, the doctor stopped by. She listened to G-ma's lungs, checked her oxygen levels. "You're improving nicely," she said. "I'm going to put in another request for a chest X-ray. How are you feeling?"

"A little better."

When the doctor left, Slash asked, "Elsa, where do you buy your clothing?"

"That boutique near my house, but I've gotten a few things online from the website you sent me."

"I'm going home to grab my laptop," Slash said. "Is the boutique near that Italian restaurant we like?"

Elsa smiled. "That's the one, but you don't have to—"

"I've got this." Slash stood. "I'll be back in a few."

Carrera held out a credit card, but she waved it away.

Jazz breezed in with Russell. Jazz eyed Slash and Carrera before kissing her grandmother on the forehead.

"G-ma, I can't believe this happened to you," Jazz said. "Are you okay?"

G-ma nodded.

"Hey, man," Russell said to Carrera. "We came as soon as we heard."

They're a we, now?

Russell walked around the bed, extended his hand to Slash. "Russell Fitzpatrick. I'm running for US Congress. A seat opened up in the great state of Virginia, and I'd love your vote."

Slash raised her eyebrows as she shook his hand. "Slash."

"I'm sorry?" Russell asked.

"That's her nickname," Jazz said, and rolled her eyes.

"Jazz's dad told us about the fire," Russell said. "G-ma, did you leave something on, like a burner?"

Instead of heading out, Slash sat in the bedside chair, clasped G-ma's hand. Carrera couldn't miss the shift in her energy. With a ramrod-straight back, her gaze ping-ponged from Jazz to Russell, then back to Jazz. No longer chill, she had a stance that screamed, "Don't fuck with me." He loved that about her. Without question, her loyalty was to his grandmother, bar none.

She's a pit bull.

"What's *she* doing here?" Jazz asked.

A growl shot from Carrera. "Slash ran into the house and rescued G-ma. She saved her life."

"Hometown heroine," Russell said. "We should feature you in my campaign ad."

"God, no," Jazz blurted. "I'm in that ad, and there's no way I'm doing it if she's in it."

"Jazz is very grateful," Russell said, putting his arm around her. "She's just upset about what happened, right Jazz?"

"Of course," Jazz said, her voice tight. "I'm soooo glad you're okay, G-ma. We drove by the house on our way here. It's not good."

Tears filled G-ma's eyes, and Carrera's heart broke. His grandparents had lived in that house for decades. Even after G-pa passed on, G-ma had refused to leave.

Now, she didn't have a choice.

"We're going to salvage whatever we can," Carrera said. "And G-ma's moving in with me." He shot his grandmother a smile. "It's gonna be fun."

G-ma pointed to Slash.

"What?" Jazz asked. "Why are you pointing at her?"

"Slash is moving in with us too," Carrera said.

Jazz narrowed her gaze at Slash. "*You're* moving in with them?"

"Whatever Elsa wants, Elsa gets, right?" Slash said to G-ma.

"What do you say to doing that TV spot?" Russell asked Slash. "I can have my campaign manager—" He chuckled. "That's you, Jazz. Why don't I handle it myself? Can I count on you?"

"No," Slash replied.

Russell's gaze hovered on Slash. "Too bad. You would have given my campaign that winning boost. I'm sure of it."

"When do you get released?" Jazz asked G-ma.

"We don't know," Carrera replied.

"If there's anything you need, just let us know," Russell said with a smile. "We're happy to help." He regarded Slash. "Good to meet you. Don't forget to vote for me." Then, he extended his hand to Carrera. "It's good to be a part of the fam."

What the hell?

"What does that mean?" Carrera asked.

"Your sister and I are getting serious," Russell said. "If we get married, I'm thinking of changing my name to Santini. I mean, it carries a lot of weight. Russell Santini, United States Congressman." He puffed out his chest. "That sounds fantastic!"

With a cheesy grin, Russell dipped down, kissed G-ma's forehead. "Godspeed."

Carrera flicked his gaze to Slash. She arched an eyebrow at him before sliding her attention back to Russell.

When they left, Carrera shut the door. "What the hell was that?"

"That was your typical sleazebag politician," Slash said.

"Amanda May, why don't you do the TV commercial?"

Slash sat back down, clasped G-ma's hand. "You'll find out

just as soon as we bring you back to Carrera's." She winked. "And you won't believe it."

"Oooo, secrets. I can't wait," G-ma exclaimed.

Carrera had no intention of discussing their real work with his grandmother, but when her face lit up, Carrera knew to trust Slash.

If anyone knew what she was doing, it was her.

THE FOLLOWING MORNING, G-ma entered Carrera's home with him and Slash. No longer required to use supplemental oxygen, G-ma had been released with instructions to follow up with her health provider if she had any lingering symptoms.

"Thank you for taking me in," G-ma said. "I've never been homeless."

"You're not homeless," Carrera said. "How are you with stairs?"

"I'm okay."

"I've got a bedroom on the first floor with an en suite bathroom that's yours, or I've got my bedroom upstairs, along with two more."

"Where's Amanda May sleeping?" G-ma asked.

Carrera slid his gaze to Slash. "Upstairs."

With me.

G-ma wandered into the first-floor bedroom, meandered back out. "I like it down here."

Yesterday afternoon, Slash had left the hospital, returning three hours later with new clothes for his grandmother.

"Once you get settled, we can look at your new clothes," Slash said. "I can return what you don't like or what doesn't fit, then we'll order everything else online."

"I'd like some coffee," G-ma said, "then we can do a show-

and-tell." She smiled at Slash. "Do you remember when I'd take you shopping—"

Slash smiled at the memory, and her joyous expression tugged at Carrera's heart.

"I'd come out of the dressing room and model everything for you," Slash said. "You were so generous with me. You bought me an entire wardrobe."

"And now, you're doing it for me," G-ma replied. "When can I see my house?"

"Whenever you feel up to it," Carrera said. "The arson detective wants to talk to us, and he said the structure isn't safe to enter."

"Elsa, I stopped by and found these." Slash pulled G-ma's jewelry box and her purse from a carry bag.

G-ma's face lit up. "You're an angel."

Slash wiped off the soot, set her items on the kitchen table.

G-ma checked her wallet. "Everything is here."

Carrera made coffee while G-ma went through her jewelry box. "Nothing was taken. I'm relieved about that."

Once the coffee had brewed, Slash filled three mugs, set them on the kitchen table.

"Are you up to talking to the arson detective?" Carrera asked them.

"Absolutely," G-ma replied.

"Bring it on," Slash said.

Carrera put the call on speaker. Rather than get into it on the phone, the arson detective told them he'd swing by in the hour.

While Carrera made breakfast, Slash helped G-ma get settled in her new bedroom. This had to be traumatic for his grandmother, but she was rolling with the changes like a champ.

Like a Santini.

Slash

SLASH WAS beyond ready to talk to the arson detective. She needed to play this one like the doting granddaughter and not like a woman hell-bent on revenge. Just thinking about how someone tried to kill Elsa made her blood run cold in her veins.

After yesterday's shopping spree, she'd swung by the charred remains of Elsa's home. It was both heart wrenching and terrifying to think that Elsa could have died in that fire. The west side of the home lay in waste. Large piles of rubble, burned furniture, charred remains were all that was left. The east side—the side where she'd found Elsa—was intact. The walls, the furniture, and everything in the kitchen were covered in a thick black layer of soot and dried chemicals from the fire-hoses, but the items hadn't disintegrated to ashes.

While they ate breakfast on Carrera's screened porch, Slash tried to relax, but her nerves were shot. She kept reminding herself that Elsa was okay. There didn't appear to be any evidence of permanent lung damage, and Elsa had a wonderful place to live while her home was rebuilt.

"Elsa, do you want me to pick up your lotions, shampoo, and makeup, do you want to go shopping—"

"Online is easier," Elsa said. "I can use whatever Carrera has for a few days." Then, she clasped both their hands. "Thank you for taking such good care of me. Now, tell me what's going on with you two."

"Going on?" Slash asked.

"I haven't heard a single cuss word out of either one of you. You had a date last night on a Carrera cruise boat. Slash is staying here—"

"I'm here because of you, Elsa," Slash said.

"I want you here," Carrera said.

"Are you dating again?" Elsa's expression was filled with so much anticipation that Slash laughed.

"We've been working together on a case," Carrera said. "I've fallen in love with Amanda May, and I've been waiting for the right time to tell her."

Elsa grinned. "I think you just did."

His gaze fell on hers. Excitement coursed through her.

"I love you, Slash," he said.

The love that passed between them felt solid. This time it felt different.

Is this it? Is he the one?

"Are we doing this?" Slash asked.

"I hope so," Elsa said, grinning.

"We're doing it," Carrera replied.

As she stared into his eyes, her heart had found its forever. "I love you too."

He kissed her. She kissed him back.

"This is a very happy day," Elsa said.

Slash regarded her. "You're amazing. You lost everything, yet you're so happy about us."

"I didn't lose everything," Elsa said. "I have my family and I have my health. Those are what matter the most."

Slash's eyes grew moist. "You can't leave us. I would be a wreck without you."

Elsa swatted her arm. "You're tough as nails. Strong, independent, and fierce. *You* saved *me*, not the other way around."

"We saved each other," Slash said.

"We're together again, like we were all those years ago," Elsa said. "But this time, Carrera Santini, you will do the right thing. Yes?"

"Yes, ma'am," Carrera replied. "Slash has always been the love of my life, but my anger got in the way."

"Use that anger to hunt down criminals," Elsa said.

Slash's phone rang with a call from Z. "It's work. I'm gonna take this inside."

"Hello, Z," she answered as she made her way into Carrera's office. Once there, she put the call on speaker.

"Hello, Slash," Z said. "I heard about the fire. How are you doing?"

"I'm fighting mad. What's going on?"

"We need to move in for an arrest at the club."

"Dammit," she said. "Not yet, Philip."

"We've got confirmation of prostitution. Why hold off?"

"We don't have the owner," Slash said. "I've got a POI named Greg. If I find him, I'm confident he'll lead us to the missing women."

"If we shut down the club, we cripple the owner. No income stream, no women to stalk."

"I don't like that," she pushed back. "He could start plucking women from the general population. How 'bout we put a little heat on him, and we bring in an investigative reporter to do a story on these women? And we interview women at the club."

"Hmm, that might work. Flush him out."

"And when we do, I'll be there to catch him."

"I'll ask Sin to contact Alexandra Wilde to do the interview."

Her phone flashed with a call from Luciano. "We good?"

"I'll be in touch." Z hung up.

She put Luciano's call on speaker. "Hey, are you coming over?"

"Later today," Luciano replied. "How is she?"

"Amazing. She hasn't shed a single tear."

"She's a Santini." Slash could hear the pride in Luciano's voice. After a pause, he said, "I found Elwood Tosh."

A strange mix of emotions washed over her. Fear morphed into anger... then hatred. And finally, courage.

"Do you want him?" Luciano asked snapping her back to the present.

"Yes."

"Where are you?"

"Staying with Elsa at Carrera's." His deep chuckle made her smile. "What?" she asked.

"When are you going to admit you're in love with him?"

"I did this morning."

"Finally," Luciano replied. "I'll tell you about Tosh when I see you. You *cannot* do this hit alone. Understood?"

"Got it."

"See you later."

"Luciano, thank you." She hung up and turned around.

Carrera and Elsa were standing there, their mouths agape.

Oh, boy.

"The arson detective is here," Carrera said. "He wants to talk to you."

"How much of that did you hear?" Slash asked them.

"Enough," Carrera said.

Elsa walked over to the white board, crossed her arms, and started reading their notes. Then, she turned toward them. "Your house is far more exciting than mine."

"Not a word, G-ma," Carrera said as he ushered them out, pulling the door closed behind him.

"Not a word," Elsa promised as they went into the kitchen.

The detective was head-down on his phone typing out a text. When finished, he said hello to Slash.

"You saved Mrs. Santini's life, but I have to lecture you about *not* running into a burning building."

A smile tugged at the corners of her lips. "Save it, Detective. I would do it all over again, even with the lecture."

"Mrs. Santini, you have a doorbell camera," the detective said to Elsa. "Can I get videos from last night?"

"I'll send them over, but there's nothing," Carrera said. "Whoever started the fire steered clear of her front door."

"My investigators found the point of origin," said Detective Milholland. "It was on the ground, west side. A rag soaked in some type of accelerant. We found a second rag in the back, also on the west side."

"My bedroom and guest room are on that side of the house," Elsa said.

"Do you know if you'd turned those lights on?"

"My bedroom light was on, but the back room was dark. I was downstairs, in my family room, watching the news, and I fell asleep. When I woke up, the room was filling with smoke. I jumped up, hurried toward the front door, but I must've passed out because the next thing I remember is being outside."

"The fire was started between ten-forty-five and eleven-oh-five," said the detective.

"I know you both rescued Mrs. Santini, but I have to ask where you were at that time."

"We were at the Blue Suit club," Carrera said.

"Both of you?" the detective asked.

"Yes," Slash replied.

"Are there any witnesses who can confirm that?"

"Yes," Slash said. "We ran in to *save* her, but you consider us suspects?"

"I'm just doing my job."

"That's ridiculous," G-ma said. "Utterly ridiculous."

Slash regarded Carrera. "What do you think?"

Carrera nodded, once. "Tell him."

Slash retrieved her handbag and showed the detective her FBI badge. "I'm on undercover assignment at Blue Suit, and Deputy Director Santini is making sure I don't become the club's eighth victim. If you start asking around, you'll blow our cover, put us in danger, and the seven women who've gone missing from there will likely stay missing." She arched an eyebrow. "Are we on the same page *now*, Detective Milholland?"

"Understood," he replied, before addressing Elsa. "Mrs. Santini, is there anyone who stands to gain financially if you hadn't survived?"

"Only my executor knows the details of my will," she replied.

"Who is that?"

"My grandson, Luciano Santini. He's very wealthy, so please don't add him to your suspect list."

The detective regarded Slash. "Could the arson have anything to do with your case?"

"Why go after Elsa?" Slash replied. "Why not come after me or Carrera?"

"I have no answers yet," he said. "I'll keep you posted as we sift through the debris. I'm hoping Mrs. Santini's neighbors saw or heard something."

"What about my grandmother's things?" Carrera asked.

"The stairs are unreliable. The second floor is severely compromised." He thanked them and showed himself out.

Elsa made her way toward Carrera's office.

"I think we've got ourselves a new team member," Slash said as Elsa vanished around the corner.

"Looks that way," Carrera said.

Alone in the kitchen, he pulled her into his arms. "You have my word that I'll do right by you." He dropped a searing kiss on her lips.

She hitched her arms around his neck, kissed him back. "I believe you, but if you don't, I'll do to you what I'm going to do to Elwood Tosh."

"What would that be?"

"Slit his fucking throat," she replied.

20

THE STAKE OUT

Carrera

Carrera and Slash pulled up alongside G-ma as she read over the whiteboard.

"This is a very interesting and disturbing case," G-ma said. "Amanda May, what are you doing at the club?"

"I'm bartending," she replied.

"Are you posing as a customer?" G-ma asked Carrera.

"Something like that," he replied.

After a beat, G-ma regarded Carrera. "Why did Amanda May call you Deputy Director Santini. What happened to being a Special Agent?"

"I got a promotion," he said.

"Isn't a Deputy Director an executive?"

"Yes," he replied.

"What's that all about," G-ma asked.

"Luck," he replied.

She smiled, her eyes crinkling in the corners. "I'm sure I'll pick up plenty just by listening."

Slash chuckled. "I'm sure you will."

. . .

THAT EVENING, he and Slash went upstairs to get ready. Tonight, they were staking out the club. If Greg showed up, they'd attach a tracker to his car. Carrera added G-ma to his security system before he and Slash went upstairs to change. She stopped at his spare bedroom.

"This is me," she said.

"Why are you in here?" he asked.

"It's a room." She walked in, tugged off her shirt, and wiggled out of her skintight jeans.

His woman in a sexy, lace bra and matching panties had him raking his gaze over her. "I want you in my bed."

Slash tugged on a form-fitting black shirt and skintight pants that hugged her toned thighs. After pulling her hair into a ponytail, she covered her head with a black knit cap. Next, she slipped her switchblade into her pocket, pulled her Glock from her go-bag, checked it before returning it.

"Let's rock this," she said.

"It's a stake out, not a kill mission," he said.

"Either works," she said with an amused smile.

Her playfulness lit his insides on fire. Not that long ago, they were throwing shade at each other every chance they could get.

"Luciano Santini is approaching the front door," the computer said.

"What's he doing here?" Carrera asked.

"Keeping Elsa company. We'll be gone for several hours, and I don't want her to be alone."

He kissed her forehead. "Very loving."

"Go change. I'll meet you downstairs." She leaned up, pressed her lips to his and kissed him good.

Five minutes later, he found them sitting in the family room. Luciano had brought a bottle of Santini Chianti, poured himself and G-ma each a glass. As expected, his cousin looked sharp in a black Santini sport coat, black shirt, black pants.

Luciano rose from the sofa, pulled him in, and kissed both his cheeks. "It's like last night never happened. G-ma is a ball of energy."

"Keep an eye on her," Carrera said.

"I got this," Luciano replied. "G-ma, what are we gonna do?"

A smile wrinkled her face. "Drink wine, tell stories."

"Stories?" Carrera asked.

Luciano flashed a grin. "I make up stories about being an assassin and tell her about the bad guys I take out."

"I'm not so sure you're making up those stories anymore," G-ma murmured.

Luciano hitched an eyebrow. "Why's that?"

Carrera and Slash exchanged glances.

Luciano shook his head. "Slash, did you have me on speaker?"

Slash stayed silent.

"Don't scold her," G-ma said. "I won't say a word." She waved Carrera and Slash off. "Go."

"Can I have a word?" Slash asked Luciano.

"I'm interested," G-ma said.

"No," Luciano replied.

They walked into his home office, shut the double doors.

"I had my suspicions your cousin was doing more than running his company," G-ma said to Carrera. "Do you work with him?"

"G-ma—"

"Never mind," she said. "I already know the answer."

Slash and Luciano returned to the family room.

After saying goodbye to G-ma, Carrera and Slash left out the garage. To his surprise, her motorcycle was parked beside his. "I thought you stopped riding."

"Never, but I've been too busy to ride."

"How'd you get it over here?"

"My magic carpet."

"Smart ass."

"I rode it over, walked home, packed my stuff, and drove back in my ALPHA SUV." She flashed him a smile. "It wasn't difficult. What *is* difficult is finding Greg and the arsonist so I can slice their fucking hearts out."

"Tell me how you really feel?" he quipped.

"Angry as hell," she bit out. "Now, let's go find a monster."

At the passenger door of his SUV, he caressed her cheek with the back of his finger. "What about time for us?"

"Always," she replied as she squeezed his ass.

After she got in, he let his gaze linger on hers. "I love you. Damn, that feels good to tell you that." He kissed her, shut the door, and got behind the wheel.

They drove to The Blue Suit Club, parked in a lot across the street. She moved to the cargo area of the vehicle where she pulled out her night binoculars. He moved to the back seat, pulled a small container from his go-bag.

After extracting a tiny robotic fly, he paired it with his phone, cracked the back window, and piloted the spycam onto the B in Blue, angled it toward the parking lot, and activated it.

"How often do you have to charge that?" she asked.

"This one's solar powered."

"Isn't that a Crockett Wilde invention?"

"Yeah. You know him?" he asked.

"No, but I've read about him."

"He's a great guy. Super innovative."

"Sin's gonna ask his wife to do a story about the missing women."

"Smart. Your idea?"

"Yup."

"That'll piss Karen off."

"I hope it does," Slash bit out. "I want to put heat on Greg and flush him out of hiding." Slash peered through the night binos. "What about a mini drone in the orgy room?"

"We can try, but Crockett didn't think it would work in a red room. Too dark."

"It's dark out now," she said.

"There's lights on the building and in the parking lot."

They grew silent, watching out the tinted windows. He loved having her by his side, loved partnering with her on this case.

"Luciano found the foster parent who was molesting the kids," she murmured.

"The one Jilly warned you about?"

"Yeah. His name's Elwood Tosh. According to Luciano, that was an alias, one of several. He's bounced around the DMV. He's also fostered children in Ohio, Pennsylvania, and Tennessee."

"Was he reported?"

"Several times, but he'd leave town, find another unattached woman, move in, and start collecting foster kids again. Since he's never even been arrested, he's not in the system, not on law enforcement's radar."

"Are you sure you want to go after him?"

She lowered her goggles. "I heard him sexually assaulting the other kids, more than once. It was soul-crushing and terrifying, and he hadn't even touched me. When I ran, I promised myself that I would hunt him down and kill him. That crazy vow drove me into law enforcement. There are so many monsters out there, but this is the one I always knew I'd take out."

"Luciano told you not to go alone," he murmured.

She peered through the binos. "There's a man exiting his car. Two o'clock."

Using the drone's camera, Carrera homed in on the clubber. "Not him."

"I have bloodlust for Elwood Tosh," she whispered.

"Take me with you," he said.

She peered over at him. "I'll think about it."

When Greg hadn't shown by one-thirty in the morning, they called it.

On the ride home, she said, "I'm coming back tomorrow night, and the next, and the next, until Greg walks though that front door."

"I'm surprised he hasn't asked you into the playroom," Carrera said. "Especially if he was checking you out."

"Why?"

"You're the most beautiful woman in the club."

She cracked a smile. "You are *biased.*"

"Hell, yeah."

"Maybe he's got a type, and I'm not it."

"What do the seven women have in common?"

She grew quiet. "They all have dark hair."

"What else?"

"Hmm." She paused for a few seconds. "They're average height, average build. No kids, no boyfriend. Some have room-mates, some live alone."

"You don't fit that. You're blonde, muscular, stronger than most, and you have a boyfriend."

She flashed a smile. "I've been *purchased* for free use."

He drove into the garage, killed the engine. In the dark car, he glanced over. "I've got something I want to show you."

She chuckled. "I'm sure you do."

"Take a sunrise ride with me tomorrow," he said. "On our bikes."

She leaned toward him. They shared a kiss. "I would love that."

He waited for the garage door to close before they retreated inside.

G-ma slept on the sofa, beneath a throw blanket. Luciano

stood in the dark screened porch, staring into the night. He turned, strolled inside.

"Any luck?" Luciano asked.

"No," Carrera replied.

"That would be too easy," Luciano said.

"What trouble did you two get into?" Slash asked.

"We had a little wine. I entertained Elsa with my stories."

"Now, she knows they're true," Carrera said.

"She always knew," Luciano said. "She just never said anything."

"About that job," Slash said, "Carrera's riding shotgun."

Luciano nodded. "Good choice." He regarded Carrera. "We'll sync up after the July Fourth holiday."

"Aren't you coming to my party?" Carrera asked.

"The one swarming with ALPHA Ops?" Luciano smiled. "No, thank you. That cruise wouldn't end well, for anyone."

"You like them," Carrera said.

"As people, but at the end of the day, they're officers of the law."

Carrera chuckled. "What the hell are you talking about? They're vigilantes."

"I'll think about it," Luciano replied.

"Can you stay the night?" Slash asked.

"What for?" Luciano asked.

"Carrera and I are going for a sunrise bike ride," she replied. "I don't want to leave Elsa home alone."

"I'll be fine," G-ma said.

They turned toward her. She was sitting up, watching them intently. "If I'd known what was *really* going on, I would have moved in here years ago." She rose, kissed Luciano. "Tonight was fun. Love you, Lulu."

He smiled. "I love you, Elsa." He slid his gaze to Carrera and Slash. "If you need me to come back in the morning, I will."

"Go," G-ma said. "I'm fine."

Luciano left, shutting the front door behind him.

"Computer, lock all exterior doors and activate the security system," Carrera said.

"Doors locked, security system on," replied the computer.

"Today has been a very busy day." G-ma said goodnight before retreating down the hall and closing the bedroom door behind her.

Scooping Slash into his arms, he climbed the stairs. She caressed the back of his neck, her gaze locked on his while heat infused his chest. He couldn't wait to love her, watch her unravel in his arms.

He entered her bedroom, made his way into the bathroom. "Grab that toothbrush. You're coming with me."

Her gaze darkened. "Should I fight you every step of the way?"

"No," he replied. "You should come willingly."

Her lips tugged up at the corners. "That sounds like an invitation I can't refuse."

She plucked her toothbrush before he strode down the hall.

In his bedroom, he set her down, wrapped her close, and kissed her. His insides roared to life, but more than their physical connection, his heart had found its home.

Having her here with him completed him.

In the diffused light, he helped her out of her clothes. Slash in black lingerie turned him hard as steel, but he wanted to take his time, appreciate her and love her, before falling asleep with her cradled in his arms.

She pulled off his black Henley, unbuttoned and unzipped his tattered, black jeans. As she tugged them down, she pulled his boxer briefs over his erection, then knelt in front of him.

Desire pounded through him. The need to be with her sent a rush of blood to his already hard shaft. With gentle fingers, she stroked and teased, then licked its sensitive head.

A growl rolled out of him, piercing the silence.

She didn't make a sound as she took him into her mouth. As she caressed him, taking him further in, her soft coos had him gritting his teeth. The frustration and fury faded away, leaving only glorious pleasure.

She pulled off, wrapped her arms around him. Kissed him long and hard, and so damn good. Then, she broke away and pushed him back onto his bed. With catlike speed, she was on him, his cock enveloped in her warm, sexy mouth while her teeth raked over his engorged flesh. As she continued to suck and lick, she slid her finger over his anus.

More arousal sprang through him and he let out another throaty moan. She never inserted her finger, just teased the sensitive skin between his butthole and ball sack. With whisper-soft moans, she pursed her lips around him and started moving faster. He grabbed her hair away from her face, fisted it in one hand and warned, "I'm gonna come."

Everything turned frenetic. Her pace quickened, her ardent moans urging him on. An explosion of ecstasy shot out of him, the euphoria soothing his fury-filled soul.

So much pleasure. Pleasure he didn't deserve. As he floated back to earth, he fastened his gaze on the one woman who could rocket him into the stratosphere. The one woman he'd loved and hated for most of his life.

The one woman he'd cherish for the rest of his days.

~

Slash

SLASH'S CLIT was throbbing so hard, she thought she'd pass out from arousal. She was burning up, her insides on fire with a desire so strong, she kept forgetting to breathe. But rather than rush to orgasm, she wanted to play.

She lay next to him, propped on her elbow. As she stroked

his chest and abs with her fingernails, she leaned down, kissed him. He plunged his tongue into her mouth, rolled her onto her back, and kissed her with a ferocity that had her undulating beneath him.

When he slowed the kiss down, she opened her eyes. Even in the dark, she couldn't miss the passion in his. Then, a smile, filled with so much love, she wondered if she was dreaming.

He caressed her cheek. "Forever," he murmured.

That snapped her back to reality like a freezing cold shower. "Whoa, baby, you gotta slow down."

"I lost fifteen years. Not losing another second."

She ran her fingers down his cut arms, appreciating his bulging biceps beneath soft, tanned skin. Even in the dim light, she could see the black ink of his tats.

He was right. They had lost so much time, but looking back wouldn't change a thing.

"Tie me up and blindfold me," she said.

His eyebrows jutted up. "I thought you said you didn't like being tied up."

"You were listening."

He smiled. "Yes, I was."

"I've never *trusted* anyone enough to be restrained."

He folded her in his arms, married his lips to hers, and kissed her with his entire being. When the embrace ended, he stared into her eyes. "I got you."

He retreated into his closet, returning with several neck ties, then told her to lie on her back widthwise across the bed.

"Arms over your head," he said.

He tied her wrists together, tucked the extra material under the mattress to hold her in place. Excitement coursed through her, her heart rate quickening with anticipation.

"Spread. Your. Legs."

He secured one ankle in place with a tie, then did the same for her other leg.

She loved how he took control, how he could make her tremble from the intensity in his gaze and the grittiness in his voice.

"Safe word," he said as he planked over her.

"Yellow and red."

Standing behind her, he bent over, kissed her. "I'll stop when you get close to coming."

Tingles shot through her. "I love edging."

He covered her eyes with a neck tie, kissed her again. Once, twice, then he moved away, leaving the air cold in his wake.

Anticipation had her senses at high alert. She tried calming her breathing, but she was too aroused. His, however, was slow and strong.

His fingers trailed down her neck, her chest, across a nipple, then past her abs to her pussy where he passed over her clit, caressing her thigh and her calf. On a growl, he licked and sucked her big toe. One-by-one, he sucked them all, while she squirmed with carnal delight.

He trailed his tongue up the inside of her thigh to her pussy, his warm breath making her moan. Everything was magnified by the blindfold and the ties binding her to the bed.

Submitting to him meant she was giving him control. A simple act of trust to show him he was forgiven. Would he know that?

He ran his tongue over her opening, around her clit, then nothing. He was still on the bed, but he wasn't touching her. A surge of frustration had her arching up, desperate for more. Always more.

Then, his beautifully sculpted lips attached to her nipple, gently sucking and licking her tender flesh. Her moans filled the silence, while her clit throbbed with passion.

"Everything about you turns me on," he murmured. "Every fucking thing."

"Thank you," she whispered.

"I hated that about you," he said.

He licked her other nipple, teased the first one with tender strokes of his thumb. Teasing and teasing until she couldn't stop thrashing, begging him to relieve her suffering.

More than anything, she loved his personal brand of sexual torture.

He kissed her shoulder, nibbled her ear, bit the lobe. The sharp sting of pain made her whimper.

"Pain, pleasure?"

"Both," she rasped.

He rolled her onto her side, slapped her ass. Another whimper. Then, he rolled her onto her back, raked his hands down the sides of her torso, igniting erogenous zones she didn't know existed. Everywhere he touched—her elbow, the back of her knee—came alive, her skin tingling, her senses on high alert. His gritty growls slicked her pussy.

Every caress sent her to flying closer and closer to the sun, her body burning, her insides throbbing so hard, she needed to warn him away.

"I'm dying for you," she whispered.

He stopped touching her and the thrumming eased. His absence left her with a heightened sense of expectation. Every second he wasn't touching her was torture.

Sheer torture.

He opened a drawer. He ripped open a condom packet. Then, silence.

"You're so beautiful," he murmured.

She imagined him staring down at her, her naked body on full display. Then, he climbed on the bed, planked over her, but didn't touch her. He brushed his lips to her ear. "I will love you forever."

She melted.

He seared her with a passionate kiss and her need skyrocketed. When their kiss ended, he left a sensual trail of kisses

down her body, until he stopped at her sex. He licked her opening, twirled his tongue around her clit, slid a finger inside her
heat.

"Ohgod," she groaned.

One, two, and three digits entered her, and she started
gyrating on the bed again. Her insides roared to life, the lust
returning with a whoosh of energy.

"So tight, like a virgin," he rasped.

"Yessss," she hissed. "A virgin."

The build was intense, the orgasm barreling toward her.

"Stop if you don't want me to come," she warned.

He withdrew, leaving her teetering on the edge, her insides
throbbing so hard, she couldn't think.

"Breathe," he whispered.

She took a slow, soothing breath.

"Again," he murmured.

One more slow inhale, slow exhale.

As she calmed down, he whispered, "Talk to me, baby,"

"I'm a ball of nerves."

"I'm going to untie you so I can take you from behind."

"Okay," she replied, her insides tightening in anticipation.

He ran gentle fingers through her hair, kissed her forehead,
her lips. Then, he removed the ties from her wrists and ankles.

"On your knees."

She rolled over, raised her ass, and waited. The head of his
cock at her opening, then the glorious slide as he entered her.

"So good," she bit out. "So, so gooooood."

Slow, deep thrusts sent streams of pleasure shooting
through her. He ran his hands down her back, then one more
smack to her ass.

"Mmm," she moaned as the sting heightened her arousal.

He thrust and thrust, deep, then shallow, before reaching
around and fondling her breasts. A pinch to both nipples had
her racing toward another orgasm.

"Gonna come," she said.

With absolute precision, he stopped. Hands gone, cock gone. He moved, then gently removed her blindfold. "Sit on me."

He was in the middle of the bed, his fiery gaze waiting for her. She crawled over to him, straddled him on her knees, and lowered herself on his shaft.

"Oh, yes," she groaned as the euphoria spun through her.

He stared into her eyes with a hunger that left her breathless. They came together in a powerful kiss. Tongues thrashing, their feral moans and groans had her panting. She raked her fingers down his back while gliding faster and faster on his shaft. He cupped one breast, grabbed her hip with his other hand.

And he took control.

She stared into his eyes, their kisses ravenous, their sounds primal.

"I'm coming," she murmured.

Mind-numbing ecstasy destroyed her, overtaking every cell of her being. Spasm after spasm of pure pleasure sent her reeling as she surrendered to the one man she could *not* live without.

"I'm coming, baby," he growled.

He married his lips to hers and claimed her with a searing kiss.

Without question, she was his.

When they stilled, they gazed into each other's eyes.

Love surrounded her... until reality invaded her perfect moment. She was as vulnerable as she'd been all those years ago. Fear hovered, but she didn't latch on. Nothing would ruin this.

As if sensing her feelings, he said, "I meant what I said. I will love you forever, and *always* put you first."

The fear floated away, replaced with confidence. She returned his smile. "I love you too."

Moments passed before she pulled off him. Together, they went into the bathroom, got ready for bed. Rather than sleep in the other bedroom, she stayed.

No words needed.

In bed, he folded her into his arms.

"This is it," he murmured. "You know that, right?"

Silence.

"I love you with my whole soul," he said.

She lifted her face, peered into his eyes. "You haven't said that to me in a long time."

"I never stopped feeling it."

Neither did I.

THE NEXT MORNING, they were out the door at five-forty-five. Both wearing leathers, motorcycle boots on their feet.

They mounted their bikes, pulled on their helmets, and rolled into the driveway as the sun teased the horizon with the day's first light. After the garage door closed, they started their engines, and headed out.

Slash loved riding, loved that Carrera was riding alongside her.

The July Fourth Holiday week brought light traffic as they rode out of the sleepy neighborhood, onto the main road, continuing to the GW Parkway. She loved riding her Bandit, loved the breeze flowing past her, the freedom that came when flying down the road on a motorcycle.

Carrera on his Triumph Bonneville Speedmaster was total eye candy. More than anything, she had someone who shared her love of riding.

He signaled, slowed, turned into an overlook on the parkway. She pulled in, parked beside him. They had the place to themselves. After dismounting, they removed their helmets. He clasped her hand, walked down a path. Below lay the rushing waters of the Potomac. She found a boulder, perched on top. He stood alone, peering out at the stunning vista, the sun bursting forth on a new day filled with promise.

Despite everything going on, she paused to appreciate the beauty. As she took in the stunning view, she thanked God that Elsa was safe. She recommitted to doubling-down on finding the monster who was snatching up women and doing God-knows-what with them.

A chill streaked down her spine, but she didn't want to lose the gift of the moment, so she shifted her sights toward Carrera. He was studying her intently as he made his way over.

He eased onto the boulder, brought her hand to his lips, kissed her fingers, then her palm. "I love this."

"Me too."

"This is good for us."

They sat in a peaceful silence, their fingers entwined, their breathing in perfect sync.

"Babe," he said.

She turned toward him.

"I'm going to ask you to marry me."

Her heart leapt for joy, but she needed to be the voice of reason.

"You gotta take things down. Way down."

"I'm not asking you now." Then, he flashed that killer smile that made her heart skip a beat. "I would if I thought you'd say yes."

"You have one speed."

"Full throttle. You know that."

She inhaled the fresh air, her gaze locked on the rushing water below. She loved him enough to say yes, but they were just finding their footing again. They sat in silence for another ten, but reality crept back in. She had seven missing women to find, an arsonist to catch, and a pedophile to kill.

"I could stay out here all day," she said, "but I've got to work."

"Did I tell you I'm having a Fourth of July party on one of my cruise ships?"

"You mentioned it to Luciano."

"Will you be my date?"

"Sounds fun." After a beat, she said, "But I feel the pressure of these cases."

He pulled her onto his lap. "Work will always be there. There will always be bad actors who need to be caught or taken out. That won't end. You gotta promise me one thing."

"What?"

"We put *us* first." He kissed her cheek. "After these cases, there will be more. I don't want us to be that couple who puts work first."

"You're right, but my work is a big part of who I am."

"I'm asking for balance. What we're building will be the *best* part of our lives, and I don't want us to lose sight of that."

"I can do that." One more kiss before she pushed off his lap.

Hand in hand, they returned to their bikes. There, she noticed a silver, two-door coupe parked near the lookout exit. She pulled on her helmet, flipped up the wind shield. "How long has that car been there?"

He glanced over. "No idea. Why?"

"No reason."

They mounted their bikes, started them up, and headed out. As they approached the car, it sped away, but not before she got a glimpse of the driver.

Alarms blared in her head.

The driver's face was covered in a ski mask.

For fuck's sake, we're being tailed.

21

THE PROPOSAL

Carrera

The ride home was just as much fun as the ride to Great Falls. The view from his side mirrors was ten times better than the road ahead of him, and he kept stealing glances at Slash. For most of the journey, she rode behind him, but closer to his house, she pulled up alongside.

Back in the garage, they removed their helmets. The divot between her eyes was deeper than expected, especially since they'd been out riding.

"What's going on?" he asked.

"It's nothing."

He ran the back of his hand down her cheek. "Tell me."

"That car at the lookout... the driver was wearing a ski mask."

"What the fuck? Did you get the tag number?"

"They sped out. I didn't want to race off and try to catch them. Not on the parkway. Now, if that had been the beltway, I would have caught them."

"Wasn't it a two-door?" he asked.

"Yeah, silver coupe," she said as they entered the house.

The delicious aroma of pancakes filled his nostrils. In the kitchen, G-ma was busy at work.

"Are we having family over?" he asked.

"Just us. How was your ride?"

"Great," he replied.

After breakfast, he drove G-ma to her house. He was impressed with how she stayed strong despite the charred remains. They salvaged what they could, loaded up his truck, and returned home.

Slash was holed up in the office the rest of the day.

That evening, Alexandra Wilde called her. Twenty minutes later, she emerged from his home office with a relieved smile on her face.

"It's all set," Slash said. "Alexandra's going to the club after the holiday weekend to talk to Karen."

"Karen won't like that," he said.

"No, she won't, but her ego's pretty inflated. She might like the attention. I gave Alexandra the total scoop on her."

"How'd you handle ALPHA?"

"Alexandra said would never divulge what she knows or her sources," Slash explained. "Her focus is the missing women."

Carrera's phone rang. "It's the arson detective." He answered, put the call on speaker. "Santini."

"Mr. Santini, I'm calling with an update," said the detective. "I spoke to a few of Mrs. Santini's neighbors. No one heard anything. Two have security cameras and they said they'd check for anyone walking by the house. It's going to take a little longer to get the report back on the accelerant. Has anyone contacted your grandmother out of the blue? Someone who heard about the fire and wanted to see how she was doing?"

"Just family," Carrera replied.

"Sorry I don't have more information."

"Thanks for the call." Carrera hung up. "He's got nothing."

"Something will turn up," G-ma said. "Nobody burns down a house and disappears."

THE NEXT EVENING, Carrera entered Blue Suit ready to execute their plan. He'd worn a body-hugging, short-sleeved shirt that stretched against his muscles, and tight pants. Slash had suggested he show off his tats, something Karen had never seen. She also told him to bring his helmet inside with him. This Carrera had a gritty, more dangerous vibe. Slash was confident Karen—and every other woman in the club—would be drawn to him.

He didn't give a fuck about them. He was doing this—all of this—for Slash.

He slid onto a barstool, set his helmet on the stool beside him, ordered a top-shelf whiskey, neat.

"If you're looking for Slash, she isn't here," said the bartender.

"No problem," he said. "I'm Claude."

The bartender nodded. "Bradley."

Carrera sipped the drink while Bradley waited on other clubbers. Five minutes later, Alexandra Wilde pulled up beside him. He glanced over, did a double take, and shot her a smile.

"Alexandra, Claude Amos," Carrera said.

"Claude, good to see you."

He set his helmet on the bar. "Join me."

"I'm sorry your story got delayed," she said. "The magazine publisher pushed it back a month."

"All good. What brings you by?"

"Several dancers here have gone missing."

"That's not good."

"I wanted to interview some of the employees."

Carrera waved over the bartender. "Can you talk to journalist Alexandra Wilde?"

"'Bout what?" Bradley asked.

"The dancers who've gone missing."

Bradley furrowed his brow. "What are you talking about?"

"Yeah, seven women who worked here all vanished," Alexandra explained.

"We've had a high turnover lately, but the GM said they'd ghosted."

"I'd love to get you on the record," Alexandra said.

"Let me get Karen." Bradley made a call. "Hey, boss, a reporter has some questions for you." Bradley hung up. "She'll be right over."

A quick minute later, Carrera caught Karen beelining toward the bar.

Turning toward Alexandra, he murmured, "Here we go."

"Bradley!" Karen called out. "Where is she?"

Bradley pointed to Alexandra.

Karen pulled up behind Alexandra. "I'm Karen Woodside, General Manager. What's going on?"

"Alexandra Wilde." Alexandra mentioned the television station she worked for, along with the nationally syndicated crime show that she hosted. "I'd like to talk with you about the women who've gone missing from Blue Suit."

Karen steeled her spine. "What women?"

"Seven dancers have gone missing in the past five months," Alexandra replied. "Are you the owner?"

"I run the club."

"The public needs to know there's a predator out there."

Though Karen looked genuinely surprised, Carrera wasn't assuming her innocence.

Karen's attention jumped to him, then she checked out his tats. Slash had dressed him, and she'd been right.

Her cheeks flushed and she beamed. "Mr. Amos, hi." Then, she glanced at Alexandra and her smile fell away. "Are you two together?"

"I'm here alone," Carrera said. "Ms. Wilde interviewed me a few months ago and we just ran into each other."

"I did an extensive piece on Mr. Amos for Uber-Wealth magazine," Alexandra said. "His picture will be on the magazine cover."

Karen flicked her gaze to him. "What do you do?"

"Read the article," he replied.

Alexandra leaned toward Karen. "Just between us... he's being modest. Mr. Amos is filthy rich and very available. He's got three homes, one in the Riviera, one in..."

"Palm Beach," Carrera added. "And a third in Malibu."

"Oh, wow," Karen whispered.

"Karen, you want these missing women found, don't you?" Carrera pushed.

"They're not *missing*," Karen said. "They ghosted on me."

"Then you should talk about that," Carrera urged. "If you don't, the club will get a bad rep."

Karen nibbled her finger. "I'm not sure about this."

"I can come back and speak with the owner," Alexandra said.

"No, that won't work," Karen replied.

"Why not?" Alexandra asked.

"I'll stay with you, make sure things go smoothly." Carrera flashed Karen an encouraging smile.

She held his gaze for an extra beat.

C'mon, take the damn bait, for fuck's sake.

"We can talk in my office," Karen said.

As Carrera pushed off the stool, he caught Alexandra's eye.

As they made their way through the club, Karen asked, "Where's your free-use girl?"

"I'm not sure that's working out," he said.

"Why's that?"

"I need variety," he replied.

With a definite pep in her step, Karen entered her office.

She sat behind her desk, steeled her spine. He and Alexandra eased into guest chairs. Alexandra set her phone on the desk, hit record. "How long have you been running Blue Suit?"

"Turn that off," Karen said. After Alexandra did, Karen continued. "I started last year. Before that I was with ALPH—"

"*Karen*," Alexandra said, cutting her off. "you have a chance to be a hero,"

"Me?"

"If these women didn't ghost, don't you want to be the reason they're found?"

Karen's upper lip curled. "They ghosted, but whatever."

"You said you're partners with the owner," Alexandra continued. "Who is that?"

"I can't say."

"Why not?"

"I was told not to," Karen replied.

Are you fucking kidding me?

Alexandra read the names of the missing women.

"Who's your source?" Karen asked.

Alexandra tucked her hair behind her ear. "Police have questioned you about these women, but—"

"Look," Karen snapped. "I don't have time to chase down these women. They aren't on payroll, so they either work their shift or they don't. Some are hustlers, others show up whenever. I've got to manage the servers and the bartenders, deal with the cooks, stay on top of inventory, handle drunk customers, and sanitize the VIP rooms."

"Don't you mean VIP *room*?" Carrera asked.

Karen stilled, her eyes narrowed. "No. I mean VIP *rooms*, Mr. Amos." He couldn't miss the bite in her voice. "People go missing every day. Do your damn story, but keep my name out of it."

"Can I speak with your dancers?" Alexandra asked.

"Absolutely not," she said. "I don't need them panicking over nothing."

"If your interview helps find these women, maybe you'll get your old job back," Carrera said.

A coldness poured from Karen's eyes. "I'm stuck here, running this shit nightclub. This is my life, and all because they accused me of impeding an investigation by withholding evidence." She glared at Alexandra. "*That's* your story."

"What is?" Alexandra asked.

"A federal law enforcement agency that doesn't exist on paper," Karen bit out.

"Right now, I'm following up on these women." Alexandra rose from the sofa, dropped a business card on the desk. "When you're ready to talk, let me know." She turned to Carrera. "It was good to see you. I'll let you know when your story publishes."

Carrera stood. "I'll walk you out."

"Mr. Amos," Karen blurted. "Are you coming back?"

"My private jet is waiting," Carrera replied. "I'm flying to Palm Beach for the holiday. Enjoy the Fourth."

"I'll be here," Karen said. "With the losers."

Outside, Carrera walked Alexandra to her car, gave her a hug. "Thanks for doing this."

"There is a story here," Alexandra said. "I'll do some digging."

"That would be great because we're not getting anywhere."

"We? I thought you'd been promoted to King of the FBI."

Carrera chuffed out a laugh.

"No worries about Karen's comment on the secret agency," Alexandra said. "I'm *not* following up on that. Sin would murder me in my sleep."

Carrera wasn't surprised Alexandra knew about ALPHA. Her husband, Crockett, and Sin had been close friends for decades.

"Tell Crockett I'm using a Spy Fly."

Alexandra smiled. "He'll love that. We're sorry we can't make your holiday river cruise."

They said their goodbyes, and she drove away. As he made his way to his motorcycle, he checked the Spy Fly video, but Greg hadn't entered the club all evening.

Where are you?

He pulled on his helmet, mounted his bike, and rode into the night.

While the set-up with Claude Amos and Alexandra been a good idea, he hadn't learned anything new. Karen wasn't talking, she was sticking with her story, and she was protecting the owner. For a woman who ran her mouth about ALPHA every chance she got, she was tight-lipped as hell about everything else.

ON THE FOURTH OF JULY, at seventy-thirty in the evening, Carrera's boat cruise party was well under way. The Potomac River excursion had started with cocktails at five, they sailed at six, sat down for dinner at seven. His guests were seated inside, though a few had ventured outside to take in the sights as they rolled slowly down the river.

He and Slash were seated at a table with G-ma, his dad, his cousins Luciano and Teddy, his sister Jazz and her boyfriend, Russell.

Nearby, Sin and Evangeline were dining with Dakota and Providence. Stryker and Emerson were at a table with Cooper and Danielle, and Jericho and Liv. Right next to him were Hawk and Addison, Prescott and Jacqueline, and Rebel and Brit. Like every year, he'd also invited his entire staff at Carrera cruises. For those who'd opted to work, they were paid extra for working the event.

He chuckled.

"What?" Slash whispered.

"All that's missing is the President."

"I'm sure he'd love a few hours on a Carrera cruise. Don't forget Z."

"I am Z," he murmured.

She caressed his shoulder. "You're baby Z, like baby Yoda." She gave his shoulder an affectionate squeeze before letting go.

"You really know how to build a guy's ego," he said.

"You don't need my help with your ego, but, how's this? Baby, you're one of the most powerful, influential men in law enforcement." She arched an eyebrow. "That's actually the truth."

"Crazy huh?"

"Maybe I was smart to hitch my wagon to you."

"I hitched my wagon to *you*," he said. "Let's not forget who really holds all the power."

The playful gleam in her eyes made him smile.

She held the power, and she knew it.

Tonight, she looked so stunning he couldn't keep his eyes off her. She'd worn her hair up in a twist, a simple black halter dress, and open-toed stilettos. Around her neck, she wore the diamond necklace he'd bought her.

"Elegant, beautiful, and all mine," he whispered.

The servers appeared with trays of desserts, hot pots of coffee, and flutes of champagne. When the servers finished, he stood, his champagne flute in hand. Conversations continued until Jericho whistled.

"Speech time," Jericho thundered.

The chatty group fell silent.

"Thanks, brother," Carrera said. "Happy Fourth. We're celebrating our country's day of independence, but it came with a lot of bloodshed, a tremendous loss. But I promised you last year that I would keep my toast positive—"

"Bless you," Luciano said, and the group laughed.

"We're living fast-paced lives, raising families, running successful companies. I appreciate that every year we come together for our own celebration. Thank you to my employees at Carrera Cruises, especially to my Dad for stepping up—"

His dad cleared his throat, glanced over at Jazz.

"It's all good," Jazz said with a smile. "I loooooove my new job."

"I'm glad it worked out," Carrera said to his sister. "Congratulations to Gracie on her promotion."

Gracie raised her flute to him.

"To my close friends, I love you all. Nothing I wouldn't do for any of you."

"Same," Rebel replied.

"We love you, brother," Hawk added.

"To my family," Carrera raised his glass. "Love you guys."

"We love you, cuz," Teddy replied. "Especially the free cruise, great food, and open bar."

Everyone laughed.

"To Slash." He raised his glass. "The best part of my life."

"Who-hoo!" Brit cheered. "That's the best news."

"To Carrera and Slash," Addison added. "We love you guys."

Lots of clinking glasses while they toasted to the evening.

Before he sat, he kissed Slash.

"Thank you," she murmured.

With the annual toast over, conversations resumed.

Russell stood. "Excuse me." He waited until all eyes were on him. "Hi, I'm Russell Fitzpatrick, long-time friend of Carrera's." He grinned. "I hope ya'll don't mind if I make a little speech of my own." He smiled at Jazz. "Jazz, you were always Carrera's annoying baby sis, so I put up with you when we were kids."

The group laughed.

"Now, you're the most important person in the world to me. I hope you say yes." He knelt, opened up a ring box. "Jasmine Santini, will you marry me?"

She squealed. "Yes! Oh, yes, I'll marry you!"

He slid the ring on her finger and stood. They shared a quick peck before he grinned at the group. "The future Congressman Santini and Mrs. Santini."

Silence.

No applause.

Everyone was staring at everyone else. Carrera jumped his gaze from his grandmother to Luciano, then back to his sister who looked deliriously happy.

"Don't you mean Fitzpatrick?" Luciano asked.

"Nah, bro, I gotta go with Santini. I mean, Fitzpatrick. Who the hell are we? A bunch of nobodies."

"Congratulations," Jericho boomed as a thin applause filled the cabin.

"When's the big day?" Carrera asked.

"I'd love a long engagement and a fairytale wedding," Jazz replied. "What do you think, Russ? Next year?"

"Why wait?" Russell replied. "When you know, you know. I'm thinking in a week, maybe two, down at the courthouse."

Jazz's joyful expression got slapped off her face. "Wait, what? You can't be for real."

"And I'd love for Carrera to be my best man," Russell said as Jazz tugged him back down.

"We have to talk about all of this," Jazz said.

Carrera eyed his grandmother. She looked as surprised as he felt. Rather than say anything disparaging, he forked into his dessert. "Nothing says the Fourth of July like a piece of apple pie."

The ship dropped anchor in the river and the captain announced the fireworks would be starting soon. As everyone made their way outside, Russell beelined over.

"Pretty exciting, huh?" he asked, his focus fixed on Slash.

"Congratulations," she replied.

Jazz joined them. "We're going all the way to the White House, right honey?"

Russell beamed. "With the Santini name, there's no stopping us." He shifted his attention to Carrera. "You and Slash, that's cool. So, Carrera, I gotta ask... will you be my best man?"

Carrera stood, extended his hand. "Sure thing."

As he slid his gaze to his sister, he couldn't help but wonder if Russell's motives were pure. But he didn't want to make something out of nothing. If his sister was happy, he was happy for her.

If Russell was using her, he'd have to answer to the Santinis

When it came to his family... blood was thicker than water.

Much, much thicker.

22

LOVE

Slash

The following evening, Slash exited her SUV, and made her way toward Jericho Road. Jericho Savage's popular restaurant was known for its fall-off-the-bone ribs and killer fries—as well as line-dancing.

Slash was frustrated as hell and obsessing over Greg. Who was he? Why was he so difficult to track down? What did he do when he wasn't at Blue Suit? Did he have anything to do with the missing women?

So many questions, but no answers.

If she didn't uncover something about him—or find a new person of interest—ALPHA would move in for an arrest on the prostitution.

Maybe that's for the best.

The prostitution—or whatever the hell was happening in the back room—would stop. She could return to ALPHA and focus on training with BLACK OPS.

To make matters worse, there were no leads in the arson investigation. Absolutely nothing.

She hoped her evening with Jilly would help dispel some of her frustration. As she made her way to the entrance, several groups of people were waiting outside. She opened the door, walked into the popular eatery, and stopped short. The restaurant was jam-packed with people waiting to be seated.

Jilly said she'd try to get there early, but Slash had arranged for them to eat at Jericho's private table. She stopped at the hostess stand.

"Slash," she said. "I've got a res at Jericho's table."

As the hostess checked, Slash glanced around. Jilly was at the bar, waving her down.

"Hmm," said the hostess. "There's a group eating there now. Let me see what I can do."

The hostess handed her a pager.

The bar area was four-deep. Some were eating at the bar and at the nearby tables, while others were nursing drinks while waiting to be seated.

As she got closer to Jilly, a guy in a ball cap—who'd been standing next to Jilly—walked toward the back of the restaurant. Slash slipped into his spot.

"Hey," she said.

"There you are." Jilly hugged her. "Did you see the guy who was just here?"

"Not really. Why?"

"He's a customer from Blue Suit. Before the holiday, he asked for some private time in a VIP room. When I told him no, we ended up chatting at the bar."

"Is that usual?" Slash said.

"Oh, sure. Some just want to talk, but most are hoping you'll change your mind and go into a private room with them." Jilly rolled her eyes.

"Was he one of your regulars?"

"No, I just talked to him that one time," Jilly said. "After we talked, he tipped me $500."

That got Slash's full attention. "What did he look like?"

"I would never have remembered, but I just saw him."

A hit of energy charged through her. "He's here?" Slash pushed off the stool, stood on her toes and searched the crowd.

"Yeah, but he went to the men's room," Jilly said.

"White guy with a beard and mustache?"

"Yeah, that's the one."

"I'll be two minutes. If he comes back, keep him talking, but do *not* leave with him."

Jilly grimaced. "I'd never leave with some random guy."

Slash bulled her way through the bar, her gaze sweeping the eatery in search of her target. Once in the main dining room, she did a broad sweep for a man in a cap, then circled back to anyone with a beard.

That's half the damn restaurant.

She strode to the men's room, pushed open the door. Two guys at urinals glanced over.

"You're in the men's," said one of them.

"Have you seen a guy in a ball cap, beard and mustache?" she asked as she strode toward the stalls.

"I'm busy peeing," said one.

"Nope," said the other.

She looked under the door. Though she saw no legs, she kicked open each door to ensure he wasn't standing on the toilet.

"Dammit," she bit out.

She left the restroom, strode into the large dance hall at the back of the restaurant. Country music filled every corner of the room while a large crowd strutted in unison to the beat. She did a quick check for a bearded guy, but didn't see anyone that resembled Greg. She spotted a man sitting in the corner with a beard and mustache, but no cap. As she got closer, she saw he had a receding hairline and looked much older than her target.

Out she flew, pausing to check the smaller dining rooms. No luck finding Greg.

Fuck. Fuck.

Her pager buzzed. She hurried back to Jilly. "Did he come back?"

"No, but I saw a guy in a cap heading toward the exit. He might have left."

Slash charged through the crowd. Once outside, she hurried into the parking lot.

She was aware that she must've looked insane, but she didn't give a damn. She scanned the area, but didn't see him.

She pulled her phone from her back pocket, called Carrera.

"Hey, babe," he answered. "How's dinner?"

"I think Greg was here," she said. "I didn't get a visual, didn't get him in a vehicle either. Can you see if you can pull surveillance—"

"At Jericho Road?"

"Jilly ran into some guy here who fits Greg's description."

"I'll ask Jericho for parking lot video."

"Thank you."

"Alright, babe, try to chill. Don't forget G-ma's French fries. I love you."

"I love you." She hung up, returned to the hostess stand.

"Sorry about the mix-up," the hostess said. "Jericho's table is ready."

She retrieved Jilly, followed the hostess to the horseshoe booth tucked in the back corner. After the server introduced herself, she asked who knew the owner.

"I do," Slash replied. "He's a close friend of my boy—my man. Whatever."

Jilly and the server laughed.

"I don't know what to call my boyfriend either," said the server. "Mr. Jericho said that dinner is on the house. Can I start you off with a glass of wine or something from our bar?"

"I could use a shot of something," Slash mumbled.

"Sure thing," said the server.

"No, just a glass of sauvignon blanc." Slash said.

"Chardonnay," Jilly replied.

The server left, and Slash scanned the room. When her gaze fell on Jilly, her brow was knitted together.

"Not gonna lie, but you scared the crap out of me back there," Jilly said.

"Run me through it again," Slash said. "You got here first."

"Yeah, I got here first." Jilly leaned close. "What is up with you?"

"My gut says that guy has something to do with the missing dancers."

Jilly stared at her for an extra beat. "Didn't you warn me about someone?"

"Yes, after Deb went missing. White guy, wild hair, beard, mustache. Goes by Greg. What's this guy's name?"

"I don't think he told me."

"Did he want you to leave with him just now?"

Jilly swallowed. "He asked me if I was alone. When I told him I was meeting someone, he invited me for dinner tomorrow."

That's him. That's Greg.

Her pulse kicked up speed. "What did you tell him?"

"I told him no," Jilly replied. "Slash, I don't go out with customers."

"If you see him again, *anywhere*, text me. I don't care what time it is," Slash said. "Just because he tipped you five-hundred doesn't mean you owe him a thing."

"If there's one thing I know for sure," Jilly said, "I don't owe any man anything."

Slash breathed for the first time all evening. Jilly was safe. Jilly was smart, and Jilly was not going to be this monster's next victim.

The server returned with their wines and four small appetizer plates. "Sorry for the wait. It's crazy tonight." She smiled. "But it's always like this. Anyway, Mr. Jericho always makes sure his guests get these appetizers. Are you ready to order?"

"Ribs and Fries," Slash said.

"Two," Jilly agreed.

"And I need a large fry to go," Slash said.

When the server left, Jilly said, "I didn't know you had a boyfriend."

"The relationship is new," Slash said. "My first love has circled back around."

"Gotta love a recycled man."

Slash laughed as she glanced around the restaurant.

Is Greg still here watching me or did he bolt? Was Jilly his target?

Anger lodged in her heart. She sipped the chilled wine, letting it roll down her parched throat.

I will never stop hunting you. Never.

An hour and a half later, Slash pulled into Carrera's garage. With the bag of fries in hand, she entered the house.

Laughter from the kitchen drew Slash in that direction. Sitting around the table were Carrera and Elsa. To her surprise Jazz and Russell were also there, a chocolate Pistachio cake in the center of the table.

This oughta be interesting.

"There she is," Carrera said as he rose from the table. After giving her a kiss hello, he asked how her dinner was.

"Super chill," she replied.

"Is that bag for me?" Elsa asked.

Slash set the bag on the table in front of Elsa, pulled a plate and the bottle of ketchup from the fridge. "Enjoy."

Elsa got busy munching on fries. Slash wanted to start reviewing the surveillance video at Jericho Road, but she'd have to wait until Jazz and Russell left.

"We're talking about the wedding," Carrera rose from the table, held up the coffee pot. "More?"

Jazz and Russell declined.

"These are the best," Elsa said between bites.

Slash pulled a mug, set it on the counter in front of Carrera. While he filled it, she offered a smile, but her thoughts were still anchored on Greg. Carrera kissed the top of her head.

"You two are super cute together," Jazz said. "It's totally weird to see you like this. I mean you've been hating on each other so long." She regarded Slash. "I'm happy for you. I mean that."

Slash nodded, grateful Jazz had finally stopped thinking of her as the she-devil.

Russell's phone rang. "I've got to take this." He pushed out of the chair. "Russell Fitzpatrick." He meandered toward the front of the house while talking.

"G-ma said you moved in here," Jazz said to Slash.

Here comes a ration of shit.

"Just until your grandmother is settled," Slash said.

"You're not leaving," Carrera said.

"I agree." Elsa pushed the plate away. "I'm going to save some for tomorrow."

"They never taste the same the next day, G-ma," Jazz said.

"Do you want some?" G-ma asked.

"No, I'm stuffed from lasagna," Jazz forked a bite of chocolate cake into her mouth. "Russell surprised me. He'd planned to campaign all evening, but he got home in time for dinner."

"When's the special election?" G-ma asked.

"Two weeks," Jazz replied. "He's so far ahead in the polls, there's no way he won't get elected." After a beat, she said, "Slash, can I talk to you real quick?"

"Go ahead."

"In private."

Slash had been leaning against the center island. She glanced at Carrera before following Jazz onto the porch.

"Can I ask you a question?" Jazz began.

"Go for it."

"It's about men... I haven't had a ton of boyfriends, but they all wanted sex. Russell, well... he wants to wait until we're married."

"How do you feel about that?"

"I'm not a super sexual person, but I thought we'd at least see if we're compatible. I mean, we don't even make out that much."

"Have you talked to him about it?"

"I mentioned it, but he's so busy with the campaign that we usually just see each other at his campaign headquarters."

This was the first actual conversation she'd had with Jazz. A sliver of hope filled her heart.

Maybe Carrera's family won't condemn me for the rest of my life.

"He told me he thinks of me like the Madonna," Jazz continued. "I'm pure, and he wants me to stay that way."

"Even after you're married?" Slash asked.

Jazz shrugged.

That's fucked up.

"Do you spend the night together?"

"No," she replied. "We have dinner at his restaurant."

"What do you talk about?" Slash asked.

"The campaign, our lives in politics, how famous we're going to be."

Yup, this is messed up.

"Marriage is supposed to be forever," Slash said. "I know people get divorced, but if you pick the right person, you'll *want* to be with him." She held up her hand. "I know I'm the last person you want to get marital advice from—"

"I had a talk with G-ma on the river cruise," Jazz said. "She asked me to stop being a B to you. She said that you risked your life for her, that you've endured our crap for fifteen years, and you deserve our respect. Then, she said that Carrera is in love with you and he isn't falling out this time, or she'll kill him herself."

Slash laughed. "That sounds like Elsa Santini, doesn't it? Have you talked to your friends about your relationship with Russell?"

"I talked to my friend, Gracie. She told me that every couple is different, and that we have to find what works for us, even if that's different from everyone else."

"That's good advice," Slash said. "What do you want to do?"

Jazz started moving her hips like she was playing with a hula-hoop.

Slash laughed as Russell poked his head out. "Ready to take off?"

"Gotta go," Jazz said. "Thanks for talking. Maybe we can become friends, you know, one day."

"Maybe we can," Slash replied as they headed inside.

After Jazz and Russell left, Carrera said, "Jericho sent me the surveillance from earlier."

They entered his home office, sat side by side at his desk.

To her surprise, Elsa wandered in. "What are you looking for?"

Slash offered her chair to Elsa, then retrieved one from the kitchen. "A White guy in a ball cap with a beard and mustache either going in or coming out of Jericho Road."

Carrera started the surveillance, and they watched for the man. Every time they spotted a guy wearing a cap or someone with facial hair, Carrera would stop the video.

"There," Slash said. "That's Jilly."

They watched as Jilly made her way through the parking lot, entered the restaurant. Moments later, a lone man in a ball cap and sunglasses walked into the restaurant parking lot, head down.

"That's him," Slash said.

Carrera stopped and enlarged the image. Unfortunately, that turned the man blurry, but he snapped a pic anyway. "I'll load it into Stryker's IDware program."

"This is so exciting," Elsa said.

As the software program searched for a match, Carrera started the video. The three sat huddled around the laptop.

"Let's review this on your monitor," Slash suggested.

On the big screen, she studied the man as he made his way inside. "He's got no tats, no jewelry. He's wearing a dark blue shirt and blue shorts, and he fits right in."

Ten minutes after that, Slash pulled in, found a spot, and parked. As she watched herself, she blurted, "I've never seen my walk before."

"You've got swag, baby," Carrera said. "Sexy swag."

"Very confident," Elsa added.

Five minutes after Slash entered the restaurant, the man hurried out. As he made his way through the parking lot, he glanced over his shoulder.

"Did you see that?" Elsa asked.

"I sure did," Slash replied. "Is he checking to see if I'm following him?"

"Looks that way." Carrera stopped the video, snapped a pic, and uploaded that into the facial recognition software.

"He saw me at Blue Suit," Slash said.

"That wouldn't send him running scared," Carrera said. "If anything, wouldn't he want to talk to you?"

"If he's the one taking the women, then no," she replied. "I'm not his type."

Concern filled Elsa's eyes. "Are you in danger?"

Slash smiled. "I hope so."

"Stop messing with me like that," Elsa replied.

Slash wasn't joking, but she said nothing more. She would assume this man was dangerous until shown otherwise. Even so, she wasn't afraid. She'd spent most of her sixteenth year living in absolute fear. Once she moved in with Elsa, she promised herself that no matter what, she would never allow fear to rule her life again.

Carrera resumed the video. The man continued walking, head down, out of the parking lot, disappearing from sight.

"I'll request traffic cam surveillance," Slash said.

"This is nothing like my crime shows." Elsa patted their hands. "Okay, kids, I'm off to bed."

"Elsa, thank you for telling Jazz to be nice to me," Slash said.

"She wasn't supposed to say anything." After a beat, Elsa's expression fell. "I'm concerned he's using her for the Santini name."

"She told me something in confidence," Slash began. "About her and Russell."

"Tell us," Carrera said.

Slash looked from him to Elsa. At a crossroads, she stayed silent. Betraying a confidence *wasn't* something Slash did.

"We won't say anything," Elsa said. "If you're concerned about her, we should know."

"They've never been intimate," Slash said, "and Jazz doesn't know if they're sexually compatible."

"Maybe he wants to wait for the honeymoon," Elsa said.

"She told me he thinks of her as a Madonna," Slash confided.

"I had a friend whose husband was similar," Elsa said. "After their last child was born, he started having multiple affairs. That's not good. G-pa and I had a strong relationship in that department."

"Not an image I need," Carrera said.

Elsa bit back a smile. "Sexual intimacy is part of life."

"Their entire relationship is centered around his work—" Slash's thoughts came to a screeching halt.

Ah, fuck. Fuck me. That's just like Carrera and me. We're completely focused on work.

Her heart dipped.

"What?" Carrera asked.

"I thought you should know, that's all," Slash said. "Please don't—"

"Not a word," Elsa said.

"I'm *not* getting involved in Jazz's sex life," Carrera said.

Slash kissed Elsa on her cheek. "It's been a long day. I'm gonna say goodnight." She left the room trying to squelch the emotion that made her heart hurt.

She and Carrera were also uber-focused on work. Was that all this was? A relationship of convenience?

23

BREAKING THE RULES

Carrera

Carrera logged out of ALPHA, closed his laptop. "What just happened?"

"Go ask her," G-ma said.

Carrera alarmed the house, went upstairs in search of Slash. The guest bedroom door was closed.

Knock-knock.

A few seconds passed before she opened it. She wore a bathrobe, but no smile. "I'm not staying in your bed."

"That's not why I'm here."

"I'm about to jump in the shower."

"What happened back there?"

She stared into his eyes for several seconds. "Lemme shower first."

"We can talk on the porch off my bedroom."

One nod, then she shut the door.

He showered, pulled on gym shorts, and waited outside. Several minutes later, she joined him on the small screened porch off his bedroom. Standing side by side, he clasped her hand, but said nothing.

"What we have is no different than Jazz and Russell," she said breaking the silence.

Nothing could be farther from the truth, but disagreeing would put her on the defensive, push her way, and make her think she wasn't being heard.

Instead he said, "Because we're focused on the cases?"

She peered over at him.

In the moonlight, her blonde hair glowed like an angel, her electric blue eyes the beacons guiding him home.

"That's it exactly," she replied. "We hated each other, start screwing for work. Now, we're living together. You say you love me, I've said it back, but how well do you really know me?"

"I know that you're passionate about your career, you're loyal to your friends, to Elsa and Luciano. I know you're fearless and a total badass. Riding your bike frees you, the water is your happy place. You make love to me with an intensity that turns me into a beast. You're very smart, very observant," he said. "But I know you bury your feelings, you would feel abandoned if Elsa died. You're the best kisser. The. Best. Kisser. I know how you move when I'm inside you, and I know how to unleash your inner wild."

"That's a lot."

"Your lipstick is light pink and you wear smoky eye makeup, but only at night. At work, you wear a little blush on your cheeks... and the same pink lipstick. You're never without your switchblade."

She unearthed it from the pocket of her robe, and he smiled. "Like a security blanket." After a beat, he said, "you're terrified of trusting me, with good reason." He turned toward her, captivated by the light emanating from her eyes. "We are *nothing* like Jazz and Russell."

Even the darkness couldn't hide her true feelings. The

tension in the hand he'd been holding fell away, her jaw stopped ticking in her cheek. She breathed deep, releasing an audible sigh.

"I would *never* have sex with anyone for work," he said. "I did it because it was you. I wanted to do whatever it took to get back in your life."

"Sex is a pretty strong motivator," she pushed back.

He handed her his phone, told her his password. "Check my apps. I'm not on any dating sites, I have no social media accounts. I went to Blue Suit because I was semi-stalking you."

That made her smile.

She didn't check his phone, so he took that as a sign that she trusted him.

Or she doesn't care.

He held her gaze. The longer he peered into her eyes, the more he knew her truth.

She cares. She cares a lot. That's why she's questioning me, questioning us.

"I'm all in with you," he said. "One-hundred percent. I meant it when I said you hold all the power. If anyone knows how much I like control, it's you." He kissed her cheek. She didn't push him away, so he dropped a soft kiss on her lips.

She kissed him back, once. "You've given me a lot to think about."

"The longer we're together, the more we'll learn about each other. I hope that never stops. I never want us to end."

"Thank you," she whispered and wrapped her arms around his neck.

Her kiss was filled with an intensity that rocked him to his core. But it was the love in her eyes that anchored him to her.

"I'm so in love with you, it hurts," he murmured.

Rather than assume she'd stay with him, he escorted her back to the guest room. At the door, he said, "Whenever you're ready, I'm right here."

She peered up at him, the energy swirling around them. The desire to kiss her, to carry her to his bed and love her all night long had him biting back a growl. Resisting her was hard as hell, but having her in his home was much more than comfort for his grandmother and a sex partner for himself.

It was the beginning of their life together... and it meant everything to him.

One more tender kiss before he opened her bedroom door. "Good night, baby."

Walking away from her was difficult, but he wanted her to come to him when she was ready. And not one minute sooner.

HE WOKE EARLY to go for a run before heading to the office. He found Slash in the kitchen, getting ready for a run herself.

She kissed him good morning.

He shot her a smile, kissed her back. "Sleep okay?"

"No," she replied. "Run with me."

"Love to."

They started out slowly, their pace increasing as they warmed up. At the two-mile mark, she said, "It's crazy because I'm fearless at work, and I live for the missions. But with you, I'm terrified."

"I get that," he said.

"I thought about what you said. If I don't put my whole heart into us, I'll never know. I don't like being vulnerable, you know that, but I can be a realist and still love you. I'm not going to compare us to anyone else. I'm going to trust you at your word, but more than that, I'm going to see what happens if I love you with my whole soul."

He pulled her to a stop, wrapped his sweaty arms around her, and kissed her. Already breathing hard, they were gasping for air when the kiss ended.

As if that kiss hadn't just happened, she started running again. In a few easy strides, he caught up.

"I have a favor," she said.

"Name it."

"My friend Jilly is at risk, especially if Greg is stalking her. She's about to graduate from college with a marketing degree. Would you be willing to interview her? I'm not sure she'd even want to work for your company, but I'd love to give her that opportunity."

"Sure," he replied. "If she's interested, she can send me her resume. If I think she's a good fit, I'll ask Gracie to speak with her."

She ran a comforting hand down his sweaty back. "I appreciate that."

They finished out the run hard, returned home soaked in perspiration. After a quick shower, Carrera dressed in a suit. As he was heading downstairs, he stopped in front of Slash's bedroom.

Knock-knock.

"Babe, it's me," he said.

"Come in."

He walked in to find her in a bra and panties. And his pulse kicked up speed. "Damn, you're hot."

She wiggled her finger at him. Two strides and she was in his arms. Their lips came together in a surging kiss that rocked him to his toes. He stroked her back, palmed her ass, the desire turning him hard as the kiss heated up.

Breaking away, she sucked down a breath. With her fiery gaze on his, she murmured, "I hope you kick ass today, Deputy Director Santini."

He shot her a smile, stole another kiss. "That kiss'll stay with me for hours. Tonight, you're mine."

She ran her hand over his semi. "I can't wait."

"What are you doing today?"

"Training with BLACK OPS in the morning, then I'm going to ALPHA to talk to Providence about the case. It's time to move in for an arrest."

"Have a great training." He kissed her again. "See you tonight."

He shut the door, trotted downstairs, and said goodbye to his grandmother, who was busy making breakfast.

"Aren't you eating?" she asked.

"I'll grab something later. I've got a meeting."

"I was supposed to host my friends for lunch today."

"Your friends are welcome here. Just don't show them my office."

"Of course not." After a pause, Elsa said, "Computer, lock the office door."

"Good morning, Elsa," said the computer. "Office door locked."

G-ma smiled. "That was easy."

Slash trotted down the stairs, dressed in fatigues. "Morning, Elsa."

"Hello, honey. Are you here today?"

"No."

"Are you staying for breakfast?" Elsa asked.

"Of course," Slash replied.

Carrera kissed them both goodbye. "G-ma, call me for any reason."

"I'll be fine," G-ma replied.

Slash

DURING BREAKFAST WITH ELSA, Slash said, "I'm going to put my heart out there and love him."

"You're being very brave. I'm proud of you. He'll treat you right this time."

"I'm in a training session all morning," Slash said. "I'll have my phone with me, so call me for any reason."

"Whoever burned down my house isn't going to come here in the middle of the day—"

"You wouldn't open the door—"

"Amanda May, when have I ever opened my front door to a stranger? Now, I have a great security system where the computer talks to me. Go, do your combat training. Maybe one day, I'll get to watch you."

While Slash finished her breakfast, an idea took hold. "I'm gonna get into a shit-ton of trouble, but you're coming with me."

Ten minutes later, they were out the door. Slash knew she'd hear about it from Dakota, but in this case, it was better to ask for forgiveness than for permission. She pulled down the dirt road leading to ALPHA's black site, where they held BLACK OPS training. She pulled into the hangar, brought Elsa to the entrance.

As she was calling Rebel, the hangar door opened, and he and Brit drove in. They made their way over.

"Looks like Slash has broken the rules again," Rebel said. "Good to see you, Elsa. This is my wife, Britain."

"What a beautiful couple," Elsa said. "I know I'm not supposed to be here, but Amanda May didn't want me to be alone this morning."

"I'm sorry about your home," Rebel said. "Any leads?"

"Nothing," Elsa replied.

"Slash, I heard you rescued Elsa," Rebel said.

"Hell, yeah," Slash replied. "I know Elsa's not allowed here, but I was hoping for a one-off."

"Put her in body armor and bring a chair outside," Rebel said.

Slash grinned. "Best boss ever."

Rebel overrode the system so Elsa could enter the building.

She, Elsa, and Brit made their way to the women's locker room where she and Brit suited up.

Addison entered, did a double take, then started laughing. "What is happening?"

"It's Bring Your Grandmother to Work Day," Slash said, and they laughed.

After helping Elsa into a Kevlar vest, she handed her shooter earmuffs and eye protection. Then, Slash pulled her weapons from her locker.

Elsa gasped as the women loaded up, but she didn't say a word. With her rucksack on her back, Slash rolled a conference room chair down the hall. Once outside, she put the chair a safe distance from target practice.

"You have to stay here," Slash said. "We use live rounds, so you can't roam around."

"This is the most exciting thing I've ever done," Elsa said.

Hawk, along with Sin, Dakota, and Prescott, exited out the back door.

"Elsa," Dakota said, "What are you doing here?"

"I'm not here."

Sin laughed. "Slash is behind this, isn't she?"

With a smile, Elsa zipped her lips.

"Good answer," Dakota said. "I never saw you."

The eight-person team, led by Rebel, started with a jog around the property. Everyone hoisted on their forty-pound rucksack, moved into formation, and started running. When they finished, they set down their tactical bags for sit-ups.

The morning was heating up fast and sweat was rolling down Slash's back from the intense workout.

At fifty sit-ups, they moved to push-ups. And finally, they completed the drill with pull-ups. Slash's arms burned from the strain, but she loved the extensive workouts, loved being with the team.

As target practice began, Hawk jogged over to the helipad to start his pre-flight check.

Slash glanced over at Elsa. She was sitting on the edge of the chair, riveted by their activities.

"Ready your shot," Rebel said.

Everyone lifted their rifles, aimed at the targets, and held steady.

"Fire at will," Rebel said.

The sound of multiple rounds rocketed through the quiet wooded area, muffled by her shooter's earmuffs. Rebel held up his hand. The firing ceased.

The mechanical targets were moved back, and they repeated the drill. Again and again, she hit the target on or near its center.

The whirring roar of the chopper competed for her attention, but she continued firing at the target.

Another hand signal from Rebel. They pointed their weapons at the ground, then set them aside. One by one, they made their way to the helo. Today, they climbed in, rappelled out, no rucksack. They did this several times.

And then, it was time to climb up. Slash had no problem doing it without the pack, but when it came time for the dreaded climb *with* the pack, her back muscles were burning.

She *needed* to reach this milestone. This was the one thing she hadn't been able to achieve during training.

Straining against the weight, she started the climb. Like every other time, she felt her muscles giving out at the halfway mark. Rather than stopping, like she usually did, she inhaled a deep breath, and pulled herself up. She felt like she was shredding her biceps, but she had to keep going. One agonizing tug at a time, she made it to the top. Now, she had to get herself into the body of the hovering aircraft.

Sin extended his hand. She could accept a teammate's help or she could fight to do it on her own.

Take it.

She grabbed his arm, he pulled her in, and smiled. "Nice work."

"Thanks for the assist," she said.

When the morning drill ended, the team was both invigorated and exhausted. Mentally, Slash wanted to jump around like a two-year old. She'd finally achieved a goal that had been impossible to overcome. Today, however, she'd tried a different tactic, with better results.

Even though she'd learned how to be self-sufficient, how to be self-reliant, she'd accepted Sin's outstretched hand. That was the true definition of teamwork.

They landed, made their way toward the building. Elsa stood there, applauding and beaming. "Amazing," she said. "That was like watching an action movie."

One by one, they acknowledged her as they traipsed inside. Back in the locker room, she helped Elsa out of the vest, shelved her ear and eye protection before taking a quick shower.

Minutes later, she returned.

No Elsa.

Oh boy.

She dressed in the pant suit she'd brought with her, threw on her signature pink lipstick and a little blush, then went in search of Elsa.

She was gonna get her ass kicked for sure now that Elsa was roaming around the black site unescorted. She found her nearby with Brit and Addison looking at pictures of their children on their phones.

Slash joined them.

"Can you keep a secret?" Addison whispered.

Elsa grinned. "That seems to be all I do lately."

"I'm pregnant," Addison whispered.

"Congratulations." Elsa gave her a little hug. "How long can you continue training?"

"Pretty far into my pregnancy, but I'll stop carrying the forty-pound bag in the next month."

"Congrats," Slash said to Addison before clasping Elsa's hand. "I've gotta get you home for your luncheon."

Twenty minutes later, Elsa was safely tucked at home, her friends en route to the house.

"This has been one of the most exciting days of my life," Elsa said. "Thank you for showing me a glimpse into your secret world. I will treasure that, but honey, you can't babysit me every day. You have to live your life, and I have to live mine." She gave Slash a hug. "I'll see you for dinner."

"Today was special for me too, Elsa. I loved sharing that part of my life with you."

As Slash drove toward ALPHA HQ in Tysons, her phone rang. It was Jilly.

"Hey," Slash answered. "I was going to text you later today."

"I am so pissed," Jilly said. "Where are you?"

"I'm heading to Tysons. What's wrong?"

"Will you be there a while?" Jill asked.

"All afternoon," Slash said.

"Call me when you leave," Jilly said, and hung up.

Slash pulled into ALPHA's parking lot. Once inside, she made her way to Providence's office. Her office door was open, she was on the phone, laughing. She glanced up, and waved Providence in.

"Speak of the devil, guess who just walked in," Providence said. "I love you too." Providence hung up and shook her head. "Why are my best employees total rebels?"

"I don't know what you're talking about," Slash said, biting back a smile.

"I heard Elsa had a blast this morning," Providence said.

Slash smiled. "It was a one-off, and I trust her." Then, Slash's smile fell away. "I need to talk to you about next steps at Blue Suit."

"What are you thinking?"

"I'm confident Greg is involved with the disappearance of these women. I'm waiting for surveillance from traffic cameras, but beyond that, the man is a total mystery. I think it's time to make the arrests. Karen is guilty of orchestrating the prostitution between dancers and members, but it's unclear if she has anything to do with the missing women. She insists they've all ghosted on her."

She and Providence discussed several arrest options.

"Karen's there every day," Slash said. "The VIP room is busiest on Friday and Saturday nights."

"I know you want to find Greg, but we need you back here. Your own cases aren't being worked, and local law enforcement should be searching for those missing women."

"I have one request at Blue Suit," Slash said. "I'm the arresting officer."

"I don't have an issue with that, but she'll know you were undercover. That puts you at risk since the owner is still out there."

"If he comes after me, I'll be ready."

"Let me talk to Cooper," Providence said. "His wedding is this Saturday, so he's trying to close out several things before he and Danielle leave for their honeymoon."

"I completely forgot about that," Slash said.

"Aren't you in the wedding party?"

"Sure am."

"So is Carrera. That should be fun for you guys."

"How did you—"

"Ever since he's been back, you two have been hating on each other so hard, I knew it was only a matter of time."

"There's a razor-thin line between love and hate."

"I couldn't agree more," Providence said.

Slash spent the afternoon hell-bent on finding the owner of Blue Suit. She jumped on a website that provided legal records of every Virginia business. She found no listing of any business, company, or organization named The Blue Suit Club, so she changed the search criteria to include a DBA. Also nothing.

"C'mon, where are you?" she murmured.

She entered Karen Woodside in the Managing Partner search field, hit enter, and got a hit.

"Yes."

Karen Woodside was listed as the Managing Partner of Silver Lips, located in Arlington, Virginia. It was listed as a nightclub, not a strip or a gentlemen's club. Karen had been the Managing Partner for the past five months.

Next, Slash went hunting for the previous owners. They'd relocated to South Carolina, so she called the only number listed for them.

It rang, a woman answered.

After introducing herself as MB Graves from the Arlington Business Board, Slash confirmed she was speaking with the former owner of Blue Suit.

"My husband and I owned the business for years," the woman said.

"We're updating our system," Slash lied, "and I wanted to confirm the name of Karen Woodside as Managing Partner."

"Yes, that's right."

"Did you also work with another person during the sale of Blue Suit?" Slash asked.

"No, just Karen," the woman replied.

"Is she the sole owner?"

"I thought so. Hold on, let me ask my husband." A few seconds later, the woman said, "My husband said she mentioned having a silent partner. I remember during settlement she left the room to call someone, but I don't remember who she called or why."

Slash asked a few more questions, but the woman remembered nothing more.

"I can look for Karen Woodside's number if you need to talk to her," said the woman.

"We've got it," Slash said. "Thanks for your help."

Slash hung up, pushed out of her chair, and walked outside. The humid summer air felt great compared to the air-conditioned building. While pacing, she thought about how Greg left Jericho Road, walked out of the parking lot, and disappeared.

Find him.

Determination had her yanking open the door in search of Danielle Fox. She found her working away in her office.

"Hey," Slash said from the doorway.

"Hi," Danielle said. "I've missed you around here."

"Same," Slash said. "Got a sec?"

"Of course."

Slash eased into the guest chair. "Are you ready for Saturday?"

Danielle smiled. "Ready? No, but super excited. I can't wait to finally marry Cooper. Your dress is good, right?"

"It's perfect," Slash replied. "I need help accessing surveillance cameras near Jericho Road."

As she explained who she was looking for, Danielle hopped online. Danielle Fox was one of the best hackers Slash had ever known. Even though Danielle was an ALPHA Op, everyone went to her for hacking help.

In minutes, she'd accessed several traffic cams in the vicinity.

"What date did this happen?" Danielle asked.

Slash gave her the day and time. Minutes later, Slash watched Greg mosey toward a nearby strip mall, then disappear inside the grocery store.

"What the hell," Slash said. "He's slippery."

"I have a meeting in the conference room." Danielle showed Slash how to toggle between cameras. "He's got to come back out."

"Thanks," Slash said as Danielle left her office.

Slash sat there staring at the surveillance. Five minutes turned into ten, turned into twenty. Greg never walked back outside. The longer Slash watched that damn video, the angrier she got. After fast forwarding an entire hour of video surveillance, she concluded that either he'd exited out the loading dock or he'd walked out looking like a completely different person.

Her blood pressure was through the roof when Danielle returned.

"No progress?" Danielle asked.

"I didn't see him come out, which means he left out the loading dock or he changed up his look in the store."

Danielle jumped online, her fingers flying over the keys. Slash watched in awe as Danielle tried accessing the grocery store's loading dock cameras.

"There are two cameras out back," Danielle said, "but I can't get past the firewall on either. The cameras in the parking lot are operated by the shopping center's property manager, but these two are run by the grocery store. I'll work on it some more and send you a link if I can access it."

"Can you send me the link of what I've been watching so I can review it again later?" Slash asked.

Danielle sent it over.

"I feel like I've been chasing the damn wind with this guy," Slash said. "Thanks for your help."

"Anytime," Danielle replied. "See you Friday for the rehearsal dinner."

As Slash slogged through rush-hour traffic, she called Jilly back.

"Hey," Jilly answered. "Any chance we could get together? I want to show you something."

"I'm staying with a friend. Come by and have dinner with us."

"I don't feel like socializing."

"Are you okay? Did that guy from the club contact you?"

"I'll be okay, and no, I haven't seen him."

"I want you to meet the woman who took me in after I ran away."

"Okay. I'll meet her, talk to you, then bolt," Jilly said.

Twenty minutes later, Slash stood in Carrera's kitchen inhaling the mouth-watering aroma of culinary delights.

"Elsa, it smells so good, I need a drool cup," Slash said as Carrera pulled up alongside her.

"That's some sexy talk," Carrera said.

She and Elsa laughed.

Slash lifted the lid. "Yes, your homemade red sauce." She dipped the wooden spoon into the pot and sampled it. "Your best yet."

"After my luncheon, I got busy," Elsa said. "Today's outing was the boost of energy I needed."

Carrera removed his jacket, his tie, and rolled up his sleeves. She loved watching him undress and homed in on his every sexy move.

"What did you do today?" he asked his grandmother.

"I went out," she replied.

"And?"

Slash peered into the oven. "There've gotta be thirty meatballs in there." With her gaze cemented on Carrera, she said, "Elsa came with me to training this morning."

Carrera laughed. "That's funny."

"Something happened to my friend Jilly today," Slash continued. "She's the woman who told me to leave the bad foster home. I invited her to stop by."

"I can't wait to meet her," Elsa said.

"Carrera," said the computer, "a four-door sedan parked out front. An unknown woman is walking up the driveway."

"That's Jilly," Slash said as she headed toward the front door.

"You were joking about taking my grandmother to BLACK OPS, right?" Carrera asked.

The doorbell chimed.

"Not joking," she replied. "That's why she didn't answer you. She promised me she'd never talk about it to anyone."

"Good god, woman," Carrera said, as Slash opened the front door.

"Hey, Jilly," Slash said stepping aside.

Jilly glanced from Slash to Carrera, her brows furrowed. "Haven't I seen you at Blue Suit?"

"He's there to make sure I'm safe," Slash said.

"You're her bodyguard?"

"Yeah," Carrera replied. "Bodyguard."

"This is my friend Jilly Linder." Slash wasn't sure how to introduce him. At the club, he was Claude Amos.

"Good to meet you, Jilly," Carrera said. "Come on in."

"I shouldn't intrude," Jilly said.

"Elsa wants to meet you." She tugged Jilly inside and brought her into the kitchen.

Elsa was putting garlic bread into the oven and pulling a large salad from the fridge. Elsa walked over to Jilly. "I'm delighted to meet you. I'm Elsa."

"Hi, Elsa. I'm Jilly."

"Can I hug you?"

"I'm a big hugger," Jilly said as Elsa folded her in a warm embrace.

When Elsa let go, she had tears in her eyes. "I include you in my prayers."

Jilly's eyebrows jutted into her forehead. "Me?"

"Because you warned Amanda May about that monster, she found her way to me."

Jilly looked at Slash. "I'm gonna need a little help here. Who's Amanda May?"

"I used to be Melody Donaldson. Legally, I'm Amanda Maynard, but Elsa calls me Amanda May. Now, I go by Slash."

Jilly chuckled. "I'm Jilly. Just Jilly Linder."

Carrera pulled a bottle of Santini Chianti from his wine collection, popped the cork, and set it on the kitchen island. "Wine, beer, soda, water, coffee, hard liquor? Who wants what?"

"I got fired today," Jilly said, "so I would love a glass of wine."

Silence.

"She did *not* fire you," Slash said.

"She sure did, and I recorded her crazy-ass rant on my phone." She regarded Elsa. "Sorry."

Elsa nodded. "No worries. I've heard much worse from these two, especially when they used to swear at each other."

Slash poured two glasses of wine. "We'll be on the porch."

Once outside, Slash tapped her glass against Jilly's. "Good riddance to Karen."

"I'll definitely drink to that."

A delicious melody of berries, herbs, and a blend of oak and smoky flavors erupted on her tongue as she sipped the fine wine.

"What happened?" Slash asked.

"I showed up to work the lunch shift, which I hardly ever do. One of the bartenders told me Karen was looking for me, so I pulled out my phone and started recording, but it's audio only." Jilly sipped the wine, set down the glass, and got busy on her phone. "I'll play her rant."

Jilly pressed Play.

"You need to clear out," Karen said.

"Clear out what?" Jilly asked.

"Duh, your things," Karen said. *"Your fired."*

"Fired? For what?"

"Because I said so. This is my club. I'm the queen, I make the rules, and I can break the rules I make."

Karen's cackle made Slash wince.
Jilly paused the audio. "She's crazy."
"Yeah, she is," Slash replied.
Jilly started the recording.

"The owner told me you need to go," Karen continued. *"You're expendable. I'm not. I'm very important. This club wouldn't be as successful as it is without me. I've got plenty of dancers who can fill your shifts. You've got ten minutes to clear out or I'll have security boot you out."*

"Can I talk to the owner?" Jilly asked.

"Talk to the owner?" Karen yelled. *"Why would you do that? The owner wants you gone and I'm good with that. If you're looking for a recommendation, you won't be getting one from me."*

"No problem there," Jilly said. *"You're a terrible manager. None of the girls like you."*

Another shrill cackle. "Do you think I give a crap? I don't care about any of you. I'm a superstar here and you aren't. So byeeeeee."

Jilly stopped the recording. "I spent the afternoon working on my resume which, by the way, won't get me hired by any company with cred."

"Blue Suit has creds," Slash said. "Do you like dancing?"

"No. It paid the bills, and barely."

"Who's the owner?" Slash asked.

"I've never seen anyone there except Karen."

Carrera walked onto the porch. "Anyone hungry?"

Jilly rose from the sofa. "I should get going."

"You gotta stay," Slash said.

"It's okay," Jilly said.

"We can't make her stay," Carrera said.

"No, we can't," Slash agreed. "That would be kidnapping."

"Yeah," Carrera said with a smile. "Not gonna touch that one."

"We could bribe her," Slash continued.

"You mean with my grandmother's homemade meatballs, homemade pasta, and homemade red sauce?" Carrera asked.

Slash nodded, her gaze sliding from Carrera to Jilly. "That might work. What about a job interview? Do you think that would sweeten the deal?"

"Only one way to find out," Carrera replied. "Jilly, I own Carrera Cruises. We're always looking for marketing reps—"

"The boat cruise company?" Jilly asked. "You're Carrera?"

"He's Claude at the club," Slash said, "So you can't say anything to Karen."

Jilly raised her eyebrows at Slash. "You did *not* just say that to me. The only thing I would ever say to Karen Woodside is F-you."

"Get in line behind me," Slash said.

"She didn't fire you too, did she?" Jilly asked.

"I knew her from another job," Slash said. "She did something illegal, she got herself fired, and blamed me."

"That's a story," Jilly said.

Slash said nothing as she pushed off the sofa.

"You're not really a dancer, are you?" Jilly asked.

Slash wanted to answer that question, but she couldn't, so she stayed silent.

"Let's eat," Carrera said. "We can talk about your career."

"That's so nice of you," Jilly said.

"My family owes you a world of debt," Carrera said as he held open the French door for them.

"You don't owe me anything," Jilly said.

"If you hadn't told Slash to run, she wouldn't have ended up in my life," Carrera said. "Offering you a job is the least I can do."

Carrera slid his gaze to Slash, and in that moment, she knew. She was going to spend the rest of her life with this man.

Until the end, 'til death do us part. The whole enchilada.

Jilly excused herself to the bathroom while Slash washed up and started setting the table.

"How'd I do, boss?" Carrera asked.

She set down a fork. "You did good. You did *real* good."

When they sat at the kitchen table, Elsa said grace. "Dear Lord, thank you for this meal, for our family, the family at our table tonight, and for Jilly who gave us Amanda May. In Jesus' name. Amen."

"Amen," they echoed.

The food was passed around, and they started eating.

"Elsa, this is unbelievable," Slash said. "I'm having seconds, no matter how full I am."

"It's excellent," Jilly agreed.

"Tell me what type of job you're looking for," Carrera said to Jilly.

"I'm two classes from a bachelor's in marketing with a

concentration in biz dev," Jilly said. "I love thinking outside the box on ways to grow a business. Change happens daily, so if businesses don't keep up and grow, they die fast."

The conversation continued. By the end of the meal, Carrera said, "I don't need to see your resume. I'll talk to my new executive director, Gracie. We've got a marketing spot open and we've got a few customer relations spots as well."

"What are those?"

"They talk to prospective customers and book cruises."

"Where do you find new business?" Jilly asked.

"We advertise, we're on social media, word of mouth, and a ton of repeat biz."

"I've never seen a local spot," Jilly said. "What about TV?"

"My former business partner, my sister Mara, was looking into that," Carrera said.

"What happened?" Jilly asked.

"She passed," Carrera said.

"I'm so sorry," Jilly said.

Carrera pulled out his phone. "I'm texting Gracie your name with my recommendation." His fingers flew over the keyboard before he set his phone down.

"Will I see you when I'm there?" Jilly asked.

"Probably not," he replied. "I have another job that takes up most of my time."

"Do you two work together at that *other* job?" Jilly asked Slash and Carrera.

"Indirectly," Carrera replied.

"Working at Blue Suit was a means to an end, but ever since Karen started, it's been awful," Jilly said. "I want to thank all of you for turning a bad day into one filled with love."

"I hope you'll come back," Elsa said.

"I'd love to," Jilly replied.

Carrera's phone buzzed with an incoming text. "Gracie says, 'Can't wait to talk to her,'" he read out loud.

Carrera flashed her a smile, and her heart leapt.

"Thank you," she said to him.

Despite the loss she'd endured, and the challenges she'd faced along the way, she was where she was supposed to be, with the people she was supposed to be with.

And she couldn't be more grateful.

24

THE QUICKIE WEDDING

Carrera

After Jilly left, Elsa said, "The arson detective called me. He talked to a few people on my street with surveillance cameras and asked to review them."

"Stryker's gonna help us out," Carrera said.

"I hope you find something," Elsa said.

"We will," Slash replied.

He and Slash cleaned up while G-ma relaxed on the sofa. When they finished, they said goodnight to her. To his surprise, Slash clasped his hand as they headed toward the stairs. On the second floor, she stopped in front of the guest room. "Would you like company tonight?"

"Only if it's you," he replied.

She collected a few items from the guest room before they continued on to his bedroom.

After he shut the door, she set down her things, and pulled him close. "You came through for me tonight. Thank you."

"Every. Single. Day," he said.

She kissed him. He snaked his arms around her, deepened

the embrace. This kiss was different. Not just filled with desire, but overflowing with love.

She slowed them down, dropped a soft kiss on his cheek. "Trust doesn't come easy for me, but I'm going to put myself out there with you."

He placed his hands on either side of her face, dipped down, and kissed her with such intensity, need ricocheted through him. She moaned into him, he devoured her, pulling her so close, no air passed between them.

"Too many clothes," she whispered between kisses.

"Not enough love," he replied.

"Shower with me," she said.

Hand-in-hand they walked into his bathroom. He turned on the faucet.

While the water heated, she stripped naked. Off came his shirt, he yanked his undershirt over his head, his pants and underwear gone in seconds. They came together in a whoosh of energy. Their fingers roamed and caressed bare skin, while their tongues teased and swirled together.

Into the shower they went. He stood beneath the secondary showerhead, leaving the primary for her. Water cascaded over her beautiful body and his erection bobbed up and down in approval.

She wrapped her hand around his shaft. "I've got Mr. Johnson's approval."

"He loves you."

"And you?"

"I love you more."

The water poured over them while they stared into each other's eyes. Yes, he wanted her, but he wanted to make love to her in his bed, not screw her in the shower. So, he picked up the soap, lathered up and ran his sudsy hands over inch of the woman he loved with his entire being.

As the water rinsed away the suds on her chest, he placed

his mouth over her nipple, teased her nib until it plumped. Her soft coos filled his ears as he stroked her shapely ass with a tender touch. She cupped her other breast, offered it to him, and he traced her areola with his tongue before drawing her nipple into his mouth until it too was engorged.

"Wow," she murmured. "I want you so badly."

"Turn around," he ordered.

When she did, he cleaned her strong shoulders, beautiful back, but when he slipped his hand between her butt cheeks, she said, "That's a first."

He kissed her shoulder, letting his lips linger on her heated skin. Then, he knelt and washed her thighs and calves. Touching her soothed his savage soul and reminded him how lucky he was that she loved him back.

One more kiss before he washed her hair, making sure to keep the soap away from her eyes.

"Will you always take care of me like this?"

"Always."

"Nothing is forever," she murmured.

He massaged her head and her eyes fluttered closed. As he stared at her face, he did know. Not because she was beautiful or because she was strong and smart, independent and brave, but because he'd lived without her and he knew he would never do that again.

"We are," he said.

She opened her eyes.

"We are forever," he said. "I feel it in my gut and in my heart. This second chance means everything to me. Why would I fuck this up? Even I'm not that stupid."

He delighted in making her laugh. For a man who lived to avenge his sister, a man who straddled the line of good and evil, Slash was his sanctuary.

The place where his heart and his soul had found a home.

"I love you," she said as she placed her head under the water, rinsing away the shampoo.

Hearing her tell him that would never get old.

She ran conditioner through her hair, then collected the soap to wash him. Soft hands traversed his body, her touch both soothing and titillating.

Within seconds, his erection was back. As she cleaned his shaft, a moan ripped from the back of his throat. "I love your touch."

She kissed him before turning him around and continuing to suds his body. When she finished, she washed his hair before rinsing out her conditioner.

As they dried off, she said, "I'm not on birth control."

"I'll use condoms."

"If we're an us, I'll talk to my doc."

"We're an us," he said.

Once dry, he sat on the bench and watched her dry her hair. When they returned to his bedroom, he pulled a condom packet from the box before they crawled into bed.

He pulled her into his arms and he loved her. Gentle kisses and tender touches filled with whispers of love while they moved as one beneath the sheets.

His special girl was now his forever woman.

When they cuddled close, he said, "You were my first love, and you are my last love."

"I love that."

"This is it."

"This *is* it," she replied while running her soft fingers over his chest.

JUST AFTER SIX the following morning, as he and Slash were rushing around the kitchen before work, Carrera's phone rang. It was his sister.

"Hey, Jazz," he answered.

"Hey, I've got Russell on speaker."

"How's it going?" Carrera asked.

"We're hoping you're free later this afternoon," Jazz said.

"We're getting married!" Russell announced. "Can you be my best man?"

Carrera slid his gaze to Slash who was busy on her laptop. "Don't you want the fam there, Jazz?"

"It's definitely happening fast, but we'll have a big reception after Russell wins the election," she said.

"We've got an appointment today at four at the Arlington courthouse," Russell said.

"I asked Gracie if she could make it, but her whole day is booked," Jazz explained.

While Carrera was disappointed for his sis, he was relieved Gracie wasn't bolting at the last minute."

"Maybe Slash can come with you?" Jazz asked.

"How many witnesses do you need?" Carrera asked.

"None," Russell said. "We don't need any, but we want you there."

"I'll be there," Carrera replied.

After hanging up, he asked Slash, "Babe, what's on your schedule today?"

"We're moving forward with an arrest at Blue Suit, so I've got meetings and strategy sessions at the Bureau."

G-ma entered the kitchen, still in her robe. "You two are up early."

"We've got early morning meetings," Carrera replied.

"Elsa, what are you doing today?" Slash asked.

"I'm going grocery shopping," G-ma said. "Lunch with a friend, then Luciano is stopping by."

Carrera handed her his credit card, but she refused him. Rather than get into it with her, he thanked her.

He opted to say nothing about Jazz's last-minute nuptials.

The messenger always got shot. Instead, he said, "Slash, how 'bout we drive in together?"

"I'll take you up on that," she replied.

After a quick breakfast, they were out the door and on their way to work.

"Jazz and Russell called me," he said. "They're having a quickie wedding at the courthouse today."

"Wow, that's fast."

"They invited me. Jazz asked if you'd come."

"Hmm, what time?"

"Four," he replied.

"Do you want me there?"

"Hell, yeah."

"What are you doing today?"

"Working with Z, then I'll be in my office. Come up and see me."

"You sure about that?"

"Absolutely."

"We'll see."

"So, what do you think about their wedding?" He drove over the bridge into DC.

"What do you mean?"

"Would you want a courthouse wedding?"

"I'm not sure I'm getting married, but if I did, Elsa would be there. Luciano too. Oh, and you're invited."

He chuffed out a laugh. "Damn right I'm there. I'm the one you're marrying."

"You think so?"

"I know so."

"Marriage is a big commitment," she said.

He clasped her hand, said nothing more. He wasn't in a rush. When it came to Slash, he had nothing but time.

He parked at the building in his personal space. They rode the elevator to the lobby, then made their way through security.

In the crowded elevator on the way upstairs, he clasped her pinky, gave it a little squeeze before letting go.

As the doors slid open on her floor, she said, "Have a good day, Deputy Director Santini."

"You too, Special Agent O'Reilly."

On the executive level, he swiped his keycard, and spied Sin and Z waiting outside his locked office door.

"What's goin' on?" Carrera asked.

"Peter Hirzog filed a formal complaint against you," Sin said.

Z stepped close. "You should have taken the office down the hall."

Carrera fought the urge to roll his eyes. "What's his problem?"

"You level jumped, so the Inspector General has to review the complaint," Z explained.

Carrera keyed into his office. "I'm ready to get to work."

Sin smiled. "That's the attitude. He doesn't give a damn."

"I *don't* give a damn," Carrera replied.

Sin eased into a guest chair. "I've got my team looking into it."

"What for?" Carrera said as he logged in.

"Hirzog said he knows what Luciano is up to," Sin said. "If you don't step down, he's threatening to whistleblow."

Carrera chuckled. "Let him. They won't find a damn thing." He shifted from Z to Sin, who arched a brow.

"Does Luciano know about this?" Carrera asked.

"No," Sin replied.

"Sin, are you and Carrera working with Luciano?" Z asked.

"We are," Sin said.

Carrera's stomach dropped.

"I've got eight mil tied up in his company's stock," Sin said. "Carrera, are you doing business with your cousin?"

"Yeah," Carrera replied. "My portfolio is heavily weighted with Santini stock."

"That's not what I'm talking about," Z bit out. "I don't have the time or the patience for this bullshit. If you're involved with Luciano and his alleged illegal business activities, I can't protect you."

"We don't need protection," Carrera said.

"And we're not afraid of Hirzog," Sin added.

Carrera extracted his phone from his pants pocket, called his cousin. With phone to ear, he waited for Luciano to answer.

"Santini," Luciano answered.

"I'm in a meeting with Z and Sin," Carrera said.

"Speaker?"

"No. Hirzog filed a complaint against me because I forced him out of his office."

"Nothing he does surprises me," Luciano said.

"He said he's got dirt on you," Carrera explained. "If I don't step down, he'll whistleblow."

"Figlio di puttana," Luciano spat out. "Put me on speaker."

Carrera tapped the button on his phone. "You're on."

"Good morning, Sinclair. Hello, Philip." The words sounded lyrical, coming from Luciano. "Beautiful morning, isn't it?"

Sin chuckled.

"We have a problem," Z bit out.

"Philip," Luciano crooned. "Relax. It's all good. I have one thing to say."

"What is it?" Sin asked.

"Don't give up the office. It's a power play."

Knock-knock.

"Come in," Carrera said.

The door opened. Hirzog glared at them. "Gentlemen, I'm going to ruffle some feathers."

"Peter, it's Luciano Santini," Luciano said. "You're wasting your time with me."

"I didn't spend my entire career at the Bureau to get over-looked by a novice who's still wet behind his ears," Hirzog said. "Watch your sixes gentlemen." He pulled the door shut.

As he passed the glass walls, he glared at them.

"Take me off speaker," Luciano said.

"Yup," Carrera said, phone to ear.

"He's using you to come after me," Luciano said. "Do *not* back down."

The line went dead.

Carrera eyed both men across his desk. "Let's get to work."

AT THREE-THIRTY, Carrera entered the Organized Crime Division and stopped at reception. "I'm looking for Special Agent O'Reilly."

The employee typed in her name. "She's in a meeting. If you want to have a seat, I can let her know you're here. What's your name?"

"Deputy Director Santini," he said.

The receptionist offered a tight smile before leaving his post. Down the hall he went, knocked on a conference room door. After entering, he exited seconds later.

"She asked if you can hold for five?" he asked Carrera.

"No problem." Carrera moved away from reception, sent Luciano a text.

> Are you having dinner with G-ma?

Yes

> See you then

A few minutes later, Slash emerged, her laptop bag slung over her shoulder. As she made her way toward him, he couldn't ignore her swagger. She carried herself with a confidence that was a total turn on, but the love in her eyes gave him hope for their future.

And then, he checked her out. From her tailored white pantsuit that hugged her curves to her open-toed stilettos, she was the epitome of professionalism... and she was all his.

"Deputy Director," she said.

"Special Agent O'Reilly."

As they rode the crowded elevator, the desire to pull her close and kiss her hello had him caressing her hand. Never before—not even when they were teens—was the pull this strong.

The elevator stopped on the next floor, the doors opened and Hirzog entered.

Carrera wasn't intimidated and he wasn't backing down. Hirzog was fucking with the wrong men. But to Z's point, none of this would be happening if he'd taken the smaller office down the hall.

Hirzog narrowed his gaze at Carrera. "If I were you, I'd vacate that office."

The thick tension in that small space had everyone staring at them.

Ah, for fuck's sake.

"What's the real problem, Peter?" Carrera asked.

The elevator stopped in the lobby, the doors spilled open, and everyone rushed out.

"You're fucking with the wrong man, Santini. You, Develin, and that asshole Luciano should sleep with one eye open."

Hirzog stepped off, and the doors closed. The elevator descended into the parking garage. In silence, he and Slash walked to his SUV. Once they drove out, on went their sunglasses, as the summer sun beat down on them.

"What's Hirzog's problem?" Slash asked.

"I took his office."

"So?"

"He's got a grudge against Luciano," Carrera replied.

"What does that have to do with you?"

"No idea."

"Hmm," Slash said. "A few years ago, Hirzog's wife left him."

"How do you know?"

"Luciano told me." After a beat, she said, "We're raiding Blue Suit on Friday night."

"This Friday?"

"Yeah. I'm gonna miss Danielle and Cooper's dress rehearsal."

"Do you have a date for the wedding?" he asked.

"You," she replied matter-of-factly.

At the red light, he leaned over. She smiled as their lips came together.

"I can get through all this BS at work, as long as I have you by my side," he said.

She laid her hand on his thigh, sending a jolt of energy pounding through him.

Fifteen minutes later, he parked near the Arlington County Courthouse. Once inside, he texted his sister.

"They're on the third floor," Carrera said to Slash.

Upstairs, they knocked on the judge's chambers. A middle-aged Black man opened the door. "Come on in, I'm Judge Gadson."

They introduced themselves, shook the Judge's hand. Russell and Jazz stood nearby.

Jazz was smiling, Russell was not.

Wedding jitters?

Carrera hugged his sister, shook Russell's clammy hand. Slash said hello.

"Is everyone ready?" asked Judge Gadson.

Russell handed Carrera two gold wedding bands. Simple and lightweight, they felt more like aluminum than actual gold.

As the judge began, Carrera clasped Slash's hand.

"Do you have vows you'd like to say to each other?" asked the judge.

"Yes," they both replied.

"Jasmine, why don't you say yours first?" suggested the judge.

"Russell, I love you. I love that we work together, love that your dream has become mine. I will support you and take care of you, listen to you, and be there for you. We have our whole lives to get to know each other and I'm excited to spend mine with you."

Carrera handed her the ring and she slid it into Russell's finger.

"Russell, you can recite your vows to Jasmine," said the judge.

"Jazz, things happened fast for us," Russell began. "I appreciate how committed you are to my success, how hard you work to help me achieve my dream—*our* dream. I'm excited for our life in politics, in giving back to our community, and to the nation. Thank you for your loyalty."

What the fuck was that? It sounded more like a campaign speech than a wedding vow.

Carrera squeezed Slash's hand. She glanced up at him. He met her gaze, before she returned her attention to the bride and groom.

Russell swung his gaze over to Carrera. "Did you want to say something?"

Nothing like being put on the spot.

"Russell, take good care of my sister. Be her partner, put her first. Love her with your entire heart. Jasmine, I'm happy you found your person, someone to love, to go through life with, to share your joys, your struggles, and your challenges, knowing he'll be there every step of the way. We wish you both the best."

Tears rolled down Jazz's cheeks and she whisked them away. "That was beautiful, thank you."

"You're welcome," Russell replied.

Slash squeezed Carrera's hand. They both knew Jazz was talking about *his* speech, not Russell's. The judge pronounced them husband and wife. They shared a chaste kiss, Russell thanked the judge, and they left his chambers.

That was the fastest, most emotionless wedding Carrera had ever witnessed.

In the hallway, Carrera suggested they come to the house for dinner. "You can share your news with G-ma."

"That sounds great," Jazz replied.

"You go ahead, wife." Russell grinned. "That sounds funny. Wife."

"You're my husband." Jazz furrowed her brow. "Crazy."

"I'm gonna head back over to campaign headquarters," Russell said. "I'll text you later to see if you're still there." He gave her one quick peck before he took off.

Carrera's heart broke for his sister.

"Congratulations," Slash said to Jazz. "Your grandmother and dad are going to be so happy for you."

The three walked out. As Jazz headed to her car alone, Slash said, "I can follow you if you want to ride with her."

"I'm good, but thanks," he replied. "I gotta ask... what the hell was that?"

"A quickie wedding," Slash said.

"What's the rush?"

"If he changes his name to Santini before the election, you'll have your answer."

"If he's using my sister, I'll fucking kill him," Carrera growled.

~

Slash

AT THE HOUSE, Slash changed into a T-shirt and running shorts. Back downstairs, she spotted G-ma and Jazz talking on the porch. Carrera was at his desk in his home office.

He glanced up. "Yo, mama, where you headed?"

She poked her head in. "Downstairs to lift."

"Need a spotter?"

"You can check on me, if you want."

"Carrera, Luciano Santini is headed up the walkway," said the computer.

"I'll let him in on my way downstairs." Slash made her way to the front door. After she opened it, Luciano stepped inside.

"I like seeing you here all the time," Luciano said. "Is my cousin treating you like a queen?"

That made Slash smile. "He is."

"Are you going for a run?"

"Downstairs to lift. I need specs on that job you told me about." She was referring to Elwood Tosh, the foster-care monster.

"We'll talk after dinner," Luciano said.

"Jazz is here, so now is better," Slash pushed.

"There were numerous complaints filed against Tosh, but he denied them," Luciano murmured. "He went off the grid for a while, moved back a year ago. He lives in Springfield, and he's mooching off some woman who didn't foster kids, but he's got her doing it. He used to foster teens, now they're between nine and twelve."

"Ohgod," Fury made her blood boil. "That makes me sick to my stomach."

"He's using two different aliases. AJ Allen and Jason Mullen."

"How is he getting away with this? Isn't Family Services verifying?"

"He has no criminal record, the kids are too terrified to say anything, especially now."

"Address?"

Luciano rattled it off.

Carrera's dress shoes clicked on the marble floor, the air crackling with energy the closer he got.

Carrera pulled his cousin in for a bro-hug. "What's the word?"

"He's prepping me on Elwood Tosh," Slash said.

After Luciano finished briefing them, Slash retreated downstairs to work out. As she was finishing up, Carrera trotted down wearing nothing but a pair of workout shorts. A groan ripped from her throat as she drank him in.

Solid, defined muscles *everywhere.* A rock-solid chest with perfect pecs, eight-pack abs that made her fingers tingle, and thick, striated thighs she could gawk at for days. But it was his bulging biceps that she melted over... every damn time.

All muscle, all man, all mine.

She sauntered close, curled her hands around his biceps. "You got some serious guns on you."

He wrapped his hands around her arms. "So do you."

He kissed her. She kissed him back.

"I'm going for a run," she said.

"I'll go with," he replied.

"Stay and workout."

His sad face made her smile.

"I'll have my phone and my switchblade. You know my route. Back in twenty."

She let her lips linger on his before she broke away.

"You taste good," she said.

"You taste like more," he replied.

In the bedroom, she strapped her cell phone to her armband, curled her fingers around her switchblade. G-ma, Jazz, and Luciano were on the porch, so she headed out.

Engulfed in July's heat and humidity, she took off, increasing her speed after a few minutes. She rounded the corner and continued toward her townhouse, turning left at the end of the street.

A silver two-door coupe was parked near her house.

Slash took off in an all-out sprint, but the driver sped away. She eyed the Virginia license plate catching the last two numbers.

One and five.

Anger jumped to the surface.

Who are you and what do you want?

Pushing hard, she continued running full-tilt to the inter-section. The silver car was gone. As she finished running her route, frustration replaced her runner's high. Back at Carrera's, the kitchen was bustling with activity. Elsa and Jazz stood at the stove while Luciano was grilling on the deck.

"Hi guys," Slash said.

"How was your run?" Elsa asked.

"Good. I'm gonna take a quick shower."

Rather than head upstairs, Slash entered Carrera's office, extracted her ALPHA laptop from her computer bag, and logged in. She opened the familiar site, requested all Virginia tags ending in one-five. On her way out, she pulled the office door shut.

"Computer lock the office door."

"Hello, Slash," said the computer. "Office locked."

She went upstairs to shower before dinner.

Twenty minutes later, everyone was seated outside on the porch, and the conversation quickly turned to Jazz's wedding.

"Where are you living?" Luciano asked.

"In my apartment," Jazz replied. "Russell hired a contractor to upgrade the bathrooms and kitchen before I move in. The house is forty-years old and he said it needs a face lift."

"Do you like his house?" Slash asked.

"I've only seen it from the outside," Jazz explained.

What?

"He's never invited you in?" Carrera said.

"No, but it's not like we spend a lot of time hanging out," Jazz replied. "We're busy campaigning, going to events, meeting and talking to constituents all the time."

"Have you met his family?" Slash asked.

"He and his dad haven't talked since his parents got divorced, and his mom died while he was living in Boston," Jazz explained. "But now he has my family."

The conversation remained light all through dinner. When they finished, Jazz took off.

In the kitchen, Elsa and Luciano sat huddled around her laptop at the table while Slash and Carrera cleaned up. When they finished, they retreated into his office. She logged into her laptop, checked the results of her license plate search. Carrera pulled a guest chair around, sat beside her.

She started to get up. "You sit in your chair."

He ran his hand down her back. "That one's more comfortable."

"Thank you." She eased down. "When we rode to Great Falls, I saw a two-door silver coupe—"

"Ski mask," he said.

She nodded. "I saw the vehicle today, near my house."

Up went his eyebrows. "Why didn't you tell me?"

"This is the first chance I've had," she said.

"Babe." He pointed from her to him. "Partners."

She nodded. "Point taken. Virginia tag ending in one-five." She spun the laptop toward him. "Fifteen-thousand possible matches."

"You're being stalked," he said. "Going forward, we stay together."

"That's unrealistic," she pushed back. "I got this."

Carrera opened his laptop. "Stryker was able to lift videos from surveillance cameras in G-ma's neighborhood."

"Now, we're getting somewhere." She slid close. "Show me whatcha got."

A devilish smile filled his face. "I will as soon as we finish up here."

"There's my sexy motivation."

Turning their attention to the videos, they reviewed them one by one. Most were cars returning home or heading out. There were videos of rabbits, deer, and even a family of foxes. But there wasn't a single video of a person walking anywhere near Elsa's home.

At ten o'clock, Luciano stopped by to say goodbye. They went back to watching videos. Elsa came in to say goodnight at eleven-thirty. They continued working until one in the morning with no luck.

"Are there more videos?" Slash asked.

"Yeah, a few," Carrera replied.

"I gotta call it," she said. "We'll pick this up tomorrow night."

In bed, she cuddled close. "I can't believe I have no energy to love you."

"You're loving me right now," he replied as he caressed her bare back.

As her eyes closed, the silver coupe flashed in her mind. Someone was watching her every damn move.

While she loved being independent, loved that she was fearless, she wasn't stupid. If Carrera wanted to watch her six, maybe she shouldn't be so quick to reject him.

"I like that you have my back," she murmured.

"Always," he replied as she drifted to sleep.

25

THE ARREST

Carrera

T he following evening, Carrera was determined to make progress finding the arsonist. The detective had contacted Elsa that afternoon with an update. The accelerant was a common mix of gas and kerosene dumped on the home before a match was lit. Beyond that, he had nothing.

"We got this," Slash said after walking into his home office with two mugs of freshly brewed coffee. "Leaded." She set his down, sat beside him.

He sipped the hot drink, pulled up the video where they left off the night before. After watching several minutes of five fox pups playing in a neighbor's front yard, he wanted to put his fist through a damn wall.

She rubbed his back. "Wow, you are tight." Standing behind him, she massaged his shoulders, running her knuckles along his knotted muscles. "Breathe."

"I am breathing."

She leaned around, kissed his cheek. "Breathe in *slowly*."

Several minutes passed while she massaged away the tension.

"Feels great."

"Tomorrow's the big night," she said. "We're making arrests at Blue Suit."

"If Greg's your guy, you might be shutting him down too," Carrera said. "He won't have a readily-available group of women to go after and he might not feel confident outside his comfort zone."

"I hope you're right," she said. "I'm so frustrated I can't find him."

"You will," he said. "I know you. You'll never stop searching for him."

She finished massaging his shoulders and sat back down.

"Thank you, babe," he said.

He felt like they were chasing their tails, the constant pressure a source of angst. Even so, he wasn't giving up. He would always fight for his family, for those he loved. Whoever tried to kill his grandmother would regret the moment he lit that match.

He pulled up another video. This one was of a backyard filled with flashing fireflies. "Dammit. I don't have the patience—"

Just as he started to close the video, she said, "Wait, what's that?"

They continued watching as movement emerged from the wooded area behind the house.

"That's a person," Slash said.

"That's just some shadow," he pushed back. "Looks like rustling leaves."

"No, that's someone walking from the woods into the yard," she said. "They're in black with a black ski mask."

He paused the video, enlarged it, but still couldn't see anyone in the shadows.

"Where's that house?" she asked.

He checked the long and lat coordinates. "Two blocks from G-ma's." He opened another window, pulled up a map.

She leaned over him, her beautiful scent surrounded him, and he breathed her in. "I love how you smell."

Soft fingers caressed the back of his neck. "Thank you, baby."

He loved that she'd called him baby, loved that they were a couple. Now, his life had meaning beyond his work.

"Here's what I'm thinking," she said plucking him from better thoughts. "There's that little shopping center near Elsa's house. I think they parked there, walked through the woods, and hugged the tree line that backed up to the houses." She pointed to specifics houses on the map. "If any of these houses have surveillance, let's check them out."

He zoomed in on the map, got the street name, and went searching for those videos. Four homes had front-facing cameras, three had rear-facing. He picked one and viewed the video.

The first yielded nothing. He repeated his efforts on another home with a backyard camera. Also nothing.

When he opened the last one, excitement pounded through him. "We got a hit."

"I see," she replied.

A lone person walked by in full view of the camera. In his hand, a gas can.

"There it is." He could hear the smile in her voice.

"Nice work," he said.

"Yeah, we got it goin' on, don't we?" She kissed him once before turning her attention back to the computer.

"One kiss? That's it?"

She stroked his thigh. "One now, the rest later."

Motivated to find the arsonist, he went in search of the

surveillance Stryker had pulled of the shopping center. There were over twenty files of the parking lot.

As if sensing his frustration, she said, "I'll drive." With gentle fingers, she took control the mouse, clicking on the first link.

He sipped the now-cold coffee. "Refill?"

"I'm good, thanks," she said, laser-focused on the video.

With mug in hand, he walked into the kitchen, dumped the cold liquid into the sink, and filled his mug.

Back in the office, he sat beside her. Despite the late hour, Slash was determined.

"Nope," she said. After viewing the next video, she mumbled, "Not that one either."

More watching, more eliminating.

He kept his attention glued to the screen while they reviewed video after video. She clicked on the next one. It started playing.

"We got it."

They watched as a silver, two-door coupe parked in a dark corner of the lot. A lone person exited the vehicle, their ski mask already in place. He pulled a small gas container from the back seat and headed toward the woods.

"That's the car that's been following me." She zoomed in on the license plate. "It ends in one-five."

This time, however, the entire license plate number was in full view. She dragged her laptop over, logged into ALPHA, and plugged in the tag number. While the system searched, she regarded Carrera.

A slow, sexy smile filled her face. "They are so fucked."

"You're a beast, you know that?"

"I love when someone fucks with me," she said. "They have no idea who they're dealing with. When my parents died, I was gutted and utterly lost."

Sadness crept into his heart. "I'm sorry. I'm sorry for the part I played."

"I had to dig deep. I had to force myself to never give up hope, even though I was scared." She lifted her yoga pants. Strapped to her ankle was her switchblade. "Once I armed myself, I got my foothold."

"Did you ever use it?"

She stared into his eyes for so long, he knew her answer, but he waited to see if she'd tell him.

"Three times." A shadow fell over her eyes. "Some things from our past need to stay there and some things are better left unsaid." The fear and the fury in her eyes dissipated.

She'd been through hell, then he'd tossed her to the curb.

"I don't deserve you," he said.

"Only time will tell." Then, she shot him a little smile. "But... if I were betting on us, I'd say we'll go the distance."

"I *am* betting on us, because I know we will."

They came together in a tender kiss, interrupted by the bing of an incoming email.

The license plate inquiry had a match. They grew quiet while they read the results.

"Whoa," she blurted.

"No fucking way," he said.

~

Slash

WHILE SLASH'S closest friends were having a blast at Danielle and Cooper's dress rehearsal, she was suiting up alone in ALPHA's locker room. On went her combat shoes, her body armor, her gun belt. After tucking her Glock into the holster, she left.

She couldn't wait to make the arrest.

She'd been so fired up about it, she hadn't slept much. Turned out, that had worked to her advantage. Carrera had kept her well entertained half the night.

That man has got it going on.

She spent the day coordinating logistics with FBI SWAT Team lead Neil Eggleston and Arlington County's Police Detective Rosario. With their plan in place, they agreed to meet at ten o'clock.

Once at Blue Suit, she called them both. Neil's SWAT teams and the vans were two minutes out. Detective Rosario had just parked.

When SWAT pulled in, two vans drove out back, two parked at the entrance. Slash exited her SUV, but she didn't pull her weapon from its holster. Guns in a nightclub were a last resort. She had every confidence the men in SWAT gear were a menacing enough sight that no weapons would be needed.

Slash met Eggleston and Rosario at the front door.

"Let's get this done," she said.

The three, backed by SWAT personnel, marched into the main room of the club. The place fell eerily silent, all eyes on the formidable group of LEOs who made their way through the crowd. She said nothing, made eye contact with no one. A group of members beelined toward the exit. She let them go, her focus on arresting one woman and her illicit customers. The SWAT teams would arrest everyone in the playroom, then escort them into the waiting vans.

With Carrera's access card in hand, Slash stopped in front of the Management Only door, swiped the card, the light turned green, and they stormed in.

Like any Friday night, the room was filled with nude and semi-nude clubbers having their hedonistic fun with the dancers and other members.

"FBI!" she yelled. "Everybody down on your knees with your hands up!"

As soon as the SWAT team dispersed to make their arrests, Slash led Rosario and Eggleston to Karen's office. Excitement pounded through her. She could not wait to take this woman down.

Knock-knock.

Karen opened the door, her gaze jumping from Slash to Rosario to Eggleston. Her face went ashen white while her beady eyes shot daggers into Slash.

"You motherfucking bitch!" Karen started to shut the door, but Slash stopped it with her foot, then bulled her way inside.

"Karen Woodside, you're under arrest for racketeering, specifically taking money in exchange for sex between members and dancers," Slash said. "You have the right to remain silent. You have the right to an attorney. If you cannot afford an attorney, one will be appointed to you. Do you understand these rights as they have been read to you?"

"Fuck you," Karen bit out.

"Do you understand them?" Detective Rosario asked.

"Of course I do. I'm not stupid. I used to be law enforcement. Who are you today, Slash? Why don't you tell them who you really work for?"

Detective Rosario glanced over at Slash before handcuffing Karen.

Slash wasn't fazed. There was nothing Karen could say that would affect her. If Karen didn't keep her mouth shut, it would only work against her, especially if she started blabbing about ALPHA.

Slash lifted Karen's laptop off her desk, tucked it under her arm.

"I need to make a phone call," Karen said.

"At the detention center," the detective said, as SWAT Agent Eggleston led her through the club.

The music had been turned off, every dancer stood frozen on a stage, shocked expressions plastered on their faces. A lot of the clubbers had cleared out, but those who stayed still hadn't moved out of their seats.

As Karen passed Bradley, the head bartender, she yelled, "Lock up on your way out."

Slash was incredulous. Karen's loyalty to the club was unmatched.

It's Greg. Her loyalty is to Greg.

Maybe Karen would strike a deal in exchange for information about Greg.

A handcuffed Karen was placed in Detective Rosario's vehicle while SWAT agents loaded everyone from the back room into the vans. Slash followed them to the police station.

When Rosario brought Karen through booking, Slash stayed by her side.

"This isn't going to stick," Karen said. "My boyfriend will post my bond, then he'll hire the best attorneys in the area."

Rosario put Karen in an interrogation room and uncuffed her.

"Can I get you a coffee? How 'bout a bottle of water?" the detective asked.

"Yeah, like that's gonna fix this fucking problem," Karen hissed, rubbing her wrists.

After Rosario shut the door, she and Slash observed her from a room around the corner.

"She didn't stop talking the *entire* ride over," Rosario said. "She blamed you for getting her fired from some top-secret law enforcement agency she called ALPHA."

"Not exactly." Slash let the words roll out. "Karen Woodside withheld information in a serial killer investigation. The case wasn't even mine, but I was asked to keep an eye on her. She got fired, blamed me."

"Anything to this top-secret group, ALPHA?"

"First time I'm hearing that one." Slash's phone buzzed with an incoming text. After reading it, she said, "He's here. I'll bring him up, and we'll go in together."

Detective Rosario nodded. "I'll be right here."

Five minutes later, Slash, Detective Rosario, and Arson Detective Milholland entered the interrogation room. Karen was pacing in the small space.

"Can I make that call now?" Karen asked.

"After we talk," Rosario said. "Have a seat."

Karen sat.

Detective Rosario sat across from her, Slash and Detective Milholland sat in chairs near the door.

Slash opened her laptop on the cued-up video, set the computer on her lap facing Karen, and hit Play.

Everyone in the room grew quiet while Karen watched the video. The first one Slash played was of a person dressed in black with a ski mask dumping the accelerant on the foundation of Elsa's home, outside her bedroom window, then in the back beneath the spare bedroom.

"What the hell is this?" Karen barked. "This doesn't have anything to do with me."

"Watch," Slash said.

After striking a match, the person mumbled something before tossing it onto the accelerant. They vanished around the back of the house. Twenty-nine seconds later, the person ran toward the house next door. Since the neighbor's front porch lights were on, the person in black was clearly visible as they ran from the burning building.

"You set it, then ran *away*," Slash growled. "I ran *in*."

"That's not me," Karen insisted. "I have an air-tight alibi. I'm at my club every night."

Next, Slash played the second video, the one in the parking lot. After the person in the two-door coupe parked, they pulled on a ski mask. For three brief seconds, the person's face was visible.

"You can't prove that's me," Karen said.

Slash pulled up the close-up of the car's license plate number, then Detective Rosario set a single piece of paper on the table in front of Karen.

"That's from the DMV." Rosario recited the license plate number, then read who the vehicle was registered to.

"So what?" Karen blurted. "There's no proof that's me. Someone took my car—without my knowledge, by the way—and torched some old lady's house."

Relief shot through Slash. Per usual, Karen had dug her own damn grave.

"How'd you know who was in the house?" Detective Milholland asked.

Blabbermouth Karen Woodside pursed her lips, lowered her head, and stared into her lap.

Silence hung in the air for several tense seconds.

Slash had the arsonist, but she didn't have motive. "Why did you try to murder Elsa Santini?"

When Karen raised her eyes, her killer stare drilled into Slash. "You got me fired from a job I was amazing at. The best in the biz, baby." Pausing, she flicked her head, and her hair flew away from her face. "You ruined my life, so I wanted to return the favor. I decided to go after your adorable little grandmother. Then, you ran in to that burning building and rescued her. I could not fucking believe that."

Karen glared at Detective Milholland. "Happy? She caught me. What a fucking hero. Blah-blah-blah. Let's all kiss Slash's ass. The whole thing makes me want to hurl."

Despite the anger coursing through her, Slash didn't react. She sat unmoved, letting the silence—and the truth—speak for her.

She had won. Plain and simple. And it felt so damn good.

"Detective Milholland, she's all yours," Slash said.

"Karen Woodside, you're under arrest for first degree arson and for the attempted murder of Elsa Santini," Detective Milholland said.

A deep sense of satisfaction filled Slash's soul. Sometimes justice did prevail.

SATURDAY LATE MORNING, Slash and Carrera parked in front of Elwood Tosh's Springfield home, owned by his current girlfriend. Tosh had been living there ever since he'd slithered back into town.

Unlike her arrest last night, she and Carrera were going into this situation blind. She didn't have access to Social Services records on any of the minors in the home, but her random welfare check should help answer her questions.

She just needed to stay in character and not slit Tosh's throat the second she laid eyes on him.

Determination coursed through her as they exited her SUV, made their way up the walkway of the split-level home. In Tosh's case, outside appearances were deceiving. The yard was freshly cut, the bushes trimmed, the flower garden bursting with vibrant colors. The exterior of the home presented well, but she knew the horrors lay behind closed doors.

She needed to gather everything she could about Tosh, so she could plan her hit with exact precision.

One car was parked in the driveway, a second in the carport. With any luck, both Tosh and his girlfriend would be home.

"Ready?" Carrera asked as they stepped up to the front door.

"Nothing like confronting the devil." She rang the doorbell.

A moment later, a pleasant-looking woman, who looked to be in her forties, answered. "No solicitations, please."

"Ms. Corlan, I'm Evelyn with Fairfax County Department of

Family Services," Slash said. "I'm here to do an unscheduled welfare check on the minors in your home."

Judy Corlan stepped back. "Come in."

She and Carrera entered the house, the rank odor of garlic and onions hung heavy in the air.

A man moseyed into view. Though she hadn't seen Elwood Tosh in fifteen years, she recognized him immediately.

Hatred and fury sliced through her.

No longer a terrified teen, Slash squared her shoulders. Elwood Tosh could no longer hurt her.

Now in his fifties, Tosh colored his hair a too-dark brown. He had a cluster of moles on his cheek and the least expressive eyes she'd ever seen. Dressed in jeans and a T-shirt, he'd gained a little weight, but otherwise looked the same.

Refusing to smile at him, she said, "Hello, are you—"

"This is my boyfriend, AJ," Judy Corlan said.

"What's this about?" Tosh asked.

"Social Services is doing an unscheduled check," Judy said.

Two small children ran into the foyer. The little boy came right over, but the girl hung back.

Ohgod, they're so young.

"Are these your children?" Slash asked.

"These are the foster kids," Judy replied. "Wouldn't you know that?"

"I have you down as fostering *older* children," Slash said. "Unfortunately, there was a mix-up in our system. The employee who entered data was making a lot of mistakes. It happens, sometimes."

Tosh nodded along.

"I'm glad you said something about the mix-up," Judy added. "First time, we fostered teens—"

"The sweet spot is between ten and fifteen." A demonic smile filled Tosh's face. "Old enough to wipe their own asses, but young enough to have a little fun with 'em."

A growl shot out of Carrera.

"If you prefer older, why didn't you refuse these children?" Slash asked.

The little boy held up a toy. "Can you play?" he asked Carrera.

"Sure, buddy," Carrera replied.

Judy led them into the living room. A few toys were scattered on the floor. While Carrera sat on the floor to play with the children, concern swept through Slash. She needed to get these little ones away from Tosh as soon as possible.

"Why didn't you tell the agency you couldn't take them?" Slash repeated.

"I was at work," Judy said. "AJ just took 'em."

"I made a mistake," Tosh said. "Thought I'd try out young kids, but they're too much work."

"We'll have them removed right away," Slash said.

"Good," Tosh said. "When can you bring us older ones?"

"Actually," Judy cut in, "I'm headed out of town tomorrow morning to visit my sister in Alabama. I'll be gone until Wednesday. Me and Elwood, we've been fostering nonstop. I work six days a week, so I need to take a break—"

"I'm here all the time," Elwood interrupted. "I'll take care of 'em."

Bile rose in Slash's throat. The thought of him alone with any children made her sick to her stomach.

Slash snapped a few pictures of the children. "How old are they?"

"Shouldn't you have all this?" Tosh asked.

"Like I said, the system shows you having older children," Slash said. "Lucky for you I stopped by."

"Yeah, I guess," Tosh grumbled.

"The boy is four, the girl is three," Judy said.

"What are their names?" Slash asked.

"Owen and Layla," Judy replied.

"If you have their medical records, can I see them?"

"Sure." Judy left the room.

Tosh glared at her. "We've never run into this much confusion before."

"The more you help us now, the faster we'll get these kids replaced for you."

"Yeah, okay. I like that," Tosh said.

The children started laughing. Carrera had built a tower with the soft blocks, then tipped it over. He was so good with them, so patient. As she returned her attention to Tosh, she prayed he hadn't laid a finger on them.

"What do you do with the kids all day?" she asked him.

Judy returned, handed Slash the paperwork. "We just got them a few days ago. I took off work. It's been kind of crazy."

Slash snapped pictures of everything. Both children were healthy, no known allergies.

"They're siblings," Slash said. "And their parents were killed in a car accident."

"Why aren't the kids with family?" Carrera asked.

"I was told they was having trouble locating anyone," Tosh replied.

Carrera stood, a child tucked under each arm like bundles. Both were giggling.

"If they puke, you clean up the mess," Tosh said.

"AJ, they're fine," Judy said.

Slash didn't want to leave the toddlers, but she couldn't take them. With a heavy heart, she walked through the house with Judy. The home was neat, the children slept in twin beds in the same room. Judy appeared to be a caring, responsible person. But her issue wasn't with Judy, it was with that monster Tosh. Back in the living room, she concluded the interview.

"We'll have the children picked up as soon as possible," Slash said.

When Carrera set the kids down, they went back to playing together.

"Do you want us to call or text to arrange a pick-up?" Slash asked.

"I'm here all the time," Tosh replied. "The faster you can place 'em, the happier I'll be."

"We'll make it our top priority," Carrera said.

They showed themselves out. As Slash drove away, pain sliced through her.

"You don't think he's hurting those babies," she whispered.

"I hope not," Carrera replied.

"How are we going to get those kids out?" she asked.

Carrera made a call.

"Hey," Sin answered. "I look forward to seeing you tonight."

"I've got Slash on speaker," Carrera said, "and we need your help."

"Go," Sin said.

Carrera explained the situation.

"I've got connections," Sin said. "Let me make some calls."

"Sin," Slash said, "I'm going back there when the guy is alone."

Silence.

After a beat, Sin asked, "When?"

"This Sunday, late."

"That's a small window," Sin said. "Foster care doesn't move that quickly, but I'll see what I can do. What are the kids' names?"

"Owen and Layla," Slash replied. "They're siblings. I snapped pics of them and their medical records. We'll get that over to you."

"I'll let you know." Sin hung up.

Slash stopped at a red light, handed her phone to Carrera, and told him her password.

"I'm forwarding to Sin and to me," Carrera said.

When he finished, she clasped his hand.

"I'm terrified for those little ones," she said.

"We're doing everything we can, short of taking them ourselves."

"I'm not ready to be an instant mom. I know that's selfish—"

"It's okay."

"Do you want to take them?" she murmured.

"As adorable as they are, I don't think it's a smart idea."

"Do you want children?" she asked.

He was silent for a minute. "It's not something I think about much. We need time together before we decide about kids. How 'bout you?"

Relief coursed through her. "Same."

"If we did have kids, we'd make kick-ass parents."

She laughed. "I hope so. It's the most important job in the world."

26

THE WEDDING, FINALLY!

Carrera

Saturday late afternoon, Carrera pulled up to Hotel Dillinger, handed the valet a folded bill, and made his way around the SUV as Slash got out.

Cooper and Danielle's wedding was finally here. He couldn't be happier for them, couldn't wait to kick back and relax for a few hours with his woman... and his friends.

With their wedding clothing in garment bags, they made their way inside and upstairs to the suites. He walked her to the bridal suite and kissed her goodbye as Rebel and Brit turned the corner.

"You two are too cute," Brit said.

"Hey," Slash said.

"Did you make the arrest?" Brit asked.

Slash smiled. "Yes, and it felt great."

"How'd she do?"

"Blabbed nonstop," Slash replied.

"Congratulations," Rebel said. "You must be relieved."

"Yes, to the arson and prostitution, but no to the missing women," Slash said. "Alexandra Wilde's news story airs on Monday. I'm hoping we get some legit leads."

Rebel kissed his wife before the women vanished inside the suite.

As Carrera and Rebel entered the groomsmen suite, Rebel asked, "How's your new job?"

Carrera hung his garment bag on the rack. "Going great. I've already managed to piss someone off."

"I'm sure you've pissed off a lot of people, you level-jumper you."

Carrera laughed.

Cooper and Stryker were chilling on the horseshoe-shaped sofa in the suite's living room. The men rose, everyone hugged it out.

"Congratulations, Coop," Carrera said. "You had a record-long engagement."

Cooper laughed. "I've been ready to marry Danielle for years, but life got in the way. Thanks to this guy"—he squeezed Rebel's shoulder— "everything here is first class."

"Thank you, brother," Rebel said.

"I heard you and Slash finally kissed and made up," Stryker said.

The guys laughed.

"I'm a lucky guy," Carrera said. "Stryker, you saved us with the video surveillance."

"How'd that go?"

Hawk, Prescott, and Jericho walked in.

"Karen Woodside got arrested," Carrera said.

"Again?" Hawk asked.

"For what?" Jericho asked.

"Prostitution at Blue Suit, first degree arson, and attempted murder," Carrera said.

"What the hell?" Prescott blurted.

"She wanted to get back at Slash, so she torched Elsa's house, hoping she'd die in the fire," Carrera continued.

"Pure evil," Jericho said.

"That's fucked up," Hawk said.

Stryker opened a bottle of chilled champagne and poured bubbly into seven flutes. With glasses in hand, they toasted the groom.

"To Cooper," Stryker said. "We love you, brother, and we wish you the best."

"Happy wife, happy life," Hawk said.

"Amen to that," Jericho added.

The men clinked glasses and sipped the champagne.

"Thanks for standing up for me," Cooper said to the group. "We've had each other's backs for a long time, known each other even longer." He raised his glass. "To my brothers."

They tapped flutes.

"How's everyone taking your promotion at the Bureau?" Cooper asked.

"Most don't know," Carrera replied. "Peter Hirzog is furious."

"Why would he care?" Rebel asked.

"Career agent." Carrera flashed a smile. "I took his office."

Jericho draped his arm over Carrera's shoulder. "Bro, why do you always poke the bear?"

"Because he can," Prescott said, and the group cracked up.

As the guys got ready, Carrera wondered how long he'd wait before he asked Slash to marry him.

"How long did it take you guys to know you'd found your person?" Carrera asked.

"I knew the minute I saw Brit," Rebel answered.

"I loved Addison before I was ready to love anyone again," Hawk replied.

"Are we talking about Slash here?" Jericho asked.

"Yeah." Carrera tugged on an undershirt, pulled his tuxedo shirt from the garment bag. "I'd marry her today—"

"Join us," Cooper said.

"Tonight?" Carrera asked.

"He's getting married in an hour," Stryker said. "He doesn't know what he's saying."

The guys laughed.

"I appreciate the offer, Coop," Carrera said, "but I'm gonna marry her on one of my cruise ships."

"The man knows what he wants," Prescott added.

"I sure as hell do." After a beat Carrera said, "I want to run something by you guys."

"Go for it," Jericho said.

Carrera gave the guys the short version of Elwood Tosh and the toddlers in his home, finishing with, "Sin is checking with his connections at family services. We need the kids removed ASAP."

He pulled up the pics of the little ones, handed his phone to Jericho.

"They're adorable." Jericho passed the phone to Hawk.

One by one, the guys looked at the pics of the children.

"They're siblings," Carrera said. "Owen is four, Layla is three. Their parents were killed in a car crash."

"Lemme talk to Liv," Jericho said. "Maybe we can foster them."

"That'd be great," Carrera said.

"Do they have grandparents?"

"Unclear at this point," Carrera replied.

As soon as the men finished getting ready, the hotel's wedding planner escorted them downstairs to a side ballroom where the bridesmaids were waiting.

Carrera scanned the room of beautiful ladies—all wearing black off-the-shoulder gowns—and found his target.

And his heart jumped into his throat.

Ohmygod, she's stunning.

Slash's dress hugged her curves in all the right places. Her hair was sculpted into a French twist, her long bangs framing her beautiful face.

Moving as a pack, the men made their way to their women.

When Slash swept her gaze over the guys, she locked on his. Her smile filled her face as he pulled up in front of her.

"You are gorgeous," he said.

"I clean up well," she deadpanned.

"Breathtaking in that dress, and I'm gonna enjoy undressing you later."

She stepped back, gave him a slow once-over. "Nice," she said. "You in a tux is giving me a lady boner."

Laughing, he clasped her hands. "It's my pleasure."

The wedding planner entered the ballroom. "Hello, beautiful people," she called out.

When the chatter continued, Jericho's piercing whistle silenced everyone. "Settle down."

"Thank you," said the planner. "Okay, so our beautiful bride is in a room nearby and our guests are anxiously awaiting. Is everyone ready?"

They were.

"Wonderful," she said. "I need my groom and his parents. Cooper?"

Cooper, his dad—in his wheelchair—and Cooper's mom made their way over.

"Are you ready to marry the woman of your dreams?" the planner asked Cooper.

"Been ready for years," Cooper replied.

"Best man?" called the planner. "Where are you?"

Stryker walked over. "Let's do this, brother."

After the wedding planner placed Cooper between his

mom and dad, Cooper offered his mom his arm and placed his hand on his dad's shoulder.

Stryker and Emerson stepped in line behind them, followed by Jericho and Liv. Next up, Hawk and Addison, Prescott and Jacqueline, and Rebel and Brit, with Carrera and Slash finishing off the bridal party.

The wedding planner and her assistant opened the double doors in the back of the ballroom, and orchestral sounds floated from the room.

Cooper and his parents headed down the aisle.

"Hi," someone murmured behind Carrera and Slash.

They turned to see Danielle, flanked by her mom and dad. The bride's elegant white dress flowed behind her, her radiant smile lighting up her pretty face.

"You look beautiful," Slash said.

Danielle beamed at them.

"Your man's waiting," Carrera said. "Let's get you married."

Slash slipped her hand around Carrera's bicep, gave him a squeeze. "All man, all muscle, all mine."

"Always," he murmured.

Over two hundred guests craned to see as the wedding party made their way down the aisle.

He peered down at Slash. "I love you," he murmured.

Her gaze found his. "I love hearing you tell me that." She winked before refocusing her attention on the guests.

At the end of the aisle, he kissed her cheek before they separated.

The traditional processional music began, the guests stood, and Danielle began her journey toward her forever man. Carrera glanced over at Cooper. He was beaming, but it was the look of love in his eyes that stood out the most.

In addition to the heartfelt speeches that were given by a few friends and family members, the wedding celebrant talked about the importance of forgiveness and the healing power of laughter. When it was time for the bride and groom to recite their vows, the room became pin-drop quiet.

As Danielle recited hers, Carrera thought about a life with Slash. Would they stay in his home or buy one together? Would his grandmother continue to live with them? Would Slash even marry him? Would they have children?

He looked beyond Cooper and Danielle, his eyes resting on Slash. Her gaze had softened as she watched Cooper promising his bride that he would treasure her forever, that he would spend his life loving her and making her smile. Slash swiped away a tear before she looked in his direction.

He was waiting. If she would have him, he would do right by her... for the rest of their lives.

After the rings were exchanged, the newlyweds came together in a long, loving kiss.

Cooper faced the guests. "Yes! *Finally!*"

The room exploded in laughter.

With huge grins, bride and groom made their way down the aisle as husband and wife. Two by two the wedding party filed out behind them. As he and Slash came together, she clasped his hand. "That was beautiful. I loved their vows so much."

"You're a softie," he murmured.

"Shh, don't tell," she replied. "You'll ruin my badass rep."

Once they exited the ballroom, the wedding planner ushered them into a side salon where the photographer started taking impromptu pictures as the close-knit circle of friends hurried over to congratulate the newlyweds.

At some point, the photographer asked Carrera and Slash to pose. Carrera stepped behind her, wrapped her in his arms, and said, "Forever and ever."

She craned her neck in his direction, her eyes filled with love.

The photographer snapped several pics. "Beautiful," he said. "How long have you two been together?"

Slash turned to the photographer, who continued clicking away.

"Not long enough," Carrera replied.

"I could tell," the photographer said. "I've been doing weddings for years, and I've gotten good at being able to spot the couples who'll stay together."

"We're getting married ourselves," Carrera said. "Can I get your contact info?"

"Okay, wow," Slash said.

The man handed him a card. "Judge for yourself when the pics come back, but honestly, you guys were easy. If the love is there, the camera will find it."

When the photographer moved on, Slash said, "Congrats on your engagement. When's the big day?"

"Whenever you say it is," he said before folding her in his arms and dropping a light kiss on her lips.

As the photographer was positioning the wedding party for group shots, Jericho and Liv hurried over.

"Liv and I will foster the children," Jericho said.

"What?" Slash asked.

"I showed the guys the pictures of Layla and Owen," Carrera explained.

Slash hugged them. "What a relief. That's a big commitment."

"We can handle it," Liv said. "Our hearts broke for those little ones. We're happy to take them."

Carrera pulled out his phone. "I'm letting Sin know."

"I'll grab two car seats in the morning, then pick you guys up," Jericho said.

"I'll get the guest room ready for them," Liv explained. "Then, explain to Liam—who just turned three—that we're having Owen and Layla for an extended visit." She smiled. "It'll be fun."

After the photographer snapped several group shots of the

bridal party, they made their way toward the reception, held in the grand ballroom.

Slash walked over to Carrera, entwined her fingers through his.

"You are amazing," she said. "Thank you, babe."

He flashed her a smile. "You can thank me later."

She laughed. "Yes, I can, and I will."

27

REVENGE

Carrera

Sunday morning, Jericho parked in front of Elwood Tosh's house. The front windows were wide open. Carrera looked inside, but couldn't see anyone.

As the three made their way to the front door, Tosh yelled. "Shut your damn mouths and stop your fucking crying."

BAM! BAM! BAM!

Carrera pounded on the front door.

Seconds later, Tosh answered.

"We're here to take the children." Carrera bulled his way past Tosh and strode into the house.

The children were sitting on the living room floor, crying. When the little boy saw them, he lifted his hands toward Carrera. Carrera's heart overflowed with love as he swept the youngster into his arms.

"Hey, Owen." Carrera smiled at him. "You ready to get outta here?"

Owen stopped crying.

Jericho crossed his arms, glared down at Tosh. "Where're their things?"

Tosh pointed. "Upstairs."

Slash picked up Layla. "Hi, Layla. You ready to leave with Owen?" She wiped the little girl's tears from her cheeks.

Carrera smiled at both children, despite the fury that raced through him.

Carrera and Slash stood in the foyer while Jericho walked up the short staircase with Tosh. A few minutes later, he returned with a small duffle bag and a suitcase. "I got the clothes. Let's get 'em the hell out."

"I've got great news," Slash said.

"What's that?" Tosh asked.

"Would you to foster like a fifteen-year-old girl?" Slash asked.

Tosh's face lit up. Carrera and Jericho exchanged glances.

"Sounds perfect," Tosh said. "When's she coming by?"

"I'm going to rush the paperwork through," Slash said. "How 'bout I bring her by tonight."

"Can't wait," Tosh said.

"It'll be late, after eleven," Slash explained.

"Perfect," Tosh said. "I'll get her all tucked into her new bed."

A growl rumbled from the depths of Carrera. He wanted to wrap his hands around Tosh's throat and kill him himself.

"We'll see you then." Slash smiled at Layla before the three left the home.

At the SUV, Jericho placed their things in the back, then walked over to the children. "Hi, Owen. Hi, Layla. I'm Jericho. You're going to stay with me and my wife, Liv, and our son Liam." Jericho smiled at the kids. "You ready to head to your new home?"

They strapped the children into the car seats. Jericho pulled two sippy cups from a cooler. After smiling at the kids, he said, "Who's thirsty for water?"

"I am," Owen said.

"Me too," Layla agreed.

Jericho handed each of them a cup before Slash climbed into the back with them, and they took off.

Jericho talked to the kids most of the way to his house. He smiled more than Carrera had ever seen, and he'd softened his voice.

For a large, foreboding man, he looked like a teddy bear. Relief swept through Carrera.

"If things work out," Jericho said, "Liv and I might adopt them."

"Whoa," Slash said from the back seat.

"We'll see," Jericho continued. "We stayed up late talking about it. We have to find out their situation. They might have good family waitin' to take care of them. I'll keep you posted. For now, they're safe and they'll be loved."

~

Slash

LATER THAT AFTERNOON, Slash entered the Arlington detention center, flashed her FBI badge. After signing in, she was escorted to the detainee visiting room. From the moment Slash had learned Karen had tried to kill Elsa, she couldn't shake the anger.

Karen would pay for what she'd done. Slash would make sure of that.

Slash didn't give a damn about the prostitution ring, and would have moved in for the arrest sooner had she not found out about the missing women. But the attempted murder was personal. Who the fuck tries to burn down an old woman's house?

A growl shot out of her.

A goddamn sociopath, that's who.

A guard led Karen in. She glared at Slash before sitting down on the other side of the glass window.

"You must be pretty fucking proud of yourself," Karen said.

"You got an issue with me, come after me. Only monsters try to kill an innocent, old woman."

Karen's lips split into a menacing smile. Once again, Brit's motto held true.

Life's short, shit happens, people are mostly crazy.

"You don't get it," Karen said. "If I'd killed you, you wouldn't have suffered. This was all about revenge, bitch. You made me suffer. I wanted to repay the favor."

Slash glared at her. "No, *you* don't get it. You did this to yourself when you impeded an active-threat investigation."

"Oh, you mean at ALPHA!" Karen bellowed.

Those guards don't give a fuck about her blathering.

"It's time to save your sorry ass," Slash said. "I'm here to throw you one lifeline. Tell me the club owner's name and where I can find him."

Karen's shrill cackle pierced her ears.

"The last thing I would do is help you."

"Seven women went missing from your club. You were there busting your ass every single day and every single night. What did you get out of that? Not enough or you wouldn't have pocketed the prostitution money."

"I did not—"

"We're way beyond your lies at this point," Slash said. "You got ten grand from Claude Amos and you kept it. You're facing a lot of prison time. Save your own ass, or are you too stupid to do that?"

"Fuck you, you bitch," Karen spat out. "Fuck you a million times."

Slash shook her head. This woman was beyond messed up.

"Is your boyfriend, Greg, the owner?" Slash asked. "I saw him in the kink room with Deb right before she went missing. If he's involved with these missing women, are you an accomplice?"

Karen harrumphed. "For the hundredth time, those women didn't go missing. They quit! Why are you so obsessed with this anyway? Who gives a fuck!"

Fury pounded through her.

"You're behind bars and you won't even save your own sorry ass. I won't stop until I find him." She regarded Karen with cool disdain. "You didn't win, and neither will he."

Slash pushed out of the chair and left.

As she headed into the parking lot, she bit back a smile.

The bait had been set. All she had to do was wait for Greg to take it.

Instead of going back to Carrera's, she drove to BLACK OPS, stopping to grab dinner on the way. After parking in the hangar, she shouldered her computer satchel, grabbed the food, and made her way to the retina scanner. The light turned green, and inside she went.

To her surprise, she heard voices coming from one of the offices. Following the sound, she walked down the corridor, glancing into empty rooms until she stopped in front of an open doorway.

Carrera was on speaker phone. He flashed her a smile as she walked in.

"I appreciate your help, Malcolm," Carrera said, as Slash set her items on the desk.

"Who should we contact, Deputy Director Santini?" asked the man on the phone.

"Special Agent O'Reilly and me." After providing their contact info, Carrera hung up.

"Hey, babe." He pushed out of the chair and kissed her hello. "That was the detention center. We'll be notified if Karen has visitors."

"You're handy to have around, Deputy Director," she said.

He leaned his ass against the table, kept his hands anchored on her waist. "How'd it go?"

"Like we expected. Karen wouldn't give up the owner, wouldn't comment on Greg, and she doesn't give a damn about the missing women."

"You're not surprised, are you?"

"No, but I *am* surprised she doesn't want to save her own ass. I can't figure out why she's so loyal to Greg. It's not like he's her husband."

"Maybe he is. We don't know anything about him."

"With any luck, she'll give him a heads up. I reminded her that I caught her, and I told her he's next."

Concern flashed in his eyes. It was subtle, but she caught it. "You don't think I can take him, do you?"

"I do, babe," he said, "but if he kidnapped seven women and left no trace, you can't underestimate him."

"I'm not afraid."

He shot her a smile. "Eyes wide open."

"Always," she replied. "Ready to work?"

"Let's do this."

After opening her laptop, she said, "I've been waiting fifteen long years to take out this monster."

While they ate, they talked strategy. Kill missions had to be exact, they had to be quick, and they could leave no trail.

"We probably shouldn't even be here," Carrera murmured. "This isn't an ALPHA-sanctioned hit."

"We can't talk about this at home—I mean, your place. Elsa loves studying the white board. She's fascinated by the cases.

You should've seen her the day I brought her out here for train-ing." Slash chuckled. "She was on the edge of her seat. I've never seen her so locked-in on anything."

His gaze drilled into hers.

"What?" she asked.

"You called my house home."

"I corrected myself."

He smiled. "Move in with me."

"I kinda have."

"Most of your things are still at your place. What about selling or renting your townhouse?"

She leaned back in the chair and studied his face. He was serious.

"My favorite part of the day is waking up next to you, and my other favorite part of the day is loving you in my bed, then falling asleep with you in my arms." He kissed her.

She appreciated his honesty, loved his romantic side.

"It's going to take months before Elsa's home is rebuilt," she said. "I'm gonna be straight-up with you—"

"I hope so," he said.

"She likes living with you—with us," Slash said. "I never thought she was lonely. She's got a life, activities, friends, but she seems happier with us."

"She told me she doesn't miss the stairs," he said. "What do *you* think about her living with us?"

She smiled. "You're slick."

He pointed to himself. "Me? Nah." He paused. "What do you think about moving in, for real?"

Slash had fallen deeply in love.

Should I tell him?

Yes, tell him.

"I'll move in," she said. "And make us official, but *only* so you'll stop asking me."

He laughed. "That'll work."

"I love that Elsa is with us. I adore her so much." Slash's eyes grew moist with emotion, and she cleared her throat. "I love you, Carrera. I know you're my person. You've always been my person."

He placed one hand on her cheek, the other around the back of her neck, beneath her hair. "I will love you fiercely for the rest of my life."

She melted from his words and the tender way he held her, but the love shining in his eyes made her feel like she'd finally come home.

She tapped her laptop. "Okay, let's focus up."

It was after eleven when they finished strategizing. Like any kill mission, she went over best-and-worst-case scenarios.

She appreciated that Carrera didn't take lead. Despite his alpha tendencies and his need for control, he understood that this was her mission.

"We have a saying at ALPHA," she said. "We go in together, we come out together. That includes a body bag."

"Jesus," he muttered. "That's not happening."

"No, it's not, but we put everything on the table."

Once finished, they suited up. On went their Kevlar. Both pulled on a double holster, both attached a silencer to their primary Glock, then placed a secondary weapon in the other holster. Like a second skin, her switchblade was already tucked in the leather sheath around her ankle.

In her go-bag, she replaced the smoke bomb, her helmet with night goggles, and her ski mask with a plastic tarp. She tied her hair in a ponytail, pulled on a black, knit cap, handed a cap to Carrera.

Slash made a call. Luciano answered.

"We're leaving," she said.

"You're clear," Luciano replied.

The line went dead.

Luciano had shut down the home surveillance systems in Tosh's immediate neighborhood.

She and Carrera were armed, and they were ready.

They walked down the hall in silence, made their way into the hangar.

"I'll drive," he said.

After placing her bag in the back seat, she slid into the front. He covered the front and back license plates with a deflector. Once the large hangar door closed, they rolled out. As they headed toward Springfield, she removed the heart necklace he'd given her and stored it in the glove box.

He opened the sunroof, and she stared into the night sky dotted with twinkling stars. She appreciated that he stayed silent so she could focus on the mission, running through the scenarios in her mind, ensuring that each one ended with the death of Elwood Tosh.

But taking another's life came with a heavy burden on her soul. Life was precious, something to be revered. She went into law enforcement to protect and to serve, but she spent her days chasing evil.

The atrocities of others bled into her nightmares, into her life, into every decision she made. The stench of the wicked clung to her daily.

Tosh was a predator who preyed on the innocent, the gullible, the defenseless. The worst kind of evil. And because he was cunning, he'd never been caught. Didn't have a record. In fact, he was probably viewed as a good Samaritan, offering up his home and his time toward those who needed a helping hand.

A growl ripped from the depths of her soul.

The hunger for revenge had festered for too many years. Tonight, she would take out one of Satan's helpers, and she could not fucking wait.

It was almost midnight when they drove into Tosh's quiet

suburban neighborhood. Carrera killed the headlights, backed into Tosh's driveway. The front light was on, an upstairs light too. The blinds in the front room were open, but the room was dark.

He clasped her hand. "I got your back."

"And I got yours."

They pulled on their black gloves and exited the SUV. She grabbed her go-bag before quietly closing the vehicle doors. On the front porch, she rang the bell.

Seconds later, Tosh opened the door. "Where is she?"

Slash brushed past him. "Waiting in the vehicle."

Carrera entered the house, shut the door, and killed the outside light.

Tosh eyed their body armor. "What's going on? Where's the girl?"

"We've had some complaints about you, so we want to clear those up before we bring her inside," Slash said.

"Complaints? Like what?"

Slash's fingers tingled to take him out, to end it, to move on, but she needed closure. She needed to say what she couldn't all those years ago.

Carrera strode into the darkened living room, closed the blinds, then bolted up the half-flight of stairs into the front bedroom. The upstairs went dark, and he returned, a Glock in his hand. Tosh's eyes grew wide.

"Goddamn, is this a robbery?"

Slash grabbed his arm and forced him into the living room. "I don't want your crap,"

Carrera turned on a small table lamp, bathing the room in dim light. She shoved him into a chair and glared down at him.

"You're raping and sodomizing your foster kids," she ground out, the long-held anger burbling to the surface.

Even in the low-lit room, fear flashed in his eyes. "Those brats are makin' shit up. I've never laid a finger on any of 'em. I give 'em a home, a hot meal, and this is how they show their appreciation? By making up shit lies?"

"Fifteen years ago, I was one of those kids," Slash said. "My parents were killed and I got put into the system. You were molesting and assaulting the kids in the house."

"Fuck you," he rasped, his voice rough like dirt.

"I heard them," Slash continued. "I heard one of them begging you to stop. I heard another whimpering. In the dead of night, while they were tucked into their beds—vulnerable and alone—you committed violent, unspeakable acts."

Tosh looked at Carrera. "She's a fucking loon. Crazy bitch. You and me, we's guys need to stop her."

"Shut the fuck up," Carrera growled. "You're the worst kind of evil."

"It's my word against yours," Tosh said.

"Last words before you meet the devil," Slash said.

"I loved every moment of my life," Tosh said, his voice gruff, his eyes filled with hate. "I loved earning their trust, loved forcing myself on them. They're so helpless, so fuckin' terrified." A maniacal smile split his face. "I had a never-endin' stream of victims parading through. If a kid complained, I was on the run. Then, I'd find some lonely woman, show her a little attention, convince her to foster kids, and I was back in business."

"You're the fucking devil," Carrera bit out.

"I am." Tosh lunged for Slash, but she jumped away. He reached behind his back—

With lightning speed, Slash whipped out her blade, plunged it into his heart. Tosh dropped to the floor. She pulled her Glock and squeezed the trigger—*POP!*—hitting him between his eyes.

They had to work fast.

Carrera locked the front door. She pulled out the tarp from her bag, and they laid Tosh's body on it. She removed her knife, cleaned off his blood with his shirt, then Carrera checked Tosh for weapons. He had a gun tucked into the back of his pants and a cell phone in his pocket. Carrera left the gun and the phone on the chair. After they wrapped his body, they carried him outside through the carport. Carrera opened the back of the SUV and they placed Tosh's body inside.

They were gone in under five.

Once Carrera hit the main road, he turned in his headlights, opened the sunroof. The ride was filled with the sound of air rushing inside the vehicle.

She breathed deeply. It was over. A fifteen-year-old promise had been fulfilled. Tosh could *never* assault another child, ever again. His victims would never know that someone had finally stopped him. She was no hero, she was a villain in her own story. Despite her actions, she had no regret, and she would spend eternity in hell if one innocent child was spared his heinous acts of violence.

In the dark vehicle, she bagged their gloves, clasped her heart necklace around her neck. When she peered over at Carrera, he met her gaze.

"I dragged you into my nightmare," she said.

"I walked willingly," he said. "Our lives will always be complicated, but as long as we've got each other, we can get through anything."

"I'm beginning to think you're right."

For years, revenge had been her guiding force. Maybe it was time to free herself from the bondage of her past and set her sights on her future... a future with the man sitting right beside her. A man who would stop at nothing to show his allegiance and his loyalty.

In the blink of an eye, her entire life had come full circle.

28

MARRY ME

Carrera

Carrera needed to give Slash space, but he also wanted to check in with her. What had happened between her and Tosh had been intense.

He drove down a street, passed a convenience store gas station, turned right, then a left, and another right before he stopped at the gate and tapped the intercom buzzer.

"I'm here," said the familiar voice.

"Delivery," Carrera said.

"Name?"

"Pied Piper."

The gate opened, Carrera drove through, and around back.

Like every other time, the metal fire door had been propped open. He and Slash unloaded the body, carried it inside, set it on the floor.

CK shook Carrera's hand, eyed Slash. "Howdy, ma'am."

She tossed him a nod.

After they unwrapped the body, he and CK set him on the

cold slab. Slash removed the black gloves from the bag, set them on the body.

"You staying?" CK asked.

Carrera held out folded bills. "Always do."

The door to the incinerator opened. Tosh was rolled in, the door closed and bolted shut.

"I'll be in here." CK walked into his office, shut the door.

Carrera sat on the nearby bench while Slash stood there unmoved.

"You want to sit with me?" he asked.

When she did, she let out a deep breath.

"How are you doing?" he asked.

She tugged off the knit cap, pulled out the ponytail, raked her fingers through her hair. "I'm doing."

"You want to talk about it?"

"I stopped a predator," she murmured, staring ahead. "A monster who changed my life. But... if he'd been a good man, I wouldn't have run. I wouldn't have met Elsa, I wouldn't have met you. Because of him, I spend my life hunting evil." She peered over at him. "I feel no remorse for what I did."

He ran his fingers through her long hair, caressed her back. "Maybe it's time to put your past behind you."

She nodded. "Maybe it is."

Carrera

FIRST THING MONDAY MORNING, Carrera turned on the big screen TV in his family room. Slash sat on the sofa, G-ma by her side. Alexandra Wilde's story was about to air on the early-morning national news show.

After the anchor introduced her, Alexandra said, "This case deserves national attention. In the past six months, seven women have gone missing from the recently-closed gentlemen's club, The Blue Suit Club in Arlington, Virginia, just outside the Nation's Capital."

Pictures of all seven women were plastered on the screen.

"Yes!" Slash said. "That's great."

"According to the undercover agent handling the case, the general manager *insisted* that all seven simply ghosted on their jobs," Alexandra continued. "Rather than accept that answer, the agent has made finding these women a top priority. In a twist, the general manager, Karen Woodside—a former law enforcement officer—was arrested for running a prostitution ring out of the back room."

"I hope this blows our case wide open," Slash interjected.

"Family and friends are anxious for the safe return of all seven women," Alexandra continued. "If you've seen any of these women, please contact the FBI or local law enforcement in your area."

The anchor turned to Alexandra. "This is an important story that the public needs to know about, and you've got more to share."

"I do," Alexandra said. "I've spoken to several dancers at Blue Suit who talk about a man named Greg. He's White, between thirty and forty with brown hair, and a beard and mustache. He appears shy when speaking with the women and he claims to work for the CIA. He offers the dancers five-hundred-dollar tips for private conversations. The FBI is eager to speak with him."

"Fifteen hundred people go missing every day," said the news anchor. "I'm glad you're shedding light on this important topic." She paused. "We'll be right back."

Carrera muted the TV as Elsa hugged Slash.

"I'm so proud of you, I can't stand it," Elsa said.

Slash laughed. "I had a partner, Elsa. Don't forget about him."

Elsa hugged Carrera. "Excellent work, both of you. I hope this story makes a difference. Do you have a picture of this Greg man?"

"No," Slash said. "Unfortunately, not."

"Congratulations, babe," Carrera said before kissing her. "I'm headed to work."

"Same," Slash replied. "Elsa, what are you doing today?"

"I'm having a pool party," Elsa replied.

"For real?" Carrera asked.

"Yes, I've invited my friends for lunch, and we're going swimming."

Carrera smiled. "Have fun."

He and Slash left through the garage.

"Let's go riding this Saturday," Carrera said. "We'll get up early, get out of the city."

"I love that." She kissed him goodbye. "I'm at ALPHA all day. Stryker's attempting to hack into Blue Suit's surveillance system. I'm hoping we can find a video with Greg in it."

One more kiss before they each drove away.

As Carrera headed to work, Liv Savage called.

"Hey, Liv, how are things going?" Carrera asked.

"As my new boss, I wanted to touch base with you. You know I'm a watcher, right?"

"I do."

"I'm requesting the week off. I know it's short notice—"

"I understand."

"Jericho and I are spending the week with the kids. Liam has been so good about sharing. I'm so proud of him."

"That's great."

"Owen and Layla are very sweet. Owen has asked for his mommy and daddy. I want to give them as much stability as possible."

"Take as much time as you need. You've got a job whenever you return."

"I appreciate that. Jericho talked to Sin. He removed Elwood Tosh's name from Owen and Layla's foster records, so it doesn't show them ever living with him."

"Nice. If you need Slash and me to relieve you and Jericho from the mayhem, text me."

"You and Slash, huh?" He could hear the smile in Liv's voice. "Why don't you two swing by Friday for dinner?"

"Sounds great."

"I'll text Slash," Liv said before hanging up.

He arrived at FBI HQ and parked in his spot in the garage. Rather than drag Z up, he took the stairs to the basement.

Knock-knock.

"Come in," Z said.

Carrera entered Z's small office.

"What are you doing down here?" Z asked.

"Less eyes," Carrera replied as he sat. "Liv's taking the week off, and she might need longer. How many watchers do you have?"

"Three, including her. I could use a fourth."

"Do you meet with them?" Carrera asked.

"Weekly," Z replied. "They prefer to come down here, so you might want to keep this office. The watchers keep a very low profile."

"Got it."

After typing a few keystrokes, Z turned the monitor around so Carrera could see their HR files.

Interesting.

Despite his pact with Luciano and Sin, he would *not* be sharing this information with his cousin. If Luciano saw the names on that list, it would be a massive shit storm that neither he nor Sin could control.

∼

Slash

SLASH WAS STOKED to be back at ALPHA full time. As she made her way toward her office, she said hello to two Ops.

"We missed you," said one.

"Welcome back," said the other.

She was thrilled to be there, couldn't wait for BLACK OPS training that afternoon.

After dropping her things in her office, she pulled Karen's laptop from her computer bag and went in search of Stryker. Her first stop? Emerson's office, where she found husband and wife working away.

With Danielle on her honeymoon, Emerson had the space to herself.

"Hey guys," Slash said.

"She's back!" Emerson said with a smile.

"Are you next?" Stryker asked.

"Next for what?" Slash asked.

"Getting married," Emerson exclaimed.

Rather than blow them off, she said, "I won't say no when he asks."

They both smiled so big, she laughed. "Stryker, you ready to work?"

"Born ready, baby," he replied as he pulled his long hair into a man-bun.

"I hate to kick you two out—" Emerson said.

Stryker's expression fell. "You want us to leave?"

Emerson laughed. "I'm kicking you out of my office, babe. Just my office. I'll see you for lunch."

They relocated to Slash's office. She set down Karen's laptop, then watched as he removed the hard drive, attached a cable, and plugged it into the laptop's USB port.

She opened her own laptop, logged in and started working.

She had twelve cases she'd sidelined, so she dove in and got busy.

Minutes turned into an hour before Stryker spoke. "Is this the only computer at the club?"

"The only one I ever saw," she replied.

"There's nothing," he said.

"What do you mean *nothing*?"

"Woodside kept no lists," he said. "No one to track."

"What about the members?"

"I can see member's profiles, but they set up online accounts, paid through the app."

"What about videos from the surveillance cameras?" Slash asked. "There were nine cameras total, two pointed at each stage, and one in the dressing room. None in the bar area, but they could have been hidden."

"There's nothing on this laptop that gives me access to *any* surveillance equipment," Stryker explained. "It's either cloud based, or it has its own, dedicated server. What you're looking for isn't here. There's nothing in the history that shows she checked surveillance because the surveillance doesn't exist. Not on this laptop."

"For fuck's sake," she bit out. "Karen told a detective that the cameras don't work."

"Either she's telling the truth or they *do* work, but she doesn't have access to them."

Dammit.

"Thanks for trying," she said. "And thank you for helping us catch the arsonist. You're a damn good hacker, Stryker Truman."

He shot her a smile. "Anytime."

After Stryker left her office, she worked until it was time for training. Ready to blow off steam, she packed up and drove to BLACK OPS.

But she couldn't shake the frustration that followed. If

Karen didn't have access to those cameras, then who did?

Carrera

MONDAY NIGHT, after Slash went upstairs to get ready for bed, Carrera sat on the sofa next to his grandmother.

"Since you're the secret keeper, I wanted you to be the first to know I'm asking Amanda May to marry me."

G-ma clasped his hand. "About time."

He grinned.

"I'm very happy for you," she said. "Do you have a ring? Are you giving her one?"

"I am, but I haven't bought one yet," he said. "I want us to design something together."

G-ma rose off the sofa. "Be right back."

A moment later, she sat beside him again, and held up a diamond ring. "This is my engagement ring from G-pa. Do you think Amanda May would like this? It's a solitaire stone that you could build on, if she likes it."

"I think she'd love it. Thank you."

"I'm delighted." She placed the ring in his palm.

"Why don't you wear it anymore?" Carrera asked.

G-ma displayed her gold wedding band. "I like wearing this by itself."

He kissed her cheek. "Wish me luck."

Up went her eyebrows. "You're proposing now?"

"I'm going to sleep." He pushed off the sofa, shot her a smile. "I hadn't thought about doing it now, but maybe I will."

Upstairs he went. He found Slash on the screened porch off his bedroom, bathed in moonlight. He slid the ring into his pocket, went outside.

"Hey," she said.

He stood beside her.

"I love this little room. I can see the stars. I love listening to the tree frogs." A firefly lit up as it zoomed by. "Those are my favorites."

He put his arm around her, caressed her shoulder. "I can't live without you."

"I know," she replied.

He chuckled.

After a second, she said, "I'm putting my house on the market."

His heart soared. "Babe, that's great. Do you want to stay here? Do you want us to look for a home together?"

She turned toward him. "I love your home, love that it works for the three of us. It's in a great location, and I would *not* give up that pool."

He slipped his hand behind her hair and gently caressed her neck. Touching her soft skin, running his fingers through her long hair brought him joy.

Do it. Ask her now.

He pulled out the engagement ring, dropped to one knee.

"What are you doing?" she asked.

"I meant it when I said I can't live without you. I did that for way too long. I love you so much and want to show you that, every day, if you'll let me." He held up the diamond ring. "Amanda May, will you marry me?"

Her smile lit up the night, and her eyes filled with love. The passion in her kiss was the answer he needed.

"Hell, yeah, I'll marry you." She kissed him again before he stood, pulled her into his arms, and lifted her off the ground.

Their embrace was filled with love and joy, passion and hope.

When he set her back down, she said, "I was definitely not expecting that."

He held out the engagement ring. "This is Elsa's. My grand-father gave it to her, and she wants you to have it."

She offered him her left hand, and he slid on the ring, but it only made it as far as her second knuckle.

"It's beautiful," she said. "I love that it was Elsa's."

"I thought we could design a ring around the center stone. Add more diamonds—"

"That sounds fun." Her adorable smile made him laugh. "I gotta say, I'm liking how you spoil me." She pulled the ring off her finger. "We'll have it resized and see about a design, but I might leave it like this." She draped her arms over his shoulders. "Let's get in bed and celebrate."

"I'm all in, babe," he replied.

"You're about to be," she said with a gleam in her eyes.

Slash

TUESDAY LATE AFTERNOON, while Slash was packing up to leave ALPHA, her phone buzzed with a text from Jazz.

> Guess what? The house is done. Yay! Come by and see it

Though Slash was surprised to hear from her, Jazz had been making an effort to be nice.

> Sure. I'll text Carrera

Dots appeared, then another text.

> I thought we could spend a few minutes just the two of us. I was hoping we could become friends. Russell is here, but I'm kicking him out lol. One glass of wine, then we'll meet the guys at Russell's restaurant

Slash shouldered her computer bag, grabbed her handbag, and made her way out of the building. Outside, dark gray storm clouds blanketed the sky as a light rain fell.

Damn.

She'd been hoping to go for a long run, then a swim in the pool. Thunder grumbled miles away, then a flash of summer lightning illuminated the sky. Slash jumped in her SUV.

> I'll swing by. Address?

Jazz texted the address.

> See you in 15

Her fingers flew over the keyboard as she typed out a text to Carrera.

> Babe, Jazz invited me to her house for a glass of wine. Renovations are done. She thought you and Russell could meet us later at his restaurant. Does that work for you?

After sending the message, Slash pulled up her playlist and drove out.

～

Carrera

CARRERA PULLED INTO HIS GARAGE, killed the engine, and headed into the house. G-ma wasn't in the family room or the kitchen. He glanced onto the screened porch, but she wasn't there either.

"G-ma?" he called out.

No response as he walked into his home office and set down his computer bag. His phone rang with a call from the Arlington County Detention Center.

"Santini," he answered.

"Deputy Director Santini, this is Malcolm at the Arlington County Detention Center."

"Hey, Malcolm. Did we get a hit?"

"We sure did," Malcolm replied. "I emailed you a link to view the surveillance earlier, but thought I'd confirm you saw it."

"I appreciate that." Carrera unearthed his laptop, opened it, and logged in. "Got it."

"Let me give you my direct number."

After hanging up, Carrera clicked on the video link. Greg sat down in front of the detainee window at the county jail. With the ball cap pulled down, and the full beard and mustache, Carrera could barely see him. He wore a white, collared shirt and Khaki pants. There was nothing remarkable about him, nothing that would ID him like a tat or an unusual piece of jewelry. Even so, there was something familiar about him.

A moment later, Karen was brought in. She sat across from him, separated by the shatterproof glass.

"I'm so happy to see you," Karen said. "You've gotta get me out."

Greg said something, but the camera was on Karen's side, so his voice was muffled.

Carrera turned up the volume on his laptop.

"I'm sorry," Karen said. "I have no idea when the club will be re-opened."

Greg's muffled voice made it impossible to hear him.

"Did you hire a lawyer for me?" Karen asked.

More talking from Greg.

Her expression fell, her mouth dropped open. "What do you mean, you're breaking up with me!" she screamed.

The guard stepped over. "Keep it down."

"Go to hell," Karen blurted over her shoulder before she turned back to Greg. "You can't leave me. I thought we were going to get married."

Greg spoke.

"What!" Karen bellowed.

"That's it," said the guard. "I warned you once. Time's up."

Karen shoved out of the chair and leaned down toward the metal slats in the window. "I hope you rot in hell!"

The guard ushered her out, and Greg left.

The video ended.

Carrera called the detention center.

"Malcolm Burrus."

"Malcolm, it's Carrera Santini. Are there cameras on the front of the building?"

"Sure are."

"When did the man visit detainee Karen Woodside?"

"Hold for me. I'll check."

While waiting, Carrera noticed he had a missed text from Slash. He tapped on it and read it.

> Babe, Jazz invited me to her house for a glass of wine. Renovations are done. She thought you and Russell could meet us later at his restaurant. Does that work for you?

"Mr. Santini?" Malcolm asked.

"I'm here."

"He was here, yesterday afternoon."

"Can you send me the video of him in the parking lot?"

"You got it."

"I'm gonna need that ASAP," Carrera replied.

Slash

SLASH PULLED up in front of Jazz's house, an older home in a busy section of Arlington. Rain pelted the windshield while the rumbling thunder grew closer. She turned off the wipers, cut the engine, and hurried to the front door.

A few seconds after ringing the doorbell, Russell opened the door.

"Hey, Slash, c'mon in." He moved out of the way so she could step inside. "Pretty wet out there, huh?"

The quaint living room was filled with a new-looking sofa, a matching chair, and a TV mounted on the wall.

"I heard your renovations are done," she said.

"Mostly," he replied. "Jazz is excited to move in. She's been cleaning like a fiend. I told her I'd hire someone, but she's on a tear." He laughed.

"Where is she?"

"Basement," Russell said. "I'm heading back to my campaign headquarters, but Jazz says we're meeting up at my restaurant in an hour."

He stepped outside, turned back. "Make yourself at home," he said, and shut the door behind him.

Slash's phone buzzed. She lifted it from her pocket, read the text from Carrera.

Hey, babe, Greg went to visit Karen in prison
yesterday. I'll see you at the restaurant.
Love you

I love you too.

"Hey, Slash, can you help me?" Jazz called.

Slash walked down the hall, stopping in front of the open door to the basement. The lone bulb at the top of the stairs bathed the room in diffused light.

Down the steps she went. At the bottom, the room was small, like a waiting room but without furniture. On the opposite wall was a doorway. Muted light from the room beyond beckoned her forward.

Slash walked over, pausing in the doorway.

"What the hell?"

A hand-held voice recorder sat on a table.

"Hey, Slash, can you help me?" Jazz called from the recorder.

The basement door at the top of the stairs slammed shut, followed by the snap of a lock being thrown. Then, the lights went out, plunging her in total darkness.

And dread filled her soul.

29

REVENGE FULL THROTTLE

Carrera

Carrera's phone rang.

"Malcolm, what do you have?" Carrera asked.

"Check your email."

Carrera clicked on the link. The video started playing. Greg left the detention center, strolled into the parking lot, and over to a car. Once inside, he drove away.

"Got it," Carrera said.

He hung up, rewound the video, pausing on the vehicle. After enlarging it, he homed in on the license plate. He couldn't tell if the second number was a three or an eight, so he entered both into the system.

While waiting for the results, he went in search of G-ma. He found her sitting with Jazz on the porch.

What the hell...

"Hey, sis, what are you doing here?" he asked his sister.

"Talking to G-ma, and hello to you too," Jazz replied.

"Slash got a text from you that Russell's house was finished and you invited her over for a glass of wine," Carrera said.

"I never texted her," Jazz said.

Oh, Jesus.

"What's the address of Russell's new house?"

"I... um—"

Adrenaline pulsed through him.

"What's going on?" G-ma asked.

"Faster, Jazz," Carrera said.

Jazz pulled up her phone, scrolled, then read off Russell's address. As Carrera strode back inside, he called Slash.

"Hel—" Slash's voice cut out, like she had a weak signal.

"Get out!" he screamed.

"I... Russ... trap—" Slash said.

Carrera put the call on speaker, set his phone on his desk. "Babe, can you hear me?"

Silence.

On went his body armor. He shouldered into his harness, grabbed both Glocks.

The computer binged with the results of the search. Even though he knew who owned that vehicle, he glanced down at the screen.

Dread had him snatching his phone and running toward the garage.

As he flew out of his neighborhood, he called Rebel.

"Hey, brother," Rebel answered.

"Slash has been taken." Carrera rattled off the address. "It's a house in Arlington. I'm on my way. ETA fifteen. Can your team—"

"Putting out the call," Rebel said. "Brit and I will suit up."

Carrera pressed on the gas. Despite the energy flowing through him, he stayed calm. Years of training had taught him that anxiety only made things worse. He focused on the road, on the traffic, pushing to get to Russell's as fast as he could. He slowed at the red light, checked both ways, then floored it through the intersection.

I'm on my way, babe. Fight with everything you got.

Slash

SLASH SLOWED HER RACING THOUGHTS. Panicking would make everything worse. She was alone, trapped, and without her Glock.

Slash eyed her phone. No signal.

Fuck.

She activated her phone's flashlight, turned off the recorder.

As she scanned her surroundings, disbelief washed over her. The room looked like a mini-command center. A desk sat facing a wall where four monitors hung. She tapped on the keyboard and mouse. The screens lit up, four different scenes started playing, the sound muted.

Three of the videos were from the Blue Suit Club. Each screen showed a different stripper dancing on one of its stages. She recognized all three women. Both Billiawitz sisters and Deb Weaver. The fourth screen was replaying Alexandra Wilde's news story about the women going missing from the club.

"What the fuck," she said.

On the other side of the room, a bulletin board covered the entire wall. On it were yellowed newspaper clippings. Walking over, she read the headline for the first article.

"Ohgod," she blurted as she studied the photo that accompanied the article. "No way."

"Way," said a harsh voice behind her.

She spun around. Greg stood behind her, his face angled down, evil eyes drilling into her.

As the stare-down continued, a sense of determination filled her soul. She was *not* going to die at the hands of this insane monster. Was he Russell? Was he Greg?

Confidence rose to the surface. She didn't give a fuck who he was. She was going to take him out, even if it meant dying in the process.

He pointed a gun at her. "Hello, Slash. Welcome, welcome. Let me give you the grand tour."

He flipped a wall switch, and red recessed lights filled the room with an eerie glow. Then, he gestured with the gun toward the command center across the room.

"This is where I would sit, night after night, trolling for my next victim," he explained.

"Very impressive," she said.

He nodded. "Yes, it was ingenious. By day, I'm Russell Fitzpatrick, restaurant owner, future United State Congressman, then one day... President of the United States." A faraway look softened his gaze. "I'm so close to winning the congressional election, I can taste victory."

"And how does victory taste?"

A narcissist like Russell needed his ego stroked. She needed to disarm him by playing the damsel in distress. She wanted him to think he had all the power. But he didn't. Despite the gun in his hand, she was well equipped to fight back.

"Victory tastes like more," he said. "One victory would lead to another and another and another."

"But then, there's Greg," she said. "Who are you now?"

"I'm Russell," he said. "Greg is the name I gave to my pain-in-the-fucking-ass GM—"

"Yeah, I can't stand Karen either."

"In all fairness, she did run my club well."

"Weren't you concerned about the prostitution? In the end, that's what shut you down."

He pointed the gun at her face. "*You* shut me down."

"No, Russell, Karen Woodside was your mistake," Slash said.

"I wasn't worried that anyone would ever connect squeaky-clean Russell to my sexy club. My restaurant is losing massive amounts of money, but Blue Suit was my cash cow, my pride and joy—"

"Then, you shouldn't have allowed Karen to fuck that up for you," Slash said.

Russell went to slap her, and she grabbed his wrist. "Do. Not. Hit. Me."

He jerked his hand away.

"You're a fighter," he said. "I like that. None of those women put up a fight. They were too easy." A sinister smile split his ugly face. "I'm going to have fun watching you die."

"No, that's where you're wrong, Russell. I'm going to have fun watching *you* die."

She braced, fully expecting him to pistol whip her.

But he did not.

"You're a feisty one. I appreciate that. You know, I'm the reason you got hired at my club."

Slash thought back to *after* her audition when Karen told her she *didn't* get the gig.

"I was watching Karen with you in the dressing room," Russell said.

"The surveillance camera," Slash said.

He bared his teeth in a terrifying smile. "You were good for business, so I had to sweet-talk that crazy bitch into hiring you."

With the gun pointed at her, he motioned toward the brown-haired, olive-skinned mannequin in the corner. Without turning her back on him, she walked over.

"This is my 3-D trophy box," he explained, pride spilling from his voice. "This necklace is from Terri Billiawitz. This ring was her sister Kim's." He pointed to a scarf. "This pretty thing belonged to Deb Weaver. She was lovely."

One by one, he pointed out everything he'd taken from his victims.

The longer he talked, the more time it bought her, and the more she learned. Dead men don't talk, and she needed to know everything she could about him before she took his life.

When he finished, he said, "Would you like to meet them?"

"Meet who?"

"The seven missing women you've been looking for."

~

Carrera

RAIN PELTED Carrera's windshield as he slammed on his brakes. Traffic came to a standstill. Flashing lights up ahead had him pulling down a side street and craning to see what was going on. An accident clogged the road, the police cars and ambulance blocking anyone from driving past.

Carrera glanced at the GPS. There was no way he could get to Russell's by car. He pulled over to the curb, cut the engine, and exited the vehicle. With his GPS acting as a map, he took off on foot, racing full-tilt toward Russell's. He bolted between houses, slipped on the rain-soaked grass. Pushing to his feet, he continued running.

With every second that passed, Slash was in more danger. Shoving out the fear, he wiped the water from his eyes, and he ran with everything he had.

~

Slash

RUSSELL OPENED another door that led farther into the bowels of the basement. With every step she took, it felt like she was moving farther and farther away from safety. But the need to help these women was too strong to ignore, so she walked through the door.

He flipped on the light.

The room was deep-freeze cold. Within seconds, she could see her breath.

A small prison cell sat to her left. To her relief, it was empty. Across the room, a black, plastic tarp hung like a shower curtain suspended from a rod.

He pulled back the curtain, and she gasped.

Ohmygod, it's a death chamber.

All seven victims were seated at a round table, their frozen bodies staring with lifeless eyes. They were all wearing brightly-colored dresses.

A combination of bile and fury rose inside her from a dark place long buried. From her short time on the street, she'd seen and experienced things that most people never do. She had lived through hell, but these poor victims were frozen in theirs.

This was the dark hour of her soul.

If she didn't take his life, he would take hers.

After he had taken his victims, he had killed them, then positioned them like they were at a tea party. Seven friends around a table, their tea cups filled with a murky-looking, icy liquid. Small biscuits had been placed on dessert dishes. Biscuits that they would never have a chance to eat.

Turning to face him, she stared into the eyes of the devil. Rage filled her soul, determination had her fingers twitching. She needed to be swift, and she needed to be exact.

"You are one sick fuck," she said.

He threw his head back and laughed.

She dropped, pulled up her pant leg, unsheathed her switchblade. As she pushed off the cement floor, she lunged.

BANG!

The bullet ripped into her, but she did not stop.

She plunged the knife into his chest as hard as she could, not stopping until the blade disappeared inside him.

"That's from me," she said.

She twisted the knife. "And that's for them."

Carrera

CARRERA HEARD the muffled bang as he shot out the front door lock. He threw open the door, strode into the house, clearing the living room and kitchen at breakneck speed.

"Slash!" he screamed. "Slash, where are you?"

He rushed down the hall, stopping in front of a bolted door. After throwing back the lock, he ripped open the door, flipped the switch, flew down the stairs.

His Glock at the ready. His senses on ultra-high alert.

The next door was also locked.

BANG!

He shoved open that door, eyed the wall of monitors of strippers dancing on stage. His attention jumped to the bulletin board and the mannequin in the corner. He strode to the next door, turned the handle.

Unlocked.

He flung open the door, swept the room.

Slash lay on the floor. Russell lay ten feet away, Slash's switchblade buried in his chest, blood pooling around him.

"Ohgod," he blurted.

He knelt in front of her, felt her carotid. Relief washed over him. She had a pulse, but she'd been shot. He yanked off his rain-drenched shirt, moved away to ring it out, then applied pressure to her wound.

Her eyes fluttered open and she smiled. "There's my partner."

He breathed. "How's my love doing?"

She craned her head toward Russell, then winced. "I'm doing a hell of a lot better than he is. But he got me."

"Yeah, chest, by your shoulder."

"I need to stand."

"You need to go to the hospital."

"Help me."

Immobilizing her shoulder, he helped her sit up.

"Whoa, I'm a little light headed," she said. "I can apply pressure to my wound."

"Seriously, babe."

Rebel and Brit bolted in.

"Jesus," Rebel said.

"What the hell," Brit murmured.

"Slash's been shot," Carrera said.

"I'm on it." Brit pulled out her phone.

"No signal down here." Slash started to get up.

Brit rushed out of the room as Carrera supported Slash so she could stand.

Slash

Searing pain shot through her, the discomfort traveling through her chest and down her fingers, but she had to push forward. Despite the frigid temps, they weren't finished in this hellhole. Not yet.

Pushing past the pain, she took a deep breath, then another.

"Confirm he's dead," she said.

Rebel felt Russell's carotid. "Gone."

With support from Carrera, she stood over to Russell. "I want my switchblade back." When she started to bend, pain shot through her and she jerked upright.

"I got it." Rebel yanked out the blade. "Straight through the heart."

"It was him or me," she said while Rebel cleaned the metal and folded it shut.

"Where does it go?" Rebel asked.

"Right ankle."

Rebel slipped the blade back into its holder. "The police will need that as evidence."

"Not happening," she said as she slowly made her way toward the women posed around the table. "Here they are. All seven missing women."

"I'm having trouble wrapping my brain around this," Carrera said.

"Russell had delusions he was going all the way to the White House," she said. "He believed that, all while hiding his *true* self behind Greg."

Carrera walked over to Russell, ripped off his fake beard, and dropped it on his chest.

"He loved killing his vics, keeping them close to him while he trolled for new women," Slash continued.

"What's with the mannequin?" Rebel asked.

"He displayed his trophies rather than hiding them away in a box," Slash answered. "We did have one thing in common."

"What was that?" Carrera asked.

"We couldn't stand Karen."

Brit hurried into the room. "First responders are on their way. Let's get you out of this horror chamber."

"Your motto holds true again," Slash said to Brit.

Brit recited her mantra. "Life's short, shit happens, people are mostly crazy."

She needed to get upstairs, but she wanted Carrera to learn the horrible truth about Russell. "I have to show you something," she said to him.

Carrera kept a firm grip on her waist as she walked him

over to the bulletin board and pointed to the first article and the accompanying photos.

Carrera

CARRERA'S HEART DROPPED. Pinned to the board were three photos of his sister Mara. He read the headline.

Falls Church Woman Murdered
Police Have No Suspects

He skimmed the article. Then, he eyed all the other newspaper clippings about how the case had gone cold. Making sure he had a firm hold of Slash, they walked over to the mannequin. As he studied each of the items, his gaze came to rest on a charm bracelet. A birthday gift to Mara from G-ma. Each of the siblings had bought her a charm.

In that moment, the fury that darkened his days and haunted his nights came flying out in a roar. His childhood friend was a serial killer. A brutal monster masquerading as a smiling, friendly politician ready to serve. A charmer who helps little old ladies in exchange for the massive power his political position would yield.

After removing the bracelet, he turned to Slash. "You're my hero."

"Hardly."

"You took that monster out without any help from anyone. I am in awe."

"She's a beast," Rebel said. "And that's why she's on the rescue team."

"I'm no different from the three of you," she said. "It was him or me... and it's not my time to die."

Two medics and a police officer came rushing into the room, stopping short at the mere horror of it all.

"Which one of you was shot?" asked the medic.

"Me," Slash replied. "But I can walk out."

Carrera's heart broke for his sister, Mara, but he was grateful his family would finally have closure.

Slash winced as she climbed the stairs. He wanted to take her pain, but for reasons he couldn't explain, he knew she wanted to feel the weight of this. She wanted to honor all eight victims by shouldering what they could not. He wasn't just mouthing off words when he told her she was his hero. She really was.

Upstairs, Slash sat on the stretcher, and the medic got her set up with an IV.

"I'm going to need your statement," said the officer.

"I'm Special Agent O'Reilly, FBI," Slash said. "I'll give you my statement after they get this bullet out of me."

The officer nodded. "We'll talk later."

They loaded the gurney into the ambulance, and Carrera jumped in with her. On the ride to the hospital, he held her hand. She'd been through a terrifying ordeal, yet she remained rock solid through it all.

She had his utmost respect. She was the strongest, most self-sufficient person he'd ever met. It would be the greatest blessing of his life to build a life with her. Without question, she was his person, and he was the luckiest man in the world.

As they pulled into the hospital, he made himself a promise. There wouldn't be a day that passed where he didn't show her how much she meant to him.

They wheeled her into triage, and he stayed by her side. After X-rays, the doc told her she'd need to have the bullet surgically removed.

"It's a clean shot," said the surgeon. "We'll have you out in no time." The doctor turned to Carrera. "She's going to be just fine."

Carrera smiled. "Yes, she is."

"Remove my blade," she said to Carrera.

Carrera unstrapped the knife holder, pulled if off her, and held the knife. "This'll be waiting when you wake up."

After kissing her goodbye, he said, "I love you, babe."

Her smile sent a bolt of lightning through him. "I love you too."

En route to the waiting room, Carrera called Luciano.

Slash

SLASH GLANCED around the dimly-lit hospital room. Carrera was seated in a chair beside the bed. Brit and Rebel sat on the small vinyl sofa near the window. Luciano stood in the doorway, like a guard, while Elsa and Jazz were seated in chairs on the other side of the bed.

"Hey," Carrera said, capturing her hand in his. "Look who joined the party."

Elsa leaned over her and kissed her forehead. "My angel, you had a very busy day."

One by one, everyone let her know how much she was loved.

Her gaze locked with Carrera's and she smiled. "How'd I do?"

He dropped a soft kiss on her lips. "You did great. The surgeon extracted the bullet and said you'll make a full recovery."

Luciano stood at the foot of her bed. "I will never, *ever* get on your bad side."

The group laughed.

"Should we tell them our good news?" Slash asked Carrera.

"I think that's a great idea," he replied.

"We're getting married," they said in unison.

The smiles and cheers warmed Slash's heart. She'd never envisioned her own happily ever after, because the only person she wanted to spend her life with had been Carrera.

As they shared a smile, he dipped down and kissed her.

"I will love you forever," he said.

"And I will always love you back," she replied.

THREE DAYS LATER, Slash walked into the Arlington County Detention Center, Carrera by her side. Carrera stopped by to thank Malcolm for his help.

"I run Carrera Cruises," Carrera said to Malcolm. "Call my office, ask for Jilly. She's expecting your call. If you're interested, you can bring a guest and enjoy one of my cruises. Brunch, dinner, whatever you want."

Malcolm grinned as he shook Carrera's hand. "All I was doing was my job, but I appreciate the gift."

"You helped catch a serial killer," Carrera said.

"Wow, maybe I should try my hand at law enforcement," Malcolm said.

"Maybe you should," Carrera replied handing him a business card. "Let me know how I can repay the favor."

Their next stop? The detainee visitor center on the third floor. Malcolm escorted them, and they said their goodbyes.

After Slash and Carrera were seated, Karen was led in by a guard.

She rolled her eyes as she sat in the chair. "Back again. I'm not talking."

"I'm not here for information," Slash said. "I wanted you to know that your boyfriend Greg was actually Russell Fitzpatrick," Slash said. "He was running for US Congress."

Karen's eyes flashed with surprise. "Liar."

"I don't care if you believe me," Slash said. "I wanted you to know the full story."

"You don't deserve this," Carrera said. "You blamed Slash for getting fired, but you fucked up your own life."

"Go to hell, Claude Amos," Karen bit out.

"Russell was watching the dancers from his house, then going to the club in his disguise," Slash continued. "There, he got to know the women, built trust, and brought them home. He murdered all seven women. They were discovered in his basement, in a walk-in freezer he used to keep their bodies intact."

"Ohmygod," Karen blurted, her face turning ashen white.

In order to get closure, Slash wanted the extent of Russell's crimes to be well known. She also wanted the families to get the closure they needed, and she wanted everyone to know what kind of monster Russell really was.

"He was using you," Slash said. "He was using everyone. Recently, he married someone—"

"WHAT!" Karen bellowed.

The guard warned her to pipe down.

"He married a woman for her last name," Carrera said. "He was obsessed with winning the congressional seat so he could springboard to the White House, but he needed the club to feed his addiction."

Karen was stunned into silence.

"He was a serial killer," Slash said.

"Is he in prison?" Karen asked.

"No, he's dead," Slash replied.

"Good," Karen bit out. "I thought he loved me. I thought he was going to marry me."

"I want you to do something," Slash said.

Karen regarded her across the glass. "What?"

"Stop blabbing about ALPHA. Have respect for an organization you were once a part of. Operatives risk their lives to take down monsters like Russell. Show some *discretion* for a change and keep your damn mouth shut."

When Karen didn't respond, Slash regarded Carrera. "I'm ready."

They stood.

"I'm not coming back," Slash said. "You'll see me at your trial."

She shot Carrera a smile. "I'm ready to go ring shopping."

"You're marrying Claude Amos?" Karen blurted.

Slash slid her gaze from Carrera to Karen. "Yes, I am. I got my happy ending, and if you'd done the right thing, you would have found your prince charming too."

"I don't believe in fairy tales," Karen said.

"Neither did I," Slash replied. "But my prince found me anyway."

EPILOGUE

Three months later, Early October

Carrera

Carrera sat in Z's former office in the basement of the FBI building watching a horrific, top-secret video. A terrorist group was executing seven civilians at an undisclosed location somewhere in the United States.

Fury flowed through him while his blood iced in his veins.

He'd seen enough and stopped it. He would have sent BLACK OPS, but there was no one left to rescue.

He had options for going after these monsters. An ALPHA kill mission, or he could offer it to Luciano who would make the problem go away without any government involvement.

His phone alarm started chirping.

He turned it off, eyed the time. His decision could wait. He had something much more pressing to do. After shutting down, he slipped his laptop into his computer bag, locked his office, and took off toward the underground parking garage.

Most days, he worked upstairs. Better visibility, easier access to the Director, and it was always entertaining to watch Peter Hirzog go up in flames whenever they got within ten feet of each other.

While Carrera still didn't know what had crawled up Hirzog's ass and died, he was confident it went beyond office location. In fact, Hirzog met with the Director every chance he could, so moving down the hall hadn't affected his interactions whatsoever.

Z had been right about keeping the basement office. Everything he did required the utmost secrecy. Upstairs, someone was always popping in. His position came with a lot of power... and a lot of responsibility. He could never allow anyone to see what he saw, to witness some of the evil atrocities happening day in and day out.

The nightmarish images of hate and destruction ate away at his soul. Fortunately for him, his home life balanced things out.

Carrera walked into the underground parking garage, slid into his SUV, and drove out. It was four in the afternoon. Time to head to the yacht. Excitement had him refocusing his thoughts on today. After all, it was one of the most important days in his life... in their life as a couple.

He parked in the marina, made his way over to the star of his fleet, the sixty-foot ship used for special events.

Like weddings.

That made him smile.

Once aboard, he was relieved to see that his crew was busy getting ready. The staff was setting the white cloth-covered tables, the bartender and his small staff prepping behind the bar. The chef and her cooks were whirring around the galley. He found his dad relaxing on the helm.

His dad rose, hugged Carrera. "It's your wedding day, son. It means a lot to me that you and Slash want me to be such a big part of it."

"Are you ready?"

His dad chuckled. "Are *you* ready?"

"So ready," Carrera replied.

He retreated into one of the large cabins below reserved for the groom and his groomsmen. He showered, threw on a T-shirt and shorts. No point getting his suit wrinkled.

The next hour was a total whirlwind. Jericho arrived with Hawk and Prescott. Stryker walked in with Cooper and Rebel.

The attendant delivered a bottle of champagne, opened it, and filled seven flutes. Glasses in hand, the guys toasted him.

"Congratulations," Rebel said.

"To Carrera and Slash," Jericho added.

"We're happy for you, brother," Hawk said.

The guys clinked glasses, sipped the bubbly. One more sip, and Carrera set down his flute. "Thanks for today. I love you guys like brothers."

"Is your actual brother here?" Prescott asked.

"No," Carrera replied. "He hasn't been back in years. I wasn't surprised he couldn't make it."

"Where is he?"

"Last we heard, Costa Rica," Carrera replied.

The guys started getting ready. Black suits all around, with black shirts and black ties. Once they were ready, they left the cabin, found the photographer, and posed for pics on the stern.

"We look like a bunch of gangsters," Stryker said.

The guys laughed.

"We kinda are," Jericho murmured. "What's the difference between us and the monsters we go after?"

"Better looking," Hawk replied, and the guys cracked up.

"Richer," Prescott said.

"Those drug lords are rich as fuck," Cooper said.

"You mean, we're in the wrong line of business?" Rebel said. "I wish you'd told me that ten years ago. What the hell are we gonna do about that now?"

"Never too later to jump to the dark side," Jericho joked.

The bridesmaids—also in black—joined the guys on the bow. More pictures were taken by the photographer.

"Did the bride bolt?" Carrera asked the women.

"No way," Liv replied.

"She's super excited," Brit said.

"In a laid-back, totally cool way," Addison said.

"So calm," Emerson said.

"She looks stunning," Danielle added.

Carrera smiled. He could not wait to marry Slash. Couldn't wait to call her his wife.

They decided to have a small, intimate wedding with their close circle of friends and a few family members on a Carrera cruise ship, then enjoy dinner while the vessel rolled down the river.

Sin and Evangeline, Dakota and Providence said hello before taking their seats.

Jazz walked in, Jilly too. Both sat down. Next, his cousins Gabriel and Teddy. Though Teddy hadn't apologized to Slash, she still wanted to include him on their special day.

Carrera's dad announced that everyone had boarded, then took his seat at the helm. The crew untied the boat ropes from the pier, and the yacht left the slip, heading toward the Potomac River.

As they motored slowly down the river, Carrera couldn't wait to see his bride. Couldn't wait to hold her hands, gaze into her crystal-clear eyes and exchange their vows.

This day was a long time in coming... yet it felt like yesterday when he first met the quiet girl who'd moved in with his grandmother. Yesterday, but also a lifetime ago.

So much had changed... mostly him.

He'd loved her, then he'd hated her. Now, she was his entire world and he couldn't live without her. Fortunately, he didn't have to, because she felt the same about him.

~

Slash

SLASH STOOD GAZING out the window of the bridal cabin while Elsa and Luciano relaxed on the sofa. They were enjoying a glass of champagne, but she wanted to abstain until dinner.

Like the groomsmen, Luciano wore a Santini black suit, black shirt, and black tie.

All the women in the bridal party had commented how calm she was. She couldn't understand why she'd be anything *but* calm.

Her heart was full of love, she was marrying the only man she'd ever truly loved, and she was surrounded by her close friends. Yes, she wished her mom and dad could have been there, but she didn't dwell on things that could never be.

Luciano shifted his attention from Elsa to Slash. "You look stunning, mio angelo."

"Grazie," Slash replied.

Santini's personal designer had created a fitted satin silk wedding gown that flared at the bottom with a simple train that flowed behind her. She wanted elegant and streamlined. And that's exactly what she got.

"Does Carrera know you're not in white?" Luciano asked Slash.

"No, it's a surprise."

"It's perfect for you," Elsa said.

Luciano sipped the bubbly. "For the record, I'm not getting married—"

"Don't say that, Lulu," Elsa said. "That makes me sad."

Luciano smiled. "But if I were to marry, I would hope my bride would wear black. You're rocking that dress, Slash."

She smiled. "I tried on a few white ones, but they weren't

me." She glanced down at the Santini original. "This gown is exquisite. I mean, seriously stunning."

"Thanks to you, I have my first designer line of clothing for women." Luciano slid his gaze to his grandmother. "Elsa, you look beyond beautiful."

Elsa beamed. "This Santini original is like nothing I've ever worn."

The dress was perfect, but Slash would have been happy marrying Carrera in a simple black dress. What mattered most was the man. And the man she was marrying was the *only* one for her.

As she watched the city roll by, her heart felt at peace.

Even though work had been crazy busy, and she'd just returned yesterday from a BLACK OPS mission in London, she was totally in the moment. Marrying Carrera was her happily ever after, something she believed would *never* happen.

How wrong was I.

Slash glanced down at her engagement ring. She and Carrera had left Elsa's solitaire stone unaltered. While Elsa had encouraged her to add a diamond halo, Slash liked the simplicity of it. She loved that the ring had once been Elsa's, and now it was hers. A treasured family heirloom.

Also something Slash never believed she'd ever have again.

Family.

She moved the ring to her right ring finger. After the ceremony, she'd place it back on her left hand, paired with the simple, gold band.

The boat slowed, then stopped. The rumbling sound of the anchor being lowered into the river was her cue. She regarded Elsa, then Luciano.

And she smiled.

"It's time," Slash said.

"I never asked..." Luciano said, "are you changing your last name?"

"Carrera and I talked about that," Slash replied.

"And?" Luciano asked.

"I'm doing something unconventional. I'm dropping Maynard, adding Santini, but I'm also adding May as my middle name."

She and Elsa shared a smile.

"Now, you really are my Amanda May," Elsa said.

"And a Santini." Luciano opened the cabin door. "With that name comes a lot of responsibility... and a lot of enemies."

Maybe so, but Slash wasn't scared.

They walked toward the stern. Once there, Slash clasped Elsa's hand, then wrapped her other hand around the crook of Luciano's arm. Pausing, she scanned the guests and the wedding party, searching for her man.

And when she found him, her heart leapt.

Wow. So handsome.

His gaze radiated love, as her own happiness coursed through her.

Carrera's dad stood to the side while the wedding party formed a horseshoe against the back of the ship, facing the small group of seated guests. Instead of the men on one side and the women on the other, Slash asked that the couples stand together. Husband and wife, side by side.

The music began, the seated guests rose. She made her way down the aisle toward Carrera, whose gaze never left hers. When she came to a stop beside him, she kissed Elsa's cheek, then Luciano kissed both of hers. Luciano escorted Elsa to their seats.

She acknowledged her close friends with a smile before she turned her full attention on her man.

He clasped her hands. "You are beautiful. Just stunning."

"You too, babe," she murmured.

His dad introduced himself and welcomed everyone. "As the ship's captain and a proud dad, it's my absolute honor to officiate my son's wedding. And I couldn't be happier for him and Slash." Addressing the couple, he continued. "Today is the beginning of your life together. Going forward, you are a team. Together you can work through anything, take on life's challenges, and experience life with a forever love. Talk through your issues, and remember to laugh." He paused. "Who has the wedding rings?"

Luciano rose, handed Carrera the gold band.

"Carrera, would you like to pledge yourself to Slash?" Carrera's dad asked.

Carrera let his gaze float over her face. "Slash, I love you with my whole heart," he began. "Today, in front of our family and closest friends, I promise to put you first. *Always*. You are the love of my life, and every day we are together will be a good day. Forever will never be long enough with you. You are my world and I adore you."

They shared a loving smile before Carrera slid the wedding band onto her finger. "Forever."

"Slash, would you like to say your vows to Carrera?" his dad asked.

Slash stared into his eyes. "Carrera, you are my forever love and that will never change. We've got a good thing. Let's always remember that. Marriage means something... to both of us. I will love you fiercely, I will love you always. I will love you with my whole soul."

Luciano offered her the ring, which she slid onto Carrera's finger. "The circle of this ring symbolizes the circle of our love and our life together. Never ending."

Paul Santini proudly pronounced them husband and wife.

Carrera placed his hands gently on her face and kissed her. The love flowed and she smiled. When the kiss ended, she kissed him back.

"Hello, wife," he murmured.

"Hello, husband."

The photographer swung into view and they smiled at the camera. "Like I told you when I met you, the camera loves you two."

Carrera kissed her cheek, whispered in her ear. "You are beyond stunning." He lifted her hand, kissed her skin. "Ladies and gentleman, my gorgeous, smart, badass wife, Slash Santini."

The guests and wedding party applauded and cheered.

She laughed as their friends gathered around offering their best wishes and congratulations. A few minutes passed before she broke away.

"Where are you going?" Carrera asked her.

"Elsa," she replied.

She sat next to Elsa, clasped her hand. "Now, we're family."

Elsa patted her hand. "You've been mine since the moment God brought you to me."

"Welcome to the fam," Luciano said but his gaze was focused on the shoreline beyond her.

Slash glanced over her shoulder at the banks of the river. A shock of adrenaline charged through her.

Someone was watching them, their face hidden behind high-powered binoculars.

"Are they watching you or me?" Slash asked Luciano.

"Me," he replied matter-of-factly. "She's watching me."

Nine Months Later, Early July

Slash

SATURDAY AFTERNOON, Carrera parked at the curb in Old Town, Alexandria, cut the engine. "The house looks great."

"Different enough that I can let it go," Elsa said.

Slash exited the SUV, opened the back door for Elsa, and

helped her out. Together, they walked toward Elsa's home, the For Sale sign staked in her front yard.

"Are you two absolutely sure?" Elsa asked. "Because I don't want to sell this, then find out you don't want me living—"

Slash put her arm around Elsa. "Why would you ever move back in here when we're having so much fun together?"

"You'd lose access to our home office," Carrera added.

"Who would help me solve my cases?" Slash asked.

Elsa smiled. "Okay, that was the last time I bring it up." She keyed open the front door, and they stepped inside. The smell of fresh paint filled the air. The gleam from the new hardwood had them removing their shoes.

"The contractor did a great job," Carrera said.

In silence, they walked through Elsa's empty home the final time before the open house later that afternoon. It looked phenomenal, but it wasn't Elsa's home. Not anymore. Elsa's home was with her and Carrera.

As they meandered through, it became clear to Elsa now too. After finishing the final walk-through, they locked up, and left.

Next stop, Jericho and Liv's adoption party for Owen and Layla.

"I forgot my gift," Elsa said.

"They're all in the back," Slash said. "Yours too."

Slash had bought several toys for all three of Liv and Jericho's children, and she couldn't wait to spend the afternoon with everyone. Owen and Layla had adjusted well, but the one who loved having siblings the most had been their biological son, Liam.

Slash loved being around the little ones, but she wasn't ready to talk babies with Carrera yet. As of late, she'd been training hard for a mission in Turkey, and she was eager to head over there, rescue the group of American hostages, and get the hell out.

"I heard from the D.A. about Karen Woodside's trial," Slash said. "I'm meeting with her team next week."

"When's the trial start?"

"Not for a while, but they're ready to start prepping their witnesses," she replied.

He clasped her hand, kissed her skin. "You'll do great."

"I heard she's been on her best behavior, but she's not getting away with anything this time. Last time, she got time served and was released. I'm going to make sure that doesn't happen again."

~

Carrera

ON THE RIDE to Jericho and Liv's home, Carrera's phone rang.

"Santini," he answered. After listening, he said, "When did this happen?" More listening. "I'll handle it." He hung up, then made another call. "It's a go."

He set his phone in the cup holder before glancing over at his wife. "Luciano."

Slash raised an eyebrow. "Who's he taking?"

Her phone rang and she answered. "Hello. Understood." She hung up.

"He's taking me," Slash murmured. "Are you working this one?"

He nodded, once.

"When?" she asked.

"Tuesday, three in the morning," he whispered.

She shot him a little smile. "We've had our eyes on these guys for a while."

"I *can't* hear you," Elsa called out from the back seat. "Talk louder."

He and Slash chuckled, but stayed silent. Elsa already knew

plenty, but there were certain things she was *not* privy to. Kill missions and anything to do with Luciano topped that list.

Slash fixed her eyes on the road, rolled her shoulders back. This was his wife moving into mission-prep mode. Tonight, they'd strategize. Tomorrow, she'd spend an hour or two at the shooting range.

He parked in Jericho and Liv's long driveway. In they went, loaded down with plenty of presents. Slash and Elsa went in search of the little ones while Carrera sought out his guys.

They were huddled out back, on the patio.

He joined them, congratulated Jericho on the adoption. Then, as he expected, the conversation moved to their missions. Despite their close-knit bond and their loyalty to their women and families, these seven men walked a razor-thin line between good and evil.

He knew it. They knew it too.

Truth was, someone had to hunt down and eliminate evil. If anyone was up to the missions, it was ALPHA. At the end of the day, they hunted down the worst of the worst because they were the best of the best.

After catching up, he went in search of Slash. En route, he spotted Elsa chatting in the living room with Jericho's grandmother.

He found her in the playroom. Three Savage kids, two Hawk children, two little Dillingers, and one Armstrong.

Jacqueline, Prescott's wife, was expecting their first, and Liv was pregnant as well. It was mayhem. Pure insanity as the children played together like siblings.

Slash was sitting on the floor playing a game with Owen and Layla. When she saw him, she smiled. That was the invitation he needed to join them. He eased down beside her.

"Uncle Carrera," Owen held out a toy, "you can play."

"Thanks, bud."

After joining in, he glanced around the room. A room filled

with so much laughter and love. Friends who'd formed a second family that shared in each other's joys and sorrows and always had each other's backs.

When they finished playing, he and Slash rose.

"They are so happy here," Slash said as tears pricked her eyes. "I love knowing that, although tragedy struck them at a tender age, they're going to be okay."

"I know someone else who walked that same path once," he said while pulling her into his arms and dropping a chaste kiss on her soft lips.

"Get a room, you two," Hawk said as he walked in.

Slash and Carrera laughed.

"Daddy, come play with us," Axel exclaimed, and Hawk disappeared into the fray.

"What do you think of all this mayhem?" Carrera asked her.

"I love it, and I think I'm ready."

"Really?"

"But... we should double-down on practicing, just to make sure we get it right."

He stole another kiss. "I *love* the way your mind works, baby."

"What about you?" she asked. "Are you ready?"

"Hell, yeah. If anyone's going to have a Santini, it's gotta be us."

One more kiss before she pulled the soccer ball from the corner of the room. "Hey, kids, who wants to head out back and play soccer with Auntie Slash and Uncle Carrera?"

All the kids jumped up, big grins on their adorable little faces. "I do! I do!" they screamed.

With the soccer ball tucked under her arm, she clasped his hand. "Let's go have some fun."

As they led the children through the house, Carrera said, "I love you, babe."

She gave his hand a tender squeeze. "I love you too," Slash replied with a smile.

Another Happily Ever After by

Stoni ALEXANDER

~

A Note from Stoni

THANKS SO MUCH for reading FURY.

When you read one of my novels, you step into my imagination. It's an intense place to be. Sometimes I tell my beloved husband, "You just hear what I *choose* to tell you. There's a lot of sh*t I <u>don't</u> mention."

My fascination with good and evil probably would have made me an excellent therapist, or an ALPHA Op, but my path lay elsewhere.

I first fell in love with Slash in VENGEANCE, Cooper and Danielle's love story, but I had no intention of writing a novel about her... until my readers started asking. Even with all the requests, I moved on in my Vigilantes series. Next, came Jericho and Liv, then Hawk and Addison, and Prescott and Jacqueline. When I started writing Rebel and Brit, Slash showed up again, bigger than life. A badass ALPHA Op who was wildly independent, fiercely loyal, and just a little crazy.

It was time.

Turns out, my readers were right.

This story came flying out! Turns out, I didn't realize how much I needed to tell her story. It was raw and filled with a realness that touched my soul in a whole new way.

And don't even get me started on Carrera. I'm having a serious book boyfriend hangover for this man. He had to work very hard to prove himself worthy of Slash and to show her he was no longer the stupid teenager she'd fallen madly in love with. This was so much fun for me to write.

The Vigilantes series continues with Luciano Santini—my gorgeous, sexy, suave, filthy-rich, assassin. *Evil never looked so good...*

For updates on my next book release, sign up for my occasional newsletter at StoniAlexander.com, or follow me on Amazon.

Back into my imagination I go...

Cheers to Romance,

Stoni Alexander

NOVELS BY STONI ALEXANDER

THE TOUCH SERIES
The Mitus Touch

The Wilde Touch

The Loving Touch

The Hott Touch

In Walked Sin

Dakota Luck

THE VIGILANTES SERIES
Damaged

Vengeance

Savage

Wrecked

Broken

Rebel

Fury

BEAUTIFUL MEN COLLECTION
Beautiful Stepbrother

Beautiful Disaster

Available on Amazon or Read FREE with Kindle Unlimited

ABOUT THE AUTHOR

Stoni Alexander writes sexy romantic suspense and contemporary romance about tortured alpha males and independent, strong-willed females. Her passion is creating love stories where the hero and heroine help each other through a crisis so that, in the end, they're equal partners in more ways than love alone. The heat level is high, the romance is forever, and the suspense keeps readers guessing until the very end.

Visit Stoni's website:
StoniAlexander.com

Sign up for Stoni's newsletter on her website and she'll gift you a free steamy short story, only available to her Inner Circle.

Here's where you can follow Stoni online. She looks forward to connecting with you!

amazon.com/author/stonialexander

bookbub.com/authors/stoni-alexander

facebook.com/StoniBooks

goodreads.com/stonialexander

instagram.com/stonialexander

Made in the USA
Monee, IL
11 August 2024

63585295R00298